THE
HUNT

THE
HUNT

BY MEGAN SHEPHERD

BALZER + BRAY

An Imprint of HarperCollins*Publishers*

Balzer + Bray is an imprint of HarperCollins Publishers.

The Hunt

ISBN 978-0-06-224308-9 (trade bdg.)

Typography by Michelle Taormina
16 17 18 19 20 PC/RRDH 10 9 8 7 6 5 4 3 2 1

First Edition

To the Highland Books community,
my home away from home for many years

1

Cora

SIX STEPS LONG BY six steps wide.

Cora must have paced the perimeter of her cell a hundred times. There was no clock. No window. No way to tell if she had been there for three days or thirteen—not that time even passed the same way on the space station. The only objects in the room were a stiff plastic-like blanket that always felt cold, a toilet, a water spout she could drink from, and a glaring ceiling light that never turned off.

Sitting in the corner, legs pulled in tight, she splayed her hand across the black observation panel set into the wall. Her nails against the smooth surface looked jagged and gnawed.

We have taken you for your own good, the Kindred had said.

We are your saviors, they had said.

She pressed her fingers against the black panel, one at a time, one for each of the five friends they'd separated her from. Lucky. Leon. Nok. Rolf. Mali. Weeks ago, they'd been strangers caged together in an artificial Earth where they were observed like wild animals behind bars. The experiment hadn't lasted long.

Neither had Cora's failed escape.

Stupid, she thought, *to think I could ever escape from them.*

When she took her hand away from the panel, traces of moisture from her fingers clung to the glass before vanishing.

Five gray spots against the blackness.

Five stars against a dark sky.

Five notes that might begin a song.

But not stupid, she thought with resolve, *to believe we're any less than them.*

She closed her eyes and took a deep breath, concentrating on focusing her senses. She could still remember, deep in her bones, what it had felt like to trigger her telepathic ability. It had started as a dizzying wave and distorted vision, and then—*yes, there*—she had been able to sense a figure standing on the other side of the wall, and—*yes, again*—she had even been able read Cassian's thoughts. It had only happened once, though she had tried in vain to make it happen again.

She stared at the black panel, again trying to sense behind it, though her neck ached and her eyes were bleary and worries kept itching under her skin, reminding her such abilities were unnatural. Freakish, even. Back on Earth, she'd be committed if she claimed to sense things with her mind. Back on Earth . . .

But there might not even *be* an Earth anymore.

"Wishing on stars never got me by," she sang to herself quietly. Lyrics had always helped her clear her head of her worries. In songs, she wasn't a freak, just a girl far from home and the parents, brother, and shaggy old dog she missed more than anything. "Wishes, and hopes, and kisses good-bye . . ." She traced her finger in an arc against the panel, composing lyrics that faded as soon as they'd been written. "I wished to stay stronger, instead I got . . ."

Her voice went hoarse with lack of practice, but her finger kept writing:

M-O-N-S-T-E-R-S.

The letters faded until there was nothing but blackness.

For a second, maybe two, that dizzying sensation started to creep over her again. Her vision blurred at the edges. She almost sensed that something was moving beyond the walls, or maybe *someone*, or maybe several someones.

The walls and floor began to vibrate. The rumble rose through her legs, making her heart trip and thunk, and she shoved to her feet, startled. The vibrations grew into a hum that filled the room. The hair on the back of her neck rose as if someone's warm breath were whispering against it, and she clamped a hand over her nape.

Concentrate, she told herself. *You can sense what's out there. You did it once. You have to do it again.*

The ceiling lamp grew so bright she had to squint. Light came from the walls too, as they split apart in intricate puzzle-like shapes that revealed a doorway. More light poured in from the opening, coating her skin with warmth. She flinched and shielded her eyes.

Footsteps.

Then, voices.

Someone was speaking words she didn't recognize, in a monotone voice. The Kindred's language. She tensed, fearing why they might have come. And then a clearer voice, in English, cut through the light.

"Stand."

A shadow eclipsed her.

She blinked her eyes open cautiously. Black eyes looked back at her—no pupils, no irises, just puddles of oily black, set into a woman's face the color of burnished copper. Tessela. One of the guards under Cassian's command.

Cora gasped at the sight of a familiar face. "Tessela! Please, let me out—"

"You are guilty of disobeying Rule Two and Rule Three," Tessela said mechanically, as though Cora was just another troublesome human. "Of attempting to escape your enclosure. Of lying to the Warden."

Cora blinked against the light. "That isn't the whole story. You know that."

Tessela grabbed Cora's arm with shocking strength and hauled her to her feet, then released her and stepped away. Another Kindred stood in the doorway, dressed in a uniform so dark a blue it was nearly black, with the most intricate knots she'd ever seen running in twin rows down the front. He stepped into the light and she drew in a sharp breath. Fian. Another of Cassian's team. The first time she had met him, he'd nearly choked her to death, never mind that it had been a trick by Cassian to earn her trust. She rubbed the base of her throat at the bad memory.

"If you just ask Cassian . . . ," she started, but faltered on the sound of his name. No, Cassian wouldn't help her now. Cassian had bent the rules for her when she'd had trouble adapting to her previous enclosure, but that was before her escape attempt. Before she'd found out Cassian *was* the Warden—the one manipulating her the entire time.

Light reflected off the sharp needles and gleaming metal of an apparatus in Fian's hand. Her stomach curled. The Kindred claimed they didn't experiment on humans, but she'd seen them sticking needles into a dead girl, looking for signs of evolution. It seemed the only thing the Kindred feared was that their precious human pets, whom they had so ironically sworn to protect, might one day become as clever as they were.

And we are, Cora thought loudly enough for Tessela and Fian to read it.

Tessela only blinked. "Extend your arms by your sides," she commanded.

Cora shook her head. "Where are Lucky and Mali?"

"Extend your arms." Tessela took a step toward her. "This is for your own good."

Cora ducked and ran for the wall where the doorway had been, but Fian was impossibly fast. He grabbed her arm with a twist of pain and held her hand out to her side. Tessela took the apparatus from Fian. It began to hum, probably triggered telekinetically.

"It was my idea to escape, not theirs," Cora insisted. "You can't punish them."

Tessela approached with the apparatus. Now that it was closer, it looked similar to the sensors that the Kindred medical officer, Serassi, had inspected them with, only this one had half-inch-long needles protruding from the end.

"We do not believe in punishment," Fian said flatly. "That is a primitive concept."

Cora would have laughed if her throat hadn't been closing

up in terror. What did they call being locked in the cell, if not punishment?

Tessela pressed the needles to her skin. Cora hissed as the needles suddenly moved on their own, not stiff but fluid, working their way into the palm of her hand. Too tiny to be painful, but just as uncomfortable as microscopic worms burrowing into her skin.

"Please," she gasped. "Tell me if Lucky and Mali are okay. And Nok and Rolf too. Are they still in the cage? Is Nok's pregnancy okay?" Cora gritted her teeth as Tessela pressed the apparatus to her other palm. "Just tell me!"

Tessela finished and holstered the apparatus. Cora looked down at her hands. A strange pattern of lines and pinpricks covered her palms and circled the base of her fingers like half-moon rings. The half circle on her ring finger was more prominent than the others. The pinpricks there radiated out like a star. In the cage, the Kindred had branded each ward with constellations to pair them together; but these concentric circles and rows of tiny markings had nothing to do with the night sky.

"I don't understand."

"You aren't meant to," Tessela said. "The code is for our record keeping, not yours."

Fian released her, and she sank back against the wall. She squeezed her fists, curling her fingers around the lines and symbols that now marked her as Kindred property.

With a rumble, the wall seams started to break apart again to reveal the doorway. She jerked her head up.

A new figure filled the doorway.

Black eyes.

Skin the color of copper.

A scar on his neck and a bump in the bridge of his nose—imperfections on an otherwise perfect face.

Cassian.

Focus? She could barely breathe. The first time she'd seen Cassian had been in her dreams. With his impossible beauty, she had thought he was an angel. Now she knew: he was a monster, like all of them. Looking into his mind that one time and seeing a flash of almost human-like regret for what he'd done to her hadn't changed that.

"You," she said. "All of you." She jerked her chin at Tessela and Fian. "You think you'll always be in control, but humans can be as smart as you. The minute I get out of here—and I *will*—I'm going to show everyone on this station what humans are capable of. Reading minds. Sensing things. They won't be able to deny it anymore." She hoped they didn't detect the tremor in her voice that whispered *freak* in the back of her head.

Cassian folded his hands calmly. "That would be unwise." He motioned to Tessela and Fian. "Leave us."

Fian and Tessela obeyed like clockwork, moving in unison toward the door, which sealed closed behind them. The starry light from the wall seams spilled over Cassian's skin, softly reflective, almost as if he was the god Nok had talked about from her childhood stories in Thailand.

"Fian's uniform, in case you did not notice," Cassian continued, "has the twin-knot design of a delegate on the Intelligence Council, the highest governing party on the station and a collaboration among all the intelligent species. My position as Warden is powerful, but the delegates will always far outrank me. Those of us sympathetic to the human cause have painstakingly toiled, over the course of many rotations, to infiltrate it; you should be thankful Fian is on our side, not theirs. If a true delegate witnessed you saying such things, you would never leave this chamber."

"You can't threaten me."

"I am merely telling you the truth." His head turned as his gaze skimmed over the room, lingering on her fingerprints on the black panel. "You are not the only one in danger. If they were to learn of my involvement, they would demote me to the lowest position—a star sweeper, sent to clear astral debris in a solitary ship. Ninety-five percent of star sweepers are killed by asteroid collision in their first run."

Cora balled her fists harder. Like she cared what happened to him. She wanted to hate him. She *did* hate him. And yet her mind flashed back through moments when hate had been the last thing she'd felt. He had given her stars, when she couldn't sleep. He'd saved her life, when Fian had nearly strangled her. He had stood in the artificial ocean surf, and uncloaked his stoic emotional walls, and looked at her with real eyes, not black ones, and whispered to her with real emotions, not hidden ones.

And he had kissed her.

She looked away. *Nothing here is real,* she reminded herself. *Love most of all.*

He took another step into the room. She couldn't tell where he was looking with his all-black eyes, but his head tilted toward her clenched left fist, then her right.

"I want to help you." His voice was softer. "Our goal is, ultimately, the same. If you can read even a small piece of my mind, then you know that is true."

"If you're going to apologize again, forget it," she cut him off. "I'm tired of hearing that you betrayed me for the good of humanity. That you broke my mind so that I'd evolve to the next level." She paused. "That what you felt for me was real."

But this time, he did not contradict her. He only removed a long piece of fabric from a deep pocket in his black uniform and held it out.

She took it hesitantly, too curious not to, and let the smooth fabric unroll. Straps. A hem.

An ankle-length dress.

It wasn't like the formal robes both male and female Kindred of low status wore. Nor the white sundress she had worn in the cage. This was gold and silk, richly made, and it held a faint trace of cigarette smoke and a perfume, but one that was older, not like her mother's designer scents. It was a real artifact from Earth, unlike all the re-created clothing, which smelled like ozone and didn't have the right weight.

"What is this?" she asked.

She'd expected to spend the rest of her life in the cell. They wouldn't kill her—that would go against their unbreakable moral code. But it didn't mean she wouldn't be drugged, or worse.

"This is a second chance," Cassian said evenly. "For both of us."

2

Cora

CORA LET THE DRESS'S smooth fabric fall through her hands and settle on the floor in a pool of silk. "A second chance?"

She could guess what the 1930s-style dress meant. She knew about the Kindred's menageries—private clubs that re-created different time periods from Earth—where they dropped the emotional cloak they wore in public to let their pent-up emotions run wild. Less-desirable humans were kept there as servants and oddities for entertainment. Cassian had taken her to one to warn her about what happened to children who disobeyed. It had been called the Temple, an artificial Greek palace where drugged children in togas were made to perform tricks.

Why human places, human times? she had asked him.

There is no society, nor habitat, better suited for the cultivation of experiences than the human world, he had answered.

Now, she narrowed her eyes. "Putting me in a menagerie is hardly a second chance. It's further punishment."

"I have little choice. The Intelligence Council cannot learn of your escape attempt. Fian convinced them that your enclosure failed due to technical difficulties, and that the remaining wards should be transferred to alternative facilities. Only Fian, Tessela, and Serassi know the truth." He paused. "I have made an arrangement with Serassi in return for her silence. Fortunately, Fian and Tessela have always been sympathetic to our cause."

"*Our* cause?" Cora shook her head. "I don't have anything to do with whatever you're planning." Her mouth felt very dry, and she started to turn toward the water spout, but he rested a hand against her shoulder.

His eyes, black as they were, seemed to reach all the way into her head. "You have *everything* to do with our plan. A plan that has been in the works for nearly six hundred rotations—almost twenty human years. We call it the Fifth of Five, because if we are successful, humanity will ascend to the fifth intelligent race." He ran a hand over the back of his glove, changing a setting, and then traced something onto the table. Two intersecting lines appeared, like a double helix, with five dots in the center. Whatever substance he was writing with only lingered a few seconds before disappearing.

"This is the covert symbol of the Fifth of Five. The first four points represent the current intelligent species: Kindred, Mosca, Axion, and Gatherers. The last one represents humanity. But we cannot raise humanity's position without you. I am not the first leader of the Fifth of Five initiative. Nor are you the first human we have set our hopes upon. Hundreds of Kindred have been involved in the clandestine effort to declare humanity's intelligence, spanning back generations. The irony is that you cannot even see that we are attempting to help you."

She paced tightly. "Helping us? If you want to help, why don't you try finding out if Earth still exists."

"The stock algorithm predicted POD98.6. That stands for Probability of Destruction ninety-eight point six percent—"

"Yeah, I know, chances are humans have destroyed Earth. But even if there's a tiny chance it's still there, it could mean everything to us. Our homes. Our families. Our entire world."

He looked at her with eyes that revealed no emotion. "*This* is your world now." He paused long enough to pick up the dress. "Take this. You will need it."

HE LED HER THROUGH the austere hallways that formed the public world of the Kindred's station. They passed walls that glowed with starry light, and a few open nodes like the one they had once used to board a transport, and then there was a rush of air and chatter as the ceiling opened into a three-story-high marketplace. Cora's feet slowed. She had been here before—to this very market, or one like it. It was mostly filled with Kindred vendors offering artifacts—human and otherwise—and a few hunchbacked Mosca traders with their eerie breathing masks and red jumpsuits. There was even a sole Gatherer, one of the willowy, monk-like eight-foot-tall creatures Cassian had once warned her never to look at directly.

Her eyes settled on a raised platform. It was a stage of sorts, maybe for auctioneering, about four feet off the ground. If she could distract Cassian, she could climb up there and hold a demonstration of her psychic abilities. Books and utensils from the market stalls would levitate at her command. Kindred would gasp. Fingers would point at her. And then they would have to reluctantly admit that she and all humans *were* just as capable as they were, and that they would never be able to cage her again—

Cassian stopped.

"You forget that I can read what you are thinking," he said. "A public demonstration of your telepathic abilities is not the way to achieve your goals."

He motioned toward Kindred guards posted on the upper level of the marketplace that she hadn't noticed before. "If you were to claim that humans have evolved, no one would believe you. They would ask for proof that you could not reliably demonstrate. You have the potential, yes, but not the mastery. And when you were not able to prove it, those guards would declare you mentally unstable and lock you away. Do you not remember what happened to Anya?"

Anya. The Icelandic girl Cora had seen trapped in the Temple, drugged and delirious.

"On a stage not unlike that one," Cassian continued, "Anya once performed a fairy-tale play her private owner had written. She decided to alter the script. Instead of picking artificial flowers from a vase, she levitated them with her mind. I could not stop the Council when they came for her." He lowered his voice even further. "Stubbornness can be an endearing trait, but it can also be your downfall. There is a way to get what we both want. Do not let your anger at me blind you to reason."

His words only stoked her anger more. She could feel it growing inside her, and yet a memory pushed forward. Her older brother, Charlie, shaking his head after she'd fallen out of the oak tree at the edge of their property for the tenth time in a row. He'd dusted her off and said, *You know what stubborn means?* Cora, eight at the time, had shaken her head, and he'd explained, *The definition of stubborn is to know what the right thing to do is, but not to do it anyway just to prove a point. And right now, you should really just give up.*

She clenched her jaw and looked away from the platform. "Okay. But this doesn't mean I'm agreeing to anything."

He didn't answer. Silently, he led her through the marketplace, then down into roughly hewn hallways that cut through the asteroid core itself. These dank places made up the Kindred's private world: menageries, brothels, gambling halls—places where the Kindred could safely uncloak and seek the emotional thrills they craved. A row of doorways was dug into the rock, and in front of each doorway was a podium staffed by a young Kindred male or female.

"Hosts," Cassian explained. "To greet their guests. Each door leads to a different menagerie. You're going to the Hunt."

Cora held up the old-fashioned golden dress. "So what is that, some kind of Prohibition nightclub?"

"Not exactly."

He said nothing more as they passed the first few doors. One host wore a leopard-print caveman's toga. One hostess looked like a Viking maiden. Another was dressed in a baseball uniform.

"The menageries have only recently opened for this rotation, so it is a relatively quiet time. There will not be many guests yet. They operate on a roughly terrestrial schedule of day and night, for the comfort of the humans who live here."

Cora let out a smirk. *Comfort.* "How many human days make up a rotation?"

"The exact conversion rate requires complex algorithms,

as it changes based on a variety of astrophysical factors. Humans are incapable of this level of mathematics, but suffice it to say one rotation is equal to anywhere between one and two weeks." He stopped at the sixth door. The hostess here wore what looked to be a safari uniform: khaki blouse with the shoulders cut out, thick leather belt, hunter-green skirt, with a pith helmet perched on her perfectly combed hair. Like all the hostesses, she wore glasses with eyes painted on the front, though Cora knew that behind them her eyes were uncloaked and almost as clear as a human's.

The hostess smiled stiffly at Cassian. "Welcome back, Warden."

Welcome *back*? Cora had never imagined him playing dress-up in some club.

He inclined his head. "Issander."

The hostess opened the door for them. Heat coated Cora's skin like a thick lotion. The air was muggy, as warm as the light that cast long shadows throughout the room. The calls of tropical birds reached her ears first, then other sounds: the roar of a far-off truck, low chatter and clinking of glasses, soft instrumental music.

"Be cautious." Cassian nodded back toward the door. "The Council has watchers posted through the station whose job is to report back any unusual activity. Improper relations between Kindred and humans, humans disobeying the rules, that sort of thing. Their identities are kept hidden. I do not know if Issander is a watcher, but she is not sympathetic to our cause."

"Won't that be a problem?"

"I have a plan for that."

"Sure you do. You have a plan for everything." Overhead, wooden beams rose thirty feet to form a thatched roof that supported hanging lanterns. The lodge was open and airy, filled with teak furniture draped in exotic fabrics, with amazingly realistic statues of giraffes and zebras. Along one wall, two human boys shook cocktails behind a bar. Across from the bar, billowing floor-length curtains flanked French doors leading to a wide veranda where a savanna glowed beneath a setting sun. Cora stopped, stunned. For a second it all felt too real. When she had been a little girl, she'd loved sunsets like this. She and Charlie used to race each other across the yard, laughing, trying to reach the big oak tree at the edge of their property before the sun disappeared.

Cassian nudged her out of her memories.

She blinked back into the present, remembering that everything here was artificial, even the sun. "A safari lodge?"

"Yes. The Hunt. It is modeled after early colonial expeditions. Guests come here to experience the thrill of the safari. It provides an exhilarating rush of emotions, I am told." He gestured toward the bar and lounge areas. "The lodge is where guests wait to depart for an expedition, or to relax after they return. Your job will be to entertain them while they wait." He pointed to a stage by the bar, where a microphone stood. "Singing. Playing card games. Dancing with them. Whatever they request."

The bird sounds came again and she scanned the rafters. "It's all simulated, right?"

One of the bartenders, a severe-looking boy with buzzed blond hair, gave her a long, unreadable look, but Cassian didn't seem to notice as he led her toward the veranda.

"Not entirely. The technology we use here is not the same as in your previous enclosure. There, creating realistic facsimiles that could be immediately altered required a large amount of carbon. We reserve our carbon supplies for scientific pursuits, such as researching and observing lesser species. We would never expend such resources on entertainment. That is why everything here is real. Within reason." He swept aside a curtain, showing her the wide expanse of the savanna. It seemed to stretch for miles, through grassy plains and around a watering hole. "The distance is an illusion, of course. This entire menagerie is, in actuality, not much larger than a single habitat in your previous enclosure."

She noticed that the French door's curtain was frayed at the hem. On closer look, all the parts of the lodge that had appeared luxurious at first glance now looked threadbare. Half the chairs had been hastily repaired. The floor had cracks in it. She glanced back at the buzz-haired bartender. He was pouring a drink for the sole guest in the lodge, a Kindred who hunched stiffly over his barstool. The bartender had an air of refinement about him, but that might have just been his crisp jacket with gold trim, because when she looked closer his haircut was roughly uneven, and the back of his neck was dark with grime. He looked to be about eighteen or nineteen. He had coded marks just like hers on his palms.

She turned the dress over in her hand. The gold color matched the trim on the boy's jacket. An image flashed in her head of standing onstage, singing songs like a trained parrot.

At the end of the bar, one of the giraffe statues coughed, and Cora jumped.

"Wait, that giraffe is *alive*?"

"Yes. The animals are real. We are not only intrigued by humanity; all terrestrial life holds a certain fascination for us. As you are doubtlessly aware, there are no indigenous animals in space."

The giraffe was small, probably a juvenile, and it looked sickly. It doubled over and coughed again, dripping thick drool on the Kindred guest's boot. The Kindred let out a low, guttural sound, and the second bartender, a boy with beautiful dark lashes around watery eyes, hurried over to clean up the mess. Slowly, as though he sensed her watching, the Kindred guest looked at Cora.

He had a beautiful face, like all of them, but it was twisted somehow, as if the bones beneath had been broken many times and re-formed in a way that reminded her of a tree knot. From his scowl she could tell he was uncloaked, but his eyes were so recessed that they still appeared entirely black.

A gong sounded from the veranda, and she turned. The sound of a vehicle roared.

"An expedition is returning," Cassian explained. "Watch."

Car doors slammed amid the sound of excited chatter from outside. A thin boy and a girl appeared on the veranda. They were dressed in rugged, dusty safari clothing, and Cora caught a glimpse of the same coded markings on their palms. The boy signaled to the blond bartender, who stepped onto the stage.

"Ladies and gentleman," the bartender said, though there was only the one guest, "I am most pleased to announce a record-breaking hunt!"

Though his delivery was slightly stilted, his words weren't as flat as Mali's way of speaking, so he must not have been taken from Earth as young as she had been. At his announcement, another Kindred guest came through the veranda doors, dressed in safari clothes that looked bizarre against his metal-like skin. He dragged a bobcat by one leg. A rifle was slung over his shoulder.

"The first kill of the day!" the blond boy said. "This bobcat weighs in at nineteen kilos, and let me tell you, ladies and gentlemen, these animals are fast, with a top speed of . . ."

Cora felt her head spinning as the boy went on. The bobcat's blood streaked the floor between her and the stage but was mopped up quickly by the dark-haired bartender. She rubbed her temples, feeling like she was going to be sick. "That's real blood," she whispered to Cassian. "Real rifles. You thought I'd be safe *here*?"

Cassian led her toward a row of alcoves separated from the main space by wooden screens. "I had no choice," he whispered. "You would not have lasted long in the Harem menagerie; girls never do. They would have drugged you in the Temple, and I need your mind sharp. There are fewer regulations here, yes, but that is why I chose it. We shall be able to work together privately." He gestured toward the nearest alcove, which contained a table laden with dice and decks of cards. "Kindred come here to gamble in private. It isn't unusual for them to want a human companion to serve them drinks or to play card games with. As soon as I handle Issander, no one will spare a second glance to what we do here, alone."

She glanced at the alcove with its low lighting and soft cushions. "Alone?"

Despite the fact that he was cloaked, his breath seemed suddenly shallow. She wondered if he too was thinking of the last time they had been alone, standing in the surf, when he'd pressed his lips to hers.

"For the training," he said curtly. "You will need to master your perceptive abilities if you are to succeed."

Worry crept up her back. "Succeed at what?"

He leaned close. "The Gauntlet."

3

Lucky

"I'M SERIOUSLY SUPPOSED TO wear this?" Lucky held up the faded khaki shirt, matching shorts, and dented pith helmet the girl had just handed him.

The girl giggled. She had to be at least fourteen years old, but from the way she chewed on the end of her mousy-brown braid, she seemed much younger. Behind her, two rows of cells spanned the walls like prison barracks. About half of them were occupied by wild animals: a kangaroo, a hyena, a lioness asleep in the corner.

He rubbed the bridge of his nose. For days he'd been locked alone in a tiny observation room he could barely pace in, trying to figure out what was going on and what had happened to the others. He finally had someone he could talk to, and she could only giggle.

"Listen . . . What was your name again?" he asked.

"Everyone calls me Pika." Her nails, he noted, didn't look like they had seen soap and water in years. "It's the name of a rodent. But, like, a cute rodent." She grinned, revealing a few missing teeth.

"I like animals. That's why they put me back here. At home my parents raised, um, I forget what they're called. Oh! Ferrets. They said I could start raising my own when I turned twelve." Her face fell momentarily, as though remembering that twelve had come and gone long ago. She swallowed nervously. "Anyway, I like animals."

Lucky rubbed his nose harder. "How long ago were you taken?"

"Three years," she said, then frowned. "Wait." She counted on grubby fingers that were marked with lines and circles, just like his. "Four. Maybe five. *Vampires of the Hamptons* had just started. Is that show still on? Did Tara ever hook up with Jackson?"

His head was seriously starting to ache now. "I never watched it."

Pika's face fell.

"Listen," he tried again. "Have you heard anything about a girl named Cora? She has long blond hair and—"

"They said you're good with animals too," Pika interrupted. She grabbed his hand and led him along the wall of cages toward a warren of back rooms that smelled like unwashed feet. There was a medical room, a feed storage room, and a shower room with drains in the floor—which, judging by Pika's smell, didn't get nearly enough use. He'd never imagined he'd think this, but he almost missed the cage. At least it hadn't reeked.

Pika went to the end of the corridor and cautiously pushed open a bright red door. "Take a peek," she whispered. "But don't let them see you."

The sound of music came from the door. *Jazz?* Well, after the collection of wild animals, nothing surprised him. He glanced through the crack to find a safari lodge straight out of the British

Empire, with a bar and lounge furniture and—was that a giraffe? Before he could take it all in, Pika shut the door.

"That's the lodge," she said. "That's where Dane and Makayla and the others work, the important ones. You and me, we stay backstage with the animals. Don't ever go through this door. Got it?"

"I guess—"

"Come on." She tugged him back down the hallway into the main room of cells. The lioness had woken and was flicking her tail. "What animals have you worked with before?"

"I lived on a ranch," he said, blinking. His granddad's farm felt so distant. He could barely picture the barn where his motorcycle had taken up the first stall on the right. "Chickens, horses, dogs. A stray cat."

"We don't have those here," Pika said, climbing up a short flight of metal stairs to the upper row of cages, where she went to the lioness's cell and threw in a pellet of something that smelled like rotting bread. "I've heard there's a farm menagerie somewhere, or maybe it was a rodeo. Anyway, here it's about hunting." She swung down from the upper story, landing with a thud on her feet.

"You mean the Kindred *hunt* these animals?"

Pika giggled. "Well, that's the whole point, isn't it? We're in the Hunt. Each menagerie specializes in something that helps the Kindred release their emotions. Fighting, or drinking, or racing cars . . . Here, they hunt."

Lucky gripped the bars of the closest cage to steady himself. "I thought they were supposed to protect lesser species. That's their whole moral code."

"They don't actually *kill* the animals," Pika explained, as though he were slow. "Their rifles look like ones from Earth, but they aren't. They use *these* instead of bullets."

She dug around in her dirty safari clothes and came back up with what looked like a used fireworks casing. "It knocks the animals out. Makes them go numb. Bleeds a little where they're hit, but that's it. They drag them back to the lodge, make a big show of the hunt up onstage, everyone's supposed to clap, and then they dump them back here for you and me to patch up so they're ready to be hunted again." She blinked at him like it was all supposed to make sense. "See? It's humane. They don't kill them. If they hurt them, we just make them better."

Lucky's fingers curled tighter around the bars, squeezing until his knuckles were white. He thought again of his granddad's farm, and this time the memories were clearer. He remembered his granddad hobbling out to throw kitchen scraps to the chickens and collect any eggs. When hens got too old to lay, his granddad would slaughter them and they'd freeze the meat for winter. All that death had bothered Lucky. But somehow, that seemed more humane than this.

A *thump* sounded from the long corridor. The faint sound of jazz trickled from the hallway.

Pika grinned. "Take a look!"

She hurried back down the corridor, where the red door was propped open. Two humans, a boy and a girl in safari clothes, dragged in a heavy burlap sack. They eyed Lucky with interest.

"They actually found somebody to help you back here?" the boy teased Pika. He had an Australian accent, and hollow cheeks that spoke of malnutrition.

"And he's cute," the girl said in a matching accent, appraising

Lucky, scratching a sore on her neck. "Has all his fingers and toes and everything. Prime stock, not like us rejects. What, did you fail out of an enclosure?"

Lucky cracked his knuckles. "Something like that."

"I'm Jenny. This is my brother, Christopher. And this"—she nudged the burlap sack with her toe—"is Roger."

Blood seeped from the sack, seriously creeping Lucky out.

"Come on. Dane will have a fit if we aren't back soon." Jenny grabbed her brother's jacket and they turned back to the lodge. Lucky craned his neck to look out the door, hoping for a glimpse of other human kids to see if Cora was among them, but the backstage door thudded closed. Pika reached out and squeezed his biceps, making him jump. She giggled. "You're strong. *You* carry Roger."

Dazed, he knelt by the burlap sack. He started to pick up the corner, gagging on the tangy smell of blood. He followed Pika back down the hall to one of the smaller rooms. It had a clogged drain in the floor and medical equipment on the walls. Pika pointed to the center of the room, where he set down the sack. She opened it, and he saw fur, in a pattern that he recognized.

"A bobcat?" he said. "Jesus, I thought it was a person."

"Jenny named him Roger." Pika started muttering to herself as she dug around amid the equipment in a cabinet.

Blood poured from a deep puncture on the bobcat's left shoulder. Its eyes were open and glassy. Its chest didn't move. It looked as dead as anything he had ever seen.

"Now watch." Pika pulled out a tool that looked like a long-handled plastic lighter. She grabbed a tattered cloth from a bin and wiped the blood from the bobcat's shoulder, then set the lighter-tool over the animal's wound and punched a button. The machine started whirring. Lucky got the sense that Pika had been taught to use this piece of Kindred technology in the way you'd train a child to operate a microwave: memorize which buttons to hit with no understanding of how it really worked.

The machine whirred louder and then stopped suddenly. Pika flipped it over and pulled out one of the used firecracker casings. When she ran her fingers over the wound, it was red, but healed.

"This is the most important part," she said, stroking the bobcat's stump of a tail. "You gotta make sure they're in their cage before you wake them up. Otherwise you're in trouble. At least with the big ones. Roger's pretty tame."

She struggled to drag the bobcat by its front legs back to the main room and into a cage just high enough for it to stand, with a water trough and food pellets. She locked the door with a pin, then reached through the bars and set a small package by the bobcat's nose.

She tapped her own nose. "Releases a smell that revives them. It'll take a few minutes. There are pods that do the opposite too, if you need to calm one down."

She started mumbling to herself while she cleaned up the rest of the blood streaking the floor. She didn't do a very good job. He peered into the bin where she tossed the soiled cloth and found hundreds more rags, all soaked with blood.

Lucky stared at the bobcat. The wound might be technically healed, but it still looked raw and painful. Slowly the bobcat opened one glazed-over eye.

There was pain there, and suddenly Lucky was back on his granddad's farm. He'd seen the same look in his granddad's horses when they were ill or injured. But that was different. Illnesses couldn't be helped, sometimes horses just went lame, but this . . . This was *sport*.

His fingers curled around the bars of the nearest cage, squeezing so tight his joints ached. The Kindred had healed his busted hand when they'd taken him, and now he was in danger of breaking it again out of anger.

Something in the bottom of the nearest empty cell caught his eye. A book. *The Call of the Wild.* And in a bin in the corner, there was a blanket and one of those old-fashioned ball-and-cup games.

His head whipped to Pika. "They keep *people* in these cells too?"

She chewed on the tip of her braid. "Of course. This is where we all sleep."

Her words sank in slowly. All of them—humans and animals, as if there was no difference. And maybe, to the Kindred, there wasn't.

In the cell, the bobcat's eyes were both open now, and it was breathing steadily, but it hadn't bothered to stand up. Why would it? It had probably gone through this dozens of times already. An endless cycle that always ended in pain.

Was this his life now? Sleeping in filth? Spending his days cleaning up the Kindred's messes? He looked at his nails, his breathing coming quick and unsteady, wondering how long before he was as scraggly as the rest of the kids.

The bobcat blinked.

"You said the Kindred hunt with rifles?" Lucky asked.

Pika's mumbling ended. She chewed harder on her braid, darting looks toward the red door that led to the lodge. "Don't get any ideas. The rifles don't work for us, only for the Kindred.

If you tried to pull the trigger, nothing would happen. Trust me, we've all tried." She giggled again, more nervously. "The Kindred aren't stupid."

He watched the bobcat slowly close its eyes. He sank down next to it, wanting to hide his face from Pika, his breath coming faster, the panic he was trying to swallow back. There was no going home—that's what he'd learned from their botched escape. Not for him. Not for Pika. Not for these animals either.

He gently stroked the bobcat's mangy fur.

He wished he could do more. He wished he could do *anything*. Because if the Kindred hunted animals just for sport, what did they do to humans?

The backstage door opened, and two Kindred carried in sealed crates. Pika jumped up, tugging on Lucky's jacket. "Fresh supplies!" she said, their talk of rifles already forgotten. "Oh boy! Sometimes they put in salt licks for the animals, but we get first dibs. They're *so* good. Like potato chips. Only without the chips. So basically just salt, I guess." She trailed off, mumbling to herself excitedly as she dragged him toward the feed room.

The Kindred set down the crates. "Is it only the two of you back here?" one asked.

"Yep!" Pika said, tearing open the crate.

"Do not leave this feed room until you have finished unpacking all the supplies." The Kindred exchanged a look, then closed the door firmly behind them.

4

Cora

THE *GAUNTLET.*

Cora raised an eyebrow at the word Cassian had just spoken. "Why does that sound suspiciously like something that's going to get me killed?"

Cassian motioned for her to follow him into the alcove, where they could speak privately. Through the wooden screen she could still hear the music and feel the breeze, but they were alone.

"The Gauntlet," he said, "is a series of tests used to rate species on four categories of intelligence. It is run by the Stock Algorithm, which serves as an impartial third party. Because it is a computer program, it cannot be influenced by any outside factors."

"And what does it have to do with me?"

The expression on his face softened. "Everything. It is humanity's chance to prove its value, and thus gain freedom." He paused. "However, it is true that the Gauntlet's puzzles are challenging, even dangerous. If the test were easy, it would serve no purpose. It was originally established a million and a half rotations ago, when there were only two intelligent species: the Gatherers and the Axion. The Gatherers had taken my people under their guidance long before, and taught us to improve our minds and bodies over generations, until we had mastered the essential abilities. They wanted to admit us into intelligent society, but the Axion questioned our qualifications. They are an ancient species, but secretive and suspicious. And so the Gauntlet was created to prove our worth. That is how the Kindred became the third intelligent species."

"I'm guessing that means the Mosca were the fourth. Did they beat the Gauntlet too?"

Cassian recoiled slightly at mention of the Mosca, like he had smelled something rotten. "Eventually, yes. For all their faults, the Mosca have incredible perceptive abilities. But they struggled with the morality puzzles. It took them nine tries until one of them could manage to curb his innate inclination to steal long enough to pass the test. Other species have not been as successful. The Conmarines. The Scoates. A half dozen others, in sectors very far from here. Even a chimpanzee tried to run it once—the Axion had experimented on it to give it higher intelligence. But they all failed the perceptive puzzles."

He removed a device from his pocket and twisted the end. "This is how it works." Lines of light spilled out from the device, stacking on top of each other with startling speed on the table surface to form intricate shapes. "The Gauntlet is a governance module. It is its own ship, just as our markets and research centers and private chambers are independent, interlocking ships. It travels from station to station, planet to planet, to ensure that all the lesser species through the known galaxies have a fair chance to run it. That is why it only docks at this particular station every six hundredth rotation—there are many other galaxies very far away that it must also visit. It is composed of four categories of puzzles with three rounds each. Twelve puzzles in all." The lines of light kept connecting, building, until they took shape as rooms and chambers. Cora realized she was looking at three-dimensional blueprints. She reached out to touch the image, expecting to feel only the warmth of holographic projections, but her fingers grazed a rigid surface. She pulled back her hand in surprise.

"This is a rendering of the Gauntlet itself. Note the twelve chambers. A candidate must traverse each chamber in order. Once one puzzle is complete, the chamber will allow access to the next puzzle. Naturally, they get increasingly difficult."

She leaned closer. She couldn't help but be intrigued, both by the structure of pulsing light and by what it signified—a chance, a *purpose*. As she watched, a small holographic figure no bigger than her thumbnail appeared in the first chamber, which started glowing a soft red. The figure moved to the next chamber, which glowed green.

"The colors represent the type of puzzle in each chamber," he continued. "The first represents a perceptive puzzle, red. Then intellectual, green. Then physical, yellow. And moral, blue." They watched as the figure moved through all twelve chambers, each lighting up with one of the four colors. "What you see here is the previous Gauntlet's schematic. It occurred here six hundred rotations ago—about twenty years. Four humans and two Scoates ran it, all unsuccessfully. Each time, the puzzles within the Gauntlet change. We will not know ahead of time the order of puzzles or what specific skills each puzzle will test."

Beyond the alcove screen, the sound of another hunt announcement began. Cora threw a look toward the screen, where she could just barely make out the sounds of the blond bartender speaking. "It isn't sounding any less dangerous."

"That is why I placed a variety of puzzles in your previous enclosure. You did not realize it at the time, but I was preparing each of you. The Gauntlet's intellectual puzzles could take the form of anagram puzzles like in the candy shop, or the number games in the toy store. The physical puzzles might be climbing, like in the forest. Or balance, like in the sledding course." He paused. "But there is a key difference. In your previous enclosure, you were always safe. If you fell in the forest's treetop puzzle, you would only land on soft pine needles. If you got lost in the desert's maze, there was ample water and shade. But those were merely training modules. In the real Gauntlet, there will be no safety nets. If you fall, you fall."

Cora's stomach tightened. "And you really think those puzzles trained me well enough?"

"We will have to hope so." At the look of apprehension that crossed her face, he added, "I would not have chosen you, or any of the other potential candidates, if you hadn't already shown exceptional abilities. Humans are already quite advanced in physical, intellectual, and moral development. It is the perception category that will require further training. We have just over two rotations until the Gauntlet module arrives. There is a docking procedure that takes one-tenth of a rotation, about three days. All in all, we have roughly thirty days to prepare." He pressed the device again, and the blueprints folded back up into it and flickered off.

Cora blinked at the bare table. There was something about it all that made her skin tingle in an exciting way, urging her to take this chance—but then she saw that same flash of excitement on Cassian's face too, and it killed hers.

"Don't bother," she said. "I don't need to know how, because I'm not going to run it. It's just a game to you, moving us around like chess pieces."

"You don't understand what is at stake. By the next Gauntlet, enough time will have passed that humanity's evolution will be obvious. But instead of supporting it, the Intelligence Council will suppress it. We must do this before they understand your potential, while they think it is still harmless to let you run. It must be now. It must be *this* Gauntlet. You must have a sponsor; naturally, that will be me. That is how all of this will be possible."

She crossed her arms tight, trying to act indifferent, though the allure of the Gauntlet was still fresh in her mind. "Then find a different girl to run."

"There have been other candidates—Anya, for one—but none of them worked out. Even if another human displayed potential at this point, that human would not be able to sufficiently develop his or her abilities in time. It must be you." He paused. "I want it to be you, Cora."

At the sound of her name, spoken not in his monotone voice but like that day on the beach, standing in the surf, her skin started to tingle in that dangerous way.

She turned away sharply. "I don't need puzzles or bureaucrats or scorecards to tell me humans are intelligent." She slid open the alcove screen. Beyond, the hunt ceremony had ended. A girl with dark-brown skin was onstage, tap-dancing to music, a bandage around one knee, dressed in a gown like Cora's but knee length. The girl flinched every time she had to bend her hurt knee. Cora started to step into the lodge, but Cassian slid the alcove screen shut again.

He leaned in, not stiffly anymore, the patient look gone from his eyes. "I cannot force you to run the Gauntlet, but take time to think it through before you make up your mind." And then his expression eased, and he took her hand, weaving his fingers between hers, turning her palm upward. "It isn't a game," he said. "It never has been."

With her palm toward the ceiling, the markings were an even greater reminder that she was, and would always be, a prisoner.

She pulled her hand back, trying to ignore the tingling sensation. "I'd rather take my chances with the wild animals."

Even as she said it, she knew it wasn't entirely true.

The definition of stubborn, Charlie's voice echoed, *is to know what the right thing to do is, but not to do it anyway just to prove a point.*

She snatched up the dress angrily.

Shut up, Charlie, she thought silently, glad that a memory couldn't answer back.

5

Cora

CORA WENT INTO A different alcove to change into the gold dress, and when she came out, the dancing girl had finished onstage. The girl now slouched on a stool at the end of the bar, gulping water from a cloudy glass, shaking her head at something the Kindred guest on the next stool said. Cora recognized him as the one with the eerily sunken eyes. He produced a golden token from his pocket; it flashed in the lantern light. The dancing girl hunched further, massaging the muscles around her hurt knee, but then sighed and took the token. The Kindred patted her on the head as one would a dog.

Cora's stomach turned. In the cage, she had been constantly observed, but there had been walls. The Kindred could watch but not touch. Here, there were no walls. Nothing to stop the Kindred from doing whatever they wanted to their human pets. And judging by the bandage on the dancer's knee, and the scraggly haircuts on the others, the Kindred weren't particularly interested in their pets' welfare.

Cassian motioned to the empty stage.

"I'm supposed to start singing now?" she asked. "Already?"

"This isn't like your previous enclosure. There is no adjustment period. Here you sing, or you starve." He held out his hand to help her up, but she ignored it and stepped onstage. Her bare feet crunched over sand grit and something uncomfortably sticky. She lifted the gold dress's hem, trying not to look too hard at the stains on the stage.

"What am I supposed to sing?"

"Whatever you like," Cassian answered. "We do not create music; to us, it all sounds alike. Pleasant but vague."

She stared beyond the microphone at the tables that were now cast in shadows. When she shaded her eyes, she just made out the dancing girl with her arms around the Kindred guest, the two of them dancing slowly in the center of the room.

Cassian started for the door.

"Wait," Cora whispered, covering the microphone. "You're just going to leave me here?" He was a monster, yes, but a monster she knew.

"My responsibilities as a Warden did not end when your enclosure failed. We are in the process of introducing new wards to that facility. Younger ones this time, taken from regulated preserves where they have been raised. There is hope they will adapt better than your cohort did, as they have never known Earth. We will have to suspend Rule Three until they are older, but it is an acceptable sacrifice."

"You mean they're just children?" she asked.

He nodded.

Her stomach turned again.

"You do not believe it is morally correct to take children," he concluded. "If you don't like it, then work with me to change the system. Consider what I've told you. This place will"—he looked around at the dirty floor—"give you needed perspective. You will soon realize that I am correct. If you have any hope of bettering your life, the Gauntlet is the only way. I will return when my duties allow to see if you have changed your mind."

She didn't answer. He wove among the tables and then disappeared back into the warren of tunnels through the asteroid to his life, to his job, to his responsibilities that weren't her.

For a moment, the lodge was silent. The spotlights shone in her eyes, and she had to blink to see around them. The boys at the bar and the girl dancing with the Kindred guest were watching her.

She tapped the microphone and coughed at the cloud of dust.

It looked vintage, like the kind radio announcers in old movies spoke into, and yet there were no wires. An artificial reconstruction, just like the spotlights shining in her eyes, and the smell of sticky-sweet drinks being served at the bar. She shifted in the gold dress, unused to how it hugged her body.

Before her, the Kindred audience was cast in shadows. More had arrived, and now the sounds of a dozen guests waiting filled the silence. All were dressed in artificial human clothes. The only exceptions were two Kindred soldiers in black uniforms, heading out toward the savanna. Sweat trickled down her back as she cleared her throat again.

"Wishing on a star, never thought I'd come this far. . . ." Her voice reverberated around the corners of the room louder than she'd expected. The two bartenders stopped what they were doing and turned in surprise, like they hadn't heard real singing in years.

"Across the night sky, never knowing why . . ."

The sounds of a vehicle roared in the distance; chairs squeaked as the Kindred guests twisted toward the savanna, more interested in the most recent hunt than in her song, and for some crazy reason, this angered her.

"Wanting to stay strong, surrounded by *monsters* . . ."

She knew she was pushing it, but they ignored her. Apparently, Cassian was right: for all their brilliance, subtext in song was lost on them.

The gong sounded, signaling a returning expedition. But then it sounded again. And again, haphazardly, as though someone was falling against it. Someone shouted, though Cora couldn't make out the words. A few of the guests jumped up and ran to the French doors to see what had caused the commotion. She stood on her tiptoes at the edge of the stage, trying to see over the guests' heads.

And then, suddenly, the guests parted. The two uniformed soldiers she'd noticed earlier came striding up the veranda stairs with a human boy between them. He was tall, with medium-brown skin and short hair, and he wore a safari uniform with leather driving gloves and, dangling around his neck, a set of driving goggles.

"It isn't time yet!" he yelled, as he fought against the guards. "It's too soon!"

Cora threw a look to the bartenders, who watched apprehensively, not making a move to help the boy. Three other kids came up the savanna stairs, including the same scrawny-limbed boy and girl as before, their safari uniforms caked with even more dust, eyes just as wide as they watched the boy being dragged off.

The boy locked eyes with the blond bartender. "Dane! Tell the others. We've all been lied to and—" One of the guards jabbed a device into the boy's side and he slumped, unconscious. The two guards dragged him to a red door behind the bar. One of the bartenders started to follow, but the other one—Dane—held out a hand to stop him.

For a second, the entire lodge was silent.

Cora looked around in confusion, hoping for an explanation. The guests seemed shaken but not entirely surprised. They whispered among themselves, faces wearing exaggerated masks of pity for the boy.

A dishrag flew at her, and she jumped.

"Sing, songbird," the bartender named Dane commanded. "Distract them."

But she could only stand there, lips parted. No sound came from her throat. No lyrics came into her head. It was too much, all of it. To be abandoned here, thrust onstage, witness to whatever awful thing had just happened to that boy. And on top of everything, who was Cassian to say that *she* was supposed to set humanity free?

Dane rolled his eyes and jerked his head for her to step off the stage. He put on some recorded music and ordered the dancing girl to get up there. As soon as she did, the guests seemed to forget about the incident, returning to their drinks and conversations and slow dances.

"You've got ten minutes to pull yourself together," Dane threatened Cora. "And then you sing when I tell you to sing."

The guest with the sunken eyes had been close enough to hear their conversation. His head was cocked in her direction now, as though he could see straight into the offstage shadows where they stood. He smiled slightly.

She hugged her arms, feeling cold despite the humid air, until a hand reached out from the shadows and pinched her.

6

Leon

IF THERE WAS ONE thing Leon liked, it was a full glass of vodka.

Not the fancy stuff, no. It was quantity he was interested in, and Bonebreak had plenty. As a black-market trader, Bonebreak seemed to be able to get his hands on anything from Earth or any other planet. The more Leon drank, the easier it was to overlook the fact that Bonebreak had a seriously ugly hunchback and breath that smelled like something had died. Also, that he wasn't human.

Leon tipped the dusty bottle toward the Mosca. "Cheers, mate."

"Cheers."

The Mosca's voice came in fits and starts from behind his mask. In the two days that Leon had known Bonebreak, he hadn't seen his face once, or the faces of any of Bonebreak's underlings, who scuttled around the corners of the room. After Bonebreak had passed out drunk the night before, Leon had tried to pull off the mask to see what was underneath, only to find it was sewn into the edges of the creature's face with thick black wire.

Leon tilted the bottle up, then frowned. Empty already. "I need another bottle," he said. "This one must, uh, have had a leak."

Bonebreak groaned as he pulled himself to his feet. He scuttled around the various crates, poking and prodding through the contents. He'd set up his smuggling operation in the back half of a shipping node on a lower level that no one seemed to even remember was there, judging by the dirty halls and neglected lights. There was a bored-looking, low-level Kindred official who staffed the front of the node, collecting shipments for the level's few residents, and accepted Bonebreak's steady supply of bribes to get first dibs on the shipments' contents.

"Ah. Here." The Mosca unearthed another bottle of vodka, this one still shiny and new. "From the latest supply run." He held the bottle to his mask and breathed audibly. "Smells like Earth. Rotting plants and burning coal."

Leon shifted uneasily. "So how long ago was this run, exactly?"

"Recent enough."

"The Kindred said Earth was destroyed right after we were taken. Humans ruined it or whatever—some climate-change shit. That true?"

Bonebreak snorted behind his mask, making a sound like a wheeze. "The Kindred think they can explain the universe with their mathematics. They forget the universe was here long before mathematics was. As were we. And so we shall be long after they are all dust in space." He swiped a gloved finger along the dust-composite crate, coming away with a chalky powder.

"So . . . Earth's still there? For real?"

Bonebreak held up the vodka. "Where else would I have gotten this?"

Images filled Leon's head of his sister Ellie's apartment back in Auckland. A cramped place that always swarmed with every kid in the neighborhood, it seemed, but suddenly he missed all that chaos. "Maybe the next time you go back, you could give me a lift. You know, a little favor among friends." Leon scratched his ear, playing it off casually.

Bonebreak snorted. "Nice try. The last ship bound for Earth left four rotations ago and won't be back for, oh, forty human years." He admired the bottle. "You are stuck with us."

An uneasy feeling set up shop in Leon's head and wouldn't move out. The Kindred swore Earth was gone; the Mosca swore it was still there. He didn't trust either species, but if he had to pick sides, he supposed he'd take the one with the booze.

He reached for the bottle.

Bonebreak held it just out of his reach. "Not yet. You see, my hospitality is finite."

Leon knew an endless supply of potato chips, vodka, and a crate to sleep in was too good to be true. He'd been waiting for the catch ever since he'd fallen on Bonebreak's head two days ago and discovered the Mosca's smuggling den by accident. While running from Kindred guards, he'd pried open one of their mind-control doors with his bare hands and found a room full of human arti- facts: picture books, cloth diapers, even a crib. Baby shit. He'd hidden in the crib for two days, until he'd thought he'd go crazy if he had to stare at pink penguin bedding any longer, and then suddenly woke up to find himself in the utter dark, breathing chalky air, caged inside the crib, which had been crated up and was moving. He nearly broke his hand punching his way out, only to find himself in a system of claustrophobic tunnels that eventually spit him out onto a hunchbacked alien in a red jumpsuit with a mask sewn into his face. Bonebreak's underlings had seized him.

At his scared face, Bonebreak had just cackled. *Do not worry, boy. Any enemy of the Kindred is a friend of mine.*

Now, Leon blinked at Bonebreak's opaque mask, wondering what the trader was going to demand in exchange for not turning him in to the Kindred.

"I know how this works," Leon said. "So just skip the part where you claim you're looking out for my best interest. We've got guys like you back home. My uncle, for one. So tell me what I have to do, and I'll do it." Leon puffed up, but Bonebreak only leaned in, letting out a low hiss.

"Do you know why I am called Bonebreak, boy?"

Leon deflated a little. "Uh . . . I can guess."

"Can you? Good. I suggest you use your imagination so I do not have to demonstrate. Leave the arrogance to the Kindred, and you and I will get along much better. There is only one reason I haven't turned you in." He kicked out a thin booted leg and prodded Leon's knee. "Humans have a certain flexibility of tendons that we Mosca lack. A flexibility that permits you to . . . what is the word? Ah. Crawl. That is why you are still alive. Because your bodies allow you to crawl, and ours do not, and that is a useful skill in a station full of very low tunnels."

Leon narrowed his eyes at the hunchback Mosca. "No way I'm going back in those tunnels. It was rank as hell, and it's too easy to get lost with all those twisty corners. I'd probably suffocate trapped between levels and rot."

"That is unlikely." Bonebreak stroked the chin part of his mask. "The debris-cleaning traps would kill you long before you'd suffocate."

"*Traps?*"

"I'm surprised they didn't kill you already. They're stationed at random intervals, set to be triggered by anything other than an official package. They release a burst of flammable gas that incinerates anything that shouldn't be in the tunnels."

"Like me," Leon added.

Bonebreak cocked his head. "Like you—if you are not careful."

Leon scrubbed his face, grumbling to himself about all the ways he was going to die on this station. "So you want me to risk my life to steal for you, eh? Crawl around booby traps like some spy shit?" He scratched his chin. "What's in it for me?"

Bonebreak cackled again. "Your life." Bonebreak's underlings, huddled around the edge of the room, cackled too.

"Yeah, well, I can do a hell of a lot more than crawl, see? I escaped the Kindred. I didn't even know the traps were there, and still avoided them. I'm good. And I'm not risking my life for a few stale potato chips."

Bonebreak eyed him with contempt. "What do you want?"

Leon paused. "I want you to radio those supply ships out there, the ones going to Earth. I want to know . . ." He pictured his sister, Ellie, and his nieces and nephews who used to play Godzilla with him, and his dad who he'd never visited in prison, not even once. "I want to know if my family is . . ." His throat seemed clogged all of a sudden.

But then a wave of anger swept him up, and he turned away.

No. It didn't matter if Earth was still there. Did he really want to know if his sister and his nieces and nephews were dead? "I want a place on your crew. A proper bed, not a damn crate. I'm sure you can smuggle that out of somewhere. And I want half of what I steal for you."

Bonebreak stared at him from behind the mask. "A quarter."

"Deal." Leon reached for the bottle of vodka, but Bonebreak held it back.

"There is one more thing. To be a part of our crew requires a sort of . . . initiation." He held his hand open, and one of his underlings skittered forward and placed a curved, jagged-looking sewing needle there. Leon's stomach shrank.

Bonebreak slowly threaded the needle with the gummy black wire that held their masks to their faces. "We'll start with a small piece of shielding on the upper arm, since you can breathe without the aid of a mask. The thread is coated in cobalt toxin; it keeps the skin from grafting to it. It's only moderately poisonous. We've never actually used it on a human before, but you're a big fellow—I think you'll be fine."

Leon paced, eyeing that heinous needle. Bonebreak wanted him to be exactly what he had been on Earth: filth. A criminal. A bad guy. The Kindred had thought he had potential to be some-thing more—damned if he knew why. Cora had thought so too.

He looked out into the blackness of the shipping tunnel. Somewhere, it connected to them. Cora. Mali. Lucky. Nok and Rolf, wherever the Kindred were keeping them. Lucky would have put on his damned white knight suit of armor and gone to rescue them all.

But Leon wasn't like Lucky.

Leon wasn't a hero.

And anytime he had ever tried to help someone, he'd only ended up hurting them more. He grabbed the bottle of vodka and drank until he could barely remember Cora's name, or Mali's pretty face, and let the Mosca set a molded piece of shielding against his shoulder.

Bonebreak raised the needle.

No—he wasn't a hero. He was a smuggler. And, apparently, now an official member of Bonebreak's crew.

7

Cora

CORA CLAMPED A HAND over the place on her arm where she'd been pinched, and spun to find herself looking at a girl dressed in safari clothes, with long black hair tied in unkempt braids, and a permanent scowl.

"Mali!"

Dane tossed Cora a warning look from behind the bar. She dropped her voice, fighting the urge to throw her arms around her friend. "I didn't know if I'd ever see you again."

Mali wore the same safari uniform as the other kids, but with a driving cap over her braids, and thick leather gloves just like the boy they'd dragged away had worn. As soon as Cora saw them, uneasiness bloomed in her stomach. "Is everything okay? What happened to that boy?"

"I do not know," Mali said. "Cassian puts me here early today. He makes me a driver. The boy they take away is also a driver. His name is Chicago. He teaches me to steer the trucks this morning. They go on a track, the same circle again and again until we find an animal to shoot. The guards come for him and he starts yelling. The other safari guides look scared, but they tell me to pretend nothing happens."

Cora glanced toward the bar. The Kindred with the sunken eyes was still watching her with that creepy smile.

"Have you seen Lucky?" Cora asked. "What about Leon? Nok and Rolf?"

"I hear nothing about them." Mali suddenly latched onto Cora's wrist with clawlike fingers. "Do you remember your promise."

Cora's arm stung all over again. "Promise?"

"Anya." Mali's short nails dug deeper into her skin. "My friend. We make a deal in the cage: I help you escape and you help rescue Anya."

"Yeah, I remember," Cora said, biting through the pain. "But it isn't like we can just stroll over there and get her. We're trapped."

Mali squeezed even tighter.

"Fine!" Cora hissed. "If there's any way to do it, then we will. Now, stop clawing me."

Mali released her and then gave her flat smile, friendly again. "Good. We will talk more. After work."

She started to leave, but Cora jerked her chin at the Kindred with the sunken eyes. "Hang on a minute. That Kindred keeps looking at me. Do you know who he is?"

Mali scratched at a bug bite on her neck. "His name is Roshian. Makayla tells me about him this morning. Ignore him. He is harmless."

"Makayla?"

"The one who dances."

Before Cora could ask more, Dane beckoned her back onstage, and she didn't dare disobey him again. The platform was smeared in fresh blood from the hyena. She looked back at the audience. Roshian had started dancing again with Makayla, stepping on her toes hard enough to make her grimace.

Their eyes met over the girl's shoulder, and he smiled again. Ignore him? Even if she could, there were thirty more just like him. Watching her. Judging her. Maybe just waiting to drag her off too, like they had Chicago. She stepped up to the microphone again, but this time her voice was shaking.

Back home, her dream had been to become a songwriter. She'd secretly scrawled lyrics in her journal after her parents had gone to bed, about what it was like to be trapped in the life of a senator's daughter. She'd close her eyes and imagine a stage where she could sing what she wanted to, make people understand through her lyrics, be free in the spotlight to sing the words in her heart.

Now she had a spotlight.

And all she could think of was the bruises and watery eyes of the other kids, injuries she and Mali would probably have soon too.

As she grabbed the microphone, the last thing it felt like was a dream.

"HONORED GUESTS, THE HUNT is closing."

Cora's throat was hoarse by the time the hostess finally announced that the Hunt was closing for the evening. The lights dimmed, and the few remaining Kindred guests departed. The dark-haired bartender cleaned the lounge in a rush, tossing her a rag to wipe the last traces of the animals' blood off the stage.

When she finished, the other humans had gone. She looked up at an eerily empty lodge. Clipped footsteps came from the direction of the veranda, where the hostess appeared. Cora started—though she was dressed in the same costume, it wasn't Issander. Now Tessela wore the safari dress, and as she approached Cora, she gave the hint of a smile.

"Tessela," Cora whispered. "What happened to Issander?"

"You must have more faith in Cassian," Tessela said. "There was a chance Issander was a spy, so he had her replaced. I will try to protect you, but only so far. The Council cannot suspect anything. Now, come." She signaled for Cora to follow. Cora trailed her through the backstage door, which led to a corridor that smelled of both astringent and straw, like a stable. Tessela handed Cora a block of dry cake-like bread and then showed her into a two-story room lined with cells.

Cora stopped abruptly. There were wild animals in half the cages, and human kids in the other half. The dancing girl, Makayla, was on the second story. The dark-haired bartender was near the bottom corner.

"Here!" a voice yelled. "There's an empty cage here."

That was Lucky's voice! Cora whirled toward the sound. Behind his cell bars, his dark hair was just as rumpled as his safari clothes, but a little longer than she remembered. Weeks must have passed since she had seen him.

"Bring her over here," he said, gripping the bars tighter. He nodded toward an empty cage two down from his own, directly below Mali. In the cell between them, a small white fox curled at the bottom.

Cora stepped into the cell, and Tessela closed and latched the gate. It was a simple metal latch that Cora could have easily reached through the bars and unlocked, but Lucky made a signal for her to wait. She looked away, self-conscious. She hadn't looked in a mirror in weeks, but besides tangled hair, what did he see when he looked at her? The girl who'd assaulted him in the cage? The senator's daughter he'd sent to prison?

Or someone who'd once been a friend?

She dared a glance up. With his hair shaggy like that, he looked more like the boy she'd first seen on an artificial beach, looking as utterly lost as she was. She had liked that boy. She just hadn't liked what the cage had later twisted him into—someone complacent.

But as soon as Tessela left, his hands squeezed the bars tightly. There was a determination written on his face that told her that boy on the beach had never truly vanished, and it lifted her spirits.

"We can't get out," he said, and nodded toward the cell doors. The overhead lights clicked off, and a blue light clicked on above each of their doors. "Lightlocks. The other kids told me about them earlier today. They're run by perceptive technology. They don't unlock until the morning." He paused. "It's good to see you."

"You too," she said quietly.

From the cell above her, Mali stuck down a hand and waved.

In the faint blue glow, Cora couldn't quite read Lucky's face.

His hand went to his temple absently, the spot where she had once slammed a ceramic dog into his head to escape him. But then he reached out for her. She did the same, but five inches of space kept them apart. She was just about tell him that she was sorry for everything that had happened, when a deep voice interrupted her.

8

Cora

"LADIES AND GENTLEMEN, IT looks like we have a new girl."

Cora turned toward the voice in the darkness. Two hands grabbed the bars of her cell and rattled hard, making her jump. A boy's face pressed against the bars, grinning maniacally.

The blond bartender, Dane.

"Boo." He let out a laugh.

He took a yellow yo-yo out of his pocket and started tossing it up and down, up and down, carefree as though they weren't all prisoners. As though one of them hadn't been dragged off by guards just hours ago for no discernible reason, yelling about lies. The blue glow reflected on the boy's buzzed head, hair a shade darker than her own, hooded eyes that cast shadows almost like the Kindred's.

"Welcome to the Hunt, songbird. You're the third new cast member we've gotten today—we met the others this morning. What's your name?"

"Leave her alone," Lucky said.

Dane tossed Lucky a searing look, eyeing him up and down. "Friend of yours? Ah, the one you were asking Pika about. She must be. Not too many blondes around here. You must have someone powerful looking out for you, songbird, or they would have already sold your hair. I bet it was that Warden who brought you here."

"He's no friend of mine," Cora said.

Dane raised an eyebrow. "That's too bad. You'd do well to have powerful friends. A Warden on the outside, me on the inside."

Cora pushed to her feet, dusting grime off her hands. "How'd you get out of your cell, anyway?"

"Within these walls, *I've* got the power."

"The most powerful of the powerless," Lucky muttered.

Dane shot him another look, this one darker. "Not powerless. Not at all. The Kindred have entrusted me with all kinds of power you know nothing about." He threw the yo-yo again and snapped it back. "I'm Head Ward, which means I run this place after hours. I've been here the longest and the Kindred grant me privileges, like a key to my cell that can override the lightlocks, in return for keeping things nice and peaceful backstage. Let me introduce you to our ensemble cast." He swept an arm out toward the other shadowy faces. "Directly above you, we have the other new girl, Mali." He leaned in close and dropped his voice. "A strange one, talks funny, but it seems you already know each other. I saw you whispering together in the lodge. I let it slide because you're new, but I'd better not catch you chatting in public again." His hooded eyes flashed with warning, before he grinned again suddenly and turned back to the wall of cages.

"Next to Mali is the hyena, and then there's Makayla, from Vancouver, who you'll be sharing the stage with." In the faint light, Cora barely made out the dancing girl with the bandage on her knee giving her a wave, and then twisting her hand around to shoot Dane the bird behind his back. Cora barely hid her smile.

"Then the two giraffes in the tall cell in the corner," Dane continued, "and that's Pika next to Roger, the bobcat. Pika runs the show back here during the day." A dirty girl chewing on her braid paused in stroking the bobcat's tail to wave vigorously. "And our three antelope in the other tall cage, and the kangaroo and lioness along the top row. Shoukry's there on the bottom next to the zebra; he's from Cairo. He bartends with me, as you saw today. Jenny and Christopher are on the bottom too—siblings from Australia. They work out on the savanna, leading the expeditions. And then there's our other new addition, this pretty boy with an attitude." His eyes lingered on Lucky's cage, one corner of his mouth turned up in a cryptic smile. "And between you two is our arctic fox. From Canada, I believe. It likes to chew on anything it can get its teeth around. And then there's you. And me, of course, in the cell between Makayla and the hyena. I was rescued five years ago from Cape Town."

Cora raised an eyebrow. "Rescued? That's what you call being abducted?"

"Precisely. I've been running this place ever since," he added.

"Ever since you failed out of one of the enclosures," Makayla muttered loud enough to be heard across the room. Dane snapped his yo-yo back sharply and tossed her a look.

"So here's how it works." He pointed to a clock above the doorway. It looked like the industrial clocks that had been scattered throughout Bay Pines, except there was only one hand, and instead of having twelve numbers, this clock was divided into four uneven slices. "That's how the Kindred keep time for us. Right now it's on Night—the longest block of time. That little sliver next to it is Morning Prep, when you change clothes and eat breakfast, but you have to hustle because it's just a few minutes. The big block next to it is Showtime. That's when you march out there and sing and smile and do whatever the Kindred want you to do. I run the bar and make the announcements, and I'll be keeping an eye on you. Then it's the final block of time: Free Time. About an hour, give or take, and it's a privilege that can be revoked for bad behavior."

Cora rolled her eyes. "You seem awfully proud for a guy who's betraying his own kind."

The shadows around Dane's eyes deepened, so only the faintest glimmer of lights reflected in his irises. "Better to be working with the Kindred than against them."

She snorted.

Dane started pacing. "What do you think, ensemble? Is she going to make it to Armstrong with an attitude like that?"

"Not a chance!" Pika yelled back.

Cora raised an eyebrow. "What's Armstrong?"

Dane stopped his pacing abruptly. He turned toward them with an incredulous look. "No one's told you about Armstrong yet?"

"We've been locked in a fake world," Cora said. "We haven't gotten out much."

The smile crept back onto Dane's face. "Allow me to enlighten you, then. Armstrong is the closest thing to home we have. It's an uninhabited asteroid, a small moon. Well, uninhabited by Kindred or the other intelligent species, that is. It's home to displaced humans. A nature preserve, if you will. It's where the Kindred send all the good boys and girls when they grow up. We put in our hard time as teenagers, and if we behave, we're taken there when we turn nineteen. We're free to govern ourselves, do whatever we want."

Cora eyed him warily. "The Warden told me about that place once," she said slowly, "only he didn't say it was paradise."

Dane smirked, undeterred. "I thought you didn't trust a word out of our kidnappers' mouths."

Cora narrowed her eyes, and Dane matched it with a thin smile. "Like I said, with that attitude, neither of you will ever see Armstrong. Do you know what they do with the ones who turn nineteen and *haven't* behaved?"

Lucky, next to her, went still. An eerie quiet spread from the other cast members, who shifted uneasily in their cells.

"What?" Cora asked warily.

"I don't know," Dane said, and pointed toward the corridor. "But each one of those rooms in there connects to a drecktube. It's where we dump the animals if they die, and all our trash. The bad kids go in there and they never come back. You saw it yourself, today. The boy those two guards dragged off, Chicago. Until this morning, he occupied this same cell that you're in now. That's his blanket you're hugging, as a matter of fact. He's always been a problem—never wanted to clap when the guests told him to clap, never polished the rifles on time." His voice lingered in a way that made Cora wonder if he was telling the truth. Shoving kids down a trash chute didn't sound like a very Kindred thing to do.

"So behave yourself, songbird," Dane continued, "and sing

for that Warden of yours, and one day maybe you'll go to Armstrong instead of the alternative."

He stowed the yo-yo in his shirt pocket and climbed up the stairs to his cell. Pika tried to snatch the yo-yo from his pocket, but he slapped her hand away. She curled in her corner, sucking her braid, whining softly.

From two cells down, Lucky was still strangely quiet. It was as though all his anger had suddenly emptied, and Cora didn't know why, or what had changed. She wished she could see into his mind.

She slid her hands around the bars.

Well, maybe she *could*.

She'd read Cassian's mind once, though unintentionally. She hadn't tried to read minds while trapped in the six-by-six cell, simply because there'd been nobody to practice on. But now she had a roomful of test subjects, and a boy whose thoughts she desperately wanted to read.

She closed her eyes, concentrating. Before, when she had read Cassian's thoughts, her mind had been completely blank. Broken. That wasn't the case now, but maybe she could quiet her mind enough.

Her thoughts reached out for Lucky, hoping to connect. And for a second, she thought she got a glimmer of something. It was shrouded in an overwhelming feeling of uneasiness. A number, maybe.

The number 19? Was that right? He must have been worried about Chicago and what Dane said, but there was something more. . . .

She got the sudden, eerie sensation she was looking into a hazy mirror. Or maybe more like watching herself on an old video recording, her hair extra bright, the dark circles under her eyes gone. Cherry petals were fluttering around her.

Her cheeks blazed. *He was thinking of her.* She quickly severed the connection into his mind. It had been wrong anyway—she shouldn't have done it without his knowledge. Her heart pounded as she wondered if he could somehow tell what she'd done.

But then he sighed, and rolled over, and there was nothing.

She stretched out a hand instead and tried again to reach him through the bars, but they never would be close enough.

9

Nok

"THIS IS YOUR NEW home."

Serassi rested a hand on the knob of the red front door of a two-story house.

Nok placed her palm flat on her belly. With the other, she squeezed Rolf's hand. They stood in a cavernous warehouse so large that the walls were hidden in shadow. It was nearly empty except for two structures: the house with the red front door, and tiered rows of theater benches facing it.

Serassi twisted the knob.

The house was filled with heavy wooden furniture, a blocky television set, cabinets that looked painted on. Nok got the sense that she and Rolf had been brought to an enormous dollhouse, or maybe that they'd been shrunk down to doll size. She pushed back the paisley living room curtains, expecting to see opaque observation panels instead of windows. But here, the windows were real transparent glass, though beyond was only the empty warehouse.

The house is perfect in every way, she thought, *except one.*

There were only three walls.

She turned to where the fourth wall, the front of the house, should be. Open space gaped, facing the tiered spectator seating in the same way that a theater was open to the audience. Carefully, Nok walked to the edge of the living room, where the floor ended abruptly. It was about a four-foot drop to the warehouse floor below. From the house's upstairs level, the drop must be closer to fifteen feet. She let her bare toes curl over the edge. She could jump off, but where would she go? Wherever the warehouse doors were, they would be locked.

Bright lights suddenly turned on from the direction of the seating area, and she shaded her face. *Who* exactly was going to watch them?

"Nok." She turned at Rolf's call. He stood at the top of the living room stairs. His fingers were holding the handrail tightly, but they weren't tapping. He'd shaken that bad habit during their time in the cage, and for a second, he looked like an entirely different person than the twitchy genius she'd first met. "You should come see this."

She followed him up the stairs, so nervous that her own fingers nearly started twitching. The entire house consisted of only four rooms, stacked two on two like a perfect cube, with a small cutout for a bathroom. Downstairs was a living room and a kitchen large enough to fit a dining room table. Upstairs there was a bedroom and a spare room, mostly empty now except for a rocking chair and a few boxes.

She paused in the open doorway.

Unassembled parts of a crib were leaning against one of the boxes. A tangled mobile of stars already hung from the ceiling, perfectly still in the windless room. She took a shaky step inside, touching the mobile to make it spin.

A nursery—or at least the start of one.

The mobile spun faster, or maybe the spinning was in her head. She suddenly felt like she was back home in London, trapped in front of flashing camera lights, a too-small dress riding up her hips. She felt sick and turned, but jumped to find Serassi blocking the door.

"I don't understand," Nok said, breathing hard. "You said we weren't capable of raising our own young. You said you were going to take away the baby."

Serassi eyed her calmly. "That was my original assessment, yes. We reproduce by collecting Kindred DNA and matching it for optimum genetics. The offspring are not born, but raised in communal grow houses from infancy through first-decade aging. As chief genetics officer, I have been working to engineer a similar system with humans. Soon, natural reproduction will be as obsolete for your kind as it is for ours. Your child might very well be the last born of natural means."

She almost looked pleased with herself, but then she blinked, as though she had forgotten something important, and cocked her head. "Though after observing you in your previous enclosure, I realized I might be missing a valuable opportunity to study authentic prenatal care in its natural habitat. Our knowledge of your child-rearing culture has heretofore been collected by studying artifacts: instructional books, videos, and recordings. I've learned that your kind has traditions that are never written down. It is my intention to observe these informal practices here."

Nok stumbled through her words. "So . . . we can keep the baby?"

Serassi's dark eyes swiveled to Nok's belly. "As long as you prove yourselves useful to our research purposes."

"And if we don't?" Rolf asked tensely. "You cut the baby out of her belly and kill us?"

"The moral code prevents us from killing you," Serassi answered, though from the way her voice lingered, whatever the alternative would be didn't seem much better.

A pain shot through Nok's belly. Was it true? Would they really take Sparrow away before she was even born and raise her in some alien incubator somewhere, watched and documented just like Nok had been for all those photographers back home? "You're monsters!" She lunged toward Serassi, but Rolf held her back. His muscles had grown from all the sledding and gardening in the cage, and he stopped her from clawing at Serassi.

"Don't," he whispered. "She's stronger than us. Think of Sparrow."

Nok let out a frustrated cry and spun away, breath coming fast. She pressed a hand to the base of her neck. The Kindred had fixed her asthma when they'd abducted her, but she still felt the ghost of tightness in her lungs.

She stormed into the nursery. Rolf followed her, glancing back at the open door.

"At least we're safe for the time being," Rolf said.

"Until when?" she asked. "Until we can't teach them anything they haven't already learned from books? Rolf, I don't know anything about raising a baby. It won't take them long to figure that out. A month, maybe two, and they'll take her away as soon as she's developed enough."

She glanced over at the crib and felt sick all over again.

"I won't let it come to that." Rolf rested his hands on her shoulders.

They went back into the hallway, but Serassi had vanished. They found her downstairs, inspecting a microwave oven that kept dinging despite the fact that nothing was cooking. If she was upset that Nok had nearly tried to claw her face off, she didn't show it.

"Do this for Sparrow," Rolf whispered.

It gave Nok something to hold on to, and she took a deep breath and turned to Serassi. "What about the others?"

Serassi straightened. "None of the others are expecting a child, so there is no reason for them to be here." She nodded toward the staircase. "You will find suitable clothing in the bedroom upstairs. Try to ignore the observers and act as naturally as you would if you were in your former lives. This habitat has been left open so the observers can ask you any questions they might have about what you are doing and why. Answer their questions promptly. Otherwise, you are free to live as you choose."

The tight walls of the living room pressed in toward Nok.

"Where is Cassian? Can we talk to him?"

Serassi returned to inspecting the microwave. "If you believe that Cassian will take you away from this place, you are mistaken. He needed to hide Cora's escape attempt and his own role in it from the Council. Tessela and Fian are two of his supporters, and thus they agreed to lie. But I care nothing for his mission. And so he offered to give me the two of you and your baby for my own research purposes, in exchange for my silence." Serassi closed the microwave door. "I am the one you answer to now."

Nok closed her eyes, pressing a hand to her throat.

"We have simulated day and night for you," Serassi continued. "I will return tomorrow to perform the first round of tests, along with my fellow reproductive scientists. We expect you to comply with the mission of this facility and act in a way befitting parents-to-be. Cook meals and dine together. Prepare the house for your coming child. Follow whatever customs you would on Earth. And, most importantly, focus on your health. For the baby."

Her eyes, once more, went to Nok's belly.

Nok pressed her hands tighter to fight against the sense that Serassi was already communicating with her child; that Sparrow somehow already belonged more to this creature than to Nok.

Serassi left through the red front door, which seemed a bit farcical; she could have stepped down through the missing wall. Once she was gone, Nok threw her arms around Rolf. She wanted to burst into tears, but they didn't come. "How much time do we have until Sparrow is developed enough that they could take her away?"

"I can't be certain," Rolf said. "Their time works differently. In the cage, I had started to work through the calculations—it's an algorithm based on the speed of the rotations of this station and the gravitational pull of nearby planets. But then . . . Well." His face went dark. "It didn't seem to matter anymore."

Nok didn't need to ask him what he meant. She and Rolf had both gone a little crazy in the cage, convinced that the unlimited candy and video games were paradise.

"Can you try to figure it out again?" she asked, squeezing his arms. "We need to know how much time we have to . . ." Pressure built behind her eyes but she still didn't cry. This time, she wasn't going to go along blindly, letting people order her to pose this way and that. She was done being a living doll. ". . . to *escape*. Sparrow is not going to grow up in this dollhouse with an alien for a mother. She's going to grow up with you and me—far away from here."

10

Cora

IT WAS A NOISY night. The brother and sister from Australia whispered to each other from their neighboring cells, and once Dane fell asleep, Pika started grumbling aloud to the bobcat's tail about the yo-yo. The only quiet corner was Mali's and the hyena's, and Cora wondered what Mali must think of all this. Like Dane, Mali had once sided with their Kindred kidnappers. But that had changed when she'd learned Anya was alive—and the Kindred had lied about it.

"Cora," Lucky whispered. "You still awake?"

"As if I could sleep." She tapped on the bars above her. "What about you, Mali?"

Two arms and a head appeared, upside down. Thin as she was, Mali had to be the only one who could squeeze her head between the bars. "I do not sleep either."

"Where have they been keeping you?" Lucky asked.

Cora told him about the six-by-six cell, and the grimaces on both his face and Mali's said they were all too familiar with it.

"I do not think they have caught Leon," Mali said. "He might come back for us."

Lucky snorted. "He won't."

The disappointment on Mali's face was plain to see, even upside down. In the cage, she and Leon had been matched. An arrangement that Leon had resisted, to say the least, and yet Cora knew that the Kindred had matched them because they were more alike than he wanted to admit.

Cora reached up and squeezed Mali's dangling hand.

Lucky's voice dropped an octave, as though he knew he was treading dangerous ground. "They said the Warden brought you here. He didn't hurt you, did he?"

Cora felt her heart beat just once, painfully, as if someone had reached into her chest and squeezed out all the blood. Had he hurt her? He'd *decimated* her.

She clenched her jaw.

"I'm fine." She squinted into the darkness. "Are there black windows here? Are they watching us?"

"Not as far as I can tell. It isn't like the cage, where they watched us all the time. They don't seem to care what we do, as long as we don't cause trouble. Wait until you get a good look at this place during the daytime. It's a dump."

Mali grunted her agreement. "We are not prime specimens anymore."

Cora glanced toward the other cells, listening to the faint sounds of shifting bodies as the others slept. She pulled her blanket tighter. *Chicago's* blanket. What had he done to merit being dragged off on his nineteenth birthday, instead of being sent to Armstrong?

And what were the Kindred's lies he'd been yelling about?

"I don't know if I believe a word Dane says," Cora said, "but we can't stay here."

Lucky let out a harsh laugh. "We tried to escape. You know as well as I do how that played out."

"I'm not talking about escape," Cora whispered. "Cassian has a different plan. There's a series of tests that's happening in a few weeks. If I run them and pass, humans will be granted intelligent species status. They won't be able to cage us anymore. That's why he put us here, to train me in psychic abilities secretly so I can pass the tests."

Mali, her long braids dangling toward the floor, let out another soft grunt. "You speak of the Gauntlet."

Cora nodded.

Lucky stared at her with an unreadable expression in the blue glow. "Psychic abilities?" There was a strange undertone in his voice. She couldn't shake the feeling that words like *freak* were circling around in the back of his head.

"Will you do it," Mali asked.

"I didn't say yes," Cora said. "I can't bring myself to trust him. He had me completely fooled before. You have no idea how awful it is to even be around him, the constant reminders that he was lying the entire time."

Lucky didn't respond right away, and she realized her connection with Cassian was probably the last thing he wanted to talk about.

"The Gauntlet is dangerous," Mali said. "Eleven humans attempt to run it before. None still live."

"They died in the puzzles?"

"A few. The physical challenges are difficult, but the moral and perceptive ones are most dangerous. They can break your mind. Some humans go insane and die after."

"What kind of puzzles were they?" Cora asked.

"No one knows," Mali said. "There are rumors that the moral tests form impossible choices: for example, a human is placed in a room with a caged lion that is dying of starvation. The human is told to save its life, but the only way to do that is to free it so it can eat *you*. The perceptive puzzles are even worse because they force the brain to work in unnatural ways. Pushing a weak mind to perform telekinesis can rupture the tissue."

"And this is what you plan on doing?" Lucky asked.

"I'll be better prepared than the people who have run it before," Cora said, trying to sound confident. "That's why I'll train with Cassian, so I *don't* lose my mind." She took a deep breath. "He said it's the only way we'll ever be free. Maybe he's right."

"Well, I know *this* isn't right," Lucky said. "This place. The things they do to these animals is sick. And there's something wrong with these kids too. Everyone's half starved and bruised. Who knows how many kids have vanished before Chicago. Or how soon the rest of us will." His face turned very serious.

"What's wrong?" Cora asked.

He pinched the bridge of his nose. "Remember what Dane said about turning nineteen?"

Cora nodded slowly.

"My nineteenth birthday is October twenty-first. We were abducted from Earth on July twenty-ninth. I don't know how much time has passed exactly, but it's got to be close. And if what happened to Chicago is true . . ."

The significance of his words wove their way into Cora's head. Nineteen. The age the Kindred determined that a human went from child to adult. Her eyes went to the supply room with the drecktube.

"Shit," she whispered.

"I'll turn nineteen any day now and be taken away, and then Mali will, and then you." He jerked a hand back toward the cell block. "And everyone else."

"So the Gauntlet's our only option." Cora shifted, anxious. It wasn't just the idea of working with Cassian that bothered her, or that ache in her head when she tried too hard to use her abilities. It was the weight of what it meant. Humanity's freedom resting on her shoulders alone. What if she failed?

And then again, what if she *succeeded*?

"There could be a third option," Mali said quietly, still hanging upside down.

Cora's head jerked up. "What do you mean?"

"The Gauntlet tests competitors in twelve puzzles. If the competitor successfully passes all of them, each tester, known as a Chief Assessor, inputs his approval into the algorithm at the end of the examination. It is a simple process: they approve you or they do not. The exact mechanism is similar to turning a key. Technically, one does not beat the Gauntlet by beating the puzzles. One's success is registered when all four keys are turned."

Cora still looked at her blankly.

"I am saying that you do not have to run the Gauntlet," Mali explained. "You do not have to complete a single puzzle. You must only make the testers turn their keys. It is a . . ." She seemed to search for the word, her arms gesturing upside down. "Loophole."

"How's she supposed to do that?" Lucky whispered. "These aren't exactly creatures you can pull a gun on and make demands."

Mali smiled thinly. "You take control of their minds."

For a second, Lucky and Cora just stared at her. Cora started to laugh a little deliriously, wonder if she'd heard wrong. "Not even the Kindred can control other people's minds."

"Anya can," Mali said, and then corrected herself, "Anya *could*. I see—*saw*—her do it. If we free Anya, she can teach you. It is not a complex skill to learn, if one has already achieved mind-reading ability. It is merely a modification—a trick. She can teach it to you in a matter of days."

"Cheating is too risky," Lucky said. "We'll think of something else."

But Cora didn't answer right away. She picked up a deck of cards Chicago had left behind and riffled through it anxiously. She hadn't touched a deck in months—not since Bay Pines detention center—and the shuffle felt comfortably familiar.

"She might be onto something," Cora argued. "They already think we're criminals. Maybe that's what makes us smarter than them—we aren't restrained by logic and rules. We can be clever. We can cheat. They can't." She held the deck tightly in her hands. "This way, we don't have to trust Cassian. We can betray *his* trust this time. I'll let him train me; I'll let him submit me for registration, but there's no way I'm going to actually run. The minute I stand up in front of the testers, I'll cheat my way to freedom. For all of us."

Upside down, Mali smiled.

In the darkness, Cora could feel Lucky's gaze searing into her. She remembered the kiss they'd shared beneath the boughs of the weeping cherry tree. She had thought she could love him then, but that was before she knew the truth about his mother's death and her father's crimes. Before the cage had twisted him into someone who thought life in an elaborate zoo was paradise.

"I still don't like it," Lucky said. "But I definitely don't like the idea of you going through tests that could rupture your brain, or get you eaten by a lion, or mangled in some physical test."

She bit hard on the inside of her lip. She could smell the rankness of the cell block. Unwashed kids, sick animals, and, beneath it all, the tang of blood.

All night, she toyed with the deck of cards like it was a rosary, whispering prayers and fears and hopes as she shuffled. At Bay Pines, she'd had a cellmate named Tonya who everyone called Queenie because of the queen of hearts tattoo on her shoulder. Queenie's mom had been a sous-chef in Las Vegas, and her dad a card counter at the blackjack tables. He had taught Queenie and her brother to count cards and he'd put them on his team. It wasn't illegal, at least not technically. But there had been an argument with another patron. Accusations of more serious cheating. A fight that resulted in two card dealers in the ICU and Queenie sent to juvie.

But were you really cheating? Cora had asked.

Queenie had snorted and tossed a jack of spades at her bed. *Of course we were.*

Queenie taught her how to hide spare cards in the loose folds of her khaki uniform. It had started out of boredom, two insomniacs locked together in a cinder-block room until the seven-a.m. bell, but then, after two Venezuelan girls beat up Cora in the library, it became necessary. She needed protection, and for that she needed extra commissary credits, and to get them she needed to win at cards. Cheating had been dangerous then, and it would be even more dangerous now. But a thrill raced up Cora's nerves every time she imagined taking the Gauntlet and twisting it on its head: proving humanity's intelligence not through the Kindred's system, but through her own.

But that meant doing the one thing she'd sworn she'd never do, the thing she couldn't stomach even the idea of.

Trusting Cassian again.

11

Cora

AFTER A FEW DAYS, Cora discovered why no one bothered with the shower: the water was ice-cold, and besides, who was there to stay clean for, when the low lights of the Hunt hid all the grime? She learned the hard way that she had to fight her way first thing in the morning to the feed room, or she'd get only crumbs. Already, not even a full week in, she had bruises from being elbowed by the others.

"Take this." Mali thrust a threadbare blanket at her, just before the clock clicked to Showtime. "You are cold last night. I hear you shivering." She frowned and scrunched up her face. She was missing a tooth from where she'd gotten in a fight with Pika the night before over the only magazine, an old *Seventeen* with half the pages torn out. "I mean . . ." She scrunched her face up more. "You *were* cold. I *heard* you."

Cora hugged the blanket close. "You're doing good, Mali. Thanks for this." Mali smiled, seeming pleased with her progress toward acting more human.

The clock clicked to Showtime.

"Already?" Makayla yawned from behind them. "I seriously could have used another hour of sleep." She took a step, wincing on her bad knee.

"You okay?" Cora said, nodding toward the bandage.

Makayla gave a dark laugh. "What, my knee? Yeah. I did it to myself." She stretched her leg out, wincing slightly. "You know that clingy guest, Roshian? He decided I'm his personal pet. He used to take me out on the savanna every day and ask me to run. Thought the exercise was good for me after I'd spent the night in a cramped cell, you know? Like he was doing me a favor. It got old fast, so I smashed my knee into the cell bars. Thought it might get me out of dancing too, but no such luck."

Cora's own knee ached with phantom pain. "Couldn't the Kindred heal you?"

Makayla rolled her eyes. "They wouldn't expend the extra effort. Not on us." She shouldered open the door.

The low lights and chatter of the Hunt spilled out. It looked like afternoon already, the artificial sun lowering over the savanna horizon. A few Kindred guests were already there, waiting for their servers and entertainers. Cora's eyes immediately scanned the room for Cassian, but he wasn't there, and she felt slightly disappointed. He hadn't returned since the first day. Lucky had once accused her of being captivated by their caretaker—and maybe he was right. She'd told herself after Cassian's betrayal that any attraction was over. And yet, anger or love, it was still Cassian who consumed her thoughts.

She followed Makayla toward the stage. One Kindred guest

perched on a stool at the bar. Two danced stiffly together, even with no music. Another was seated at a table near the stage, his eyes sunken and dark. He stood as soon as they entered, as though he had been waiting.

Roshian.

He stepped toward Makayla, petting her head. "Has your knee improved, girl?"

Makayla bent down to massage her knee—with an exaggerated wince. "I think I need to stay off it another few days at least. A real shame."

Roshian looked displeased. He picked at his human clothes, blinking a little fast with black eyes that were only slightly cleared at the edges. He was uncloaked, Cora knew. All the Kindred, even the hostess, were uncloaked in the menageries. If he hadn't been, he'd have sensed Makayla's hatred of him in a second.

His eyes shifted to Cora.

"You." His voice was different from the other Kindred's. They tended to act a little loopy when they were uncloaked, almost like their flood of emotions made them drunk, but Roshian seemed completely in control. "You are new, girl."

"Um, yeah."

"Such unusual hair," he mused. He wrapped a curl around his finger, running his thumb over the strands delicately. "Blond hair can catch quite a price on the trading floor. The Axion believe consuming parts of the lesser species gives them strength. Your hair would be quite a trophy." He spoke so casually, comparing her hair to the heads of wild game that hunters displayed on their walls. Her stomach turned at the thought.

"You must be eager to stretch your legs," he continued. "I

could take you to the savanna, where you could run. I would like to see how fast you are."

"Um . . ." She glanced at Makayla, who only gave a slight shrug, as though to say, *Good luck.* Makayla signaled to Dane to put on some music, and she began leading dancing couples in stiff swaying motions around the lodge. Roshian's eyes slid to the nearest dancing couple, and Cora prayed he wasn't going to ask her to dance.

From the corner of her eye, she saw the main door open. She caught sight of a familiar figure over Roshian's shoulder.

"Cassian! I mean . . . it's the Warden. He just arrived and I promised him a . . . a dance." She awkwardly managed to extract her hair from Roshian's hand. "Sorry."

She hurried toward Cassian, fighting the urge to wipe her hair where Roshian had touched it. Cassian, dressed in a charcoal suit with the jacket slung over one elbow, looked perplexed at her sudden enthusiasm to see him, particularly when she rested her hands on his shoulders.

"Dance with me," she hissed.

His expression grew even more perplexed, but he set down his jacket and stepped closer. Canned music pumped out of the speakers behind the bar, something with a clarinet and a woman's languorous voice.

"I had to get away from Roshian," she whispered. "He seriously creeps me out. Honestly, this whole place does. It's—"

"Wait." He nodded toward the nearest pair of dancers, who were only two tables away, and then pressed a hand to the small of her back, guiding her in the dance closer to the billowing curtains of the veranda, until they were well out of earshot.

"It's freezing at night," Cora continued. "There isn't enough food. And these guests treat us like slaves, unless they like us, and then it's even worse."

Cassian raised an eyebrow. "I told you this place would give you much to consider. Have you changed your mind, then?"

She went silent as the dance continued, their feet quietly chasing each other's, his hand warm against her back. Her plan with Mali and Lucky was still fresh in her mind, as was Mali's warning that running the Gauntlet puzzles could make her go insane. No, she would prove humanity's intelligence in a safer way—*her* way— by cheating. But in order to do that, she still needed Cassian to get her in front of the Gauntlet testers.

"Cora?" he prompted.

They were in the open on the veranda now. Alone. She tried to calm her heartbeat. It unnerved her to see him like this, in human clothes, with almost-normal eyes, and such fluid movements as he guided her around the veranda.

"Maybe," she said slowly. "Tell me what the perceptive training would involve."

"Sessions between you and me here in the lodge, and practice on your own." He was so close that just a whisper brushed her ear. "In the past, the Gauntlet's perceptive puzzles have primarily tested candidates on telekinesis, such as rearranging floor tiles to spell words with only one's mind, or making objects levitate into a basket. If you can achieve levitation of a medium-sized object twelve inches in the air for thirty sustained seconds, I believe you will have a chance of passing whichever test they give you. I can teach you to do that. But, as time is limited, we will have to work diligently and, of course, secretly."

He nodded toward the guests visible through the veranda doors. "There are Council members in there even as we speak. They cannot learn of what we are doing."

Her palms were sweating, leaving dark marks on his shirt. "Why do they even care? I thought the Gauntlet's whole purpose was to give lesser species a chance to prove our intelligence. You even said humans have run it before."

"Some have, yes."

"And did their participation have to be so secretive?"

"No." He swung her around, so her back was to the lodge. "The difference is, no previous human candidates had a chance of succeeding until now. The Council is not interested in stopping humans from running the Gauntlet. But they are interested in stopping humans from *beating* it."

"What are they so afraid of?" she asked.

"The Council has a vested interest in keeping humanity a lesser species. Their official stance is that humans are lesser because you primarily act on emotions, not logic. You expend your resources unsustainably. You incite war. If you were to gain intelligent status, you might damage the delicate system of universal governance we currently have."

"And unofficially?"

He glanced toward the veranda doors. "If you had kept a species caged for centuries, and then suddenly gave them the key, along with access to lawmaking and transportation and weaponry, wouldn't *you* fear what they would do?"

He let her go, abruptly, and reached into his pocket. He took out a pair of dice, holding them up to the sunlight. "That is why they cannot know what you are capable of. Not yet."

Her palms felt empty without the solidity of his shoulders beneath them. The dice looked different from the others that were scattered around the lodge. The dots on these dice glowed with a faint blue light.

"I have fitted these dice with amplifiers like the ones we use to control the doors. They make telekinesis easier, especially during training. And this way, if anyone happens to observe us, it will appear we are simply playing tabletop games."

He set the dice on a table just inside the veranda doors, next to a basket of old-fashioned metal jacks and dominoes.

"And why do *you* care?" she asked more quietly. "This is our battle, not yours." She realized, as she spoke the words, she was actually curious.

He pressed a hand against her back again, drawing her once more into the charade of dancing. He whispered, "Was there nothing you cared about outside of yourself, on Earth? No greater cause?"

She pulled back far enough to level a stare at him. "I was busy enough keeping myself alive in juvie."

"Then let us look at your brother, Charlie, for example. I've read from your memories of him that ever since he was five years old he donated half his allowance to save polar bears in the Arctic. Why? It makes no logical sense. He never met a polar bear. If he had, it probably would have killed him. He did it because he did not want to live in a world without a diversity of life. He did it because, even at that young age, he knew it was the right thing to do." He led her farther from the lodge, out toward the edge of the veranda where the wind off the savanna ruffled her hair.

"So humanity is your polar bear?"

"It goes far beyond that. Unlike Charlie with his bears, I have met humans. I have seen exactly what the universe would lose without your species. And I know what it feels like, personally, to be powerless. To have others judge you based on false perceptions. I was in a low weight and height percentile when I was a youth. I was constantly overlooked. No one predicted my potential, not even the algorithm. That is why I first started to work with humans, when I was the age for a work assignment."

She couldn't help but slide a hand to the muscles beneath his shirt. "I have a hard time believing you were ever small."

He gave the trace of a smile. "I grew bigger." He drew her an inch closer. "And now I do have power. I am not overlooked any longer. And soon, you will not be either." His eyes searched hers. She still wasn't used to seeing him like this—with eyes that were cloudy, but had irises flecked with color.

She stepped faster and faster in the dance, lies mixing with truths until she wasn't sure which was which. "I trusted you," she confessed. "I cared about you. You stood in that ocean and told me you'd help us escape, when all the while you had guards stationed to capture us. I'd have to be a fool to trust you again."

Were they really spinning as fast as it seemed? His face remained placid, his steps so calm and easy.

"Do not let my mistakes stop you from achieving something important. I believe in you—in all humans. Your species has the capacity for such rich emotions; selfishness and greed, yes, but also truth and forgiveness and sacrifice. When you believe in a cause, nothing can stop you. If anyone deserves to be the fifth intelligent species, it is you."

She looked away. His words were making her feel things

she didn't want to. She was here to lie, after all. Eventually, to betray him.

He drew her closer still. "I felt you inside my head, Cora. You read my thoughts. And you liked the power that came with that. You think you're unnatural, but you aren't. You're exceptional."

The sun felt as though it was burning even brighter. The veranda seemed to be swimming. She let go of him abruptly and clamped a hand on the nearest table to steady herself.

His shadow was cast next to her. "It killed me to betray you," he whispered. "The last thing I wanted was to push you away. I wanted to hold you close, like we were dancing just now, feeling your arms around me—"

"Stop," she whispered.

His breath brushed her cheek. "I don't have to be your enemy."

She gripped the edge of the table hard. Somehow this had all gotten out of control. The sun seemed to grow brighter until it was blinding.

"I understand you," he continued. "And I want you to understand me. I want you to stay awake at night thinking about me again, like you used to. It was so difficult not to go to you, those nights, and answer every question you had, and ask you a thousand of my own."

She remembered those nights in the cage. Nok would be snoring at her side, the boys asleep on the floor and Lucky downstairs keeping watch, and Cora would stare at the black window, wondering about the creature behind it with the black eyes, more curious than she should have been.

"Say yes," he whispered. "We can change the world, you and I."

With her eyes closed, she could almost believe he wasn't

Kindred at all. Just a young man whispering into her ear on a warm summer day. A rush of feeling found a crack in her head and flooded into her heart. Conflicting emotions pushed against each other in her chest, as her vision went blurry.

"Yes," she whispered. It had been the plan all along—agree to work with him, only to betray him later. And yet this didn't feel like a lie.

He brushed her cheek.

That spark.

Her eyes snapped open at the same time something tugged in her mind. *No.* She looked through the curtains at the other dancers, Makayla and Roshian, Jenny and another Kindred. Cassian was no different. This was a man who'd betrayed her. A creature who had kidnapped her.

Her vision went white with anger.

Suddenly Cassian let out a hiss and jerked away. Cora jolted, blinking hard, trying to calm down the rush of fury running through her. When her vision finally cleared, she saw him clutching his left hand. Blood seeped from his palm.

She blinked, confused.

A spiky metal jack flashed in the sunlight. One of the jack's sharp points was embedded deep in his metallic skin—skin that was nearly impossible to pierce.

"Why did you stab yourself?" she blurted out, her head still throbbing.

"I didn't." He looked at her carefully. "*You* did. You were so upset that . . . it doesn't matter why. What matters is that you moved it with your mind."

She stared at the welling blood in his palm. She'd wanted

to hurt him, as he'd hurt her. She'd wanted him to feel pain—and he had.

She reached for a curtain to steady herself. This wasn't like when she had used her abilities before. This wasn't a pleasant sensation of power, but pain and dizziness and bile rising in her throat. "I . . . need . . . to sit down."

Her breath started to come too fast. For weeks she'd been trying to capture this sensation again, but now it was too much, too fast, too sudden. It had felt right, before, but now it felt dangerous. She shoved the curtains away, stumbling into the lodge. Makayla stopped dancing with Roshian. Dane looked up from the bar.

Everyone's eyes went to the dark blood dripping slowly from Cassian's hand.

She looked around desperately.

The entrance was sealed. There was nowhere to go. From one of the lounge tables, the Council members and Fian watched her intently, their card game forgotten.

Oh god. Not now. Not while they're watching.

Her head ached. She concentrated on not moving anything else, not making the lights flicker, not doing anything to give herself away in front of them. More blood dripped on the floor. Bright red.

She touched her nose and her fingers came away wet.

Then she crumpled to the ground.

12

Leon

LEON STUDIED THE MAP that Bonebreak had scribbled on the torn-out page of a paperback novel. The lines were as shaky as the creature's voice behind the mask, jerking and twisting and sometimes ending randomly, supposedly showing him the way safely through the supply tunnels from Bonebreak's shop to the sector that housed the Axion delegates.

Deliver this provision pack to them, Bonebreak had said, handing Leon a damp wrapped package. *And don't open it.*

Well, no danger there. From the faintly rotting smell emanating from the package, Leon was the opposite of curious to know what was inside. He'd heard rumors of the Axion's penchant for body parts—pretty depraved beliefs for a supposedly highly evolved species.

The air in the tunnels was so thin his lungs ached. He wheezed hard and shoved the map in his back pocket, then crawled down the tunnel, following a track that blinked with faint lights.

His left shoulder still ached from where they'd sewn on that rubbery shielding to brand him as one of them.

Bottom-feeders, he thought. This kind of sneaking-around-in-ducts shit was meant for someone small, like Rolf. Leon was as cumbersome as a rhino and about as loud and—

He stopped.

Ahead, a thin line near the bottom of the tunnel shimmered like sparkly fishing wire. He inched closer and adjusted the headlamp Bonebreak had given him. It was attached to the upper half of a Mosca mask, and it smelled like death. The light shone on the shimmering wire. Not wire, exactly. It was clearly broken in places, more like a hologram or laser beam catching the chalky air.

It had to be one of the cleaner traps Bonebreak had warned him about. Trip it, and he'd combust in a ball of fire.

Slowly, he eased a leg over the trap, his muscles shaking. If only there were more air to breathe. As it was, he felt so light-headed. *Pull yourself together,* he ordered himself, easing one hand over the trap, then the other. A bead of sweat rolled off his forehead and fell toward the trap.

He cringed, bracing for an explosion.

But the drip landed a fraction of an inch to the left. Dizzy with relief, he eased his other leg over, and then collapsed against the tunnel wall, breathing hard.

"Try to clean me," he muttered. "You can clean my ass, is what you can clean." He dug in his pocket for a shard of chalk and marked the wall on either side of the trap with a cartoon bomb. He shone the headlight to admire his artwork.

Not bad.

After more crawling, and two more cleaner traps that

he marked with pictures, he reached a point where the tunnel changed to roughly hewn rock, though the bluelight track continued on unabated. The surface was dusty against his hands. Ahead, the tunnel led past a handful of small metal doors.

"Well, shit. This isn't right."

He pulled out Bonebreak's map but didn't see anything that indicated little doorways in a row. The map was useless. Bonebreak was probably trying to lead him straight to his death.

A whirring sound made him look over his shoulder. A square package was coming down the tunnel, guided by the bluelight, just high enough off the ground so it wouldn't trigger any cleaner traps. He knew the Kindred had all kinds of crazy powers, but seeing a floating box hurtling toward him was still too weird to process, until he realized the tunnel was so tight that there wasn't enough room for the package *and* for him. He crawled faster, sweeping the headlight left and right to search for any of the nearly invisible traps. He finally reached the indentation for the first small doorway and threw himself into it just as the package hurtled by.

He pressed his back against the door, waiting for the package to pass. Okay, *hurtled* might have been an exaggeration. The package still hadn't even passed by yet. FedEx was faster than this.

He settled back against the doorway to wait, and sniffed the thin air. Was that . . . horse shit? And were those . . . voices? Yeah, voices. Coming from behind the door. He pressed his ear against the crack. One voice was masculine and almost familiar. Leon made out a single word.

Zebra.

Zebra? Well, why not. By now he was used to weird shit. At least the voices were speaking English. He sniffed again, and it smelled stronger. He pressed his ear against the door, trying to muffle the sound of his wheezing.

"I'll put the zebra back in its cell," the voice said. "Mali needed your help anyway."

Leon's hands started shaking. He recognized the voice now. It was Lucky. And Mali must be close too. Mali, the crazy girl with stringy braids and ninja moves who, somehow, though he'd never have imagined it in a billion years, he actually kinda liked. *Liked* liked. He'd refused to acknowledge it in the cage, but that was what happened when you had weeks with no one to talk to but Mosca: You accepted tough things about yourself, like an undeniable attraction to a weirdo.

He raised a fist to bang on the door, but stopped. The last time he'd seen Lucky and Mali was when he'd abandoned them, unconscious and sopping wet, on a control room floor. There was a strong chance they wouldn't be thrilled to see him again.

But still. It was Mali.

He raised his fist to knock.

He stopped again.

What if there were Kindred on the other side too? It didn't seem likely; Kindred didn't seem the type to hang around manure, zebra or otherwise. Lucky and Mali were probably locked in some jail or fake world behind that door; they probably needed him. He should knock.

But again, he didn't.

Sweat dripped onto the chalky rock floor. What was he thinking, anyway? Rescuing them from some zoo-themed jail was a heroic thing to do—and he only looked out for himself. Back in Auckland, when he was just a tyke, his dad had taken him aside right before they'd locked him in prison. *There's nothing in the world more important than kin,* he'd said, and pointed to the tattoos on his face that told the history of their family's achievements. *Your brothers steal, you steal with them. They fight, you fight with them. They go to prison, you go to prison too. Everyone else in the world can go to hell, but not your kin.*

And Leon's only kin on this station was Leon.

Slowly, heart pounding, he drew a zebra-stripe symbol next to the door with chalk, so he wouldn't mistakenly stumble upon them again. Then he crawled away. He turned one way, then the other, trying to get away from the voice in his mind urging him to go back and help them. He crawled past the next few doorways, sniffing. He swore he smelled campfire smoke, and then later, strawberries, and stopped to make marks next to each of the doorways. He continued crawling down random tunnels, just barely avoiding another cleaner trap. Screw the map. And screw Lucky and Mali and the others. *They aren't kin,* he told himself again. He just wanted to breathe some fresh air. Gulp it down, like a man dying of thirst would drink water. These tunnels were so tight. Were they getting smaller? Chalk was getting everywhere. It tasted ashy, almost like something burning. The air had taken on the smell of smoke, not the pleasant campfire smell from before, but like something roasting and rotten. He pressed a hand to his nose, his eyes bleary with the smoke, and took a corner too fast.

Something zapped his arm.

A cleaner trap!

There it was, that thin sparkly line, and his hand right smack in the middle of it. His throat closed up, but no ball of gas came. No flames.

And then he saw why.

Just ahead in the tunnel, curled in a ball, was the charred body of some kid who had already triggered the trap—it must not have been reset yet.

Leon jerked his hand out of the trap's laser light, eyeing the charred body with a grimace. Judging by the smell, it had been there a few days, at least.

He crawled closer, shining his light on the body hesitantly. A black kid about his age, arms covering his face. Most of his clothes were too charred to be recognizable, though they were made of a khaki material with a lion emblem on the pocket. Leon nudged a pair of half-melted goggles around his neck. Part of the boy's skin oozed off, and Leon gagged and stumbled toward the closest door.

"Gross gross gross."

He shoved the door open a crack. Blessedly, it led to an empty hallway.

Fresh air came pouring in, smelling like ozone, and he gulped it greedily, trying to get the smell of burned skin out of his nose. He should climb out, figure out where he was, deliver this reeking package, and go drown himself in vodka until he'd forgotten everything he'd just seen.

He started to open the door farther.

But then he thought of that lion emblem.

The boy wasn't far from the door where he'd drawn the zebra-stripped symbol. Lions, zebras—it didn't take a genius to guess the dead kid probably came from the same place where Lucky and Mali were being kept. What if Lucky and Mali ended up in the tunnels too? Would he be crawling over *their* charred bodies next?

He slammed the door closed. In the cage, he wouldn't have hesitated to leave them behind. But something had changed. *He* had changed. For the first time in his life he had . . . friends. Friends who he'd rather not have die in a ball of fire. And in a way, he realized, his dad had been wrong. Friends mattered too.

Grumbling, he turned around. He retraced his chalky marks through the maze of claustrophobic tunnels, back toward the door with the zebra-stripe symbol.

Maybe—just this once—he could be a damn hero.

13

Cora

CORA BLINKED AWAKE TO find herself staring at the dead, black eyes of a deer.

She sat abruptly, nearly knocking heads with the mousy-haired girl who Dane had called Pika. She was in the backstage cell block. A dead deer lay nearby on the floor, half covered by a burlap sack. Pika absently stroked its snow-white tail.

"What happened?" Cora pressed a hand to her head. The deer's blood made her remember other blood—Cassian's blood—and the gleaming sharp point of the toy jack.

Lucky swam into her vision. "You blacked out," he said. "Your nose was gushing blood. Cassian carried you back here and Pika revived you."

The girl held up a greasy package that smelled like lemon, before heading to the medical room. Mali took her place, forehead knit in concern.

Cora sat up, wincing, blinking so her vision would refocus,

and looked at the clock. Free Time, about halfway over. The other kids were spread out in groups around the room. Christopher was reading from a dog-eared paperback by the feed bins. Makayla was twisting her hair into tight balls, using the reflection of a metallic wall as a mirror. Shoukry and Jenny played dominoes around a makeshift table. Dane came in with a saw, ignoring Cora, and grabbed the dead deer's legs. He dragged the deer into the corner, where he began hacking at its antlers.

Lucky leaned closer. "What happened to you out there?"

Cora squeezed her temples, keeping her voice low. "I told Cassian I'd work with him, but then I got overwhelmed. There were some game pieces. A jack, the kind with the sharp points." She remembered Cassian's touch on her cheek. "I . . . couldn't stop myself."

"You *stabbed* him?"

Mali leaned in on all fours, sniffing around Cora like an animal. She gave a flat smile of satisfaction. "Yes. She stabbed him with her mind. This is why her nose bleeds."

Cora tossed a look around. The last thing she needed was the whole ensemble knowing her secret.

"Is this true?" Lucky asked. For a second—just a second—fear flashed in his eyes, as if he was looking at some freakish imitation of a girl, but then he blinked, and his eyes were only filled with concern.

"Has she died yet?" Dane called from the other side of the room. He kept hacking at the deer. When Cora narrowed her eyes at him, he smirked. "Oh. Still alive. Congratulations."

She jerked her chin toward the saw. "I thought they didn't kill the animals."

"Not for sport." Dane threw his weight behind the saw to break off an antler. "But this one was old. Organ failure. An exception to the moral code."

"Why cut off the antlers?"

Dane wiped a speck of blood off his forehead. "Won't fit down the drecktube with them attached." He unceremoniously bagged the deer in the burlap sack, unlocked the tube with his key, and shoved the deer down the same drecktube that Chicago had probably disappeared down.

Pika sighed deeply. "Poor little deer. It had such a cute tail."

Cora pitched her head down. Memories of the gleaming jack and that *tug* in her mind shot through like streaks of pain. The sound of the backstage door opening came, but she couldn't bring herself to look up at the bright lights again.

"She looks sick," a deep Kindred voice observed.

She jerked her head up. With her hazy vision she didn't see more than a tall figure at first, and her head throbbed harder—if it was Cassian, what would she say?—but then her vision cleared. A dark-blue suit with twin knots down the side. A face with a sharp wrinkle cutting down his forehead.

"She's fine," Lucky said quickly to Fian.

"I will be the judge of that." Fian looked around the filthy room, as though one wrong step could get him contaminated. "Come with me, girl. I need to investigate this incident."

She glanced at Lucky. They both knew that Fian was on their side, a secret member of the Fifth of Five initiative, but she was still wary.

Fian motioned for her to follow him into the shower room, which, with its groaning pipes, was the best place to talk in private.

He cast one look at the dirty drain and stepped carefully to the cleanest spot on the floor.

"Why are you really here?" she said, once they were alone.

"Cassian asked me to check on your condition. He wishes to see you himself, but he thought you might prefer to speak with someone else."

"Because of the whole stabbing thing, I assume."

Fian only blinked.

She slumped against the wall. "You can tell him I'm fine. And despite what happened, I haven't changed my mind. I'll run the Gauntlet. We can begin training as soon as he wants."

Fian pressed a hand against each side of her head gently. She tried not to recoil as he tilted her head up to inspect the dried blood rimming her nostrils. "Your mind needs time to heal first. Four days."

"That's too much time. Cassian said we only have thirty days to train and"—she did a quick tally—"at least five have already passed. The module must be halfway to the station by now. I can't afford to lose another four days before it docks."

"Three days, then. But that's the soonest. You cannot run the Gauntlet if your mind ruptures." His words had a ring of finality, but he didn't leave. Instead, he cocked his head, eyeing her up and down.

"What?"

"You still do not trust me."

She gave him a hard look. "It's a little hard to get over the fact that you nearly killed me once."

He looked down at his hands and then closed his eyes. For a second it seemed like he was meditating, but Cora had seen this before. The change that passed over them when they uncloaked. Facial muscles easing. Joints loosening slightly. When he looked up again, his eyes were clearing.

"I've uncloaked so we may speak honestly," he said. Even his voice was different. Not quite as deep, words blurred together a little more. "I'm not in the habit of apologizing to humans, but for you, I will. You need to understand how much we are all risking for this initiative. For *you*."

Her hand drifted to the base of her throat where he'd strangled her, as she nodded for him to go on.

"Cassian has spent nearly ten human years infiltrating higher ranks, and I've spent the last five. He became a Warden so he could find an ideal human candidate. I became a delegate, so I can work from within the Intelligence Council. If we're found out, we'll be as good as dead."

"I'm risking a lot too."

"I know that. Cassian knows that. But the other initiative members . . ." He glanced at the doorway. "Some are less certain of your potential. They want to know specifics of which perceptive abilities you have achieved, and to what extent."

Her headache had returned. She started pacing, blinking hard against the pain. "Ask Cassian."

"You don't understand our ways. As a delegate, I may be his superior on paper, but not within the Fifth of Five initiative. We don't ever question our superiors. Which is why I'm asking you." He stepped closer. "*I* don't need reassurance. I believe in you. But the others don't know you."

"The fail-safe exit," she said, somewhat warily. "In the cage. I sensed that the exit was hidden beneath the ocean." She didn't mention the time she'd sensed Kindred standing behind a panel, or the time she'd read Cassian's mind. Another thing Queenie had taught her: always keep your best cards close, even with people you think are your friends.

"That is all?"

"Yes."

He smiled. "I am sure Cassian will be able to further develop your abilities, but in the meantime, the others will be reassured. I will inform Cassian that you will be ready to resume training once your mind has healed." He squeezed her shoulder a little too hard. "We are on your side. Remember that."

As soon as he left, Cora slumped back against the wall. She rubbed her head, wondering if what he'd said about her mind rupturing was true. How far would she have to push it for that to happen? Would the damage be permanent?

A knock came from the shower room drecktube.

She stared at the drecktube door in surprise. It was waist high, locked so the wards could only open it a few inches to dispose of garbage. Hesitantly, she bent down.

"Chicago?" she whispered, feeling like she might be going insane. "Is that you?"

And then the door swung open, and she shrieked and stumbled back.

Massive shoulders. Short dark hair. A faded gray T-shirt covered in white, chalky dust. Black tattoos swirled around his left eye.

"Hi, sweetheart," Leon said.

14

Cora

CORA CLAMPED A HAND over her mouth. "Leon!" She hadn't expected to see him again, especially not here, especially not covered in grime. She threw her arms around him.

"I heard you chatting with your new friend," he said. "Figured I'd wait for him to leave before stopping by for a visit. Kindred are the jealous sort, you know."

"I knew you'd come back for us!"

The shower room door cracked open, and she swiveled her head around in alarm, but it was only Lucky and Mali, peeking their heads in.

"Cora?" Lucky said. "You shouted. I thought—" But then he caught sight of Leon. "Holy shit."

Mali elbowed past him into the room, her eyes wide. For a second, Cora thought Mali might give Leon a hug, but she just punched at a piece of armor sewn to his shoulder. "What happened to you."

Leon rubbed his arm where her fist had made impact. "Nice to see you again too, kid." He gave Lucky a nod. "All of you. I've been shacking up with a Mosca operation. Not bad guys, actually, if you can make out what they're saying behind those masks. Bone-break, he's their leader. Reminds me a bit of my uncle. Likes vodka. Snores too." He motioned to a wrapped package on the floor that was letting off a smell even worse than the shower room drain. "They're black-market dealers. They use the drecktube tunnels to smuggle their stuff around the station, and humans are the only ones flexible enough to crawl around in there."

"Have you been looking for us this entire time?" Cora asked.

He rubbed the back of his neck. "Uh . . . yeah. Sure have."

"How did you come up through the drecktube?" Lucky asked. "It's locked."

"Not from the inside," Leon said, but then scratched the back of his head as if avoiding something. "Actually, I, uh, found something in there. Someone. Sort of like a, well, dead guy. Don't know if he was a friend of yours."

Cora and Lucky exchanged a look. "Was he wearing driving gloves?" she asked. "And goggles?"

Leon nodded. "Charred up bad. He shouldn't have been down there, eh? Those tunnels are death traps if you can't navigate them."

"He didn't go down there intentionally," Lucky explained. "His name was Chicago. The Kindred threw him down there. They do that to humans when we turn nineteen."

"If we have misbehaved," Mali clarified.

Leon eyed Mali warily, as if he was worried she might attack him again, but then his hand itched at the spot on his neck where the markings that paired with hers used to be.

"Listen," Cora said in a rush. "If you can pass through the drecktubes safely, then we need you to do something important." She told him about the Gauntlet and their plan to cheat it, which elicited a rare nod of approval from him. "But we need a girl for it all to work," she continued. "Her name is Anya. She's being kept in the Temple menagerie. Short blond hair, about ten years old, missing some fingers. We're going to have to get her out of there somehow. See if you can break into their backstage area. If you find her, leave a mark with that chalk on the floor here, so we'll know. Be careful. Don't let anyone see you."

"Tell her that you are friends with me," Mali added. "She will trust you more."

Leon raised an eyebrow. "Friends, is that all?"

Mali only blinked stiffly, and Leon seemed disappointed.

"Have you seen Nok and Rolf?" Cora asked, but he shook his head. "Try to find them too. We need to make sure they're okay."

Leon rolled his eyes. "Anything else? Chocolate milk? Gumdrops?"

Someone drummed on the shower room door sharply. "Cora." It was Dane. "Get out here. Break's over. Who's in there with you?"

Cora shoved Leon back toward the drecktube. "Go. Quick." He grumbled as he climbed in. She paused, holding the door open for a second. "It's good to see you, Leon."

He gave a reluctant half smile. "Yeah, sweetheart. You too."

She closed the drecktube just as Dane opened the door. He froze when he saw her and Lucky standing so close, and Mali off to the side. His eyes slid over Lucky, tracing the shape of his body as though looking for imperfections. "What's going on in here?"

"Nothing," Cora answered quickly. "Sorry. I'm going."

She started down the corridor and opened the backstage door, letting in the sounds of birds and clinking glasses, but a hand stopped her.

Dane had followed her. "Hang on, songbird. A word."

Her heart thudded with fears—had he heard Leon?

"Look, I'm not blind," he said, and then nodded back toward the shower room. "I can guess what that was. You wanted to sneak off to be with Lucky, and have Mali stand guard. Well, I can't blame you—we don't get many guys looking like *him* around here. But we're here to work, and that's it. Any privileges you had before—to date, to eat when you want, to take long baths—are over now. You gave that up when you failed out of your last enclosure."

Making out? That's what Dane thought this was about? She clenched her jaw against the ripple of anger that surged up her throat. "Got it," she said tightly, but he didn't let her go. She had seen how Dane's gaze had lingered over Lucky, when he tended to the animals with such care, and especially when he took his shirt off to wash himself in the water trough.

"So just keep to yourself," Dane said. "And we'll be fine."

The ball of anger twisted harder in her stomach. If he thought he had a chance with Lucky, he was going to be greatly disappointed. Even if Lucky did like boys, he wouldn't go for Dane in a million years.

"Right," she choked, and pushed her way into the lodge.

FOR DAYS, CORA CHECKED the floor around the shower room drecktube obsessively, but there were no chalk messages from Leon. Maybe he had run into trouble finding Anya, or maybe he'd just abandoned them, like he had before. She could think of nothing but their plan, as she stumbled through her duties and rushed through her songs. On the days when Council members were there, her stomach curled. She watched them play cards and thought back to Queenie in Bay Pines and the Venezuelan girls they cheated together. Those girls never caught on. With luck, the Council wouldn't either.

When Cassian finally returned, she couldn't help but notice he wore gloves. She wondered if his palm was still wounded from the metal jack, or if he'd worn them as protection in case it happened again.

He spoke briefly to Tessela, who nodded and came to the stage.

"You can finish your shift early," Tessela told her. "One of the patrons wishes you to play a game of cards." She indicated the most private of the alcoves.

Cassian was already waiting for Cora there. She sank onto one of the benches, avoiding looking at the basket of jacks. Faint sounds came from the other side of the alcove's wooden screen. Makayla's tap shoes. Clinking glasses from the bar. The roar of a distant vehicle driving toward the savanna. She shifted, flustered and suddenly warm. Being alone with him always made Cora feel too hot, like standing outside on a summer day at noon—in danger of getting burned.

Cassian took a seat a safe distance across from her. "How is your head?"

"Better." She picked at her fingernails. "How is your hand?"

He slowly removed his gloves. The skin on his palm had mostly healed, though it was still red. "It was my fault. I provoked you, though it was not my intention."

She reached out and placed her hand over his, hoping the gesture would relieve any suspicions he might have. "It doesn't matter. I agreed to run the Gauntlet, and I will."

He looked up at her touch, and for a second she feared he'd sensed her lie. But then storm clouds in his pupils darkened, and he leaned forward as though gravity was drawing him closer. "I know it is not easy for you to trust me again," he said, "But I knew you would agree."

She tilted her head, curious. "Did you?"

"Forgiveness, mistakes, determination—all human values I have known and appreciated. But I've learned more about humanity after watching you. Something that I first observed on Earth but never quite understood until now. Perseverance. Or rather, perseverance in the face of the illogical."

For a second, her mind turned back to being ten years old, standing bruised beneath an oak tree, and Charlie lecturing her about being stubborn.

"You mean not giving up?"

He nodded. "To us, that is an unfathomable trait. The decisions we make are carefully weighed. In the cage, you should have given up many times. You didn't, even when it defied logic. And most incredibly of all, not giving up was the right decision."

"It wasn't," she argued. "It didn't work."

"Your escape did not succeed, true. And yet not giving up was the *right* decision. It made you stronger. That is what fascinates me. If it had been Kindred wards, they would still be there, running puzzles for the rest of their lives. It makes me not want to give up either. Not just in my head, but also in my heart." He pressed a hand to his chest, and she felt her own heart start to thump. "When I weigh this decision to train you to run the Gauntlet, logic tells me it is not the wisest choice. And yet I believe it is right."

Another memory returned to her, this one from a year ago. Their father had forbidden Charlie to take flight lessons. *Too dangerous for an eighteen-year-old,* he'd said. So Charlie had gotten a job after school at a call center to pay for the lessons, and on weekends when he was supposed to be working with a college prep tutor, he'd driven to a small airstrip outside Richmond. *Dad will be furious if he finds out,* Cora had said. *You told me yourself, you have to know when to give up.* Charlie had just shaken his head. *You have to know when* not *to give up too.*

She still rested her hand over Cassian's. She remembered the first time she'd felt the electricity of his touch, how he was so much warmer than she'd expected. For a second, she forgot this was all an act.

She cleared her throat. "We should get to work."

He blinked as though he'd forgotten why they were there too.

"Of course." He took out a pair of amplified dice, working one die between his fingers. "Telekinesis is the first thing we are taught." He set the die on the table and concentrated. It suddenly slid toward him, all on its own, as though someone had given it a shove.

He set it back on the table.

"Focus first on the shape, memorize it, so that if you closed your eyes you could still picture it. Then simply give it a tap with your thoughts, as you would with your finger."

Cora stared at the die. Hard and compact, just like her anger had been. The anger was still there, buried down deep where she would never forget, but she was finding it harder to direct that anger at the man seated across from her.

She thought about tapping the die.

Nothing happened.

She wrinkled her brow and concentrated harder. Her vision started to blur, and the room felt like it keeled to the left, though she knew it wasn't moving. She ignored her shifting perceptions and focused on the die.

Tap.

Again, nothing happened, and in frustration she reached out and flicked it with her finger.

Cassian shook his head slowly. "That is cheating."

"Well, the result's the same."

He replaced the die in its starting position. "Intelligent species are interested in more than results. We are interested in processes. Doing things in a correct, efficient, logical manner. Cheating does not fit into that."

Cora picked up the die, toying with it. That was what it came down to, wasn't it? The end result. If she ran the Gauntlet by the Kindred's rules and won, humanity would be freed. If she cheated, the end result might be the same, and yet it wouldn't be the same at all—it would mean so much more because they'd have achieved it their own way.

By her count, there were only twenty-one days before the Gauntlet module would arrive on the station along with the non-Kindred delegates. Cassian would expect her to run the puzzles correctly, efficiently, and logically. His world would be thrown into chaos when she cheated. Everyone's would. But then, finally, maybe the Kindred would understand that just because humans didn't do things their way didn't mean humans weren't intelligent.

"Right."

She focused again on the die.

Once she felt like she had the corners of the die firmly in her head, she tapped it mentally again.

It moved. Hardly more than a wobble, but it moved.

She let out a cry of surprise. "It worked!"

Cassian smiled. "A good start." He set the die back in the center. "Try again."

Concentrating was harder this time. He smiled so rarely that it was distracting. She had to try to put him out of her mind and just feel the shape of the die, and *tap*.

The die slid clear across the table, fell off, and bounced against the wall.

"Did you see that?" She jumped up without thinking. "It really worked—*ow!*"

Pain suddenly ripped through her brain. Cassian leaped up, pressing a hand to her back, the electricity from his touch warming her.

"Breathe," he said. "Slowly. You need to send oxygen to your brain."

But the headache didn't abate, and she sank onto the bench.

"Perhaps that is sufficient for today," he said with concern. "Your mind is not yet fully healed from before. Keep one of the dice. Practice at night. But do not strain yourself."

She tucked a die inside her dress, then stood and headed back toward the lodge.

"Wait, Cora. One more thing." Still clutching her head, she

turned to find him right in front of her. She stared at his chest, the button-down shirt that was so human, so real. A thread was loose. "I won't betray your trust again. I promise."

Her heart beat once. Twice. Three times.

"I believe you," she lied.

She opened the screen. The lounge was nearly full, and all the sounds made her head swirl as she wove between them to the stage, where Makayla was just finishing a dance.

"Sorry you had to cover for me," Cora said.

Makayla put her hand over the microphone, muting it. "No worries." Her voice dropped. "The other day it looked like Roshian decided to make you his new favorite. Glad I'm off the hook, but for your sake, I'm sorry."

"I can handle him."

But her thoughts were on Cassian, not Roshian, as she climbed onstage and watched him leave through the main door, speaking a few low words with Tessela. He glanced back once at her before leaving and gently pressed a hand to his heart. *It makes me not want to give up either. Not just in my head, but also in my heart.*

Cora cleared her throat. She started to sing a song she'd written in juvie about four walls and no sky, but changed her mind. She sang an old song instead, one Charlie used to listen to as he'd sneak off to the airstrip.

It was about soaring high and never looking down.

And the lyrics made her feel as powerful as Cassian's words had. For the first time, she almost felt the thrill of being onstage that she'd always dreamed of. It didn't matter that none of the

Kindred guests were listening. Makayla was listening. Dane and Shoukry at the bar were listening.

And *she* was listening.

And for once, she believed her own words.

15

Mali

MALI'S DAILY SCHEDULE WAS always the same. Operate one of the safari trucks for the charade of hunting, ready the guests' artificial rifles, help the other tour guides bag the catches. The only difference today was, when she showed up for work at the garage, Lucky was waiting for her.

"You are not supposed to leave backstage," she said, confused.

"I couldn't stand another minute cramped up in that room. I don't know who smells worse, Pika or the animals. Dane gave permission. Said it was a good idea anyway to have someone else trained to drive."

Mali raised an eyebrow. She had asked Dane to switch her job assignment from driver to rifle handler, once. He'd only laughed and told her she was lucky she wasn't cleaning toilets. Apparently, Dane felt differently when it came to granting Lucky favors.

She jerked her head toward the truck. "You ride in the passenger's side."

They drove in silence to the far edge of the savanna with Jenny and Christopher bouncing along on the back bumper. The guest—Roshian—sat in the backseat. She glanced at him in the rearview mirror. Even uncloaked, he was always so eerily stiff. She had spent thirteen years living with the Kindred, so she knew how to be stiff too, but today her feelings were harder to mask, ever since seeing Leon a few days before, especially when he'd said, *Friends, is that all?* As though he had wanted something more. Not long ago, she wouldn't have understood what he meant. But after having watched Cora and Lucky together, and Nok and Rolf, she understood.

It made her smile, just a little, deep inside.

She glanced at Lucky. He was gazing out at the plains, drumming his fingers on the side of the truck. Ever since she'd been around the other kids, she'd craved the ability to act like them—speaking so smoothly, laughing frequently—so *human*. She took one hand off the wheel and drummed her fingers on the side of the truck too. It felt good. Natural. But then her thoughts turned to what Leon had said about working with the Mosca. They were the ones who had taken her from Earth. She remembered being chained to a stake in a market, as the Mosca cackled and taunted her.

There were good and bad Kindred.

Good and bad humans.

But the Mosca . . . they were *all* rotten.

The vehicle jostled, and Christopher and Jenny clutched onto the back bumper, trying not to get jolted off. A low hiss came from the backseat.

"Focus on your driving," Roshian ordered.

Mali put both hands back on the wheel. "Sorry," she

mumbled. Beside her, Lucky gave her a sympathetic smile.

Roshian returned to scanning the savanna. "There," he said. "The hyena."

Ahead, the track split. One track led to the single hill, the other to a watering hole where giraffes and antelope often clustered. Today, a skinny hyena lay panting in the shade of an acacia tree. One of its ears was a little shorter than the other.

Mali's hands tightened on the wheel.

It was the hyena that slept in the cell next to hers. The one that would sometimes reach a paw through the bars to be scratched. She had nicknamed him Scavenger. She wished Roshian had picked any of the other animals, but she'd make up for it that night, and slip Scavenger an extra cake after he was revived.

"Hey, you okay?" Lucky asked.

"Yes. It is nothing. Get a carcass bag ready." She nodded toward the glove box.

She continued driving to the end of the track, where the truck stopped automatically. Jenny and Christopher started readying the rifles. One was a compact model for close-range shots, the other a long-range scope.

Roshian stepped onto the parched soil, but he waved away the rifles that Christopher offered him. He strode twenty feet off, scanning the horizon, motioning for Christopher to stay close, as Jenny slid into the shade of the backseat.

Lucky unfolded a fresh canvas bag as they watched from behind the windshield.

"He's so short," Jenny whispered. "He has to be the smallest Kindred I've seen. I think he has a Napoleon complex." Roshian beckoned toward the truck again, and Jenny sighed and opened the side door. "Probably wants a freaking parasol now."

Once Mali and Lucky were alone in the truck, Mali asked, "What is a Napoleon complex."

"When a short guy makes up for his lack of height by being a dick," Lucky said.

Mali considered this. *Dick.* She'd have to remember that word. She tried to focus on cleaning the dust from her driving gloves, but her eyes kept creeping back to Roshian. He was arguing with Jenny, who looked displeased.

"Why do you wish to see the animals being shot," Mali asked.

Lucky looked at her with surprise. "I didn't come along because I wanted to see them shot. Backstage, all I ever see is the stunned animals. Bleeding, bruised messes. Or else cramped up in their cages at night. I wanted to see them differently, for once. Out in the open." He paused. "Even if none of it's real."

Mali looked back at Scavenger. He licked a paw slowly.

"You care about the animals as much as you care for people," she concluded.

He shrugged. "I'll always care a lot about you guys, and, hell, even Leon. Even *Dane.* I've tried to help, where I can. I even thought I could lead, once." He paused, squinting at the giraffes in the distance. "But it's different with the animals. Who's looking out for them? We're all so focused on setting humanity free, but even if Cora beats the Gauntlet, it wouldn't change anything for the animals. *They* don't have a champion. *They* don't have a chance to prove their worth." He let out a sigh and started picking at some marks carved in the truck's dashboard.

Mali blinked at him. "You."

"Me what?"

"You asked who is looking out for them," she explained. "You are." She paused, considering if she was using the correct tense. "You can." And then reconsidered again. "You *must*."

Lucky leaned back, as if he'd never quite considered this. Outside, Roshian and Jenny were still arguing. They called over Christopher, who rested his hands on his hips, shaking his head. They argued more, and at last Christopher gave in to whatever Roshian wanted. He came back to the vehicle and wordlessly dug through his expedition bag before returning to Roshian with a rifle.

"Why does Roshian want a different gun?" Lucky asked.

"I do not know. I do not recognize it from the armory. I think he brought it himself." She glanced sidelong at Lucky. She didn't need to tell him that was against the rules.

Ahead, Roshian cocked the rifle.

Jenny turned away, her face pinched.

Under the acacia tree, Scavenger had picked up their scent. Some of the animals, the newer ones especially, would run at first whiff of a predator. But Scavenger had been through this countless times before and just laid his head back down. Christopher picked up a dusty rock to rouse Scavenger into a run that would make things more sporting.

"No." Roshian's voice cut like a knife. "Leave it."

"But it will be too easy to shoot—"

"*Leave* it."

Christopher let the rock fall. He paced back to the vehicle, chewing anxiously on the inside of his cheek.

Mali leaned out the driver's-side window to ask him what was happening.

"Better if you don't know," Christopher said. "Trust me."

Mali folded her arms tight, squinting into the sun. Last night, Scavenger had slipped a paw through the bars. She'd scratched his head, and his tail had wagged.

They watched as Roshian hefted the rifle. Scavenger's head swiveled toward them. He was panting from the heat, blinking slowly at the rifle. Just as Roshian pulled the trigger, he looked away.

Crack.

The bullet tore through the air. Scavenger flinched with a yip of pain than shot through Mali's heart, and by instinct her hand went for the door latch to run to him, but she let her hand fall. It wouldn't do any good.

Scavenger tried to stand, only to collapse. Chemicals in the simulated bullets would be spreading through his bloodstream, inducing temporary paralysis and triggering extra blood flow and bruising around the wound.

"Jesus," Lucky said softly. "This is even worse than what happens backstage."

Jenny leaned on the hood of the vehicle and muttered through the open window, "Seriously. He's one sick bastard."

Mali looked at her, but Jenny didn't elaborate.

Christopher signaled to Jenny, who snatched up the carcass bag and crossed the dusty plain to Scavenger's body. Mali waited behind the wheel, her arms folded tight. Lucky was still rubbing his finger over the words carved in the dash, looking anywhere but at Scavenger.

Christopher and Jenny started to load Scavenger into the back of the vehicle, but Roshian shook his head.

"Wait."

Roshian knelt by the carcass bag and extracted a knife from his pocket. Real metal. An artifact from Earth—highly contraband. Roshian opened the bag's netting and took out one of Scavenger's stiff front paws.

Mali threw open the drivers side door. "This is not protocol—"

Jenny reached out, stopping her. "Hey, let it go," she said in a hushed warning.

"He is going to hurt Scavenger."

"Scavenger's already dead, don't you get it? Roshian made Christopher replace the simulated rifle with a real one. Said he made some deal with Dane about it."

The flames of anger inside Mali flickered wildly. She threw a look back to Lucky, who looked as shocked as she was. Dead? Scavenger was *dead*? He wouldn't wake up later, rubbing his nose with his paw?

The flames of her anger dimmed lower, growing hotter, until they were tight as coals. She climbed back in the truck and slammed the door, flexing and unflexing her hands, as they watched Roshian press the knife point against one of Scavenger's toes.

Jenny leaned close to the window. "I think it's the kill he wants," she whispered, "not just the hunt. And I don't think this is the first time. Remember that whitetail deer that died? Dane said it was sick, but it didn't look sick to me. And he claimed he had to saw the antlers off to make it fit down the drecktube, but that tube's pretty big when it's unlocked."

Mali whirled in confusion. "What do you mean."

"Think about it—none of us ever saw those antlers again. I think Roshian wanted them as a trophy. Hunters do that on Earth, sometimes. Hang them above the television set or whatever. It's like how the Axion think certain body parts have medicinal uses."

"It is against the moral code."

Jenny let out a mirthless laugh. "Yeah. Well, no good reporting it to Dane. He's in on it."

They watched as Roshian dug the knife blade deeper. Blood seeped from the wound as he sawed at flesh and fur and tendon, then slipped the claw into his pocket. Mali flexed her own scarred fingers.

"Take me back to the lodge," he ordered, climbing into the rear seat.

Beside her, Lucky was quiet.

Mali started the truck with shaking fingers.

She had thought the Kindred were like family. Cassian, who had rescued her. Serassi, who had healed her wounds. But now, as she threw the truck into reverse and glanced at Roshian in the rearview mirror, she realized that none of them were family. Her real family was still in that desert on Earth, with the camels and the hot tea.

Cora had been right. They didn't belong here.

She glanced at Lucky. His attention was still on the carving in the dashboard. Numbers, it looked like. Or letters. "You seen these before?" he asked.

She shook her head. "Chicago used to drive this truck. Maybe he carved them while he waited for the guests to hunt."

"I think I've seen the numbers somewhere."

In the rearview mirror, Roshian snaked a hand up to his buzzed head, where a line of sweat ran down to his face. He dabbed at it slowly, all the while stroking the claw in his pocket.

Mali flexed her hand again.

Yes, he was definitely more dangerous than anyone imagined.

16

Cora

BACKSTAGE, THE CLOCK CLICKED over to indicate that Free Time had ended.

All the kids climbed into their cages. Sighs and grumbles, blankets being rolled out, Makayla kicking off her shoes and rubbing her feet. In the shadows, Cora could just make out each of their shapes as they lay down shivering on the cold metal floors.

"Good night, Roger," Jenny whispered to the bobcat.

But Cora didn't go to sleep.

Ever since that first lesson with the dice, she had met with Cassian every few days to continue the telekinesis training secretly, and she'd been practicing on her own after lights-out. Night after night, she had concentrated on the small blue dots, willing the die to move. After three nights, she could make it slide across the floor a full foot. After five nights, she could make it flip over, turning itself from 3 to 1 to 6. After seven nights, she could make it hover a half inch off the floor.

If you can achieve levitation of a medium-sized object for thirty sustained seconds, Cassian had said, *you will have a chance of passing whichever test the Gauntlet gives you.*

It was still a ways to go, she knew, but the progress was undeniable. The Gauntlet would arrive in just under one rotation, which gave her somewhere between ten and fourteen more days.

But levitation wasn't the only skill she needed to develop.

She hid the die under her blanket, waiting for the others to fall asleep. Beside her, the fox gnawed a small wooden giraffe from the lodge that Lucky must have stolen for it. She could just barely make out Lucky's silhouette in the near darkness. He leaned against the wall, blanket balled up for a pillow, arms hugged close against the cold. She guessed he was just as awake as she was.

After a few more minutes, someone started snoring. Jenny gave a soft sigh like she had fallen asleep too. Soon, Shoukry stopped rolling over and was quiet. Cora waited longer, at least another hour, just to be sure. When she opened her eyes, they fell on the blue lightlock.

It was time for a bigger challenge than dice—getting out of her cell.

She examined every detail of the lightlock. The raised circular ring in the center. The slight dent in the bars where it was attached.

Move, she willed.

She was getting light-headed. She licked her dry lips and tried again.

Move.

Something was missing; that click. The amplifier attached to the lightlock was weaker than the one on the training die. Her vision slid around in the darkness, making her feel as if the entire room was rocking like a ship. She gripped the bars on either side of the lock, steadying herself. She visualized cutting through the pain that was building around the edges of her mind. Focusing on the lock, only on the lock, until everything else vanished.

Move!

Her mind pulsed all at once, like two hands had suddenly squeezed it, and for a second, she thought, *Yes, that's it!* But the lock still didn't move. She hissed in frustration.

She concentrated harder, until her mind was screaming so loud that she was shocked the others hadn't woken. The pressure grew and grew. She felt wetness under her nose and tasted the bite of blood, but she didn't wipe it away. She was so close. She could feel the catch on the lock. There was a force holding it together. If she could just shut off that pressure . . .

Blood dripped on the floor.

Move, she willed. *Move.*

And then . . .

"Magnetic."

Her eyes flew open. Someone had spoken right in her ear. Who? Who had whispered? The fox in the neighboring cell gnawed calmly on its giraffe statue, oblivious. Across the passageway, someone snored softly. The room was just as quiet as it had been.

A coldness crept up her legs.

It had to have been Dane. He was the only one able to leave his cell. And yet his cell door was closed.

She waited, still, for several minutes. At last, the pain in her mind ebbed. She took a deep breath and gripped the bars again. It hadn't sounded like Dane. It hadn't sounded like anything really, not a boy nor a girl nor a Kindred, and certainly not Cassian.

But wherever it came from, it made sense. Magnetics. She'd been wrong to try to *move* a piece of the lock, because there were no moving parts.

Instead, she needed to *open* it.

She rested her forehead against the bars and felt out the shape of the lock with her mind.

She ignored the taste of blood.

The pain.

Her sense of balance—swaying like on a ship.

Open, she urged, and something in her head clicked.

The blue light turned off. *Off!* Her breath caught as she tried to process that she'd actually done it.

"Cora."

Another whisper, but different this time. It came from two cells down, where she could just make out Lucky's silhouette. "You cried out," he said softly. "What happened?"

A sleepy mumble came from one of the other cells, and they both froze. The mumble died down as whoever they'd disturbed fell back asleep.

She glanced at the extinguished lightlock. Hesitantly, she pushed it open. The door swung open soundlessly, and she stepped out quietly, tiptoeing past the fox, who stopped gnawing and looked up. She went to Lucky's cell, fumbling out a hand in the darkness.

There.

His hand, through the bars.

She focused on the lightlock of his door. *Open,* she urged. The light shut off and once more she was flooded with the rush of success. She climbed in silently. His hands felt for her shoulders, and her hair, as though reassuring himself she was there.

His hand brushed her face and stopped. "Your nose is bleeding."

She rested a finger on his lips to remind him of the sleeping kids. He was shaking. So was she. She stood on tiptoe and pressed her cheek against his. "I'm okay." But her whispered words were stilted.

"All this training is hurting you."

"It's worth it," she said. "Now, when Leon comes back, I can sneak away with him through the drecktube tunnels and find Anya."

"He might not come back."

"He will. Any day now, I know it. It'll all work out before you turn nineteen."

Excitement made her giddy. The thrill of all the progress she'd made. Anxious and frustrated, she kneaded his arms, her lips longing to form words to express her hope.

Instead, she kissed him.

She hadn't meant to. She just wanted to celebrate this tiny accomplishment, this one thing. He pulled back, and in the dark she couldn't see his eyes or tell what he was thinking. *That was a mistake,* she thought, and her fingers in his hair felt the bump from where she'd once hit him. But he wasn't that crazed boy anymore. And she wasn't that same wide-eyed girl anymore, either.

"I'm sorry," she whispered. "I didn't mean—"

But his initial surprise didn't last, and he kissed her back. Hard, like someone reaching out of the shadows toward a single point of light. And for a second she felt the way she had the first time they'd kissed. Back when he had been a farm boy with motorcycle grease staining his hands and she'd been so certain they would go home. He had kissed her softly, then. Not like Cassian had. Cassian had kissed like it was his first time—and it had been—and he wanted to experience everything in that single instant.

She broke off the kiss, breathing hard. She couldn't do this. Kiss one boy while thinking of someone else.

She wiped the blood from her nose.

"I don't know where that came from," she started, but he silenced her by pulling her close, pressing another kiss to her forehead.

"You don't need to explain." His voice wasn't angry. "It's this place. It's being far from home and only having each other."

His voice caught on the word *home*. She wondered if he was thinking of his granddad back in Montana. His motorcycle, rusting and covered with dust in a barn somewhere. A world she might never see again either.

"Can I stay here tonight?" She hadn't meant to blurt it out. But he was right—being so far from home made her feel like some limb was missing, and when she was with him, she felt just a tiny bit more whole again.

"Of course," he said.

They curled up on the floor of his cell, blanket pulled tightly around them.

"What do you miss most?" he asked softly.

"The sky," she answered. "And the air. How it smelled like rain sometimes, and you could see the storms rolling in from the distance." She brushed away a tear forming in the corner of her eye. "Do you really think it's all gone?"

He hesitated. She could feel his heart beating hard beneath his shirt.

"There's something I've been trying to figure out," he started. "Something I found when I went on a hunt with Mali a few days ago. It was carved into one of the trucks that Chicago used to drive."

"Wait." She pressed a finger to his lips, and he looked at her questioningly. "Do you trust me?" He gave a slow nod. "Let me try to read it from your mind."

He hesitated.

"I need to learn how to read minds if I'm going to learn to control them."

He looked hesitant. "Just promise you won't root around in there too deep."

She closed her eyes and concentrated. Her cheeks warmed as she thought of the last time she'd gone digging in his mind, and found memories of her. But this time, he was focused, too. On a word. No, a number. She could almost picture it, rough lines carved into a dashboard.

"Is it 30 . . . 1?" she asked.

His body went rigid in surprise. "Yeah. Well, close. It was 30.1, and it had the letters POD in front of it. I've been trying to figure out where I've seen numbers like that before."

Her eyes went wide.

"I know where." She couldn't keep the excitement from her voice. "POD. It stands for Probability of Destruction. But Cassian says the POD for Earth is 98.6, not 30.1. If it was just thirty point one percent, then that would mean there'd be a nearly seventy percent chance that Earth *is* still there, which would be . . ."

"Incredible," Lucky whispered.

Cora felt her heart thumping hard. "When they took Chicago away, he said the Kindred had been lying to us. Maybe, if he was the one who carved that into the dashboard, this is what he meant. Maybe he figured out the algorithm was wrong."

"If it's true, and if we could get out of here, we could go back home, tell everyone to come back with intergalactic weapons—"

She shook her head. "No one would believe us. They'd lock us up in a mental ward. Even if we could get someone to believe us, our rockets are nothing against the Kindred." She shook her head. "No, we're on our own. If we ever get free, we can't tell anyone back home what happened."

"So how do we find out if the probability is wrong?"

She paused. Cassian had insisted that the percentage was too small to even investigate, but what if Chicago was right? And what if Cassian didn't *know* that the algorithm was wrong?

"Cassian didn't want to look into it before, but this might change things."

"Cora, he's the enemy."

The word caught her off guard. *Enemy?* It was a word she'd used herself to describe him, when they'd first learned that he was their captor, and again after he had betrayed her. And yet for some reason, it didn't seem to fit anymore. "He wants to help us. And he's as convinced as everyone else there isn't an Earth to return to. But if there *is*, and if we beat the Gauntlet . . . maybe we can go home."

She smiled into Lucky's shirt. She thought of a big, rolling sky filled with clouds, a sky that maybe Charlie was flying across this very moment in a small but sleek airplane.

At least for this one night, she didn't feel hopeless.

VERY EARLY, CORA SLIPPED back into her cell. When morning came and the lights flickered on, she went about her usual task of checking the floor by the drecktube, expecting nothing.

She froze.

Today was different. Chalky words and a drawing of a hand with only three fingers had been drawn on the floor.

FOUND HER.

She heard footsteps behind her and hurried to wipe away the chalk marks just as Dane walked down the aisle for inspection, tossing the yo-yo. "Going to behave today, songbird?"

She smudged the last of Leon's message. "Of course."

"Just remember what I told you." His eyes were on her, but his head was turned slightly toward Lucky.

She smiled tightly. "Right. Keep my hands to myself. I wouldn't dream of anything else."

It was all she could do not to look in Lucky's direction.

Dane threw the yo-yo again. Cassian had said that if she did beat the Gauntlet, change wouldn't happen overnight. It would take months to establish a system to bring humans equality, with some suffering longer than others. Maybe, in Dane's case, she would make sure he was handed his freedom last.

17

Cora

AS SOON AS SHE could, Cora told Lucky about Leon's message.

"I put a note down the drecktube telling him to wait until tonight," she said, whispering across the water trough. "I'll unlock my cell again. Night lasts at least eight hours; that should be plenty of time to get Anya—"

"Well, well." Dane seemed to have been lying in wait, ready to pounce on them alone together.

Cora clenched her jaw. "We're talking about work."

He smiled thinly. "You have bigger concerns than me right now. Guards are outside. They're demanding you go with them."

"Guards?" Lucky started. "But why . . . ?"

And then his face went white.

Cora gulped down last of the ice-cold water she'd scooped from the trough, feeling it freeze her insides. The last time guards had come, they'd dragged away Chicago.

Oh no. Not yet. Not Lucky . . .

"They can't take him!" she said. "They don't have any proof of his birth date. You know how time works differently—he must still have a few days."

Her voice came out desperate, but Dane still wore that thin smile.

"Cora, it's okay." Lucky sounded full of resignation. "You and Mali, you'll watch out for each other." He faced Dane squarely, and Cora felt like time wasn't quite moving right. No, this was all wrong. "I'm ready," Lucky said.

Dane's hooded eyes flickered between them, his face very serious, and then suddenly he doubled over, fingers digging into his thighs, laughing so hard tears formed at the corners of his eyes. He straightened and clamped a hand on Lucky's shoulder, squeezing a little hard.

"Oh, that was priceless. That was wonderful. Thank you."

Cora glared at him. "It was a *joke*?"

Dane snickered a few more times, fingers kneading Lucky's shoulder. "That close to nineteen, are you? Well, it seems it isn't your birthday *quite* yet." His smile changed into something far more self-satisfied as he turned to Cora. "They haven't come for Lucky. They've come for *you*."

He dragged her toward the door before she barely realized what was going on. Lucky yelled out, but it was too late. Dane had already kicked open the backstage door and there they were: five Kindred guards dressed in black uniforms.

"This is the one," Dane said, with relish.

"Good," said a deep voice. "Escort her to the Castle." Cora twisted her head around toward the Kindred who had spoken, a man dressed in a dark-blue uniform with twin-knot rows down the front, arms folded behind his back, face pinched with that wrinkle cutting down the front of his forehead.

Fian.

Her heart pounded, daring to hope, remember his words the last time she'd seen him. *We are on your side. Remember that.* Maybe this wasn't as bad as it seemed. But then she caught sight of another Council member beside him, a stout man a generation older whose uniform bore more knots than she'd ever seen. Twenty, she counted. He had to be the highest-ranking member of the whole Council.

"What's going on?" she asked. "I haven't done anything."

"That is for the Council to decide," Fian said. He turned toward the high-ranking Council member, saying a few deferential words in their language. The Council member never took his eyes off Cora, but he nodded slowly.

The guards led her toward the door, where Tessela stood at attention. Cora twisted her head back to look at the Council member with twenty knots, who was watching her steadily. There was no emotion on his face, but a sense of danger rolled off him nevertheless.

Had one of the Council's spies seen something? Had they overheard something she and Cassian had said in the alcove? That voiceless whisper in her head . . . what if it *was* a Kindred?

They led her into the rough-hewn foyer. The hosts and hostesses of the different menageries, dressed in their ridiculous costumes, all turned to watch. But the guards led her straight past a vacant podium and into a menagerie that was dark and smelled like dust. Only faint light came from the wall seams, illuminating outlines of furniture.

"Leave us," Fian ordered the guards. "I will question her here. Tell Arrowal he will get a full report shortly."

Arrowal. That must be the high-ranking Council member.

The room filled with the sounds of boots as the guards left. Dust choked the air; there were no sounds of kids, no music or guests. Cora pressed a hand to her throat. Even after Fian's reassurances, she still had nightmares about being choked.

"What's going on?" she asked, once they were alone. "You said I could trust you."

A dim light flickered on.

"And you can," he replied.

She spun—they weren't alone. Cassian stood in the shadows, and relief made her heart thump harder, though something seemed different about him. Maybe the uniform. Maybe the black eyes.

Black, she realized. *He's cloaked.*

She quickly pinched her arm as Mali had taught her to do, letting the sting of pain shield her mind so that he couldn't read her thoughts. One slip and he would know that she planned on cheating the Gauntlet.

"I apologize for having to scare you," he observed.

Slowly, it sank in that Cassian was behind this arrest, not the Council. As her fear waned, she looked around the menagerie. The furniture was heavy and wooden. A throne. Cells made of stone and wooden beams, as in a medieval castle.

"What is this place?"

"An abandoned menagerie. The Council sometimes uses it for private interrogations, as its observation panels have been turned off. Fortunately, the Council specifically requested you be interrogated without anyone's knowledge. They do not know I am speaking with you right now."

"Interrogated for what?"

"A few days ago, I formally initiated the application process to sponsor a human participant in the Gauntlet. It caused a stir, as I had anticipated." He paced the length of the room. "There are six other candidates who have submitted applications. Two Scoates. Three Conmarines. One Temporal."

He glanced toward the doorway, as though he feared being overheard. "The Council made it known they would prefer no human participants this time, but they cannot legally prevent it. They demanded to know the name of the human competitor I was sponsoring. I refused to tell them. Now they are systematically interrogating some of the more problematic humans. Arrowal is leading the effort. He is the Kindred's chief delegate, which means he will also be the Kindred's Chief Assessor for the Gauntlet. Fortunately, Fian is his second in command."

He nodded to Fian, who turned to Cora. "Arrowal wishes to locate this individual before the testing begins, when it will be too late to stop that person's participation. Your name, among others, was mentioned as that of a potential agitator."

"Why?" Cora asked. "I've done everything they've asked. I've sung on cue and haven't broken any rules."

Cassian exchanged a long look with Fian. "They found out the truth about your previous enclosure. That it failed because of your escape attempt."

"How?" she breathed. "I thought you hid that information."

"Somehow, someone found out."

Cora swallowed. "One of their spies."

Cassian nodded slowly. "I warned you the Council could have watchers stationed anywhere. It seems my fears were correct. They have narrowed down the list of potential agitators to six, which means they will be watching you even more closely. Mali is on the list as well, and Anya, and Rolf—"

Cora jumped on the name. *"Rolf?"* Among all of them in the cage, he had been the least troublesome to the Kindred. "Why, what has he done?"

Cassian folded his hands. "Your concern right now is not to give the Council any further cause to distrust you. Dane submits regular reports about all of your behavior to the hostess. Tessela can filter them, but only so much. Now that you and Mali are on the list, they will be watching the Hunt even more carefully."

Cora was silent. She pinched herself harder.

Cassian frowned. "You are in pain."

She folded her arms to hide how she was pinching herself. "Just a headache."

"Headaches can be serious, when you're dealing with perceptive abilities."

She swallowed harder, thinking of how blood had flowed from her nose when she'd broken out of her cell. "Is that what happened to Anya? Her mind ruptured?"

"We did not realize we were doing any damage. We thought the nosebleeds and the headaches were minor side effects, not lasting—that is why we have been so careful not to push you during trainings. With Anya, it got much worse. She started to hear voices."

"Voices?" Maybe that voiceless whisper last night really was in her head—the first symptom of a brain rupture.

"Fian will return you to the Hunt," Cassian said. "Be cautious; do not give Arrowal a reason to suspect you any further."

He turned to go.

"Wait," she blurted out. "I need to ask you about something. Lucky found a code one of the other boys left behind. POD30.1."

A ripple of confusion passed over Cassian's face. He glanced back at Fian. "That is impossible."

"It means there's just a thirty point one percent chance Earth is gone, doesn't it? Not ninety-eight point six?"

"The information must be incorrect," he said, but there was a waver in his voice.

"Did you actually see the algorithm readout that said ninety-eight point six percent? If the Council is so dead set on us never gaining freedom, couldn't someone have tampered with it to make it seem like Earth was gone?"

Again, he looked hesitant.

"Look into it," she said. "Please."

He gave a slight nod, then said a few words to Fian in their language. "Fian will return you now. But, Cora, one last thing. I've read some of Dane's reports myself. He says you and Lucky are still very close." No emotion crossed his face, and yet slowly, his right hand curled. "I cannot tell you what to do, but I would suggest keeping your distance. As I have been told, romantic liaisons are a bad idea between those working together."

She cleared her throat. *She'd* been the one to tell him that.

"I understand the appeal of a bond with someone in your same situation," he continued. "But you must not lose focus. Our mission is more important than everything else. It needs to be me you trust. Me you confide in."

His hand was a fist again, by his side.

Cora's throat felt dry. He didn't even know about the kiss.

"Of course. There's nothing between Lucky and me, just friendship."

He nodded and left, but his fist never released.

18

Rolf

"SUPPER'S READY, DARLING."

Nok's voice came from the kitchen. Rolf folded his newspaper—it was from 1969 and announced the moon landing—and smoothed his hand over his tie. He smiled and took a seat at the dining room table, pulling out the chair for Nok as she carried in a tray of meat loaf. She was wearing a frilly 1950s apron with a daisy pattern, and he knew she'd rather die than put on something so hideous.

But now she smiled, set the meat loaf on the table, and sat across from him. They began to eat. "I made sure to use plenty of fresh herbs," Nok said. "Fresh vegetables are good for the baby's development. After dinner, we should practice mashing up apples into applesauce. That's the most easily digestible food for toddlers."

Rolf forced a smile. "Of course."

The newspaper, the tie, Nok's apron. Serassi had presented each object to them formally, explaining that they were real artifacts from Earth. *I want this to be as real as possible,* she had said, adding, as an afterthought, *for my research.* She seemed to have some idea that this was how human couples acted. Rolf thought she clearly hadn't watched enough episodes of *Keeping Up with the Kardashians.*

"More, darling?" Nok smiled as she served him an extra helping, but her hand was shaking.

Not far away, Serassi watched their every move.

No matter how many days passed, Rolf hadn't gotten used to the fact that an entire wall of their house was missing. In the mornings, there was usually a crowd of Kindred sitting in the spectator area, all of them cloaked and stiff. He could hear the sounds of their fingers inputting data into the computers slung around their hips as he and Nok playacted watering the house plants, reading to each other from the newspaper, putting together the crib.

He took another bite of the bland-tasting replicated meat loaf. "Mmm," he said, loud enough for Serassi to overhear. "You really outdid yourself. You're going to be a great mother."

Today, Serassi was the only one in the seating area. She was often there even after the other scientists had left. Sometimes Rolf and Nok would go to sleep, curled together in the bed, and she'd still be there when they woke. It was seriously starting to creep him out.

Nok stood to do the dishes. "Did you know that babies need to be swaddled for the first four weeks?" she said over her shoulder. "We can use any old piece of fabric. A towel, or even an old shirt—"

"Stop," Serassi commanded suddenly from the seating area. "Stop this."

There was an edge to her voice that hadn't been there before.

She stood, winding with quick steps through the empty seating into the house. She pointed to the baby care book sitting on the kitchen counter. "You are merely reciting facts from the books that we have provided to you. The information on fresh produce and applesauce is on page eighty-one in the 'Nutrition' chapter. The information on swaddling techniques is on page two hundred forty. We are already more than familiar with prenatal care that has been documented in books; this scenario is meant to teach us practices we have not found in books. Informal practices." She picked up the book and dropped it into the trash can. "But you are not teaching us anything that we do not already know."

Rolf exchanged a worried look with Nok. In his heart, he felt that same familiar twist as when he had disappointed one of his teachers. Back in Oslo, he had studied all night, every night, to make top marks. It was the only time his parents paid attention to him, rather than to his brother, who was Rolf's total opposite: a prize-winning track star.

But not anymore, he reminded himself. He might never be a track star, but he had learned coordination and balance and felt the strength in his arms that meant his life wasn't just about high marks. As Serassi leaned over them, he realized he didn't feel the desire to please anyone anymore. In fact, he felt the desire to shove his fist in her face.

"It will be different when the baby comes," he said, trying to keep the anger out of his voice. "We don't know much now because neither one of us has had a baby before. But we've both worked with children. If you let us give birth to Sparrow naturally and raise her ourselves, we will show you something new."

Nok looked at him in that loving way that always made his heart flutter a little.

"No. I do not think so." Serassi's words made his hope come crashing down again. "This scenario is not justifying its expense. I cannot continue without immediate measurable results. The fetus is nearly viable; once it is, we will transfer it to one of our grow centers. Your participation in this child's life will no longer be required."

Rolf couldn't quite process what he had heard. No longer required? *Take the child?* It wasn't until he saw the look of horror on Nok's face that it sank in.

"Wait!" Nok yelled. "Oh my goodness, I misunderstood!" She forced a sudden smile that was so incredibly out of place Rolf could only stare. "I feel so stupid! All this time I thought you meant you wanted us to *adhere* to the books." She smacked herself on the forehead. "It was just a misunderstanding! We can certainly do what you want! Can't we, Rolf?"

She seemed to be struggling not to turn her smile into a grimace.

"Yes," he answered quickly, though the lie had him flustered. "Yes, of course."

"There are *so* many swaddling techniques that aren't in the books," Nok continued. "In Thailand we do this special thing with, um, pillowcases. Cut a hole in the top for the baby's head and bind it up tight. Babies love it. Fall asleep right away. I'm sure it's not in the books—it's something my mother taught me, and her mother taught her before that. Really informal stuff, yeah?"

Rolf didn't dare move a muscle. He certainly knew Thais

didn't swaddle their children in pillowcases, but that didn't matter. What mattered was if Serassi believed it.

But Serassi only watched them, her face a mask.

"Right, Rolf?" Nok prodded. "They do something special in Norway too, *right*?"

But he only blinked. That old nervous twitch threatened to come out, and he had to press his hands against the table to keep his fingers still. "Ah . . ." But he wasn't nearly as good a liar as Nok.

"Oh yeah," she covered for him. "I remember you telling me about it once. Mothers use their wedding dresses in Norway to wrap their babies. It's a good-luck thing."

Serassi cocked her head slowly. "Good luck?"

"You know," Nok said in a rush. "Superstition."

Serassi slowly lowered her hands and typed something into the input pad around her hips. Rolf waited, barely daring to breathe, until she had finished typing.

"Superstition," Serassi said at last. "Good."

Rolf let out a tight breath.

"Perhaps you have something to teach us after all," Serassi said. "At least for the time being." She turned to leave. It wasn't until long after she had disappeared into the shadows that Rolf and Nok dared to sink together onto the living room couch.

Nok immediately burst into tears.

"It's okay," Rolf said, holding her close. "She isn't taking Sparrow away. You convinced her. You were brilliant, Nok. Truly brilliant."

"I didn't know what else to do!" she sobbed, brushing away sloppy tears. "I'm so sorry."

He blinked at her in confusion. "What do you have to be sorry for?"

"Lying," she spat out. "I made a promise to myself when they took us from the cage. I became such a terrible person there, Rolf. The things I did with Leon, that I almost did with Lucky too. I was awful to you, yeah? And the moment I realized how crazy I'd gone, I promised myself no more lies."

"This is different," he whispered. "No lies between you and me, yes. Between us and the Kindred"—he smiled—"tell as many as you want."

A grin broke through her tears.

That night, for once, they had the freedom of no eyes watching them, but Rolf couldn't shake the feeling that at any moment Serassi might change her mind. While Nok spent the evening fabricating baby-raising techniques and writing them down in a journal for them both to study, he worked on the time conversion. He'd come close to solving the equation a few days ago. There was only one outstanding integer. Maybe it was a fraction he needed.

His sum came out all wrong again, and he scribbled out the bad equation.

Think, he told himself. *Concentrate.*

He folded his legs underneath him on the couch like he used to do, slouching down into himself, letting one hand twist knots in his hair. His mom had called this his genius-at-work pose. It let him free his mind, concentrate on nothing else.

He scribbled out another sum. Wrong again.

His back ached, but he ignored it. He chewed on the inside of his cheek so hard he tasted blood. Why couldn't he solve it? In the cage, he'd been able to solve even the most challenging math problems in the toy shop. Once, after a full day of sledding, and then swimming in the stream, he'd been so flushed with confidence that he'd even solved the puzzle on the jukebox.

He sat up. That was it!

All those years at home, slouched down, he had thought the key to genius was to focus only on the mind and ignore the body. But maybe that weakened everything. Maybe the key was letting the mind and body work together.

He started pacing. Nok looked up, raising an eyebrow as he reached his hands over his head, shaking out his arms, jogging in place a little.

"Serassi isn't watching," Nok said. "You don't have to make up weird behaviors right now."

"Not weird behavior," he said. "Weird thinking."

He felt blood flow into his feet, which had gone to sleep tucked under him. He drew air deep into his lungs and let his shoulders fall back.

If the bottom integer . . .

If the negative sum on the right-hand side . . .

And then he laughed.

He fell to his knees and scrawled out a sum, and then blinked. His hands started shaking.

It matched.

"I . . . I did it," he said, and then scrawled a few more numbers. "The conversion. I figured it out. We've been here, let me see, one hundred fifty days. Which means if we conceived on the day Serassi told us, that means Sparrow is due in, um"—he snatched up one of the parenting books to consult—"approximately one hundred thirty more days. That means we have enough time to figure something out, right?"

Nok chewed on her lip, snatching the parenting book from him. "But it isn't just until the baby is born. It's until the fetus can survive outside the womb. This book says that happens at twenty-three weeks. How many days is that? Shit, carry the two . . ."

The smile faded off Rolf's face. "One hundred sixty-one days. Which means we only have eleven days until they could take Sparrow."

"*Eleven?*" she said. "That's no time at all!"

"You've got to come up with more lies. Make them think we're invaluable enough to keep around indefinitely, even after the fetus is viable."

Footsteps sounded from the shadows. Nok tensed and Rolf let her go quickly. Was Serassi already returning? One of her assistants? Nok dried her eyes on her apron, forcing a smile, picking up the dirty dishes from dinner in a rush.

"Maybe after we finish doing the dishes, we can work on the crib more," Rolf said loudly, with forced cheeriness.

The footsteps came closer.

A figure loomed out of the shadows. As big as a Kindred, but not moving as stiffly. Nok turned back to the dishes, but Rolf squinted into the light.

The figure walked through the seating area but stopped halfway. He just stood there. Didn't sit. Didn't take notes.

Finally, a voice cut through the shadows.

"Bloody hell, what are you two idiots playing at?"

The figure came forward, and the lights of the house reflected on Leon's smirking face.

Rolf started. *"Leon?"*

Leon jumped up on the porch, stepping right into the kitchen. "I've been all over the damned station looking for you two, and you've been playing house this whole time?" He shook his head, but then sniffed the air. "Is that meat loaf?"

Rolf gaped.

Leon being here could mean only one thing.

Cora must have sent him. Cora must have some new plan up her sleeve, and not a second too soon. This time, Rolf wanted in.

19

Cora

THE DRECKTUBE TUNNELS WERE even worse than Cora had imagined.

  · Frigid, thin air crept up the folds of her pajamas as she crawled behind Leon on the rough-hewn ground. She'd snuck out of her cell as soon as the others had fallen asleep, tiptoeing to the door and knocking softly, half surprised that Leon had actually kept his word when he swung the door open for her, and even more surprised when he said he'd found Nok and Rolf in some giant dollhouse. Now, as he led her toward the Temple menagerie, her knees were already red and raw; thank goodness she wore a long dress during the day, because she didn't know how she'd explain scraped knees to Dane in the morning.

    "Gotta watch out for the traps," Leon explained over his shoulder. "Almost sizzled me a few times, but I've learned their tricks now. It's the packages that are the real danger. If you hear one coming, get out of the way. Hurts like hell if you get hit with one. What do you call it, again? Making things float around?"

"Telekinesis."

"And you can really do that, eh?"

Cora kept crawling. She had told him about unlocking the cell door, and about the dice, and now she felt self-conscious. "It's weird, I know."

He snorted. "No way. Wish I could throw things around with my mind. Ooh, undress girls just by thinking about it. And stealing would be so much easier. . . ."

"*Monsters.*"

She stopped crawling abruptly. It was the same odd whisper as before. Her forehead broke out in sweat despite the frigid tunnel.

"Please tell me you heard that voice," she said.

"Voice?" Leon frowned. "You feeling okay?" He twisted around and reached out, swiping his finger under her nose. It came away with blood.

She pinched her nose distractedly. "It's . . . nothing. Let's just keep going."

"That's a lot of blood."

"Keep going." Her voice was sharp.

Leon muttered something under his breath as he paused at a few doorways, consulting his markings. "So let's say you can break this Anya girl out of her cell with your telekinesis badassery. Where exactly is she going to camp out? I'm guessing there isn't a nice secret room for her in the Hunt."

"Um, no. But I did have one idea."

At her hesitation, he turned around, eyes hooded. "No."

"Leon, she *has* to stay with you. There's nowhere else."

"I'd rather cuddle up with Kindred guards."

"It won't be forever. Just until after I've run the Gauntlet. A week or two, tops."

"Are you kidding? That *is* forever."

Cora let out a sigh, rubbing her hands over her face. If only the air wasn't so thin, maybe she could think better. Leon was the kind of guy who would take a bribe, but she didn't have any money or food or anything. What could she offer him?

"Close your eyes," she said. "Think about something you really want."

"More psychic shit?"

"I need to practice mind reading."

He grumbled a little, but closed his eyes. She concentrated on probing into his thoughts. She sensed something colorful and bright, flashing lights that almost reminded her of the arcade back in the cage. But there was something else there, deeper. A face.

Her eyes flew open. "I *knew* you liked Mali!"

He cursed. "I wasn't thinking about her. I was thinking about Assassin's Creed."

"Yeah, but not deep down. I can tell what you *really* want, way more than video games." A slow smile stretched across her face. "If you helped us out, I'm sure Mali would be very grateful."

He scowled deeper, rubbing his head as if he didn't like the idea of her crawling around in his thoughts. But after a second, he asked, "How grateful?"

"Well Anya *is* like a little sister to her. And if it was my sister you were rescuing . . ." Cora thought for a minute. "Maybe second base?"

He snorted, and then turned around and started crawling again. "Whoring out your friends now, sweetheart? Remind me not to make any promises on your behalf. Don't worry about it. Mali would probably just knock me out anyway. I'll babysit your psychic brat. That's what friends do, eh?"

Cora smiled.

"Could have used your psychic powers when I was trying to find out which door led to the Temple," he continued. "Took me forever to figure it out. I staked them all out for days until I overheard someone say something about Zeus in the last one."

They crawled to the last doorway, and he pointed to his chalk drawing.

"What's that supposed to be, a goat?" she asked.

"Goat? It's clearly a Greek Minotaur!" He grumbled as he wiped away a stray chalk mark. "If I had some proper paints, maybe charcoal pencils . . ."

He signaled for her to be quiet as he shouldered the door open a crack, holding his breath so as not to be too loud. A tickle itched the back of Cora's head.

"Beware the monsters," the voiceless whisper called. *"Dancing through the halls."*

Cora flinched. Dancing? Through the halls? Either she really was going crazy, or the person sending her those psychic messages was.

Leon cursed and immediately pulled his head back in. "Shit!"

"What's wrong?"

"It's the Temple for sure, but not the backstage area. It's the main hall and there's Kindred roaming all around."

Monsters dancing, Cora thought. *Through the halls . . .*

Was someone sending her a warning?

Tentatively, Cora peeked through the crack. It was the same shimmering Greek palace that she had visited with Cassian, only now she was looking at it from a different angle. Beyond the Kindred's boots, she could make out the ten-by-ten-foot cells with lightlocks above the bars. If she strained her neck, she could see the last cell, Anya's, and the girl's sluggish hand sticking out between the bars—missing two fingers. The hand was waving languidly, as though conducting an imaginary orchestra of dancing monsters.

Cora ducked back in.

Could it have been *Anya's* voice in her head?

"She's there," Cora said, "but there's no way we can get to her out in the open. We have to find the backstage area."

Leon rubbed the back of his head. "I know where the rest of these tunnels go, and it isn't to the Temple's backstage. Did you see how there were slots in their cells for passing things like food through? I don't think there *is* a backstage in this menagerie."

Cora's head throbbed. She felt moisture beneath her nose again and wiped it away. She peeked back through the crack. "So to get to her, I'm going to have to walk right through the menagerie, amid dozens of Kindred, and flash around abilities I'm not even supposed to have to unlock her door?"

"And carry her out," he said, eyeing her thin arms. "Don't forget about that."

"So, basically, it's impossible."

Leon closed the door and added a chalk mark that was a circle with a line through it, a symbol that looked like it marked certain doom. Then he patted her on the shoulder. "Good luck with all that, sweetheart."

20

Cora

THEY CRAWLED BACK TO the Hunt in silence. Cora's lungs were burning, making her even more irritable. It felt like the tunnel's walls were getting tighter, but it had to just be claustrophobia and uncertainty tangled up together. At least she wasn't going crazy—yet. That voiceless whisper had definitely been Anya, warning her. But if that was the case, then why hadn't Anya explained how they could break her out of the Temple?

Maybe because she doesn't know how, Cora's own voice answered back.

"I'll come back each night," Leon said. "Same system. Two knocks to say it's safe, and I'll open the door. Slip a note down the drecktube if anything changes. See if you can figure out some genius new plan in the meantime."

"Rolf's the genius, not me," Cora muttered, and then stopped abruptly. "Hang on. Rolf might be just what we need. He's brilliant. And Nok's a good schemer. Can you take me to them?"

Leon scratched his head. "They're in a crowded sector. Lots more shipments moving around. Last time I was there, I got caught between two crates that nearly dragged me into a cleaner trap." But when she tilted her head, looking at him sweetly, he sighed. "You're going to get us killed, you know that? Come on. It's this way."

As they crawled, Cora thought of the last time she'd seen Rolf and Nok in the cage. They'd been in the middle of a fistfight with each other that hadn't looked like it would end well. "You said they were doing okay, right?"

"Okay? Are any of us okay? They were alive, that's all I said. They were pretty freaked out the Kindred might take away Nok's baby. They were holding on to some sad hope they could get home and raise the baby there. Whoa. Hang on. Death trap at twelve o'clock."

He pointed ahead to a place on the floor, but Cora saw nothing until he shone his headlight on it. A glistening, nearly transparent line. He carefully climbed over it, and then motioned for her to do the same.

"Actually," she said, "Nok and Rolf might not be so off base about home. Lucky found information that there's a higher chance than we thought that Earth's still there. Cassian is going to look into it."

"That right?" Leon mumbled as he consulted his scrawled map.

"Aren't you more excited? We're talking about Earth. It means that we could have a real future. If I beat the Gauntlet, no one could stop us from leaving this station and going home."

"Sweetheart, if you'll recall, I never thought Earth was gone."

"But the Kindred's algorithm predicted it."

He shrugged. "I've never trusted nerds. I go with my gut, which always said Earth was there."

She crawled behind him, thoughts spinning. "Well, if it's true, we'll need a ship to take us there after the Gauntlet is over. Bonebreak must be have one, right?"

Leon snorted. "Don't get your hopes up. I've been asking around. Next ship won't come for another forty years. I got him drunk one night, and he told me all about the last time they helped humans. Years ago, when the supply ships used to come more frequently, the Mosca made a deal with a group of humans to go back to Earth. That was back when the Kindred took mostly adults, and I guess they wanted the smartest ones. They ended up abducting savants, you know? The kinds who can multiply insane numbers in seconds, kind of like Rolf?"

He wiggled his fingers in the air like he was working out numbers. "Well, the Kindred didn't realize half those people are even smarter than *them* when it comes to numbers. The savants figured out how to override the system, got out of their enclosures, and faked their deaths. They found Bonebreak. He was just an underling at the time. His captain took the humans back to Earth in exchange for them screwing around with the Kindred's food replicator. One hell of an expensive practical joke."

He paused to wipe chalk dust out of his eyes. "It's crazy, but I actually remember my sister talking about it. She's into crime books, you know? Said in the eighteen fifties there was this group of people who just appeared in South Africa—they were all crazy, said they'd been abducted by aliens."

"Eighteen fifties? How old is Bonebreak?"

"Really old, I think. I'm scared to see behind that mask."

"And you trust him?"

Leon snorted. "Our relationship is a mutually beneficial arrangement. I have something he needs—the ability to crawl through tunnels. He has something I need—protection from the Kindred guards, not to mention a bunch of vodka. So do I trust him? Sure, until he finds a different way to get what he needs." He grinned. "But I'm not useless yet."

He pointed ahead to a chalk mark of a dollhouse. "See? Told you I'd find it again. Nok and Rolf are up here." Eventually the tunnel smoothed out and turned to metal, and then ended.

Leon shouldered the gate open into a wide room, like a dark theater. When they crawled out, Cora saw a small house at one end—except one entire wall was missing. Leon led her close, a finger pressed to his lips. In the upstairs bedroom, Nok was getting dressed, and Rolf was toying with an old radio.

"Hey!" Cora started toward them, but Leon threw a hand over her mouth.

"Christ, sweetheart, shut up." He jerked his chin toward a row of dark seating. At least ten Kindred were there, watching Rolf and Nok. She waited a heart-pounding moment, but none of them turned in her direction. They hadn't heard her.

"How are we supposed to get to them?" she whispered.

"We wait. Rolf said they have artificial nighttimes when most go home. Serassi sticks around, but not all the time."

"I can't wait. I have to be back in my cell in the morning."

"Well, what do you want me to do about it?"

Cora squinted at the house, trying to figure it out. Rolf was still fiddling with the radio. A guy like him probably knew Morse code, and she knew it too from those long classes in Bay Pines, where she and Queenie had sent each other silent messages with flashlights from across the room while the others watched rehab videos. She focused on the radio light. *Turn off,* she willed. Her mind probed around the circuitry. There was no amplifier, which meant she had to concentrate harder. *Turn OFF.* And for a second the light flickered, just like the lightlock of her cell, and then it turned off completely. Rolf frowned, but she quickly turned it back on.

She did the same, but faster. Three times.

S-O-S

Rolf's eyebrows knit together in hesitation. He looked like he was going to call down to Nok, but froze. He glanced at the watching Kindred, and then carefully turned the radio away from their eyes.

Cora made it blink again.

I-T-S-C-O-R-A

Slowly, Rolf looked over his right shoulder, and then his left. With a tentative finger, he pointed to the corner of the room. Cora could just make out an old-fashioned typewriter; she rolled her eyes. Rolf was really pushing her abilities. She concentrated on trying to remember which keys were which from afar, and tapped her message out in the air with her fingers, pushing her mind as hard as she could to make the corresponding keys move. Without amplifiers, depressing each key felt like rolling a boulder uphill.

I NEED YOUR HELP.

She sagged with the effort. Rolf hesitated. His hand went up to push at his hair a bit like he had when Cora had first seen him in the cage. He paced a little, throwing glances her way like there was something else he had to tell her. He snatched up the radio and pried the bulb out with his fingernails, and then twisted some wires around. When he pushed a button, it blinked.

T-E-L-L-M-E

She took a deep breath and focused on the typewriter again.

HAVE TO BREAK SOMEONE OUT OF CELL
SURROUNDED BY KINDRED. ADVICE?

Rolf stared at the paper in the typewriter. He picked up the radio and pressed the buttons to send Morse code.

D-O-N-T-G-E-T-C-A-U-G-H-T

"What'd he say?" Leon breathed.

"He's being a smartass," Cora muttered.

"Yeah?" Leon seemed almost impressed. "Didn't think he had it in him."

Then Rolf signaled again.

W-E-N-E-E-D-H-E-L-P-2

And he added:

"A few days left?" Cora whispered to Leon. "What does he mean? A few days before what?"

"Oh yeah, he wouldn't shut up about that before," Leon said. "He worked out some equation of how long we've been here and how soon the Kindred could take the baby away."

"He can convert Kindred time to days? Are you sure?"

"He had a whole notebook filled with numbers."

She turned back, focusing on the typewriter, but he started flashing a message first.

C-A-N-Y-O-U-G-E-T-U-S-O-U-T?

Cora paused. "They want our help getting out of there. We could get them into the drecktube when Serassi and the researchers aren't there, but then where would they go? Unless . . ."

Leon gave a suspicious grunt.

"You already agreed to keep Anya with you. And you said Bonebreak's lair takes up a whole sublevel. There must be all sorts of spare nooks they could set up for Nok and Rolf as a safe room. There's even smuggled baby stuff, right? Cribs and diapers and things?"

"Oh, for the love of . . ." Leon rubbed his face hard. "You want the Mosca to help raise a baby? Have you listened to a single thing I've said about them?"

"I don't expect them to read bedtime stories," she shot back. "Just to give them a safe place to live until after I've run the Gauntlet, when Serassi won't have any claim on their baby anymore."

"Bonebreak gets pissed enough just having me around. For him to put up with a crying baby would take serious cash."

"How much?"

He sighed. "I'll ask."

Cora turned back to the house, concentrating on the typewriter.

AM WORKING ON A SAFE ROOM. HOLD ON.
WILL COME BACK FOR YOU WHEN READY.

And then she added:

YOU CAN CONVERT TIME?

Rolf read her message and nodded, not bothering with the radio.

LUCKY'S BIRTHDAY IS OCT 21. HOW SOON
UNTIL HE TURNS 19?

Rolf bent down to his notebook and started writing furiously, working out the equation, pushing at glasses that he no longer needed. He set down the pencil and picked up the radio. The lights flashed and flashed.

Cora let out a small sound of shock.

"What?" Leon said. "What's his spy code say?"

Rolf, maybe worried they hadn't seen his signal, flashed the lights again. A dark premonition washed over her. She willed the light to blink more, but it never did.

Three blinks.

"Only three days," she said.

21

Lucky

THE NEXT MORNING, LUCKY crouched on the backstage floor next to the zebra.

He'd meant to stay awake all night, but he must have fallen asleep at some point, because suddenly Cora had been in his cell, shaking him awake with a hand pressed to his mouth to keep him quiet. She had whispered about her trip with Leon. About Anya's voice in her head and how it was going to be harder than they thought to break Anya out. And then the worst: how Rolf had figured out Lucky only had three days until he turned nineteen.

If he was being honest, he had just been glad to see Cora again. A tiny part of him had wondered, when she'd disappeared with Leon, if maybe she'd run. But she hadn't, and she'd returned with some crazy idea to smuggle him out through the drecktube before his birthday and have him set up camp in a Mosca safe room.

Like hell, he had told her. She hadn't run, so he wasn't going to either.

Now he stroked the zebra's neck, wincing at its sunken eyes and the blood crusted around its nostrils, and thought of how Mali had said that no one was looking out for the animals but him. He rubbed the zebra's neck gently, long strokes along the direction of its hair, the same way he did with the horses on his granddad's farm when they were laid up with colic. The bullet extractor lay on the floor beside him, ready to use. Press it to the wound and in minutes the zebra would be healthy again.

But would it? he wondered. *What does it really mean to look out for them?*

After all, just having a heart that pumped and lungs that breathed didn't make an animal healthy. It only kept it alive until it could be shot all over again. Once, on his granddad's farm, a yearling horse named Newt had been attacked by coyotes. Newt had broken two legs trying to get away from them and blinded himself on a wire fence.

Get my rifle, his granddad had said quietly.

But he could recover, Lucky had said.

His granddad had taken one long look at the horse and shaken his head. *Maybe he could survive,* his granddad said. *But not without suffering.*

Lucky picked up the bullet extractor hesitantly. Part of him wanted to toss it away and let the zebra die in peace. That was a cruel sort of kindness, not one a lot of people could stomach, but he thought maybe, if his granddad could do it, then he could too.

A giggle came from the supply rooms, and he whipped his head around. Pika was in there debating aloud to herself whether zebra or giraffe tails were cuter.

Who was he kidding? If he refused to heal the animals,

Pika would just do it herself.

He clenched his jaw and set the tool against the wound, extracted the bullet, and took out a revival pod from his pocket. Its waxiness rubbed off on his skin as he set it next to the zebra's nose. The animal's nostrils twitched. Then its eyelid cracked open, showing a half-moon of milky whiteness beneath. At last, the animal jolted awake.

"Shh," Lucky said, pressing a firm hand on its shoulder. "Shh, girl. You're all right."

Slowly, its pulse returned to normal.

A sneering voice behind him ruptured the silence. "What next, you going to train it to wear a little saddle?" Dane strode into the cell block. "Bet the Kindred would pay extra tokens to see that. Maybe they'll transfer you to a circus menagerie. You could be part of the freak show."

"We're already in a freak show," Lucky muttered. "Look around."

Dane hovered in the shadows outside his cell, smirking. Then he went inside, rooted around a little, and emerged with a small notebook. "Here. A present. Now you can write down all these deep tortured *feelings* so the rest of us don't have to listen to them."

He tossed Lucky the notebook. A few pages had been ripped out, but the rest were empty. Lucky threw it aside, next to his jacket. He didn't like accepting things from Dane. He didn't like even talking to Dane. But, right now, he needed him.

"Thanks," he muttered.

"Makayla said you wanted to talk to me, so talk."

Lucky could hear the note of interest in the other boy's voice, behind the sneer. Not that he had anything against a guy liking a guy or anything, but Dane would be disappointed if he thought that's how Lucky played.

"Yeah. Yeah, it was cool of you to switch my work assignment before, and you said if I ever needed anything else—"

Pika came in, lugging a bucket of water for the antelopes and dribbling water all over the floor. Her face lit up. "Hi, Dane! You need a break? You want me to take over making the announcements? I wouldn't mind. Really."

Dane looked her up and down. "You? Onstage? The Kindred would probably mistake you for some sniveling little animal and try to shoot you. Too bad you don't weigh enough for any kind of record." He pulled out his yo-yo. "And keep your grubby hands off this. I know you've been trying to swipe it."

Pika's face fell. Her braid sagged over her shoulder, the tip slightly damp. Her eyes went bigger and bigger until she had to draw in a sharp sip of air to keep from crying.

Dane rolled his eyes. "I was kidding. Can't you take a joke?" He reluctantly pulled out his pocket square and handed it to her. "Listen. Give the feed supply room an extra scrub, the insides of the cabinets and floors and everything, and maybe I'll think about letting you play with the yo-yo tonight."

Her face lit up. "Yes, sir!" She giggled and darted off to the feed room.

Dane turned back to Lucky. "Got to give them a little hope, you know?" His voice was low, like they were old confidants. "It keeps them distracted."

"It keeps them miserable."

Dane folded his arms, leaning back on the cabinets,

appraising Lucky carefully. "You know, when you first showed up, I thought, here's a guy like me, who understands the situation and can handle the truth. But I'm starting to think you're just as blind as Pika, easily distracted by toys."

Lucky fought the urge to tell Dane to screw off. It wasn't easy.

Dane crouched down, reaching out a hand to pet the zebra, but his fingers went against the hair's direction, and the zebra flinched. "So tell me what you need that's so important."

"It has to do with time."

"You want a wristwatch? A clock?"

Lucky turned away abruptly before Dane could see how much he hated asking for another favor. He repacked the revival pods in the cabinet with his back to Dane. "Don't ask how I know this, but my birthday is in three days. I'm turning nineteen. And I'm on their throw-down-the-drecktube list, I can promise you that. I tried to escape from an enclosure. And I punched a guard once."

Dane appraised him with surprise. "I see. And you don't want to be dragged away from your pretty little songbird." Jealousy edged his words.

"It isn't about Cora." The zebra was almost revived now, and Lucky reached for the harness. "It's about not wanting to end up like Chicago."

"No one knows what happened to Chicago."

Lucky shuddered, imagining the charred body Leon had described. His hands started shaking as he slipped the harness over the zebra's head and led it to its cell.

Dane watched him work. "I'll be nineteen in just a matter of weeks, too, though the others don't know that."

Lucky closed the zebra's gate. "You've got nothing to worry

about, I'm sure. The Kindred will probably make you a prince on Armstrong, given how much you cooperate." He wiped his hands off and looked at Dane. There was a cryptic expression on the boy's face.

"Converting human time to Kindred time isn't a simple feat," Dane explained. "It's complicated even for the Kindred. They have timekeepers tasked with converting time on different stations and different planets. Roshian is one of the few timekeepers on this station. He doesn't just convert it. He keeps all the records. I could ask him to change the birth date they have down for you. Just a little change, something believable—about to turn eighteen, instead of nineteen. He owes me a favor."

Lucky eyed him cautiously. "What will it cost me?"

A smile flickered over Dane's face. He jerked his head for Lucky to follow him into his cell, which he did, reluctantly. It was filled with trinkets and books, the nicest blankets, even a robe with monogrammed initials that weren't Dane's. Dane took down a cookie tin filled with pocket squares, and he pulled back the thick cloths and a few torn-out pieces of paper. Beneath were hundreds of tokens, carefully padded by the pocket squares to silence them.

"You didn't get all of those from mixing drinks," Lucky said.

Dane closed the tin, shaking his head. "The Kindred think of themselves as being above reproach, and most of them are—given their unique concept of morality. But every once in a while you find one who's willing to bend the rules. One whose morality is a bit more tarnished. A bit more human, you could say."

Lucky folded his arms. "You mean Roshian?"

Dane nodded. "You might be aware of the fact that on occasion he hunts all the way to the kill. A *real* kill. I look the other way. He pays well. You were onto something when you mentioned Armstrong. Only I don't want to be a prince." Dane's eyes gleamed. "I want to be king."

Lucky tossed a look toward the cell block to make sure no one else was overhearing this nonsense. Pika was banging away in the feed room, and other than that, it was quiet.

"I overhear the hosts and hostesses talking, sometimes," Dane continued. "They say that on Armstrong, money is everything. The more tokens you arrive with, the more power you have. And all of this"—he shook the tin—"is going to set me up well, but I need more than money to be a king."

Lucky clenched his fist so hard that his knuckles turned white. "Let me guess. You need subjects." Now the gift of the notebook was making sense—Dane was trying to ingratiate himself.

"Not subjects," Dane said. "Associates. Even with money, it won't be easy to set myself up as a leader right from the start, with no one watching my back. But if I had someone loyal, someone I could trust, someone others inherently trust too . . . Someone who could work his way into Armstrong's society and spread the word about how fair-minded and powerful I am."

Fair-minded? *Powerful?* Lucky had a hard time keeping a straight face.

In the cell opposite them, the zebra had lain down. It was unnatural for a hoofed animal to lie like that, unless it was sick. The whole place felt infected.

"I'm waiting for an answer," Dane said.

Lucky cursed under his breath. "You promise you can get Roshian to change my birthday?"

"Yes."

"Then do it," Lucky said reluctantly. "And in return, if we're shipped off to Armstrong, I promise to tell people there whatever you want me to tell them." He told himself it was an empty promise. His mind went to the carving that Chicago had made in the safari truck's dashboard: 30.1. Which meant there was an almost 70 percent chance Earth still existed. Not much to hold on to, but something.

He heard another giggle as Pika returned from the store-rooms, and he started to go.

"Not just yet," Dane said, keeping his voice low. "Roshian's going to ask for a favor in return, and I can't spare any of my tokens."

Lucky dropped his voice even lower. "There's not much I can do from back here."

"Maybe," Dane said. "Maybe not. I think it all comes down to one question." His blue eyes darkened. "You said this wasn't about Cora. So exactly how close are you to our little blond songbird?"

22

Cora

"GOOD," CASSIAN SAID. "NOW raise them again, higher."

Cora let out a heavy breath, and the pair of dice fell to the table. They had been training almost every other day, and she'd had no idea how physically demanding levitation would be. At the start of their training, when it had been an effort just to nudge a die an inch across a table, she'd felt like her mind might rip in two. Now she yearned to go back to that simple dull headache.

Cassian reset the dice. The sounds of jazz music and clinking glasses filtered through the wooden screens of the alcove, distracting her, but not as much as her worries over Lucky. His birthday was in two days now.

She tried to put Lucky out of her mind and focus on Cassian's dice. By her count, the Gauntlet was just days away from reaching the station. Then she would have three more days while the docking procedure happened. Six days in all—not much time. Were the other candidates, the Scoates and Conmarines and

Temporals, desperately preparing like she was?

"Try it again," Cassian repeated. "Higher. You must reach twelve inches and hold it there for thirty seconds before you will be ready."

"I know. I just need to catch my breath."

Cassian's eyes flickered toward the screen. His hands kept flexing and unflexing.

"What's wrong?" she whispered.

He didn't answer at first, but then he lowered his voice. "I have been debating whether I should tell you something."

She raised an eyebrow.

He glanced in agitation toward the screen. "POD30.1. I have been looking into the algorithm's prediction records. Usually they are stored in a database accessible to all Kindred with level-five and higher clearance. But the particular results regarding Earth have been flagged with a level-twenty clearance. I cannot access them. Only delegates can."

"Fian's a delegate."

"Yes, and he has already reviewed the record at my request." He blinked a few times too many. "There were . . . irregularities. The time stamp was off. Someone modified the results. It is possible—though not definitive—that Chicago could have overheard talk of this on a safari."

"So it's true?" She felt her eyes widening. "They lied about Earth being gone?"

"We know only that the record was tampered with. It proves nothing."

But it could prove everything, she thought.

"Why would the Council tamper with it?"

"They fear humanity is at the precipice of evolution. The Council does not wish to compete with another intelligent species. But if Earth were gone, they would not have to deal with the future of humanity. Only with the handful of humans they currently have in captivity, such as yourself. Easily controllable—so they assume."

Her heart pounded. It was incredible what even this small sliver of hope could do to her morale. She pinched her eyebrows together and concentrated again on the dice. It was easiest if she let her mind probe the dice first, until she could wrap her thoughts around one as easily as if it were her own fingers moving them. She set her sights on the closest die, urging it into a wobble, then a spiral, and lifting it shakily, inch by inch, with the force of her mind until it hovered six inches. As hard as she concentrated, she couldn't get it to rise any higher.

"Mind reading," a voice whispered in her ear. *"The three little mice cheat with cheese, not with crumbs."*

Distracted, Cora let the die fall.

Anya was trying to communicate with her again, but as before, the words only came in nonsensical pieces that she could barely stitch together. Mind reading? *Cheese?* She had to get Anya out of the Temple soon, so they could speak face-to-face.

Cassian frowned. "If your head is hurting, we should stop for the day."

She glanced at him cautiously. His face was calm—he hadn't heard Anya's voice.

"No, it isn't the training," Cora covered quickly. "I just didn't sleep well." That, at least, was true—tossing all night worrying about Lucky. "I . . . had bad dreams. They were about the girl you took me to see in the Temple menagerie. The dangerous one. Anya, wasn't that her name? I dreamed she had escaped and she came here and . . . and killed all of us. I can't get it out of my mind. Could we go to see her again, just so I can reassure myself? I'm sure it would make my head hurt a lot less."

Cassian's face remained a frustratingly impassive mask, even uncloaked. "That is impossible."

"I don't see what the problem is," she pressed. "You took me there before."

He removed a small metal tag from his pocket. "When we use these temporary removal passes to get humans out of their enclosures, the activity is logged. It is not worth the risk of the Council seeing the log and growing even more suspicious than they already are. Wait until after the Gauntlet. If you win, you can see her whenever you like."

His voice was curt as he reset the dice.

She leaned forward. "I need to go *now*. Before the Gauntlet. Surely there must be some other way we could get there, without using the passes. There has to be a service entrance or something. The Council would never have to know."

"No."

"But there must be a backstage area, right? Some other way to reach her?" Cora realized her voice was growing a little desperate, as Cassian stopped arranging the dice. His head turned slowly. Even uncloaked, his eyes were dark.

"Why are you so concerned with Anya?"

"Like I said," she replied, treading carefully, "because of the nightmare."

He studied her for a long time. He was uncloaked, so he couldn't possibly see into her mind, and yet she wondered if her plan to cheat was written all over her face. She grabbed a die and gave an exaggerated sigh. "Forget it. But I'm tired of dice and cards. Can't we work on something that isn't telekinesis?" She tapped the die anxiously against the table. "The Gauntlet might test me on mind reading too, and we haven't even started."

Cassian kept his eyes on her. She could feel him trying to unravel whatever was going on in her head. His fingers toyed with the die, just as hers did. It read 6. He turned it again: 3. For a second, she wondered what it would be like to read his mind. Control it, even. What would she have him do? Bow down to her. Sing and dance on command. Or maybe—just maybe—place his bare palm over hers again, so she could feel that flush of raw electricity.

She felt her face burning, and looked away.

"There is a logical progression to these training modules," he said measuredly. "First you master nudging the dice. Then levitate them. *Then* we move on to mind reading. This process is how we will prove your higher intelligence: through measurable, documentable results. Unless you have other reasons for wanting to skip ahead?"

She bit the inside of her cheek. "No. Of course not."

He reached out as if to set his hand over hers, and for a second her cheeks flamed again, desires she could barely admit suddenly coming true. But he only took the die from her to keep her from tapping it so neurotically.

"You are anxious," he said softly.

"I just . . ." She looked away. "You're right. I do want to skip

ahead for a reason that has nothing to do with the Gauntlet."
She took a deep breath. She'd known for a few years that both
her parents were having affairs long before the divorce, but her
mother was far better at lying about it. Right before her mother
told her father a lie, she would tilt her head down and let her hair
fall in her eyes, and Cora did the same thing now. "I feel at such a
disadvantage. You know every last thing about me. You watched
me on Earth. You know about my time in Bay Pines, and you
know about personal memories, like my dog, and my parents'
divorce. There's an imbalance between us that I can't get past.
You can look into my head anytime you're cloaked, but to me,
yours is always closed off."

His hand rested so close to hers. An inch, and they would
be touching. "This is what your agitation is about? You wish to see
into my mind?" There was a trace of curiosity in his voice.

For the briefest moment, she hated herself for the lie.

"Of course." She scooted to the bench next to his, so that
their bodies were only inches apart. "The Gauntlet isn't just about
gaining new abilities. It's about proving we are truly equal. And
how can we be equal when I'm the one trapped here, and you can
leave at any time?"

The storm clouds in his eyes were moving, slowly, across
his dark irises. "I cannot change that," he said. "Until we prove
humanity's intelligence, you and all humans will always be caged."

"I know," she said softly. "But this one thing—*this* you can
change."

His fingers returned to turning the die: 2, then 4. Faster and
faster, though his face remained impassive.

"I want to know you," she whispered, "the same way you know me."

The die in his hand abruptly stopped.

Cora's heartbeat sped, even though she didn't want it to. It was undeniable, this thing between them. Always there, pulsing just under the surface. His hand was so close. So achingly close.

"Cora." In the privacy of the alcove, he could kiss her and no one would know. He wanted to. Badly. She didn't need to be psychic to know that.

A knock came on the wooden screen.

Cora jerked upright, heart racing. Through the screen, she could just make out the familiar slope of Dane's shoulders.

Cassian straightened immediately. "Enter."

Dane slid open the screen. If he found anything odd about the two of them sitting so close, dice and cards untouched on the table, he didn't even blink.

"We're closing shortly," Dane said. "Perhaps you can continue your card game tomorrow. And, Cora, I wondered if you'd mind sticking around a bit longer. The zebra was sick, and I could use an extra set of hands cleaning up. I'll have you back to the cell block before Free Time ends."

He gave a bland smile.

"Um . . . sure." Cora hurried to pick up all the cards and shuffle them into a stack. "Whatever you need. Cassian, just let me know when you want to . . . play cards . . . again."

She felt her cheeks blazing. She was in such a rush to get away that she didn't stop to think about how odd it was for Dane to ask her a favor, until he led her to the Hunt's supply closet behind the bar. To her surprise, Lucky was standing among the boxes of booze. His face looked grim.

"What's going on?" she asked, blinking hard.

"Dane and I had a chat," Lucky said quietly. "Come inside, and shut the door behind you."

23

Cora

CORA STEPPED INTO THE supply closet, squeezing between dusty boxes of booze, and inched the door closed. "Tell me."

Lucky nearly bumped into an old giraffe carving. "Dane can help us change my birthday."

Cora turned to Dane. "Let me guess—you want something in return."

Dane gave his thin smile. "Lucky and I have already settled upon my compensation. It's more about what *Roshian* wants."

Cora nearly knocked over the giraffe statue in surprise. "What does Roshian have to do with anything?"

"He controls timekeeping for the Kindred," Lucky said. "He'll tweak my records, but only for one thing."

The supply closet suddenly felt like it was closing in too tightly around her. "What?"

"You," Lucky said. And then he clarified, "He wants your hair. The same way he wants the antlers and the horns from the animals he hunts. I guess he has a special place for a human braid on his psycho shelf of lesser-species memorabilia."

Dane suppressed a laugh.

Cora's hand drifted to her hair on instinct, tangling in the curls. "I thought it was just the Axion who cared about that kind of thing."

Dane gave a shrug. "I didn't ask why he wants it. My guess is you're better off not knowing."

Her feet itched to pace, but the room was so small. "Can you give us a second to talk alone, Dane?"

Dane picked up a dusty bottle of schnapps and peeked out of the cracked door. "Five minutes," he said.

Once they were alone in the closet, Lucky ran a hand through his hair. "Listen, Cora, we can find another way. You don't have to do this."

She sank onto a box. "What other way? They'll come for you day after tomorrow if we don't, and you're too stubborn to hide out with Leon." She twisted the ends of her hair around her fist. "It's just hair."

"But who knows why Roshian wants it. Maybe he needs the DNA for something. Maybe he *is* a Council spy. Someone must have told the Council that you were behind our escape from the cage. This could be some elaborate scheme by the Council."

She leveled a stare at him. "The Kindred don't scheme. If they wanted to arrest me, they would just come take me."

Lucky shook his head. "I still don't like it."

"I don't either, but we don't have much choice. At least Tessela and Fian are usually around, in case anything goes wrong. Roshian might bend the rules every now and then, but he can't break them. He's bound by the moral code. And Dane wouldn't dare risk breaking the rules this close to his own birthday, when he's already practically got one foot in Armstrong."

"Still. It makes me nervous." Lucky's hand moved like he wanted to reach out and touch her, but he didn't, and she started toying with her own fingers. For a second, the privacy of the closet reminded her of the first time they'd been truly alone, without the watching eyes of the Kindred, beneath the boughs of a weeping cherry tree. She had seen in Lucky a boy who didn't know his own strengths. A boy who just wanted a simple life. A beach. A beer. A guitar. A boy who, like her, had had all that taken away from him.

She took his hand and pressed it against her cheek. His fingers were strong and knotty from years of farm work. The cage hadn't changed that. "Let me do this for you," she whispered.

His eyebrows knit together as though something troubled him. "For once," he said, "I want to rescue *you*. I want to make a sacrifice for *you*. After what happened in the cage, that night that I—"

He didn't finish, but he didn't have to. She remembered that awful feeling of inevitability as they'd climbed the stairs to his room and he'd started to take off her clothes with that delirious look in his eye.

"You don't owe me anything," she whispered.

"It isn't about debt," he said. His hands surrounded hers, growing warmer.

"Then what?" she asked. "We both agreed that kiss was a mistake."

"I know." He turned her hand over, tracing the markings on her hand, hesitant to continue. "But there's a reason the Kindred's algorithm matched us together. We're alike, in a way. We both need a greater purpose. You don't believe it, but it's true. The Gauntlet means more to you than you let on."

She wasn't quite sure how to answer, so she just watched him tracing the markings on her palm. "Maybe it does," she said at last.

"More important than you risking working with Roshian to save my ass."

She smirked. "Your ass is getting saved, end of story."

The tension between them had shifted, and she turned his hand over instead, tracing her eyes over the tattooed lines in his palm. "What do you think these markings say?"

"'Rejects,' probably," he concluded, and then frowned. "Yours is different from mine. Here, on your ring finger. The pinprick is a lot bigger."

She rubbed her thumb over it, almost like she could wipe it away. "I noticed before. I don't know why."

"It looks almost like a ring," he said. "The way it meets the black band around your finger. Almost like a . . ." His eyes shot to hers. "Almost like a *diamond*."

She jerked her hand away and studied it closely.

It wasn't supposed to be a glistening star, she realized. Lucky was right. Cassian must have modified her markings just slightly—just enough not to raise suspicion—to hide this human symbol there as a secret between the two of them. A diamond ring.

"That . . . that can't be right," she stuttered.

But Lucky's face had darkened. "I bet Cassian did it intentionally. He hid a diamond ring in your markings as some kind of twisted kind of declaration. A vow." He squeezed his fist, hiding the markings on his own palm.

Cora kept staring at it. It couldn't be true, could it? A tattooed diamond ring? She parted her lips to deny it again, but the door shoved open, and Dane looked in.

"Well, songbird?"

She let her hand fall. "Give me some scissors," she said quickly, ignoring the marking on her fourth finger. "I'll cut my hair off right now."

"It isn't quite that simple." Dane held up two fingers, snipping them together like scissors. "Roshian wants to do the honors himself. Odd, I know. But to each his own."

Cora glanced back at Lucky, whose face was set with worry.

"Roshian will have to make complicated conversions to change up the new date. It will take some time," Dane said.

"We don't *have* time. Lucky turns nineteen in two days."

Dane's eyes shifted to Lucky over her shoulder. "Lucky isn't going anywhere, don't worry. I'll make all the arrangements and let you know when Roshian is ready to make the exchange. It'll have to be after closing. I'll leave a signal for you onstage."

"A signal?"

"You'll know."

She ran her hand down her curls. She'd had long hair for as long as she could remember. Jenny, Makayla—theirs was shorn close, and it didn't seem to bother them. She'd get used to it, but still, how much could they snip, snip, snip away at themselves before they stopped being human and started to be something else?

"All right," she said, reaching down to squeeze Lucky's hand, and only then remembered that, after closing, Tessela and Fian wouldn't be there to look out for her.

Lucky's eyes lingered on her ring finger, and his face darkened again.

A DAY PASSED. CORA felt the time slipping away as she went about her tasks like each minute was a token falling through slats, never to be recovered. She barely knew what words she was singing, and half the time they came out as jibberish. That night, she snuck out of her cell and curled up with Lucky, holding tight to his shirt collar, as though that could keep him there.

All during the next day—Lucky's birthday—she tried to catch a second alone with Dane to ask him about the plan, but he only ignored her. She sang her first set. Then her second. Roshian wasn't in the audience but Arrowal was, with Fian and two other Council members. The walls felt even more claustrophobic than they usually did. She was nearly dizzy by the start of her final set. She stepped onstage, and stopped.

Dane's yo-yo was tied in a pretty little bow around the microphone.

She whirled her head toward the bar, where Dane was shaking a drink for a Kindred woman. For a second his eyes met hers, and he gave a slight nod. This was the signal. She sang through her set with a shaky voice, singing songs she vaguely remembered from her middle school years, innocent songs about tire swings and first loves that wouldn't give the Council any reason in the slightest to stick around after closing to question her again.

At last, Tessela announced the Hunt was closing. Cora held her breath until every Council member had left. Shoukry finished cleaning the bar, and then they were alone. Dane turned down the lamps.

"Where's Roshian?" Cora asked.

Dane untied his yo-yo from the microphone, slipping it back in his pocket. "Waiting for us."

He started toward the veranda doors, but Cora snaked out an arm. "I need to see proof first. I'm not going anywhere with you until I know Lucky's birthday is changed."

Dane took a small envelope from his pocket. She fumbled with the flap and dumped out a metal tag, engraved with the Kindred's writing. "Flip it over," Dane said.

She did, and her breath caught. A date, in English. October 21, 1998.

Exactly one year *after* Lucky was born.

Dane smiled. "I told you to trust me, songbird. You aren't the only one who doesn't want Lucky to leave. Now, this way."

They passed through the fluttering white curtains to the artificial outdoors, where she had to shade her eyes against the sun. She hadn't been on the veranda since the first day, when Cassian had shown her the savanna. She knew it wasn't real, just forced perspective and illusions, and yet her mind refused to believe that those scrubby hills didn't stretch as endlessly as they appeared to do.

Dane started down the stairs.

"Aren't we meeting him here?" she asked.

Dane jerked his head toward the savanna. "The light out there is better. Wouldn't want him to accidentally snip off an ear, right?"

She ran her fingers over the engraved tag, tucking it into her dress, and slowly followed him down the steps. She'd never been on the lower level, where the soil was sandy and patchy with dry grass. This was where the real action was, not up in the lodge. The garage, with its artificial trucks that ran along a bluelight track, and the armory, row after row of rifles. Her heart skipped a beat, seeing those guns. She knew they wouldn't work for her, and yet it seemed it would be so easy to grab one off that wall and blast her way to freedom.

Footsteps came from around the side of the garage. Roshian. Something about the way he carried himself made him loom despite his short stature. He let his eyes run down and up her body, settling on her hair. For a second, she wanted to go back on their deal. The idea of his hands on her, cutting away the hair she'd had her whole life, made her feel sick.

She glanced at the dashboard of the closest safari truck, where the rough carving had been made.

POD30.1

It gave her a small boost of hope. "Let's get this over with," Cora said.

"Yeah." Dane's voice had an odd tone. "Sure."

She looked for scissors. Neither of them seemed to have a pair, and neither seemed in a hurry either, though Dane was giving off an anxious sort of energy. He pulled out his yo-yo, tossing it distractedly. A slow, uneasy feeling started to creep up her back. They had to do this fast so the others didn't get suspicious of her absence. And did they really need to come all the way out here?

She glanced toward the veranda. Dane was standing between her and the stairs, legs spread a little wide. If she tried to bolt back to the lodge, he'd catch her in a second.

"What's going on, Dane? I thought this was about my hair."

"Oh, it is."

Slowly, Roshian took out a long black case from the truck's backseat. Cora took a shaky step backward. Roshian was bound by the same moral code as all the Kindred. As deranged and self-serving as that code was, none of them ever went outside of its boundaries. Kidnapping children was fine. Dragging them out to a savanna and shooting them wasn't.

Roshian opened the case: a rifle, this one battered and dented. Not Kindred technology. Her heart started screaming for her to get out of there.

"What's going on?" she demanded.

"I asked you once how fast you could run," Roshian said. "Unfortunately, I never got an answer, but I have studied the way you move. You are flexible, and your reflexes are fast. I would guess that you can run quite fast when pressed."

She leveled a wary look at him.

He couldn't kill her.

He *couldn't*. He was Kindred. Was this some sick joke he and Dane were playing? A game?

"I suggest you start running," Roshian said.

24

Mali

THE LODGE WAS DARK during Free Time. Mali had never liked the inside of the menagerie—she preferred the wide-open spaces of the savanna, even if it was artificial, to the smoky air with the chained animals and clinking glasses. She couldn't imagine that on Earth people really just sat around in dank rooms like this. If Lucky's theory about POD30.1 was correct and they returned to Earth, would she have to spend so much time indoors too?

She tucked the backstage door key into the pocket of her safari uniform. She'd stolen it from Dane while he had slipped out earlier, claiming he had to help Cora clean up, which didn't sound at all like Dane. So Mali had stayed behind a few extra minutes, pretending to repair the safari truck's windshield, keeping her eyes open for something suspicious. That was when she had seen Roshian sneak around the side of the garage, and she'd rushed into the garage to hide. He was up to something, and all she could think about was what he had done to Scavenger.

She'd slipped out the back of the garage and climbed the stairs to the lodge, but there was no sign of Dane or Cora or Roshian. The lodge was empty. None of the fleet trucks had been taken. She pinched herself to keep worry at bay and started to return backstage. It was a big station, and Dane's key could only get her so far. There was no way she could track down which level and sector they might have taken Cora to.

But a rustle from the bar made her freeze. Years of fighting made her body react by instinct and her muscles tensed in a familiar pattern. *There.* A shadow, moving behind the bar.

Glass shattered and the figure cursed. "Bloody hell."

Mali's muscles eased. "Leon."

He stuck his head up, grabbing for a bar towel to clean up whatever bottle he'd broken. "Mali?" His hand immediately went to smooth back his hair. "Aren't you supposed to be locked up?"

Mali walked to the bar in quick, silent steps. She pulled out a stool so she could lean in close. "What are you doing here."

"What does it look like?" He finished dabbing off the spilled liquid that smelled so sweet it made her stomach turn. "I was doing a run for Bonebreak, and it took me right by here. The lights and music were off, so I didn't think anyone would mind, eh? This bar has the best drinks of all of them." He flashed his best smile. "Want one? You and me and a few drinks could be fun."

She leveled him a cold stare. *Such an idiot. Such an attractive, stupid idiot.*

"You will ruin all our plans if someone catches you," she said.

"Eh." He dismissed her worries with a wave, then poured her a glass of orange liqueur anyway. "You don't give me enough credit. I've been crawling around this station for weeks and I haven't been caught. I even broke into Council chambers once, and tried on their ceremonial uniforms. A little stiff around the collar, but not as bad as you'd think." He downed Mali's glass of liqueur when it was clear she wasn't going to touch it. "What are *you* doing sneaking around? Miss me?"

That smile again. It almost, *almost*, made her want to smile back. But she tossed a look at the backstage door, then leaned across the bar. "I believe a Kindred named Roshian has taken Cora and I fear for her."

"*Roshian?*" Leon grunted up the name like fresh vomit. "Shit. We need another drink."

Mali narrowed her eyes. "You are aware of him."

"Oh, yeah. He's one of Bonebreak's best customers. I deliver contraband to his quarters every half rotation. All the other Kindred have quarters like army barracks, you know? Not a thing out of place. And Roshian's is like that, at first glance, but he's somehow got himself another room, a secret one, connected through a viewing screen he can open. It's filled with a bunch of human artifacts. Dude seriously likes his comic books. And all that witchcraft stuff you were talking about, powdered animal parts and antlers and shit."

Mali pinched herself, hoping the pain would help her focus, because what he was saying made no sense. "You must have misunderstood. The Kindred condemn such beliefs."

"Well, damned if I know. Maybe he's got Axion friends."

"What is in the packages that you deliver."

"I've never looked. I don't want to know what messed-up contraband guys like him want."

Mali had rarely felt this uneasy. First Cora disappearing,

now these revelations about Roshian . . .

Leon narrowed his eyes. "Why do you have that look on your face?"

"What look."

"That I'm-going-to-make-Leon-do-something look."

She leaned on the counter. "You know how to get to Roshian's quarters."

He sighed. "Here it comes."

"I want you to take me there. I want to see what is in the packages that you deliver. It might explain where he took Cora."

He held up his hands. "Okay, but I'm going to expect a thank-you at the end of this. A foot rub to start. We'll negotiate from there. And I'm taking this." He swiped a fresh bottle.

Mali let her smile come this time, despite her worry.

Leon motioned her to a panel behind the stage that was hidden by a curtain. He removed the balled-up bag of potato chips that held the panel open, and bowed.

"After you. At least I'll get a good view out of this." His gaze dropped to her butt.

She dropped to all fours and crawled in. He clambered in after her, making a ruckus as he crawled along. From his strained breath she could tell the tunnel's thin air bothered him, but she didn't mind the tight passages. For a second, Mali let herself think about what would happen if they could prove Earth was there, and if they could go back after the Gauntlet. She had asked Cora once how she could go about finding her family. Cora had said that she'd need a *phone number* or *mailbox* or *email address*, none of which Mali had, and none of which sounded like things a Saharan nomad camp would have either. But Leon might be able to help.

Leon seemed to know how to get around official requirements. And, if she was being honest, she wouldn't mind getting to know him back on Earth.

They crawled up two levels, then turned down a maze of ducts, avoiding a cleaner trap that she saw even before he did, and finally came to a drecktube marked with chalk. Leon jerked his thumb at the crudely drawn face with *x*'s over the eyes. "I do that to mark which quarters belong to assholes."

He shouldered open the narrow door, holding a finger to his lips to be quiet. But no sound came from within except the constant whir of air through the wall seams. They climbed into a set of standard crew quarters that looked identical to all the quarters she had seen for low-level officers. A single bedroom. One chair, and a table that folded out from the wall. Blue bins holding blankets and a few rationed belongings. Leon went to the viewing screen and gave it a firm jab with his elbow. It clicked open.

Mali inspected the hinges closely. "These mechanisms are very crude. It is odd that he does not protect this hidden door with perceptive ability."

They climbed inside. Leon fumbled with something in his pocket and then a light strapped to his forehead came on. The beam cut through the darkness, showing only a circle of light. Leon moved it slowly around the room so she could see everything. One wall was covered in animal heads that had been detached from the bodies and mounted on hard backings. Not just antlers and horns, but entire heads. An antelope. A deer. Mali had seen much in her life to disturb her, but her pulse had never quite raced in this fluttering, anxious way before.

"I do not understand," she said.

Leon barely glanced at the animal heads. "He's a hunter. Deer antlers. People do it all the time at home."

He spoke so casually of something so strange.

"Not the Kindred," she said. "I have never seen this."

Leon kept swinging the light, and it settled on a table where various animal parts were laid out, along with containers of chemicals and the thick black wire the Mosca used for their masks. She stepped closer, squinting at the fur in the darkness. A hyena pelt.

Scavenger.

Her stomach started to turn in revulsion. This was more than just cutting off a claw. He'd completely desecrated Scavenger's entire body. Her pulse was fluttering harder now, and she glanced at Leon, afraid he could see. Something was very, very wrong.

Leon pointed to a small desk in front of a mirror that was covered by a heavy black cloth. "I leave the packages under there."

Mali lifted the cloth, trying to calm her heartbeat, but there was only a single black canvas bag underneath. She pulled it out.

"Keep the light on it." It was closed with intricate Kindred knots, and her fingers flew over them until she had untied the final one. She looked in the direction of Scavenger's pelt on the table one last time.

She opened the canvas bag.

Leon leaned over her shoulder, the light attached to his head bobbing as he rubbed his chin. "What the . . . ?"

Mali pulled out a Kindred uniform. It was standard for someone of Roshian's rank: cerulean blue, with five knots down the side. There were also paper notebooks—artifacts from Earth—filled with writing that looked like human speech. But beneath it was something odder. A small, clear box that contained two black half circles that were soft and rubbery. And a tube with a screw-top lid, with writing in a language she didn't understand, and two heavy barbells.

Leon swiped up the box of half circles. "No way."

"Do you know what those are."

"They look like enormous contact lenses."

She grabbed him, swinging the light so that it shone right in her face, but she didn't blink. "What are contact lenses."

"We can't just magically improve everyone's eyesight on Earth. People wear them to see better. And the tube is some kind of chemical paint. Don't you get it, kid? It's a disguise. The uniform. The weights, to keep his muscles huge. Roshian is only posing as a Kindred."

Mali found a small square of plastic in the bottom of the bag. She held it up to the light. The words on it were scratched and difficult to read. *John Keller,* it said. *Medical Student, Epidemiology, Boston University.* There was a two-dimensional reproduction of a face in the upper corner; it was Roshian's face, only the skin was pink. His hair was longer. He was smiling and wearing glasses.

"He's human," Leon said.

Human. Mali glanced back at the animal heads on the walls. That explained his odd predilections. The way he kept to himself in the Hunt. Why he only seemed to have the cloaked side of his personality.

It also meant that he was not bound by the Kindred moral code.

She dropped the identification card. "We must find Cassian. Now."

"No way," Leon said. "If he sees you outside of the menagerie, he'll know we can sneak out. He'll put a stop to it. And he'll turn me in to the guards."

"This is more important. There will be no more sneaking around if Cora is dead."

"Please tell me you're exaggerating."

"I do not exaggerate." She climbed one leg back into the service passageway. "The Kindred do not kill humans. But *humans* kill humans. And I do not think that Roshian—John Keller—only wants Cora for her hair. Now take me to Cassian's quarters."

She climbed in the drecktube, and they scrambled through the tunnels, dodging packages and cleaner traps, and this time Leon didn't make a single comment about staring at her backside.

25

Cora

CORA SHIELDED HER EYES against the bright savanna sun. It glinted off the hood of the nearest safari truck, blinding her so that all she could make out of Roshian was a dark outline.

She took a shaky step backward, nearly tripping over the uneven ground. "Dane, what's going on?"

He stood at the base of the veranda steps, blocking her. "You heard him," he said quietly, tossing the yo-yo. "Run. You might have a chance."

"You brought me here to *die*?"

His eyes snapped to her. "That's up to how fast you are. I can't say I'm optimistic." He shoved the toy in his pocket, and when he spoke again, his tone was more resigned. "I'll tell Lucky that you died in an accident. I'll watch out for him. He could go far here."

She contemplated hurling herself at him, clawing his face, ripping out clumps of his hair, but it wouldn't change anything—*he* wasn't in charge.

"You!" She spun on Roshian. "If this is just about some trophy, take it! I'll give you my hair, no favors in return, no questions asked."

"It *is* the trophy I want," Roshian said calmly. "But the trophy means nothing without the hunt."

He picked up the old rifle, an enormous dark-gray monster that had to weigh twenty pounds, nothing Kindred about it in the slightest.

"Just run already!" Dane hurled his yo-yo at her feet.

She let out a hoarse cry. Her mind kept spinning, trying to find a rational explanation, as Roshian stroked the length of the rifle barrel. He couldn't do this. He couldn't kill a human. And then he rested a finger on the trigger, and her spinning mind stopped.

Apparently, somehow, he could.

"Only one way to escape the Big Bad Wolf," said Anya's voiceless whisper, and for a second, Cora was glad at least she wasn't alone. *"That's to run."*

Cora's heart throbbed harder. Anya might think in riddles, but this one wasn't hard to decipher.

Cora turned and ran.

Heat rose from the ground, turning the artificial savanna into hazy waves. Tall grass. The watering hole. Rolling hills. Not many places to hide, which was exactly how it had been designed.

Behind her came the metallic clicks of a rifle preparing to fire. Back in DC, her father had once dragged her to a shooting range for a political photo op and made her put on ear protection and fire at a person-shaped target. She had hated everything about that dank cement room of sweaty men, but she remembered one thing: it was a lot harder to shoot a moving target.

Her long dress tangled around her ankles, slowing her, and she jerked it up around her knees so she could run faster, darting and weaving to make herself harder to shoot. Her feet pounded over stone and tufts of grass, throwing up sand behind her. She ran for the closest hill. If she could get behind it—

A bullet whizzed by her side.

She shrieked and veered to the right, throwing herself behind a tree. She could just make out Roshian on the horizon, still standing by the veranda steps. He had lowered the rifle to reload. Even if the bullets were artificial, they would still immobilize her so that he could slice her throat. Her breath slammed in her chest as she dug her fingernails into the tree.

What chance did she have? He was Kindred, and all Kindred were faster, and stronger, and smarter. Tessela, Cassian, Lucky, and Mali—none of them could help her, because they had no idea that at this moment a twisted creature in a safari uniform was lifting a rifle to aim again.

"Anya," she thought as hard as she could. "Help!"

For a minute, there was nothing. The sun beat down mercilessly. It was only a matter of time before Roshian would corner her, shoot her, and cut off her hair and keep it as a deranged trophy. No one would be left to run *or* cheat the Gauntlet.

And then:

"Don't give up, little rabbit."

The words batted around in Cora's chest, giving her just the slightest amount of hope.

"How?" Cora whispered aloud.

"Make a twin."

Anya's voice echoed in her head. A twin? No, a *decoy*! That would work, but Cora had nothing except the clothes on her back. She ripped the heavy golden fabric of her dress at the knees, and then tossed it over a branch so it flickered in the wind. Anya was right. From a distance, it might look as if she was hiding there.

She shoved off and ran for the hill. A gunshot went off behind her, splintering a chunk of the tree. The torn fabric of her dress fluttered again as he fired once more.

She dropped to all fours and crawled through the tall grass. Roshian would soon realize the decoy was just fabric and follow her trail of footsteps through the sand. She needed a way to not leave a trail. If there was a river, she could wade through the water to hide her tracks. If there was a paved road, she could walk on it. But there was only sand.

"The trees offer shelter."

Cora tossed her head up, squinting into the high branches. "You've got to be kidding me."

In the cage, Lucky had taught her how to climb trees—it had been terrifying for someone with a fear of heights, but effective. Now, she gripped the lowest branch of a mango tree and swung up into the branches thick with leaves. She climbed as silently as she could, remembering what Lucky had taught her, trying not to disturb the branches as she leaped to the next tree, and then the next. The trees didn't stretch far, but she just needed them to span the sandy patch where Roshian would see any tracks she left. It would look as though she had just vanished.

The last tree ended at a grassy patch, where she dropped down and crouched low.

She closed her eyes and listened.

It was completely quiet, except for her own strangled breath.

She didn't dare look over the grass to see where Roshian was. For all she knew, he might be ten feet away, stalking her with his mind.

A twig snapped nearby, and she bolted.

Bullets ricocheted in the grass behind her, spraying sand into the air. He was just on the other side of the mango trees. She tore through the grass, flinching as it twisted around her ankles, threatening to pull her back down.

"The Big Bad Wolf is clever," Anya's voice said. *"But you have magic too. Use it!"*

Magic? Anya must mean levitation, but what was Cora supposed to do, stop the bullets with her mind? She could barely hold a die a few inches off the ground! If only there was something she could nudge, like Cassian had trained her, like a boulder perched on a cliff above Roshian. But there weren't any cliffs and the only boulders were on the ground.

Another bullet flew by her. She pivoted and sprinted toward the watering hole. At least there were rocks there, where the animals sunned themselves when they weren't in their cages, and some boulders she could hide behind. She raced onto the rocks, avoiding the water so she wouldn't leave a set of wet tracks for Roshian to follow. She dived behind a boulder and pressed her back against it, fighting to catch her breath.

No animal had ever escaped the Hunt. But she wasn't an animal. She was human, and that had to count for something. There had to be some advantage humans had that the Kindred didn't.

She heard Roshian's boots on the rocks just on the other side of the watering hole. He'd be there soon.

She thought of all the times Cassian had talked about the roots of his fascination with humanity. Curiosity. Art. Affection.

Forgiveness. None of that was going to help her against creatures with skin as thick as metal.

But not giving up—that might help. If Charlie were here, he would definitely tell her that *now* was a good time to be stubborn.

Cora rooted her feet.

The Kindred weren't completely invulnerable. Their hard, metallic skin was difficult to pierce, but what about the eyes? In Bay Pines, Cora's cellmate Queenie had once gotten in a fight on the exercise field with another girl much bigger than her. Queenie had never stood a chance in a fight, so she had gone straight for the other girl's eyes. *Cheating,* she had told Cora later, *can be useful for a lot more than just cards.*

Cora hunted through the pebbles and leaves at her feet until she found a small stick the width of her thumb, and maybe eight inches long. Hardly a match for bullets, but it was a chance. She scrambled around the boulder and found footholds to climb on top, moving slowly, making sure that Roshian was always directly on the opposite side so he couldn't see her. She pulled herself up, wishing her heart wasn't pounding so hard.

There he was.

Just on the other side of the boulder. Three feet below where she crouched, he was creeping silently, his rifle at the ready.

Three.

Two.

One!

She leaped off the boulder and landed on his back, using the momentum to sling him to the ground. He reacted fast, trying to twist the rifle around, but she was too close for him to aim. He tossed the rifle aside and drew a Kindred-issue pistol out of his holster. She struggled to keep him on the ground, clawing at his arms. Blood spurted everywhere, though she hadn't felt a scratch. He let off a shot. Pain ripped through her shin and she cried out. He'd used a tranquilizer bullet—the chemicals were already spreading through her bloodstream, starting to immobilize her. He shoved to his knees, setting the end of the pistol against her forehead—even a tranquilizer bullet would kill her this close—but she drove the stick at his face first.

"Do it, little rabbit!" Anya's voice urged.

It connected with a sickening *squish*. Roshian let out a scream that sounded impossibly human as he reached for the stick emerging from his eye socket. She stumbled back, breathing hard. Her leg was already numb. She looked down to see where she was bleeding. Her shin. Where else? Where was all the blood coming from? There was something gritty under her nails. Metallic, like tiny slivers of silver sand.

Roshian swung his head around to look for the rifle with his one remaining eye. She shoved herself to her good foot, limping, trying to get away before her entire body was immobilized. Hope surged with every footstep. The veranda wasn't far away. She might have a chance to climb those steps before the chemicals spread through her entire body. Crawl into the lodge, open the backstage door, scream until the others came running. Roshian surely wouldn't kill her in front of witnesses.

She reached for the railing. She couldn't feel her right leg at all, and her fingertips were going numb. She hobbled up, step by step.

At the top of the stairs, a bullet went off just over her head.

She collapsed to the stairs. When she turned, he was ten feet away, one hand clutched over the stick in his eye, the other eye burning with fury. "One more step and I'll shoot you in the back of the head, even if it means ruining that pretty hair of yours."

He sounded so savage, so brutal, so completely unlike a Kindred.

"*Anya,*" she thought. "*Anya, what do I do?*"

But Anya's voice said nothing now.

"Turn around," he said. "I want to watch your face as you die."

26

Cora

CORA'S LEGS WERE NUMB.

She couldn't walk. Couldn't crawl. Couldn't fight.

The safety of the lounge was so close, and yet impossible to reach.

Blood stained Roshian's torn safari uniform from where she'd scratched him. But it was too red: Kindred blood was so dark it was nearly black. And their skin was so tough that she could never tear it with her nails alone. She looked down at her hand—the jagged nails, and that gritty, silvery substance caked in them. It looked like circuitry. Minuscule metallic fibers.

Beneath the seeping blood on his arms, Roshian's skin was pale. *Pale.*

"*A wolf in sheep's clothing,*" Anya's voice whispered at the same time Cora realized it herself.

"You're human." The accusation came out as a surprise. "That's why you can kill me."

He clutched his bleeding eye harder. "An unfortunate fact for you."

He cocked the gun.

"We're supposed to help our own kind!" she yelled. "Why are you conspiring with the Kindred when they're the ones who make us live like this?" She stretched her jaw. Her throat was going numb, and it was getting hard to speak.

"The Kindred don't know what I am," he said. "No one knows, except the Mosca traders who make it possible. I was a graduate student when the Kindred took me. That was before they screened their wards, or else they would have known that on Earth I'd already killed. Deer hunting didn't quite satisfy the urge, so I studied to be a doctor. It isn't difficult to kill patients. Wrong medication. Complications during surgery."

He stepped closer, nudging her leg with his boot. Her foot flopped to the side, no longer in her control. He crouched down, prodding her shoulder with the tip of his gun, smiling grimly when she couldn't lift a finger to stop him.

"I didn't care that I'd been taken," he said. "I *like* it here. I like the Kindred. They think themselves so intelligent, but they aren't, at least not when it comes to deception. It was easy to escape from them. I've always been tall—at least by human standards. Well built. I thought, if only I had black eyes and metallic skin, I could pass myself off as one of them. So that's what I did."

She urged her body to move, but it was frozen. It was all she could do to force words from her throat. "But surely they could tell. Your mind . . ."

He ran a hand down her hair, appraising it like it was already hanging from a hook in his room. "Read my thoughts, you mean?

That was easy enough to get around. They can't read minds when they're uncloaked, and they're always uncloaked in the menageries. So this is where I stay. I have no life outside of the menageries and my quarters."

Blood kept seeping from the wound on her shin, but she felt nothing. Not a single muscle would respond to her internal screams to move. Soon, she wouldn't even be able to speak. All she would have left was her mind.

"*But,*" Anya whispered, "*not all swords are held in the hand. Real power lies in the mind.*"

"You've lived among them . . . without any . . . perceptive abilities?" Cora managed to ask.

He aimed the gun. "Flattery won't help you."

"I'm serious. Not a single . . . ability?"

His smile started to fade. "I used my intelligence alone. We're smarter than the Kindred realize, even if their mental abilities are impossible for us."

She closed her eyes.

"Oh, I know all about impossibilities." She concentrated on the stick in his eye. Maybe she couldn't yet control someone else's mind, but she could levitate small objects. She wrapped her thoughts around the stick, imagining it was her hand, and she *pushed.*

The stick jerked.

Roshian screamed.

And then she pushed again. A nudge. And another. Roshian dropped the gun. She didn't let go of the stick with her mind. She pushed it farther, steadily and slowly, letting her anger cut through the pain piercing her head, through the sound of him screaming as he crumpled to the ground, through the blood that was dribbling from her nose. He was human, and the human brain was soft and easily damaged. She pushed the stick farther, all the way, until it tapped against the back of his skull.

He collapsed facedown on the ground. Blood pooled beneath his head.

She released her hold on the stick. Her whole body started shaking, though she couldn't feel a single muscle. She couldn't stand. Couldn't move. Blood poured from her nose faster but she couldn't lift a hand to brush it away, and her skin burned, and then burned harder, and then she couldn't even feel it anymore. She knew she was crying because she could taste the tears. She might have been screaming, if her throat still worked. Her ears had gone dead too.

Then two hands grabbed her.

She looked at them as though from the far end of binoculars, small brown hands, nails as chewed up and torn as her own. Fingers pinched her arms and shook her, though she couldn't feel it. A face that was familiar. Stringy black hair and brown eyes that always looked angry, except for now. A mouth that was moving, though she couldn't hear anything. The girl took something out of her pocket. A smell, sharp and citrusy and peppery all at once, choked Cora's mouth and made her gasp.

Her sense of sound snapped back into her head at the same time as her reason. Mali. Mali was shaking her, waving her hand in front of her face. Cora heard her own breath coming ragged, half choked with blood that she leaned over to spit up. Feeling was returning to her limbs, and with it, a roar of pain. More footsteps came down the stairs. Leon appeared, looking from her to Roshian on the ground. He kicked at the body to turn it over, and gagged at the gaping eye socket wound.

"Christ, sweetheart! What did you do?" He dry-heaved into the bushes, and then wiped his mouth. "Sorry we didn't get here sooner. Cassian said the traps in the shipping tunnels would slow us down. We had to take the hallways."

Cassian was with them?

More footsteps. Heavier ones.

Cassian came thundering down the stairs. He went directly to Roshian's body and pressed his shoulder to the ground with one booted foot, as though Roshian might try to get up, and then inspected the body to make certain he was dead. Cassian's head cocked at the sight of the too-red blood.

"I had no choice," Cora choked, as her voice returned. "He tried to kill me."

Cassian climbed the stairs to where Cora was doubled over, and gently tilted her chin up to look at the blood trickling from her nose.

"You killed him."

"He kept coming. He was human—he didn't care about the moral code."

She could tell from the lack of surprise on Cassian's face that he already knew. He ran a thumb gently along the sides of her face, brushing away the blood. He was dressed in his formal Warden's uniform; he must have been on duty before coming here. "You did this with your mind. You pushed yourself too far."

"I had to. The bullet . . . I couldn't move."

His eyes shifted to her exposed shin, where blood was still flowing from the bullet wound. "This is beyond my abilities to heal. I must take you to Serassi before you lose too much blood."

She leaned forward, wincing in pain, one strap of the torn

gold dress slipping from her shoulder. A few steps off, Mali picked up a Kindred-made pistol Roshian had dropped. She inspected it closely, then aimed at the ground and squeezed the trigger, but nothing happened.

"What about the Council?" Cora said. "When Arrowal finds out about this, he'll investigate even more closely and figure out I killed him with my mind. He'll know I'm the agitator they're looking for. He won't let me run the Gauntlet—he'll probably throw me in prison."

"Let me worry about Arrowal," Cassian said.

Cora's eyes shifted to Cassian, and a new fear entered her mind.

His eyes were entirely black.

He was cloaked.

Which meant he could see into their minds. Hers was already masked with enough pain to shield her thoughts, but Mali's and Leon's weren't. Mali had enough training to be able to prevent him from reading her mind, but Leon didn't.

Cassian had to know that they could get out of their cells. That, for weeks, Leon had been hiding out with the Mosca. That they were negotiating with Bonebreak for a safe room for Nok and Rolf to raise their baby in. That all her training sessions with Cassian were only a lie, and that she had never once intended to actually run the Gauntlet.

Not helping him, but humiliating him.

She searched his eyes, but there was nothing but blackness. Did he know? Or had Leon somehow—miraculously—kept his thoughts private?

"You can't turn Leon in," she blurted out.

Cassian didn't take his eyes away from her face. "We have more pressing matters," he said, and stood. He took out the temporary removal pass from his pocket, then bent down to pick her up, but she shook her head.

"Promise me, Cassian. Leon isn't a problem. He's living in the shipping tunnels, that's all. You don't have to turn him in."

Did he know that this went far beyond Leon being loose on the station? Did he know about her plan to cheat? Did he know *everything*? She thought back to their last training session. He had already been suspicious when she'd pressed him to help her learn to read minds, until she'd turned it on him and said it was because she wanted to know him better.

Did he know that was a lie too?

He turned to Leon and said quietly, "I suggest you disappear back into whatever hole you crawled out of, and never show yourself again. Another Kindred would not be as forgiving as I. And you, Mali—return to Free Time and do not say a word about what has happened here." He turned back to Cora. "I will return to take care of Roshian's body."

"But . . ."

"I will take care of it."

His words had an edge, though his face was blank. Even cloaked, he had never been good at hiding his emotions. She didn't have to be psychic to read the anger and hurt just beneath the surface.

He picked her up as though she weighed nothing. His hand held her under her knees, flooding her with that electric sensation.

His chest against her cheek was thudding hard with his pulse, which was pounding too fast for someone supposed to be cloaked. When she looked up, his face was only inches from hers.

Just a few days ago, she had told him: *I want to know you, the same way you know me.*

He looked away from her, and she saw a flicker of something else beneath his cloaked mask. Pain.

Oh yes. He *knew*.

He carried her up the rest of the steps silently.

27

Nok

SERASSI, DRESSED IN HER white uniform with the row of
knots down the side, blinked at the three-dimensional image on
the glowing surface. "What a sweet little baby."

"Sugary," Nok corrected. She was getting the hang of this
lying thing. Maybe, if they ever saw Earth again, she'd study to be
a lawyer. "What a sugary baby, you mean. That's what we *really* call
babies, not sweet. Your books were wrong again."

They were in Serassi's genetics laboratory, where she had
taken Nok for testing. Serassi's head swiveled toward her as though
she had forgotten Nok was lying flat on the examination table with
tubes snaking into her veins. Something had changed over the past
few days. Serassi had been spending more time in the house, not
just observing it. She rarely input research findings into her hip
computer, even when Nok made up a really juicy lie about baby-
raising practices. And last night, Serassi had hung photographs of
Sparrow on all the dollhouse walls. Simulations of what she would

look like as a baby, and as a toddler, and as a little girl in a lavender dress. Serassi had superimposed herself in all the photos, like a doting mother. Nok and Rolf weren't in any of them.

Now, in the lab, Serassi dismissed Nok's correction. "Yes. Babies are sugary. Not sweet. Of course." She turned back to the three-dimensional model of the baby on the glowing surface. The image glowed a little itself, but otherwise it looked alarmingly realistic. The projected baby was crawling, which meant she had to be around six months old, if Nok had learned anything from reading all those parenting books.

She ran a hand over her belly and accidentally brushed one of the sensors. The image of the baby flickered like static on a television set and then righted itself again. Serassi punched a few more commands into her hip pad, and the baby fast-forwarded until she was twenty pounds bigger and was walking now, unsteadily, waving her little arms.

There was something in Serassi's face that hadn't been there before, as she watched the projection. Even though she was cloaked, there was a glisten of pride and desire all mixed up together that made Nok's heart race with fear.

Serassi punched a few more keys, and the toddler fast-forwarded again. Now the baby fat was gone, and the child's black hair, slightly curly at the ends like Rolf's, hung down to her shoulders. The little girl skipped in a circle.

Nok pressed her hand again against her small belly bump. The fetus was just a little over twenty weeks old, yet here she was as a four-year-old. She had Nok's eyes.

Serassi punched in another few commands and the girl's face shifted slightly. Her hair was shorter; her limbs were too.

"Hey!" Nok sat up in alarm, jostling the equipment, making the image flicker. "What did you do to her?"

Serassi gave her a slow, annoyed-looking blink. "I am running a variety of programs to see what effects various diets and outside factors will have on the child's development."

"Well, don't. It's creepy to see her change like that."

"They are all possibilities for how the baby will grow depending on what external factors I expose her to."

"*We,*" Nok said tensely. "What *we* expose her to."

Serassi leveled her a black-eyed stare, then turned back to the screen. "This is if she receives a protein-rich diet, and if I mimic her environment to be that of a high altitude." A few more buttons, and the girl shifted again, her hair slightly lighter. "This is if she receives a primarily vegetarian diet, at a low altitude, in an area with strenuous terrain."

"And if she grows up on an alien space station, eating replicated food that all tastes like chalk?"

"As far as the child is concerned, she will not even know what Earth is." Serassi's face was perfectly emotionless. "Or rather, *was.*"

Before Serassi had taken Nok away for this round of examinations in the laboratory, Rolf had whispered in her ear: *Cooperate with her. Don't give her any reason to be unhappy with us.* But Nok had never been good at controlling her temper. "Yeah," she muttered, "because it'll be totally normal to have a dozen Kindred observers watching through a missing wall of our house."

Serassi's eyes narrowed slightly. "It is not up to you to decide how the child will be raised." The image of the girl sat cross-legged, playing a game on her hand that Nok used to play, too.

"Sparrow," Nok said.

Serassi cocked her head. "What did you say?"

"Her name is Sparrow."

She was pushing it, she knew. And yet she detested that possessive look on Serassi's face. It was the same look Miss Delphine, her talent manager, had worn when she sent Nok to fashion shoots in dirty warehouses. As if her life wasn't her own.

The blue sensor above the door suddenly flickered, and Cassian entered.

Nok sat straighter—it was the first time she'd seen him since the cage. He was cloaked, and just as robotic as always, except his eyes shifted to the black panel anxiously. If Cassian noticed the projected four-year-old girl playing hand games on the glowing surface, he didn't say anything. He exchanged a few words with Serassi and then turned to the door.

"There are no observers," he said in English. "It is safe for you to enter."

Cora hobbled in, favoring one leg. Nok leaned forward so abruptly that it screwed with all the sensors and the image of Sparrow flickered wildly. Cora's hair was dirty and streaked with sweat; she was wearing a torn gold ball gown; dried blood was crusted on her left shin.

"Cora?" Nok asked incredulously.

Cora's eyes went wide. "Nok!"

Nok kicked her legs off the examination table and threw her arms around Cora. "What happened?"

Cora shook her head. "It's a lot to explain, but I'm okay. And you? You're okay?" She looked around at the lab's medical equipment.

"It's just . . . baby stuff," Nok said, glancing at Serassi. "There's this projection and . . ." But Serassi was watching her keenly, and she stopped. She wanted to tell Cora about the doll-house, about the lies she and Rolf had made up, about Serassi's increasingly possessive behavior.

But Cassian interrupted their reunion. "Cora, sit on the table. Serassi will repair your wound."

Serassi gave him a look that said she had no intention of doing anything of the sort, and they spoke in flat Kindred words for a moment. Serassi's voice went extra tight—the closest thing to an argument two cloaked Kindred could reach.

Nok pinched herself so that they wouldn't be able to read her mind and stepped out of their earshot. "Please tell me you're get-ting us to that safe room soon," she whispered to Cora. "Serassi's got this weird obsession with Sparrow, like Rolf and I don't even exist. She's going to cut Sparrow out of me and lock us away in cages any minute, I swear."

"I did have a plan, but . . ." Cora looked down at her blood-stained hands, and Nok wasn't sure she wanted to know what had happened. "But Cassian might suspect too much now. If anything happens to me, Leon will get you to the safe room." She glanced at Cassian. "Listen, don't get your hopes up, but we found a clue that someone might have tampered with the algorithm that claimed Earth was gone. We're trying to get real proof."

Nok's heart thundered. "We could go home?"

But Cassian and Serassi had stopped speaking, and Nok squeezed Cora's hand hard, a signal not to answer in case they were listening. Serassi turned to one of the cabinets, where she traced a pattern and took out the repair tool. She worked efficiently, healing Cora's wound slowly and methodically until the skin was entirely patched. If it hadn't been for the dried blood crusting Cora's foot,

Nok would never have known she'd been wounded.

Cassian turned to Cora. "We must go."

Nok threw her arms around Cora again, breathing in the scent of mud on her clothes, with only a trace of ozone. "Don't leave."

"Just hold on a few more days." Cora squeezed her hand.

It was the same quick, tight squeeze Cora had given to her the first day they had woken in the cage, with no idea where they were. At the time, Nok had been so crippled by fear that she'd barely been able to string words together. Now, she could feel how much she had changed. Instead of balling up and rocking back and forth, she could fold the fear into herself, tuck it away carefully behind a mask of indifference, just like the Kindred. There, it could grow, and fester, and give her a steady stream of anger that she could twist into strength.

Serassi ripped Cora out of Nok's arms before she could say good-bye, and shoved her toward the open doorway. The door slid closed.

Nok was again alone with Serassi.

On the glowing surface, the projected image had changed again, this time to Sparrow as she truly was, a barely developed fetus, tiny arms visible when the image wasn't flickering.

Nok's fear folded itself into a knot again, tighter and tighter.

Serassi reached out toward the projection, fingers brushing against the formless shape tenderly. "Sugary," she cooed. "Such a sugary little thing."

28

Cora

THE LAST TIME CORA had been in Cassian's quarters, everything she'd known about him had been a lie. He wasn't the low-level Caretaker he claimed to be, powerless in the face of the Warden—he *was* the Warden. So when the door to his room slid open, she expected to find chambers befitting his rank.

But there was only the same lonely chair, the same hard bed, the lone square drinking glass.

She turned to him in confusion. "I thought this room was just part of the act."

"I told you that not everything was a lie." He crossed to a cabinet and handed her a thin towel. There was no mirror in his quarters, only the dull reflection of the black panel. In it, she saw that almost every inch of her skin was caked in sand or blood or sweat.

I killed a man, she thought, and her hands started to shake. But at least it hadn't been for nothing. Lucky was eighteen now, not nineteen. Safe.

She scrubbed the towel over her face. As thin as it was, it absorbed dirt almost magnetically, and when she was done, there was no sign of her fight with Roshian except the torn dress. She couldn't possibly return to the stage in that condition, but maybe that was just as well. There were some things you couldn't come back from.

Cassian disappeared into the bedroom; the sounds of cabinets opening and closing followed. Cora sank into the single chair, staring at the empty square glass. It felt like years ago since they had sat here, drinking and sharing stories about each other's worlds. That night had been the start of something forbidden but undeniable between them, that had come crashing down when he'd betrayed her. And now here she was, her life and her future in his hands once more—but this time *she* was the one doing the lying.

He returned to the main room. He had cleaned up and was tying knots along the side of a fresh uniform. A triangle of copper-colored skin flashed from the unknotted top of his shirt, showing a deep scar there that, if extended, would match the smaller one on the side of his neck.

"You've never told me how you got that scar."

He still didn't look at her, though his mouth twitched darkly, like the memory either pained or amused him. "Perhaps I will tell you one day. Or perhaps Mali will."

"Mali was there?"

"Mali gave it to me. There was a time when she thought I was the enemy, though I was only attempting to help her. She understands that now. I am still waiting for you to reach a similar realization."

His voice had gained an edge.

He finished tying the knots, then grabbed a pair of boots from a cabinet. "I must dispose of Roshian's body. Tessela can hide it for a short period of time, but we cannot risk anyone discovering it and alerting the Council. If they were to learn of any of this, everything we've worked for would be destroyed. They would restrain you for murder—it doesn't matter that he was human. You would have no chance of running the Gauntlet. No chance of freedom. You would be lucky if you ever got to speak to another human."

"What about Roshian's rifle? It's human-made. It could be useful if anything goes wrong."

"It is too dangerous to hold on to anything that could be traced back to him," Cassian said. "But if anything ever happens to me, go to Fian or Tessela. They are ready at all times to enact the secondary plan, should it come to that."

"Which is . . . ?"

"Free humanity ourselves. Destroy the enclosures. Remove the human wards from menageries and private owners. Take them all to a neutral satellite station until we can establish a more permanent colony." His fingers flew over the thick laces of his boots. "But that would mean war. There are only several hundred Kindred sympathetic to our cause, on a station of two million. Chances of success would be minimal."

He finished lacing the second boot and then started to slide on a pair of gloves, glancing at her torn gown. "I will bring you a replacement dress. Until then, you will find clean clothes in the bedroom. Try to rest."

She could feel his agitation in every step. He was already halfway to the door.

"Wait," she said.

He stopped, the left glove only halfway over his hand, and turned slowly.

"We need to talk about what happens now." She took a deep breath. "And I don't mean now that I've killed a man. I mean, what happens *now*. Now that you've read Leon's mind. Now that you know I never intended to put myself at risk by running the Gauntlet, but meant to cheat it instead. And humiliate you in the process." She laid her hands flat on the table and seriously wished that empty glass was full of something that would make this conversation easier.

Not the slightest trace of surprise showed on his face. As she'd suspected, he had already known.

He slowly peeled off the the left glove, as though all his previous hurry had vanished. Slowly, he approached the table. For a second, Roshian's black eyes flashed into her head. Behind the disguise he must have had human eyes, and a human mind, and a human body. She wished she could brush a hand over Cassian's eyes and have him be just as human.

"I know that you read Leon's mind," she said quietly. "I saw it in your face."

His face gave nothing away.

"Uncloak, Cassian. Please. I don't want to talk to a statue about this."

For the count of a few breaths he remained motionless, though she suspected his thoughts must be churning as violently as her own. At last, he dragged over a bench to sit across from her.

"I will not uncloak," he said slowly. "Uncloaked, I cannot read your thoughts. And what I want from you is the truth. So no masking your thoughts with pain."

Before she could react, his hand clamped over hers to prevent her from pinching herself. She drew in a sharp breath. He hadn't put the gloves back on yet and the electric sensation prickled her skin.

"Leon's mind is a confusing place," he said. "It is filled with self-doubt and false bravado. I could not read all the details. Only that you never intended to go through with my plan to prove humanity's intelligence to the Council. That you were only training with me so that you could learn to control the testers' minds to cheat your way to freedom. I assume all that is true."

She swallowed. "I'm sorry," she stammered. "I really am. But I meant what I said. If you expect humanity to excel, we have to play by our own rules, not yours. I have to prove our worth my own way."

"By cheating."

"In this case, yes."

He let out a harsh laugh. "I thought your species demonstrated higher values. I thought you were ready for self-governance."

"We are," she whispered urgently. "You told me yourself how dangerous the Gauntlet puzzles can be. Isn't it the definition of being intelligent to find a way around that risk? Self-preservation? I can cheat the Gauntlet, and then, if you're right about someone tampering with the algorithm's predictions, there's a chance we could go home."

"Perhaps."

She was surprised he didn't contradict her, though there was a strangely hard edge to his voice.

"But there would be consequences you cannot foresee," he added.

"What consequences?"

He didn't answer.

"Look," she said, "you would be humiliated, I get it. But a little bruised pride is nothing compared to what you did to me. You—" Her voice hitched. "You gave me hope and then crushed it."

The wall panel hummed softly, like a trapped insect, and for a while it drowned out all other noise. Then he curled his fingers around hers. "It was all so you, and your kind, could have a better life."

"Roshian nearly killed me. Is that better?"

He leaned in. "I blame myself for not foreseeing his intentions." His hands were growing warmer. He glanced at the door, as though remembering the body bleeding out into the savanna sand that, if found, would ruin them both. "Sometimes I think the Council is right when they insist humans are of a lesser intelligence, because that is the only way to explain such a senseless plan to cheat the Gauntlet. And to solicit the Mosca's help is even more foolish. Just because Leon lives among them does not make them loyal. Everything is a whim for them, whatever they feel like that day, betraying a promise or keeping it." He shook his head. "Your plan is foolhardy."

"Maybe the Mosca aren't trustworthy," she said. "But neither are you."

"You said you forgave me."

She looked down at her hands. "I lied."

His fingers curled harder around hers. "I've done everything for you. I took you from a dying planet. I gave you a world where you could be happy. I gave you a partner who was perfectly matched for you. I'm risking everything to expand your mind, so that you, and all your kind, don't have to live like animals anymore. I am risking my life and my own freedom—as are Tessela and Fian and many others—because we believe in our mission to free humanity. We are doing this for *you*." His hands were shaking now. Try as he might, his emotional cloak was slipping. "Even now, I am bending every rule to find out if your home planet is still in existence, though we both know it would mean that I'd never see you again. And you throw it all back at me like I have done nothing."

At last, he let her go and stood. "Fian and I will bury Roshian's body. But I will not let you go through with this foolish plan to cheat the Gauntlet. Either you will agree to run it honestly or we abandon all our plans right here. You can return to the Hunt and survive as long as you can behind bars, until you turn nineteen and they drag you off to an even worse place. Tell me, right now. No lies. No deceptions. What do you choose?"

Cora's pulse throbbed in her head, too loud to think. In Bay Pines, the guards had always offered the inmates two choices. It was supposed to teach them to make good decisions. Once, Queenie got into a fight in the cafeteria, and the guards said she could either spend free period cleaning the spilled food or be dragged straight off to solitary. Queenie had just smiled and stabbed a fork into her hand, and spent the next two weeks in a cushy bed in the psych hospital watching *Friends* reruns.

Cora had learned a lesson from Queenie that day, but not the one the guards wanted: just because someone told you there were only two choices didn't mean they were right.

Sometimes you had to make your own third option.

29

Cora

"ANSWER ME, CORA," CASSIAN said. "Agree to run the Gauntlet according to my rules. There is still time. It is for your own good."

"Is it?" Her voice was dangerously soft. "We both know this is about more than the Gauntlet. You can't stand the thought of your precious pet not obeying you." She met his eyes with a challenging stare. "You can't stop thinking about that day in the ocean surf when you kissed me. I bet you even want to do it again, don't you? Feel desire, and love, and all those emotions that are denied to you. You never wanted me to be free. You want me to be *yours*." She turned her hand palm up to show the markings on her skin. "Did you think I wouldn't notice my ring finger? You modified the markings to look like a diamond ring."

He went quiet. His eyes went from her hand to her face and back again.

"You've studied humanity more than any other Kindred,"

she continued. "You know what a diamond ring means to us. *To have and to hold.*"

The muscles of his neck were tensing. He picked up the gloves again, tugging one on stiffly. "You understand nothing."

"Don't I?" She stood. "You might be wearing a mask, but I can still see beneath it."

He turned on her fast enough to make her breath go still. He would never hurt her, she knew, but it was impossible not to be intimidated by him.

He leaned in until he could whisper against her ear.

"Can you? Well then, let's both drop our masks." He closed his eyes. The muscles of his face shifted beneath his skin. Tension drained away. Jaw softened. When he opened his eyes, they had cleared into the gray storm clouds that hovered just over his irises.

He blinked.

"This is bigger than what I want, and what you want." His voice was rounder, more insistent, and it made her blood pool in her heart. "I suspected all along that you were not being honest with me, but I did not want to believe it. And I don't blame you for wanting to cheat us, after we have mistreated you. But now, you must agree to do this the correct way. Then, once this is over, I'll take you back to your solar system myself, so we can both learn the truth. And if the algorithm is right, and there is only a hole in the sky where your home used to be, you will truly know that there is no other place for you than with me."

A shiver ran down her back. "Don't talk like that."

But he leaned in closer. "You accuse me of wanting to feel lesser emotions. You're right. Is it such a crime to want to feel? I do not understand why we must always be at odds. Why we cannot be partners in proving humanity's intelligence. Why that partnership cannot cross into what I feel in my heart whenever I think of you. Why you cannot love me, and why you feel such contempt for the fact that I love you."

His lips grazed her ear on his last words. She drew in a tight breath, electricity from his touch shooting through her nerves. He turned his head just slightly, until the side of his face pressed hers. "You do not give up," he said. "And so I will not give up either. Even when it goes against logic."

He wanted to kiss her. She could feel it in every move he made.

And she wanted him to. She wanted to put aside the anger, the betrayal, the questions over the future. She wanted to forget about the murder on her hands.

But she looked away.

"No," she said. "There's a third way. You say you respect us, so prove it. Help me do this *my* way."

His hands flexed against the wall indecisively, as though part of him still wanted to kiss her right there. His face was warm against hers.

"I cannot condone cheating."

"You can. Because if you truly love me, then the only way that I could come to love you back is if we're complete equals."

She let her lips graze his ear and felt his jaw tighten in response. He let out a breath and then pulled away, hands falling to his sides. He paced quickly, one hand scrubbing over his face in indecision. For a minute, she almost regretted using him like this. But then he snatched up the other glove from the table and tugged it on, his movements tight and angry.

"Does this mean you'll help?" She couldn't keep the hope from her voice.

He gave a reluctant nod. "Yes, though you have no idea what you're asking. There are complications . . ." His voice was tense, and he dropped whatever he was going to say. "Just rest. Your mind needs it. I'll return shortly."

The door slid closed behind him.

The panel hummed, and the weight of solitude pressed in from all sides. She pressed a hand to her lips, where she could still feel a lingering spark. Her body started shaking at the thought that after everything—the murder and the argument and months of anger—they were on the same side. There would be no more secrets or lies.

She staggered into the bedroom and paced, trying to calm her heart. He had left a drawer open, and she riffled through it. Black shirts made of a liquid-metal material that was like impenetrable silk; they were formfitting on him, but when she changed into one, it fell below her hips like a loose tunic. She pressed the fabric to her face. It smelled like ozone and salt, and for a moment the lingering image of Roshian's bloody face disappeared, and she remembered standing in the ocean with Cassian, her face pressed against this same shirt.

Had he really meant his promise? Had *she*?

I could come to love you. . . .

The idea made her shiver with either nerves or excitement, and she balled up her dirty dress and shoved it into the back of the drawer, then slammed it closed. There was another drawer next to it. Curious, she tapped on it, trying to mimic whatever gesture he made to open them. She swirled her finger over the drawer's surface, trying circles, stars, crosses, and then paused. Slowly, she traced the symbol that he had drawn for her once on the alcove table. The symbol of the effort to prove humanity's worth, the Fifth of Five: a double helix with five marks for the five intelligent species.

The drawer opened, but inside she found only more clothes, a deck of cards, a few spare temporary removal passes. Then her fingers brushed something hard.

A small spiral-bound notebook.

It was cheap; the kind of thing you'd pick up at the dollar store to jot down grocery lists in. But the worn pages suggested it had been handled carefully for some time. She flipped open the cover, but there were only strange marks in pencil that varied in pressure, like the writer wasn't sure how hard to press.

She flipped another page. It was just shapes. A small circle, a large oval, something like an elongated triangle. She flipped again. Similar shapes, only more confidently drawn. One line was marked through, and another carefully drawn next to it. As she kept flipping, the shapes continued to evolve until her eye could stitch them together into something recognizable. That triangle was meant to be a tail. That small circle, an eye. By the last pages, the shapes formed a roughly drawn picture of a dog, its ears perked up.

She stared at the drawings. Had Cassian taken this from one of the abducted children? No, there was something so odd about the drawing. The lines wavered as if the artist didn't know how to properly hold a pencil.

She flipped the page again, and started. In the final drawing, there was a loop on the dog's back strung with a chain. It wasn't just any dog—it was the charm Cassian had once given her to remind her of Sadie.

He had made these drawings. Painstakingly, secretly, teaching himself how to make human marks on human paper to depict an animal from a lost world. Why? She ran through every explanation, but there was really only one that made sense.

He wanted to draw. He wanted to make art.

She closed the notebook and stowed it back in the drawer.

She lay down. The pounding in her ears abated, and she began to hear the sounds of the station. Electricity pulsing. Machinery whirring softly. Right now, he would be destroying Roshian's body to erase evidence of the murder she had committed.

Her thoughts started to unjumble as she rested. She believed everything he had said. That he loved her and wanted to prove humanity's intelligence badly enough that he would even help her cheat—a practice that went against his core nature. It made her think of her parents' marriage being held together with lies. Her mother's denial about drinking and about all those late-night sessions with her personal trainer—though she didn't seem to lose a single pound. Her father's string of affairs too, the campaign aides and the widow two houses down, and all the false promises about a stable life, about retiring from politics, when he never had the slightest intention. A relationship twisted by betrayal was no relationship at all.

But then she thought of the drawing. If Cassian was going to stand by his promise, then maybe she would stand by hers. Maybe he didn't deserve giving up on. And maybe not all relationships that started with lies also had to end with them.

30

Leon

LEON GRUMBLED TO HIMSELF as he stood over the broken-down parts of a baby crib. Bonebreak had agreed to the safe room idea, but only if Leon forfeited his cut of each smuggling run, which was extortion if he'd ever heard of it. But he'd begrudgingly agreed, and Bonebreak's underlings had taken him to this dusty storeroom that, as best he could tell from the smell, used to house rancid cheese.

"Why don't these bloody things come with instructions?" he muttered to himself, picking up a piece that might have been a railing. It was the same crib he'd busted out of when he'd first met the Mosca, pink penguin bedding and all. Beside it sat a stack of baby supplies he'd managed to scrounge. Some tiny cowboy pajamas. A bottle with dancing giraffes on it. A stack of old shirts advertising a dentist in San Diego that he figured they could use for diapers.

"Let's see, this part matches this part. . . ." He fumbled with a screw, and cursed as the entire crib fell apart again. "Well, shit."

He seriously needed a hammer, or whatever super-advanced alien tool would stick two pieces of wood together. He sauntered through the halls of Bonebreak's lair toward one of the back rooms. It was in a sector Bonebreak said was off-limits, but the hell if he was going to rebuild that crib with spit and duct tape alone.

"Hey, anybody here?" He stuck his head into a few empty rooms. "Hello?"

He riffled through a few crates but found nothing useful, and kept searching. All the doors were unlocked except the last one, at the end of the hall. He shoved it with his shoulder, but it was stuck.

He backed up, aiming his shoulder with the artificial shielding, and raced toward the door. He felt the force of the impact all the way to his teeth, but the door buckled open. He rubbed his shoulder, then pushed the door all the way open.

He stopped.

What the hell?

Bonebreak and his men stood in a circle beneath a ship. A real goddamn ship. It was a clunker to be sure, painted a pukey shade of green, but there it was. All docked, everything official. Mosca writing on the side. Spare parts and tools lined the walls. A goddamn ship in a goddamn flight room Bonebreak had told him was off-limits.

"You liar!" Leon barked. "What happened to forty years before the next ship returns?"

Bonebreak turned, and Leon caught sight of what they were all gathered around. A dead body lay in their midst. Upon closer inspection, Leon noticed the red-soled boots of the Mosca crew's former second in command. He also noticed the knife jutting out of the second's back.

"Uhh . . . on second thought, I'll come back later." Leon whirled.

"Stay." Bonebreak's voice crackled with static. He stepped around the second's sprawled arm. "This is just a little housekeeping. So. You got curious and came exploring, hmm?"

Leon held up his hands, stuttering to think, which was hard while staring at a dead body. "Just, uh, my mistake."

"Well, now you know. There is a ship. Yes. If I had told you as much, I would never hear the end of it. *Take me home, Bonebreak. I miss my family. I miss taco night. I miss my kitty-cat.*" Bonebreak made a disgusted sound from behind his mask. "Do you really think you're the first human we've worked with? I've heard it all, boy."

Bonebreak's disdain was starting to wear on Leon. He narrowed his eyes, darting his gaze between the dead crew member and the ship. "You should have told me anyway."

"You work for me, not the other way around. My second in command had a problem understanding that." He stepped right on the Mosca's dead body, whose bones snapped beneath his feet. "Do you have a problem too?"

"Me?" Leon winced as more bones popped. "Nope."

"Good. You never saw this ship, understand? If I let you return to Earth, then who is going to crawl around the tunnels for me, hmm? As you said yourself, nobody steals quite like you do." Bonebreak poked Leon's stomach with a spindly finger. "Unless you get too fat to fit in the tunnels. Then no home for you, no nothing for you, just a knife in your back."

Leon clutched at his stomach. "It's mostly muscle!"

"Silence. Do you have the payment for the last trade?"

A sinking feeling overcame him. He touched his pocket, hoping for a miracle, but it was still empty. "About that. There's a problem. The other half of your business partnership died before I could collect the payment."

Bonebreak straightened. "Roshian is dead?"

"Yeah, but not before I peeked into that black bag of his. You know what you've been supplying him with, right? The makeup and stuff? That creep was human."

Bonebreak took another step over the body of his former second in command, giving a flick of his fingers. "It is not my job to care which species my clients are. And I do not appreciate not getting paid for my shipments."

"He was dead. What was I supposed to do?"

"That's your problem," Bonebreak said, and then crunched the second in command's foot. "We're just full of problems today, aren't we, crew?"

The other Mosca, in the shadow of the ship, did not answer.

Bonebreak stooped down and pulled out the knife from the second in command's back. He slowly wiped the blood on his jumpsuit.

Leon held up his hands. "I can get the payment. I swear."

Bonebreak cocked his head. "You already owe me for that safe room. Your credit is running thin. Too thin, I think." Leon couldn't tell what expression Bonebreak was making behind the mask, but he didn't like the way the knife was aimed toward him. But then Bonebreak holstered it and signaled to his underlings. "Roadag.

Silverquake. Show the boy what he gets for sneaking around."

Before Leon could turn, a plank of something hard smashed into his face.

He staggered backward.

Blackness. Sparks. *Pain.*

He knew he shouldn't fight back. The dead second in command had probably fought back too, which was why he was in his current condition. But damned if he had ever let anyone best him in a fight. He let out a bellow and tried to slam into them, but they already had him on the ground. Hitting him with the stiff plank again and again. Pain burst across his face, then his left shoulder, then his kidney, until he was staring up at Bonebreak's ugly mask.

"Now," Bonebreak said. "What exactly did you see in this flight room?"

"Uhng. Nothing."

"And what are you going to tell your friends about the ship?"

"What ship?"

Bonebreak cackled in delight, or maybe he was just envisioning all the ways he'd stomp on Leon's cracking bones. "Good. Keep not seeing any ships."

Leon pressed a hand against his face. He stumbled back to his room, where he collapsed on his bed. At least the deal was still on. Nok and Rolf and that baby of theirs would be safe. But as soon as he closed his eyes, his thoughts returned to what he'd seen.

A ship, he thought. *A goddamn ship.*

Or rather, a goddamn *useless* ship that would never take him anywhere.

But what if it could?

And what if Cora was right about Earth still being there? He could drink a beer. Preferably while watching rugby on his sister Ellie's crappy old television set, preferably millions of miles away from hunchbacked murderers.

He briefly wondered how much it would cost for Bonebreak to give him a seat on that ship. For all the Mosca's threats, Bonebreak could always be swayed with the right price.

But no. Cora and Mali and the others were his family now. Kin. He had left them behind once and he still felt the shame of that written on his face as plainly as the tattoos.

He groaned and fell back on the bed.

He *really* missed beer.

31

Cora

CORA WOKE TO THE sound of a door opening. For a second, she was surprised to find herself in a strange bed, in a room where the lights never went off. Cassian's room. It all came back in a rush that made her head throb. She touched beneath her nose, but there was no blood this time. Just bad memories.

A sharp stick. A bleeding eye socket.

She sank back onto the bed. It still held a trace of Cassian's scent, and faint sparks of the sensation she felt at his touch—or maybe that was just in her imagination. She swung her legs off and sat up. There was no clock to tell how long she'd been asleep, nothing besides the tears that had crusted under her eyes.

Sounds of movement came from the main room—Cassian was back. She went to the doorway to watch him bend over to unlace his boots. He looked as flawless as always, robotic in his perfection, but he tugged too hard at the knots.

"Did you take care of the body?" she asked softly.

He looked up, eyes falling to his black shirt hanging on her frame. "Yes." He handed her one of Makayla's matching dresses, then glanced at the bedroom, where the blanket was twisted in knots. "You slept?"

"A little." She ducked back into the bedroom to change into the dress.

"Good," he called. "Your mind needs substantial rest after what you did to Roshian. Ideally, we would slow the training sessions, but time is of the essence. The Gauntlet module has already crossed into Kindred territory. It will be here in three days."

She came back into the main room, smoothing out the dress. "Then we should start focusing on mind reading. That's the only way I'll be able to take over the testers' minds. I've been practicing on my own and I can get glimmers of ideas, but nothing very substantial." She tugged on the hem of her dress when he didn't answer. "You haven't changed your mind about helping us, have you?"

He finished untying the knots and kicked off his boots. "No. I haven't." He ran a weary hand over his face. "But I also promised to keep you safe. From the delegates, yes, but also from your own mind. It may be possible to cheat the Gauntlet, but one cannot cheat the limitations of one's own body." He went into the bedroom. She heard the sounds of drawers opening, clothes being swapped. She nudged his boot with her toe. Traces of dirt clung to the grooves in the bottom. She imagined Roshian's body ripening in the sun.

Her stomach started to turn, as Cassian appeared in the doorway, as immaculate as always. With one look at her face, he said, "I made you a promise and this time I will die before I break it. Now, close your eyes."

"Why?"

"I only know the parts of your plan that I could read from Leon's scattered thoughts. Let me read the rest from your own mind, so I know how to help you."

She paused, still hesitant to trust him, but then closed her eyes. He rested his hands on her shoulders. She could hear him breathing steadily above the hum of the panel. And there was that familiar probing sensation in her mind that almost tickled. She could feel him scrolling through each part of the plan. Finding and freeing Anya. Learning how to control minds from her, so Cora could stand in front of the testers and make them move like puppets at her command. Leon and Bonebreak, even the safe room for Nok and Rolf.

He dropped his hands. Deep worry was etched into his face.

"What's wrong?" she asked. "Is it more training? Something else I need to learn?"

He shook his head. "Something *I* must learn. If I am to help you run the Gauntlet your own way, I must understand your methodology."

She blinked in surprise. "You . . . want to learn to cheat?"

"It is the only way I can help your plan succeed."

Cora glanced toward the bedroom door, hesitantly. "Hold on." She went back to his bedroom and took out the deck of cards she'd found earlier in his drawer, shuffling it carefully as she returned. "My cellmate at Bay Pines taught me how, over the months we roomed together. I can explain the basics. The first thing is to forget what you're trying to cheat at, and focus on *who*. I can't make these cards be anything other than what they are. But I can manipulate *you*. I can read your face and your tells—assuming you're uncloaked—and learn what is important to you, so that I can exploit that."

He leaned closer. "And what is important to me?"

Her cheeks started to warm. She focused on shuffling the cards.

"Let's say, for argument's sake, your particular weakness was pretty girls. Then while I was shuffling the cards, I'd play with my hair, give you a smile, do anything to keep you from looking too closely at how I was dealing the cards. If I happened to slip an ace under the table so I could play it later, you wouldn't notice because you'd be too distracted."

He looked at the card in her hand. "The Kindred are not distracted by pretty girls."

She lazily spun her finger around her hair. "Are you sure?" She reached out to hide the ace in her dress, but his hand snapped over hers. "That isn't fair," she breathed. "I told you what I was planning to do."

"One does not normally announce when one intends to cheat?"

"Not as a rule, no."

"So, to summarize. Step one: learn how to distract your opponent. Step two: disarm the opponent by manipulating said weaknesses." He rubbed his thumb gently over hers, and leaned closer. "Something like this?"

She cleared her throat, which had suddenly gone tight. "Yeah, something like that." She set the cards on the table. "Consider that your first lesson—and I need your help in return. We've run into a problem getting Anya out of the Temple. There's no backstage area."

He shook his head. "I am watched too closely by the Council to extract her myself." He dug in his pocket until he found a temporary removal pass. "But if you cannot get her through the tunnels, perhaps you can devise a way to go in through the front."

She pocketed the tag, though using it seemed like an impossibility with all the Kindred guests there. "Dane's a problem too. He isn't going to be happy I'm still alive."

He considered this a moment, then went into the other room and came back with Dane's yellow yo-yo, which she'd last seen abandoned on the savanna sands. "Step one," he said. "Learn how to distract your opponent."

"You're saying I should cheat him?"

"I'm saying you need to get rid of him. And if I'm starting to understand the way humans think, the best way to do that is to set up a lie. A crime, perhaps. Something that will force the Kindred guards to take him away."

"You mean frame him." She wrapped her fingers around the yo-yo, stashing it in her dress next to the tag. "That might work."

By the time they returned to the Hunt, a dozen Kindred sat in the lounge, awaiting their safari departures as though it was just a regular day, completely unaware that it was the morning after Cora had killed a man. Dane was onstage announcing the most recent kill. His eyes swung in her direction; they were hooded in the spotlight, but she could read the shock in his voice as he saw her.

"I buried the body beneath the acacia tree on the far side of the watering hole," Cassian said quietly. "It will be absorbed by tomorrow. I'll return then, and we can restart our sessions. I'll teach you to read minds. You'll teach me to cheat." He nodded toward a far table, where Arrowal sat with Fian. "Be cautious. They are always watching."

Her lips parted. With his metallic skin reflecting the Hunt's low lights, she thought of Nok's stories of the gods from the *Ramakien* with blue skin and the ability to control the winds. But Cassian was no god. She didn't want him to be. "Thank you."

He gave her a nod and left as the ceremony onstage ended.

There was a scramble as Jenny and Christopher dragged a stunned antelope backstage, but Dane remained by the microphone. He shaded his eyes against the bright lights.

"I see you there, songbird." His voice was unreadable. "Come on. Time to sing."

She stepped onstage, fighting the urge to claw his face. He smirked, but she detected an undercurrent of fear. He was guilty of conspiring to kill humans and animals—if she breathed a word about it to the Kindred officials, he wouldn't be headed to Armstrong.

"I'm surprised to see you here," he muttered, through a smile for the audience. "*Alive*, that is. Either you convinced Roshian to let you go or you offered him an even better quarry. I had an agreeable business arrangement with him. If you messed that up, I'll shoot you myself."

"Well, you can ask him about it next time you see him, though I have the feeling he won't be coming around much anymore."

Dane glared at her as he stepped down from the stage.

She squinted into the bright lights until she could make out Arrowal's silhouette at the farthest table. She smiled grimly to herself as she sang through her set. She picked old songs her grandfather had liked about card sharps and con men. In the loose part of her dress, she could feel the yo-yo.

"You won't know what's coming," Cora sang, and then the words died on her lips.

The yo-yo gave her an idea.

On her next break, she managed to slip onto the veranda and wave over Mali, who was working out of the garage.

"Listen, I only have a minute," Cora said, fumbling in her dress for Dane's yo-yo, and then scrawling a note on the back of a cocktail napkin. "Take this. Give it to Lucky next time you go backstage and tell him to do what's on the napkin. Then get in touch with Leon. Tell him we need him to retrieve all the tails of the dead animals from Roshian's room."

Mali's mouth wrinkled in confusion. "I do not understand."

Cora smiled. "We're taking down Dane. Tonight, before he can cause any more trouble."

Mali glanced at the note on the napkin, reading it quickly, and then smiled flatly.

ALL AFTERNOON, CORA SANG as though the men she was going to cheat weren't sitting right in front of her. Dane was the first step. Arrowal would get his in due time as well.

"You can run, baby," she sang, glancing at Dane, "but you can't hide. If you do me wrong, I'll get you before long. . . ."

He gave her a smirk from the bar, and she smirked right back. A second later, the backstage door slammed open.

Pika's cheeks were splotched with red. Her braid hung forgotten over one shoulder. Cora intentionally faltered in singing so that Dane would look around. The Council members turned as well, as a ripple of unease passed through the lounge.

Dane stomped around the bar. "I told you to stay backstage."

"You creep!" Pika launched herself at him. "I saw them in your cell! The whole cookie tin was full of them!"

He recoiled as her thin arms flailed around him. "What are you talking about? Get back inside!" He cast nervous looks between her and the Council members, who were now all watching keenly, except for Fian, whose head swiveled toward Cora instead.

The main door opened, as Tessela heard the commotion. She made a line straight for Dane and Pika.

"Listen, I don't know what she's—" Dane started, but Tessela dragged them both backstage as though they weighed no more than children. Arrowal started to stand, but Fian placed a heavy hand on his shoulder.

"Petty arguments," he said. "You know how humans are." Fian poured Arrowal another drink, glancing at Cora from the corner of his eye.

She gave him a hesitant nod of thanks.

"He's a monster!" Pika screamed from down the hall, and Cora just had time to slip in behind them. "It's disgusting and horrible and those poor, poor little animals!" She let out a high-pitched wail.

Cora inched closer down the hall, until she could peek into the cell room. The door to Dane's cell was open. He was pacing, red-faced, arguing with Tessela. Lucky had one arm wrapped around Pika's back as she sobbed into his shirt. Over her shoulder, he met Cora's eyes. If she'd looked away for half a second, she might not have seen his quick smile.

"I swear they aren't mine," Dane sputtered. "Why would

I want a bunch of *tails*? There were tokens in there! Someone replaced them!"

Pika made a gagging noise. "I can't believe he's been keeping tails in that cookie tin this whole time!"

Tessela picked up the whitetail deer's tail and eyed it closely. Dane started to protest again, but she took an apparatus, which looked like a pair of binoculars, out of her safari uniform. She jabbed it at Dane and he crashed to the floor, unconscious. "This boy is no longer Head Ward," Tessela informed them calmly. "Makayla will now assume that responsibility. Guards will come shortly to take him away for interrogation. No one is to touch him or the evidence in question."

"What are you going to do with him?" Lucky asked.

"It is a crime to traffic in black-market objects," Tessela said. "As we do not believe in punishment, he will be reassigned."

Reassigned? Where were they going to reassign him to, the same drecktube they'd shoved Chicago down?

Pika still sobbed into Lucky's shirt, clutching Dane's yo-yo, the string hanging down limply. "I didn't mean to find it," she choked. "He left his yo-yo on his bed. Just sitting out in the open. He never does that. I just wanted to play with it a little, but the end of the string was caught in that cookie tin, and that's when I found . . . ewww!"

Lucky patted Pika on the back, as though he wasn't the one who had planted the yo-yo. Then he detached himself from Pika and came over to stand beside Cora.

"Listen, Leon's at the drecktube door," he said quietly. "He wants to talk to you. He said it's urgent."

Cora looked at Dane's unconscious body.

She was tempted to shove him down the drecktube herself, let him get charred in the cleaner traps just like Chicago.

But no.

Whatever the Kindred had planned for him would be much more unpleasant.

32

Cora

"YOU AREN'T SUPPOSED TO come until after lights-out," Cora whispered through the slats in the drecktube door. "Anyone could have heard you."

"You worry too much." Leon cracked the drecktube open, sniffing the air. "Hey, you wouldn't have any more of those cake things, eh?"

"We barely have enough to keep ourselves from starving." Commotion sounded from the cell room, and she cursed and dropped to all fours. "Scoot over. Let me in there too."

She crawled in and gasped when he turned toward her. Dark, splotchy bruises marred the untattooed side of his face, barely visible in the glow of the bluelight track.

"What happened to you?"

"Nothing to worry about, sweetheart. A tussle."

"Did Bonebreak do this? I thought you said we could trust him."

"Don't worry about it. I'll slap some makeup on and look good as new." He flipped his hand to dismiss it, but he'd started sweating again. "Anyway, listen. I got big news. He has a ship."

"*What?*"

"I saw it by accident. He'll crack every bone in my body if he finds out I told you, but I'm crap at keeping secrets, especially big ones."

She slumped back against the drecktube wall in shock. "You mean we could go home?"

He let out a snort. "I didn't say he'd take us. I just said he had a ship."

"But he's a businessman."

"So *you* try negotiating with him."

She rolled her eyes, but her head kept spinning with the possibilities. Could they really go home after the Gauntlet was over? Assuming she beat it, humanity would be freed. No more cages, no more rules. They could go home and not a single person could stop them.

"I want to know everything you can find out about that ship, short of getting yourself murdered." Footsteps sounded outside the grate, and she went silent. "Listen," she whispered. "The Gauntlet's almost here. We can't wait any longer to get Anya."

"I told you," Leon said. "There's no backstage in her menagerie."

"Cassian gave me a temporary removal pass so we can go in through the main doors. I don't know how we'll avoid being seen by any Kindred—" She cocked her head suddenly. "Wait, what did you say before, about your bruises? You said something about makeup."

"It was a joke, sweetheart."

"No!" She sat up so fast she nearly banged her head on the top of the tube. "That's it. Only Kindred can get into the Temple menagerie, right? Think about how Roshian was able to pass as a Kindred. The weight lifting. His height. And you're even bigger than he was."

Leon looked down at his chest and flexed his muscles.

"We get the disguise kit from Roshian's quarters," she said in a rush. "We can make you look like one of them. You can just walk right in there and get Anya."

Leon looked at her like she'd gone crazy. "The hostess chick will read my mind and know I'm a fake."

"Then we'll do it after hours," Cora said. "The hostess won't be there. There'll just be the one off-duty guard who oversees all the menageries. You just flash the temporary removal pass and the guard won't ask questions. It logs the visit, but by the time anyone checks the record, you'll be long gone."

Leon scratched the back of his head. "What about those magic doors?"

She paused. He had a good point. It wouldn't look good if he approached a door and it didn't slide open automatically. "I'll have to come too," she said at last. "We'll pretend I'm another ward you're taking to the medical officer. I can open the doors ahead of you, so no one will be able to tell it isn't you doing it."

Leon muttered something under his breath about lipstick and then reached into the back of his waistband and took out a handgun. "Well, at least we have this."

Cora ducked at the sight of it. "Jesus!"

"Relax. It only works for the Kindred. Mali swiped it off

Roshian's body after he tried to kill you. But it can still be good for show. My dad did nineteen armed robberies back home and never once had to fire. People get freaked out if you just flash a gun around."

"I guess we can use any advantage we can get. I'll come back tonight."

He saluted her with the gun. When she climbed out of the drecktube, two feet were waiting for her. Her heart raced until her eyes traveled up to a face framed by shaggy dark hair.

"Lucky," she breathed. "I was afraid you were someone else."

He crouched down. "You have to be more careful."

"I know. Leon's a bad influence." She told him about their plan, and he rubbed a hand over his chin.

"You really think Leon can pull it off?"

"It's our best shot."

"Then I want to come with you. And Mali too." Lucky dropped his voice, though it was just the two of them. "I still don't trust him."

"He told me something that might change your mind." She glanced toward the door, making sure they were alone. She told him about the ship in hushed excitement, about what it could mean and where they might go. But his eyes didn't light up the way hers had.

"What's wrong?" she whispered. "I thought this was what we all wanted."

"What about the Gauntlet?" he said. "And proving human-ity's worth?"

"That hasn't changed." She pinched the bridge of her nose, wondering how this conversation was getting derailed. "All I'm saying is that after the Gauntlet is over and we've won freedom for all these people, we'll have choices. The Kindred won't be able to stop us from going home, and now we might have the means to do it."

But his eyes stayed dark. "What about Pika and Makayla and everyone? Will they be able to go back with us too?"

She blinked. "I don't know how big the ship is—"

"And what about the other humans in the other menageries? There are hundreds. Maybe more. And there are other stations too."

"I get what you're saying." She tried to keep the tension out of her voice. "But I never agreed to take everyone home. Isn't freeing them enough?"

At her exasperation, his expression softened. "I'm not trying to give you a hard time. What you're doing takes a lot of bravery. But when you made the decision to run the Gauntlet, you made a decision to stand up for humanity. That doesn't end as soon as the last test is finished. You can't flip the system on its head and then walk away to let everyone else pick up the pieces."

She wasn't sure what to say, so she paced tightly, trying to process his words.

"I know that isn't easy to hear," he continued. "I made a commitment too, to take care of these animals. As much as I miss home, I can't break that commitment just because I want to sleep in my bed again and eat a real pizza."

"Home is about more than that," she said testily. "And you know it."

"You're right—we have everything on Earth. Family. Friends. But there's one thing missing there."

"What's that?"

He paused. "Something worth fighting for."

Cora dropped her hand from the bridge of her nose and, for a second, felt a little dizzy.

His face softened. "Listen, I didn't mean to—"

"Haven't we been through enough?" she interrupted. "Cassian picked us because we were all misfits back home. Our lives were broken. Your mother's death. My time in juvenile detention. Nok being trapped by that London agency, and Leon's family in prison, and Rolf's parents' expectations. And what do we get for all of our suffering—locked in this prison for the rest of our lives."

She was suddenly aware she was shouting, and dropped her voice. "You can't ask us to sacrifice more. We need this. After we win the Gauntlet, we'll have a chance to go home and make lives for ourselves that are a little less broken."

Warm tears had gotten netted in her eyelashes. She pushed them out roughly with shaking hands. Lucky's face was unreadable; only his eyes gave any hint of what he was feeling.

"I don't want to stay here, Lucky." Her voice broke.

He drew her into his arms. She pressed her face against his chest, surprised at how fast his own heart was beating. "I know," he said. "We'll see how it goes, after the Gauntlet. We'll see how much chaos there is, how people deal with freedom. I'd never deny you a chance to go home if that's what you really want, and I wouldn't ask anyone else to give that up either. But just so you know"—he pulled back to look into her face—"I'm staying."

She jerked back in surprise. "Lucky, be reasonable."

"I'm serious. Working with these animals has reminded me of who I used to be. I went a little crazy in the cage, I know, but I'm not that person now. I've taken responsibility for these animals, and that might not seem like a lot, when you're trying to free our whole species, but that's dozens of living creatures who need me. I can't run away from them. I don't want to. I'm staying where we're needed, whether you beat the Gauntlet or not."

Cora had so many things to say, and yet couldn't seem to speak a single one of them. For the rest of the day, his words swirled in her head as she sang distracted songs while the others went about their work, a little more cheerfully now that Dane was gone. Christopher and Mali didn't get into any fights. Shoukry slipped some sugar and lemon into Cora's water as a treat. Makayla even jumped onstage and sang a song with her, though her voice was terrible.

The whole time, Cora couldn't shake Lucky's words.

Where we're needed.

SHE WAS STILL TRYING to put their conversation out of her head when it was time to meet Leon that night. Most of the animals had fallen asleep quickly, and the other humans too. She focused on opening her cell's lock, ignoring how her pain was worsening, and the images of Roshian screaming in pain.

She opened Lucky's and Mali's cells too. Wetness dripped beneath her nose but she wiped it away, hoping the others wouldn't see. The three of them tiptoed to the feed room, then knocked twice on the drecktube door.

Leon shouldered it open. "Took you long enough."

They climbed in, crawling in a single line in the maze of tubes only Leon knew, until at last they arrived at Roshian's quarters. They were similar to Cassian's; so similar that Cora's thoughts, a little heady, kept swimming back to the night before. She had promised to forgive Cassian if he helped her. Part of her wondered if maybe that's why she was so anxious to board that ship and run. Not just to go back to Earth—but to escape promises she had made.

Leon pushed open a panel to reveal a hidden room. It smelled stale, like old paper. He flicked on a lamp. Inside were stacks of books, artifacts, and a dressing table. He dumped a box out on top of the table. "This is the stuff."

Lucky riffled through the box of supplies, lifting out a uniform.

Cora inspected the other objects. Black contact lenses. The tube of metallic paste that wasn't paste at all, but microscopic metal pieces. Papers and documents marking Roshian as a Kindred, along with notes he'd meticulously kept of ways they spoke and their mannerisms. She handed Leon the contacts.

"Put these in. They have to cover your whole eye, not just the iris."

It was a hard black shell the size of half a golf ball. He groaned as he lifted his eyelid and jabbed the contact in with unskilled hands.

Lucky sighed. "Let me. My granddad wore contacts and was always getting them stuck." He fiddled around with Leon's eye, trying to find the best way to insert the lens, and finally figured out, after a lot of Leon's cursing, that he could slide it in from the top.

Leon blinked with his one black eye.

"Can you see?" Lucky asked.

"Yeah. Like sunglasses."

He groaned again as Lucky jabbed in the other one. When it was done, he kept squinting and blinking, tilting his head to try to see out of the corners.

"The Kindred don't blink much," Cora said. "You have to practice showing no emotion."

"*You* try shoving these in your eyes and not blinking."

"I don't get how this paste works." Cora squeezed the tube, and the contents came out in a single thick blob.

Mali took it from her. "It is Axion technology. They use something like this to bathe but it is white. The pieces coat the body and attract dust and dirt like a magnet. Someone has modified this so that it clings longer and added small metal pieces to mimic Kindred skin."

"Roshian's file said he was a med student studying chemistry," Cora said. "Maybe he altered it himself."

Leon grabbed the paste from Cora's hand. He slapped it onto his bare arm and, at first, nothing happened. Then it slowly started to absorb into his skin, spreading like melted butter until his biceps was a shimmering copper color, then his forearm, then his shoulder. Once it was done, Cora eyed him eerily. If it wasn't for the rumpled clothes Leon was wearing, it might have been Roshian sitting there, or any of the Kindred.

"What does it feel like?" Lucky asked.

Leon shrugged. "Like I look like a sparkly idiot."

"No, it's good," Cora said. "It's believable. It covers your tattoos, and even the bruises."

Mali dumped the uniform in his lap. "Dress yourself."

Leon started unbuttoning his shirt.

"The lotion doesn't seem to rub off," Cora said, rolling a dab of it between her fingers, "but I think it can be scratched off with enough pressure. I clawed Roshian and some of it came away with his skin. So try not to get into any fights. And think about how they walk so stiffly and solemnly, like you're in church."

Leon looked at her. "Uh . . ."

"How you *think* people act in church," she clarified. "I'll be with you the entire time. On the off chance there are still any guests there, they'll be uncloaked and only concerned with themselves. And here." She tucked the gun Mali had swiped into his uniform's holster. "Even if it's just for show."

Leon stared at himself in the mirror. "This is a really bad idea, you know that, right?"

Cora patted his shoulder. "Let's go."

He stood up, trying to move like a robot. It wasn't a bad transformation, Cora had to admit. Physically, Leon's size and strength were nearly the same as most Kindred's, and the shimmering lotion and black eyes completed it. It unnerved her, seeing a Kindred with the face of her friend. Then he spit on Roshian's floor, and Leon was Leon again.

Lucky handed him a revival pod. "Anya will probably be drugged. You'll need this to revive her. Mali and I will head back to the Hunt; we'll see you in the morning, assuming everything goes well. Good luck."

"There is one more thing," Mali said, eyeing the pod. "In her drugged state, Anya will probably not be able to tell that you are human. She has used mind control to attempt to murder every one of her Kindred owners. If you revive her, she will probably attempt to take over your mind and murder you too."

Both Leon and Cora stared at her.

"I thought you should know," Mali clarified.

"Thanks," Leon said. "I really needed that."

3 3

Lucky

BACK IN HIS CELL, Lucky couldn't sleep.

His mind juggled a dozen different thoughts. Worry that
Cora and Leon would get caught, which was hardly an irrational
fear given Leon's track record. Worry that Anya would end up dead
and the whole plan would fall apart. Worry that they wouldn't be
able to get Nok and Rolf out. And then worry that he'd completely
screwed up everything by kissing Cora.

He cursed under his breath. That kiss had been a mistake.
He should have stopped her right from the start. Hadn't he learned
anything? Cora was practically hypnotized by Cassian, despite
what she said, and she always would be. How exactly was he supposed to compete with a guy who was mix of a billboard model
and superhero? Besides, even though he'd told Cora that he wasn't
that same guy who'd gone crazy in the cage, he didn't trust himself
sometimes. The memories were too fresh of that awful night when
he had led her up the stairs to their bedroom, taken her dress off

slowly, and all the while thinking what they were doing was right.

Right. Well, he wouldn't make the mistake of kissing her again, even if his thoughts did keep circling back to how soft her lips were.

He quietly dug through his few belongings until he found the notebook Dane had given him, and flipped through the pages haphazardly. He'd filled most of them with his worries. It helped to put them down on paper, night after night, when he couldn't sleep.

His eyes skimmed over his last entry, from two days ago:

> We repaired a hurt antelope today. Jenny and Christopher dragged it in around midday; it had been shot in the shoulder. The whole animal was quivering, its eyes darting back and forth. It was a new animal—I hadn't seen it before. Pika said we should name it Sunflower, because when Jenny first let it outside, it stood in the sun with its head tilted toward it, and smiled a little. I told Pika that antelopes don't smile. Pika said Sunflower does.

Now, he flipped to the very beginning. When Dane had given him the notebook, he'd noticed that a few pages were ripped out, but he hadn't given it much thought. Everything in the Hunt was in disrepair. It hadn't been until that morning, when they had framed Dane, that he'd found those missing pages in Dane's cookie tin, stuffed between pocket squares.

Now he unfolded the pages, tilting them toward the faint light of the nearest wall seam, and read them again.

Manual Override Codes, Dane had written. *In Case of Animal Emergency*.

Lucky scanned through the list of codes and instructions. The Kindred had entrusted Dane, as Head Ward of the backstage area, with keys and a supervisory position. *The most powerful of the powerless*, Lucky remembered taunting him, and Dane's smug retort: *Not powerless. Not at all.*

Apparently, he'd been talking about weapons.

Kill-dart guns, specifically, that Dane could access in the event the wild animals caused an uproar. It seemed the kill-dart guns were locked away in a hidden panel in the medical room, but the code to access it was written right here. Not letters or numbers, but a certain shape Dane needed to trace on the wall to make it open.

Lucky practiced tracing the same symbol on the dust of his floor until he had it memorized. He went to his cell door—he had left it cracked open when he'd come back in with Mali—and closed his eyes to listen. A few kids were snoring. One of the animals was chasing dream-rabbits in its sleep. He carefully pushed the door open, wincing in case the hinges squeaked, but they never did.

He stepped out slowly. The clock above the door indicated Night was three-quarters over already; Cora and Leon better hurry. The blue glow of the lights cast a cold look over the cell room. He passed by the fox's cell, and the fox looked up at him curiously. He held a finger to his lips and took another step but tripped over a deck of cards.

The deck went skittering across the floor and he froze, one

foot still in the air. Someone grumbled in her sleep on the upper level of cages. Was that Jenny's cell? The blood rushed in his ears....

"We aren't idiots, you know," a voice said.

He jerked his head toward Shoukry's cell. The boy's face loomed between the bars, and Lucky's breath stilled. He could say that the lock of his door had broken . . . or . . .

"Don't worry." It was another voice, from the opposite direction, and Lucky spun to find Makayla looking out from her own cell. "We didn't tell Tessela before," she said. "We aren't going to now."

Snores came from the direction of Pika's cell. She, at least, was still asleep.

"You mean you've known this whole time that we can get out of our cells?" Lucky whispered.

"Makayla and I caught on pretty quick," Shoukry said. "Jenny and Christopher know too. It isn't so surprising—there have been rumors for a while about kids gaining psychic abilities like the Kindred's. Is it you, or Cora?"

Lucky hesitated, not sure if he could trust them.

"That's what I thought," Shoukry said. "Cora."

"Dane didn't know," Makayla answered. "We made sure of it. Slipped a few slivers of the reverse revival pods in his dinner cakes so he'd sleep deeply. There are benefits to being in charge of the food." She grinned in the shadows. "We know about your friend in the drecktube too. He breathes really loud."

Shit. Lucky *knew* Leon would be trouble.

"Whatever you and Cora and Mali are planning," Makayla asked, "is it going to get us out of here, maybe even home?"

Lucky looked in the direction of the drecktube. "That's what we hope. It's a long shot. But if Cora can—"

"Don't say it," Shoukry said. "The less we know, the better. The Kindred have ways of extracting information from your mind that involve lots of tubes and lots of pain. Just, whatever you're planning, don't stop. I'll cover for you the best I can."

"I will too," Makayla whispered.

"And me," another voice said, probably Jenny's. "And you can count on Christopher too."

Lucky blinked into the darkness. He had told Cora that they couldn't leave the others behind, and now he was certain. All this time, the others had been watching out for them. He wasn't sure how to express how much their trust meant, so he settled for a nod of thanks.

He moved faster now, knowing the others were on his side. He passed by Cora's empty cell, and then he was in the hallway. He didn't need to worry about being quiet, but he was all too aware of the ticking clock.

There was less light here; he could barely make out the shape of the medical room. By memory, he walked forward with his hands out until he reached the supply cabinet. He pushed it away from the wall and felt for the seams of a secret panel. When he thought he'd figured out its location, he traced the symbol from Dane's instructions.

Something beeped. The panel clicked open.

Behind it was a drawer. He held his breath as he reached in. His fingers brushed something cold and metal. A gun. He counted ten smaller ones and at least three bigger ones, though the drawer went back quite far. He took out one of the smaller kill-dart guns. It was heavier than he had expected. Or maybe that was just the weight of his guilt for not telling Cora about this. But Cora was unpredictable, and so were Mali and Leon. That Kindred-made pistol Mali had stolen was only useful for show, which had secretly relieved him. Cora and Mali and Leon working with firearms couldn't possibly end well.

He cradled the kill-dart gun in his hand, taking a deep breath. He had no intention of using these weapons against any Kindred, or against any humans either. He kept thinking of that day when he'd been about to heal the zebra and had been reminded of that sick horse on his granddad's farm.

Sometimes just surviving isn't enough, his granddad had said.

He put the gun away quickly and closed the panel door. At the time, he had thought of killing the animals as a cruel sort of kindness. One that he'd like to avoid at all costs, if possible. Hopefully he'd find another way to save them. Maybe if Cora did beat the Gauntlet, he'd be granted more authority, and could take the animals away from the menagerie and care for them properly. But in case the worst happened, he'd rather put every single animal out of its misery with his own hand than force them to continue this sick cycle of pain. As for the other kids, well, they could each make up their own minds. If it got bad enough, or if someone was wounded very badly . . . a quick and painless option could be good for them too.

He felt through the darkness for the door, and then was back in the cell block—moving faster now, glancing at the clock—and into his cell. He pulled the door all the way closed. The lightlock clicked on, casting a glow over the crumpled journal pages in his hand. He slid them into his journal and sank to the floor.

Someone was still snoring, but now Lucky knew it was

probably just an act. All these nights while he had lain awake, the others probably had too.

He kept his eyes going between the hallway and the clock. Cora didn't have much time.

The fox nudged against the bars again. He petted it, a little hard, but the fox didn't seem to mind, or to notice just how feverishly, in that moment, he hated himself for what he one day might have to do to it.

His mind raced, and he knew there'd be no sleep for him. He grabbed up the journal and the pencil nub, and started writing to get it out of his head.

> The others know. All this time, they've
> been protecting us. . . .

His pencil paused. He caught a glimpse in the faint light of the markings on his hand; coding that designated him as a human only suitable for menagerie work.

> Maybe Cora is right about what happens
> after the Gauntlet. It isn't fair to ask people
> who have already been through so much to
> give up a chance of going home. And god, I
> think about what it would be like, if we did
> get back. I'd walk into a grocery store and
> fill up three shopping carts with bacon and
> Pop-Tarts and soda. I wouldn't join the army.
> I'd take over the farm—just me and the horses
> and the stars. And Cora—if she'd come.

He flipped a page.

But then—and here's what I can't shake—
why does going home feel so wrong? And
it does. It makes me sick to my stomach.
The animals, the humans: we're all marked
the same way, might as well be brothers in
captivity. I can't picture a world where we're
free and they're not. If it comes to it, I'll do
what I have to. But I hope it doesn't. I hope
Cora beats the Gauntlet. I hope she decides to
stay.

I hope she decides to build a life here, where
we're needed.

Where I'll be.

34

Cora

"OKAY," CORA SAID, AS soon as she and Leon reached the end of a service tunnel. "Ready?"

"Do I have a choice?"

She reached up and brushed a drop of his sweat from his forehead. "It'll be okay. Put the shackles on me so I look like a prisoner."

They listened for footsteps on the other side of the tunnel door, and when it was evident that the hall was empty, Leon looked out. "It's clear."

"Hold my arm," Cora whispered. "Like you're leading me."

The foyer where menagerie doors split off was even creepier at night. The podiums to the menageries weren't staffed, the hosts and hostesses off duty. Cora adjusted her hands in the shackles, trying to wear a mix of defiance and fear in case there were any Kindred guards. It wasn't hard. All she had to do was think about the first time Cassian had taken her down this same dank hallway.

They'd only walked about twenty feet when Leon mumbled

a low curse. "Trouble. Two o'clock."

A shadow was approaching from the far end of the foyer. A female guard, patrolling the hall slowly in their direction.

"We're almost there," Cora whispered, nodding toward a doorway on the right. "That's the entrance to the Temple. Just act natural."

With the lights so low, Leon looked perfectly believable as a Kindred. She saw the guard's head cock, curious, but then Leon swiveled Cora toward the Temple doorway.

"Open it quick," he muttered. "She's eyeing us."

Cora focused on the blue sensor above the door. Her heart was racing, but this was second nature to her now. All she had to do was ignore the splinter of pain in the back of her head. As they stepped inside, she saw the female guard turn to inspect a different node but throw one last look over her shoulder.

The door closed, and Cora sighed in relief. "That was easier than I thought."

"Yeah," Leon said darkly. "Too easy. She's probably calling for reinforcements."

"Then let's hurry."

In the dark, the Temple's ornate columns weren't visible, and the cells loomed like a prison. "I don't think there's anyone observing behind the black panel," she whispered. "But just in case, manhandle me a little."

Leon grabbed her shoulder, saying some sharp words. In his disguise he looked terrifying, and it wasn't hard to shrink back. He led her down the hall to the last cell, and there was Anya, sitting on the throne, staring at the fire. Cora wondered if the girl ever slept, or if the consciousness-reducing drugs rendered sleep obsolete.

"Stand, girl," Leon commanded, trying to make his voice flat like the Kindred. "The medical officer has requested an inspection."

Anya's head slowly turned from the fire, but her eyes settled on Cora instead. In a drugged sort of way, she smiled. *"Hi, little rabbit."*

Cora glanced at Leon, but he clearly hadn't heard anything.

"Right," Cora said. "Anya, if you can hear me, we're friends of Mali's. She's sent us to get you out of here. We need for you to teach me to control minds."

But Anya didn't seem to hear. Instead, her cold gaze raked over Leon's Kindred uniform and Kindred face.

"Are you guys talking psychic stuff?" Leon whispered. "Did you tell her I'm human?"

"I can hear her voice in my head," Cora whispered back. "But she never makes much sense when she's drugged."

"Well, read her mind and see if she's going to strangle us as soon as we get her out of there."

Taking a deep breath, Cora faced Anya. Every time she'd tried to read minds—first with Lucky, then with Leon—it had come a little easier. Now she tried to reach out her thoughts like she did for levitation, but instead of dice, it was thoughts she was trying to influence.

Images flickered at the edge of her mind.

Blood.

Lots of it.

And Leon's face with its Kindred disguise.

"Did it work?" Leon asked.

Cora blinked out of her concentration. "Um, a little. She's not thinking polite thoughts about you, that's for sure. I can't tell if she knows you're human."

"No way in hell I'm reviving this little psycho," Leon said. "If she can do even half the ninja shit Mali can, I'll be dead in thirty seconds."

"How are we supposed to get her out of here if we don't revive her?"

"I'll carry her. We have the removal pass, if that guard stops us. Come on, just open her cell with your mind or whatever. This place gives me the creeps."

Cora concentrated on the lightlock set into the wall above Anya's cell. It was slightly different from the ones in their cell block, but after a few minutes she figured it out and the door swung open with her thoughts.

Anya turned back to the fire, uninterested.

Leon started to take a step inside her cell but hesitated, like he was reaching for a live cobra that was going to strike if he moved too fast. He paced to the left, then to the right, rubbing the back of his neck.

"Just grab her," Cora hissed. "She's drugged. She can't hurt you."

"Famous last words," he muttered, then took a deep breath like he was diving underwater, and threw Anya over his shoulder. Her head pitched back, lolling; her eyes were glassy.

"We'll sail to a different world," she said into Cora's head.

Leon fumbled to snap the shackles on Anya's hands, as much for show as to protect themselves from her. "Let's get out of here."

They hurried back to the entrance. Cora wondered how sane Anya really was beneath the drugs. That tear in her own mind felt suddenly more painful. She pressed a hand to her nose, trying to stave off the blood, as she focused on the blue sensor to open the door.

It slid open—and the female guard was on the other side.

She blocked the exit, as though she had been waiting for them. Her face was a mask of passivity as she slowly cocked her head, eyes focused on Anya.

Leon had been right—it had been too easy before.

Luckily, he didn't break character now. With his free hand, he held out the removal pass.

The guard took the pass, studying it closely, and then scanned it to log the visit. It seemed to satisfy her, and she stepped back to allow them to enter the hallway. Cora closed the door behind them, keeping her face calm, so the guard would think Leon had done it. As they walked away, she could feel success with every step. Ahead, just around that corner, they'd slip back into the walls and be safe.

Then the guard said something in Kindred.

Cora froze. Leon did too.

Cora frantically tried to probe the guard's mind. When she'd read Cassian's thoughts before, it hadn't mattered what language they'd been in. But all she came up with now was a cold, suspicious feeling. Panic started to seep into her, but Leon remained calm. He gave a noncommittal grunt like she had heard the Kindred do, and started walking again with authority.

One step.

One more.

The guard spoke again, sharper. Out of the corner of her eye, Cora glanced at Leon, wondering if they should run for it. The Kindred were so fast that it would take a miracle to get to the drecktube in time. There was the gun, but that was only a bluff.

They turned slowly. The guard was facing them, and she

didn't look pleased. She wore an intercom on her wrist—she could have twenty more guards there in seconds.

The guard took a step closer, head moving in measured jerks between Leon and Cora. There was nothing they could do; there were no words to answer her. Cora glanced at Leon; sweat was trickling down his face. At the same moment, the guard noticed.

Leon broke character. "We're screwed!"

The guard reached for her wrist intercom. Time seemed to slow. Cora twisted the shackles, but it was useless. There was no stick to drive through *her* eye. She spun on Leon. "Run, now! Take Anya—I'll hold her off."

"Like hell," he said.

Cora was about to throw herself at the guard when a blast of sound fractured through the hallway. She cried out, and Leon cringed. A gunshot? She twisted around to see Leon's holster—empty. Where was the gun? Another shot rang out, and the Kindred doubled over. Cora looked around frantically. Her hands were empty. So were Leon's. So were Anya's; she was still slung over his shoulder, delirious.

Who was firing the gun?

And then she saw it. Hovering in the air four feet off the ground. Still aimed in the direction of the guard, who had collapsed.

Cora jerked around to face Anya, with her drug-laced smile.

"Anya's doing this," Cora choked. "She's doing it with her mind!"

The floating gun started to aim at the crouching guard again, but Cora reached out and plucked it from the air. The smile on Anya's face fell.

"That's enough," Cora said. "Leon, move!"

They raced down the hallway. The gun felt warm in Cora's hand. She'd never imagined power like that. Levitation. Even making it shoot—that was so far beyond her own abilities that she'd thought it impossible.

They raced around the corner to the drecktube. Leon climbed in and dragged Anya in like she weighed nothing.

Cora stuffed the gun in the strap of her dress.

"Someone's going to find that guard," Leon said.

"Yeah," Cora answered, still shaking, "But not until morning. We'll be long gone by then."

They started crawling. Leon seemed to know where he was going, which was good, because Cora couldn't focus on anything. That tear in the back of her head was throbbing. Cassian had said Anya had fractured her mind beyond repair. But could a fractured mind do what she had just done?

Eventually, they saw the tube that led back to the Hunt; Leon had marked it with chalk. Cora tried not to think about the wounded guard.

They had Anya.

Cassian was on her side.

Once they had Nok and Rolf safe, she would be ready for the Gauntlet. She ignored that itch in her mind that said there was more to the Gauntlet than Cassian was letting on.

35

Cora

CORA SLAMMED THE DOOR of her cell closed.

She mussed her hair to make it look as if she'd slept, and kicked around her blanket, seconds before the morning lights flickered on. The clock above the doorway clicked onto Morning Prep.

She sank against the bars, chest rising and falling hard. She had made it. *They* had made it. It was all she could do, once the lights flickered all the way on, not to laugh out loud in joy. She pressed a hand over her mouth and whirled toward Lucky's cell.

But the joy on her face died.

He looked awful. Dark circles around his eyes, hair tangled, like he hadn't slept at all. As soon as the lightlocks clicked off, she pushed open the door. The other kids all tumbled out of their cells, trying to beat one another to the feed room. Cora bided her time until they cleared.

"What's wrong?" she asked Lucky.

He rubbed a hand over the back of his neck and glanced at

the fox. Their argument from the night before flooded back to her, his assertions that he'd do anything—even stay behind—to protect the animals, and that it was her responsibility to do the same for the kids.

"The others know," he said.

She jerked back in surprise. "How much?"

"Not everything, but enough. They've been protecting us." He glanced toward the medical room, tucking a few torn-out journal pages into his pocket. There was handwriting on them, but it wasn't his. "Did you get Anya?"

"Yeah. She's safe, but . . ." She remembered the gun floating in the air. "I'm not sure anyone around her is. She's delirious. She isn't going to be able to train me like that."

"It must be the drugs," Lucky said. "They'll have to leave her system before she can tell you how to control minds."

The clock clicked over to Showtime, and Cora's stomach grumbled, but she ignored it. Lucky rubbed his shoulder uneasily as he watched the backstage kids tumble out of the feed room, Shoukry and Christopher arguing over half a breakfast cake. His fingers fumbled again with the torn-out pages.

"What are those?" she asked.

He didn't answer. She was tempted to probe inside his mind and see what was bothering him. She went so far as to send her thoughts just to the edge of his, but flinched when she saw images of guns, darts, dead animals—all surrounded by an overwhelming feeling of sadness.

"Don't worry about it." When he met her eyes, he blinked and his weariness vanished. He gave her half a smile. "We're getting close. You're going to beat this thing, I know it."

His words bolstered her hope.

That morning, she raced through her songs as if she'd chugged ten cups of coffee. Her limbs felt light and jittery. Arrowal and the Council members hadn't come today. Roshian was rotting where no one would ever find him. For the first time in days, Cora let herself revel in a sense of hope, as she pulled Shoukry onstage and they belted out the refrain together.

"I haven't thought of that song in years!" Shoukry said with a laugh. "We used to listen to it at the roller-skating rink. It played at my fifth birthday party."

Cora squeezed his hand, beaming.

Shoukry leaned in close. "Whatever you're planning," he whispered, "we're with you."

Shocked, Cora couldn't form words to answer until Shoukry was already stepping off the stage, and by then, the front door was opening.

Cassian entered, and any words vanished in her mind.

His eyes met hers and he stopped. Suddenly she was back in his quarters, and it made goose bumps erupt on her arms. They were in this together now. No more secrets. No more lies.

He nodded toward the alcove.

Once they were in the solitude behind the wooden screen, she thought her racing heart would slow, but it only beat faster.

"We freed Anya," she said.

"Where is she?"

"With the Mosca." Cora picked up one of the cards on the table, the queen of diamonds, turning it anxiously between her fingers.

"It will take a while for the drugs to clear her system,"

Cassian said. "A full day, perhaps longer. The Gauntlet arrives tomorrow, and the tests begin the day after that. That does not leave us much time. How much progress have you made teaching yourself to read minds?"

A *thump* sounded from beyond the alcove. The music outside stopped halfway through a song. Cora glanced at the slats, but dismissed it. Makayla must be taking her break early.

"I can see images sometimes in people's heads, sense the feelings that go with them."

"I don't know how Anya goes about controlling minds, but my guess is you'll need more than that. You'll need to extract specific words, as a starting point. It isn't like levitating dice, because there are no amplifiers built into the mind. You must probe beneath consciousness, like reaching into a murky pond and finding a stone at the bottom." He took her hands, and she flinched at the sudden contact. He placed her palms on either side of his head, just above his ears. "Tell me what I am thinking."

He closed his eyes.

She scanned his face, looking for any tells or clues that might give away his thoughts. The scar Mali had given him. The bump in his nose.

She concentrated on piercing his mind's natural shield. She had only ever intentionally read humans' minds before, and by contrast Cassian's felt surprisingly chaotic. Thoughts were stacked in haphazard piles that must make sense only to him.

Out of the chaos, she sensed an image of his quarters, bare. The book he liked to read, *Peter Pan and Wendy*. Then a memory of the cage, of watching her from behind a panel as she found the bone he had planted in the desert. That memory seemed stronger than the others.

"The bone," she whispered, and felt his head nod in her hands.

"Good. And what am I thinking now?"

She concentrated again, and pictured a black sky. A snow-covered hill that would have made her shiver, but in his memory, he didn't feel the cold. One by one, lights appeared in the dark.

"Stars."

"Yes. And now?"

He had tipped his head down, so their foreheads were pressed together. She pictured an image of her own face. She was driving in her dad's car down country roads, singing softly to the radio. Her cheeks started to warm. His memories felt different when they were about her. They crackled at the edges, more alive. The image changed to waves lapping in the ocean, the two of them standing in the surf. In the memory, they were arguing. He was confused, frustrated, desperate. She had started to speak, but then he'd kissed her.

Her lips parted in surprise. "You're thinking . . . of that day—"

And then, he was kissing her again. Not in a memory—in real life.

They were so close already that it had taken just a tilt of his head for their lips to meet. A current spread to her toes, and her hands instinctively slipped from the sides of his head to his shoulders. He kissed her deeper and she slid her arms around his neck. It was wrong, she knew. She'd sworn not to do this again. And yet ever since that day they'd pretended to dance together, she'd been unable to forget it.

Her hip bumped the table, and the cards fluttered to the

floor. She broke the kiss and twisted to pick them up, but he held her tightly.

"Cora. Please. Do not push me away again."

But it was too much—the kiss, what it meant, everything. She crouched down, hair falling over her face, thankful for the excuse to catch her breath. Her fingers curled around the fallen cards. She'd stand up. She'd face him. She'd tell him it couldn't happen again. . . .

And then she realized that the Hunt had gone completely silent on the other side of the screen. No clinking glasses, no announcements from the stage. She glanced at Cassian and saw the same realization reflected in his own face.

The wooden screen jerked open.

Arrowal stood on the other side. "You. Girl. Come with us."

The blood drained from her face. Surely he hadn't seen the kiss. Behind him, Fian stood with two Kindred guards. When his eyes met hers, they flamed with warning.

Cassian was rapidly cloaking himself. "I have reserved this girl's entertainment for the rest of the quarter rotation."

"That is inconsequential," Fian said. "There has been a murder."

Cold fear crept up her body until she was nearly blinded by it.

Arrowal didn't take his eyes off Cora. "The boy Tessela arrested, Dane, revealed it during his interrogation. We scanned the environment and found high traces of carbon. A body. Roshian's body. And according to Dane, this girl was the only one present at the time of his death."

Her lips parted, but she couldn't think of a thing to say to clear her name.

"Take her to an interrogation room," Arrowal ordered.

The two guards stepped forward. Fian's eyes—looking for instruction—flashed toward Cassian, but Cassian seemed at a loss too, his face returned to a mask to hide whatever it was he was truly feeling.

"Wait." Fian stepped in front of one of the guards. "*I* will interrogate her. This matter is too important to entrust to the guards alone."

Relief flowed into her heart. Fian would protect her, just as he had before.

Arrowal nodded. "I agree. Which is why I will interrogate her personally. The mind cannot hide the truth for long. We will soon know everything."

Everything.

If they probed her mind, they'd learn about more than just Roshian's murder. They'd learn about her abilities and the training sessions with Cassian and the Fifth of Five, and god, even the kiss.

Cassian blocked the door. "No."

His command was sharp. The guards obeyed by instinct, taking a step back as though he was their commander, not Arrowal. Cora's heart pounded wildly.

What was he doing?

Arrowal seemed to tower even a few inches higher. "You question me, Warden?"

"You only saw a portion of the truth in Dane's mind," Cassian said. "You saw the events that led up to the murder, but not the crime itself. You couldn't have, because Dane was not present when it happened."

There was a subtle shift in the air that left Cora baffled. Why was he saying all this?

For a second, Cassian's eyes shifted to Fian, and Fian gave a slight nod. Cora had no idea what silent message had just transpired between the two of them.

"And how do you know that?" Arrowal countered.

Cassian didn't immediately answer.

Cora willed herself to keep breathing steadily. Fian's hand was flexing a few inches from his apparatus belt, almost like he was preparing for something. Was that what the look between them had meant? That Cassian was going to try to fight his way out of this? Enact the Fifth of Five's secondary plan that he'd told her about, launching a war?

They wouldn't last ten minutes.

"You are always trying to protect the lesser species," Arrowal said, a hint of condescension in his voice. "But this girl is no longer a ward in one of your environments. You cannot protect her against her own crimes. Now tell me how you know Dane was not present, if you were not present yourself."

Cora tossed a look at Cassian, but his face revealed nothing. She tried to probe into his thoughts, but her own mind was too fractured, her thoughts too scattered to concentrate. All she glimpsed was a shadowy image of his quarters again. She was there, her mouth moving, a card in her hand. He was thinking of the lesson where she had taught him to cheat.

"I know," he said calmly, "because I *was* present."

A lie.

Her lips parted. Fian's hand flexed again, and it all seemed to happen so fast. She pressed deeper into Cassian's head, and suddenly his head turned toward her, as though he could feel her there. The sensation of his thoughts changed. That brighter, more alive feeling came. Images of her flashed through his head. Her, standing on a beach. Her, looking out her bedroom window. Her, when she had first felt the electricity of their touch. A feeling of love was wrapped around each one, but there was something darker too.

"Why exactly were you present at a murder scene?" Arrowal asked, and for a second the room was silent.

Cassian glanced down at the queen of diamonds on the floor. As though the world had suddenly turned on its side, Cora realized what he was about to do. It didn't have anything to do with the Fifth of Five or any secondary plans. It was why he'd shown her all the images, surrounded by love.

He was going to sacrifice himself for her.

Words rose up her throat, about to tell him that he was making a terrible mistake. She hadn't taught him to lie so he could lie about *this*.

At the same time, Fian took a sharp step right behind her, as though sensing what she was about to do.

"Because it was me," Cassian said. "I killed Roshian."

36

Cora

"NO!"

The words rushed up Cora's throat, but Fian's hand crushed against her mouth. She screamed into his palm but he didn't let go, and her words became muffled protests. It made sense now. *This* was the secret look he and Cassian had exchanged. At some point they must have made plans for a worst-case eventuality like this. Cassian would confess, and Fian would prevent her from telling the truth.

"Guards," Fian commanded. "Take the Warden into custody."

Cora bucked against his hand, but it was like fighting a riptide. She met Cassian's eyes. They had gone black now.

Cloaked.

Which meant he could read her thoughts.

"Don't do this," she urged with her mind. *"You did nothing wrong."*

His face was a mask, but she could see in the flicker of his eyes that he understood.

"Take the two of them to separate holding rooms." Arrowal seemed coldly pleased by her anguish. "And watch him closely," he added. "Summon me once the interrogations are ready to begin."

Arrowal left, but Cora hardly noticed. The room kept spinning around a common point: Cassian. The heat of his gaze was nearly scalding. It was like standing too close to a bonfire, eyelashes getting singed, cheeks burning.

If anything ever happens to me, he had said, *go to Fian or Tessela. They are ready at all times to enact the secondary plan, should it come to that.* But the secondary plan was the last resort. Destroying enclosures, breaking humans out of menageries, launching an all-out war where a few hundred were pitted against an entire station.

It was madness.

"Let me confess," she urged in her head. *"Please."*

His head jerked, just the slightest movement. *No.*

The guards twisted his hands behind his back to bind his wrists with cuffs. He closed his eyes.

Suddenly her mind was flooded with an image of home. Her house with the oak tree, and the iron fence around it, feeling so real she could almost smell the fresh-cut grass. Cassian had to be projecting it there. This wasn't a training exercise anymore. This was real, and she *had* to read the words in his head.

"Home."

It came to her as clearly as it had the first time she'd heard him in her head.

"Home," his thoughts urged again. *"The POD30.1 was right—I found the original algorithm predictions. Fian will try to get you back to where you belong. To Earth."*

Her mind ached with the strange sensation of speaking in

thoughts. *"But the Gauntlet—"*

"Forget the Gauntlet," he thought. *"You can't run the Gauntlet if you've been arrested for murder. They would use it to take away even more rights. Say you are too violent. Say you are unpredictable."* Across the room, their eyes met. *"This is where you give up."*

Suddenly Charlie's voice was in her memory again, telling her that there was a time for giving up and a time for persevering.

"No!" But Fian clamped his hand harder against her mouth. Tears were rolling down her cheeks now.

Give up? She pushed the tears out of her eyes, attempting to shake her head. Not giving up was the one thing Cassian valued most about humanity.

"Take him away," Fian ordered.

She sobbed harder, fighting against Fian, even though she knew he was only playing the role he had to.

They started to lead Cassian away, but he tossed one last look over his shoulder. For a second, it felt like it was only the two of them in the room, and she remembered the first time she'd seen him. Even then—as terrified as she had been—she'd been entranced.

"I meant everything I said," his voice said in her mind. *"We could have changed the world together, you and I."*

And then he was gone.

She stared at the empty alcove doorway. The lights stung her eyes, but she didn't want to look away. This might be the last time she would ever see him. Never again to feel that spark. Never to stay up late, talking about the stars. The Kindred claimed they didn't incarcerate their own kind, but the shackles spoke otherwise. He'd be locked away forever.

For *her* crime.

She was alone now with Fian, who leaned close to speak quietly in her ear. "I will release you, but you must not run."

She gave the ghost of a nod.

Fian's face was the same indifferent mask as always. "Cassian's lies will only hold up for a few days. They will probe his mind in an interrogation and soon discover the truth. When they do, they'll come for you."

She stared at him. "So that's it? We just give up on the Gauntlet? You put me on a ship back home and then go to *war*? It's madness. You'll all be killed."

He gave her a long look she couldn't read. That wrinkle between his eyes deepened, and for a chilling second, she remembered how he had tried to strangle her. She pressed a hand against her neck, reminding herself that hadn't been real.

"There will be no war," he said. "There will be no ship back to Earth either."

Her throat threatened to close up further. "But Cassian said the secondary plan was—"

"Yes, that was his secondary plan. It doesn't mean it was *my* plan."

The chill spread up her arms as her breath came faster. She blinked at him, all her fears becoming real. "It was you," she whispered. "You were the watcher. You told the Council about my escape attempt." Anger flooded her. "Cassian trusted you!"

"That is his major fault—he trusts the wrong people. He was a fool to trust me. To trust you as well. You never would have beaten the Gauntlet, cheating or otherwise." He straightened. "But that is over now. There will be no signal to go to war. Tessela and the others within the Fifth of Five will be investigated and, in time, arrested. I shall take you to Arrowal. If you think you are safe because of the moral code, you are wrong. Arrowal has ways around it."

He pressed a hand against her mouth before she could scream. He dragged her from the alcove, kicking and tearing at his hand. The Hunt lodge had been cleared of guests. The lights were low, and the savanna's artificial sun was extinguished for the night.

Give up, Cassian had said. But he hadn't counted on this.

Cora spotted one of the baskets of jacks on the nearest table. She concentrated on moving the basket, inch by inch, until it spilled onto the floor. She threw her weight so that Fian tripped over the jacks and they both fell downward. Pain ripped through her, but she scrambled to her feet. Right behind the bar there was an entrance to the drecktube tunnels that they used for dirty napkins and empty bottles. It was small—too small for a Kindred to squeeze into, but she might be able to. She raced for it, just as Fian sprang to his feet.

Please have left it propped open, Leon, Cora begged. Her fingers connected with it just as Fian rounded the corner of the bar. She ripped at the door with her nails until it pulled open; the latch had been kept from closing by a crumpled bag of potato chips, and she gasped at this good luck. She wriggled through the gap, twisting until her hips were through. She tumbled into the darkness of the tunnel just as Fian reached for her foot, but his fingers glided off her heel.

She scrambled back. Out of the corner of her eye she glimpsed the glittering line of a cleaner trap, and froze just two seconds before she would have sprung it.

Fian pressed his face against the gap. "Those tunnels are filled with safeguards. If the shipping crates don't crush you, a cleaner trap will burn you alive."

Heart racing, she glanced again at the cleaner trap two inches from her toe. Beside it on the wall was one of Leon's chalk drawings to indicate danger.

She'd never been so thankful for Leon's artistic nature.

She crawled without looking back, stumbling as fast as she could, scanning the walls for more of Leon's markings. The air was so thin she could hardly breathe. Part of her wanted to go back to an hour ago, so that she could take back what had just happened, confess before Cassian could, tell him sooner of her suspicions that Fian couldn't be trusted.

She leaned against the side of the tunnel. She couldn't shake that last look at Cassian's face—still trying to protect her, after everything.

Somewhere on the station, it would be Free Time. Lucky would be anxiously waiting for her. Mali too. Did she dare risk seeking them to tell them what had happened? It would be nearly impossible to find the Hunt again without Leon to guide her, and besides, Fian would probably be with them already, anticipating that it might be her plan to return.

The last remnant of strength dissipated from her legs. She collapsed on the tunnel floor. Fear and regret twisted her stomach. Images of Cassian's beaten and bloody face crept into view, but no—that wasn't how the Kindred operated. Whatever plan they had for him would involve less blood, but more pain.

What about everything she had learned?

What about proving their worth?

"Little rabbits are no use if they're dead," a familiar voice said. Anya.

Cora dried her face on her arm and told herself to breathe. To count to ten. Leon and Anya were ahead, somewhere. By now, Leon would be halfway to that deranged dollhouse to rescue Nok and Rolf. But once word got out that Cassian had been arrested, the Council would surely suspect Serassi too. Leon might be walking straight into a trap.

"Follow the trail of bread crumbs," Anya's voice said. *"You'll find us."*

Bread crumbs?

And then Cora noticed another mark at the corner of the tunnel. A dollhouse, with an arrow.

Anya was telling her to follow Leon's markings.

Cora started to crawl faster.

Cassian had told her now was the time to give up, but there were some people she could never give up on. She crawled onward and hoped she wasn't too late.

37

Rolf

ROLF CHECKED THE DOLLHOUSE'S typewriter for the hundredth time. Nothing.

He paced the upstairs hallway, past the photographs Serassi had hung on the walls of herself with the baby. The smell of meat loaf wafted up from the kitchen, where Nok was microwaving their dinner.

He started down the hall, glancing out through the missing wall at the seating area. Empty, for now. He and Nok had developed a routine. The moment Serassi and the other observers were gone, they would take turns racing upstairs to see if Cora had left them a note on the typewriter.

It had been seven days since he'd last seen her, and no word.

"Nok?" he called, heading for the stairs. "When you saw her, are you sure she didn't say anything else?" He passed the nursery, glancing into it by habit, but caught sight of a shadow and stopped.

Cautiously, he approached the darkened room. His hand went by instinct toward the light switch, but something made him pause.

It *wasn't* a shadow.

A figure loomed over the crib. Nearly seven feet tall, hair slicked back in a tight knot, gazing down at the empty bedding.

Serassi.

She must have heard him calling to Nok, but she certainly didn't seem to care. What was she even doing here? She'd never snuck around the house before without their knowledge . . . at least not that they knew.

His hand fell away from the light switch.

He started to tiptoe backward, but then Serassi turned toward the window and he caught sight of something in her arms. It was wrapped in a soft blanket like a baby, but it wasn't moving. A glimpse of a tiny plastic hand caught the light.

A baby doll.

"Go to sleep," Serassi whispered flatly, in a poor imitation of singing. "Go to sleep, little sugary baby. . . ."

Rolf practically ran back downstairs, stumbling over his own feet. When he appeared, disheveled and out of breath, in the kitchen, Nok raised a questioning eyebrow.

"Serassi's in the nursery," he breathed. "I don't think it's the research that has her fascinated anymore. I think . . . I think she wants a baby of her own."

The microwave dinged, and Nok jumped.

"I told you we have to get out of here," she whispered. "Still no message from Cora?"

He shook his head. "A million things could have gone wrong.

It might just be you and me, and in that case—"

Clipped footsteps sounded on the stairs, and they instantly snapped into their well-rehearsed roles. Nok, smiling, setting out the dinner plates. Rolf opening a drawer for napkins. "I just remembered something my grandmother in Oslo used to say about a home remedy for how to get newborns to sleep," he said loudly. "It involved pickled beet juice. . . ."

Serassi darkened the kitchen doorway. Rolf turned, feigning surprise. "Oh! I didn't know you were here. We were just sitting down to dinner—would you like to join us—"

Serassi held up a notebook.

Nok's face went immediately white, though it took Rolf a second to recognize the notebook. It was Nok's, the one she hid beneath the cushion of the rocking chair in the nursery and only brought out when the researchers were gone. It was where she wrote down all the lies they made up about baby care, meticulously documenting everything in case Serassi or the other researchers were to ask about something again, and they'd need to keep the answers straight.

Rolf glanced at Nok. She was usually so quick with a lie, but now her face was slack, her lips slightly parted in fear.

"Oh, you found my journal." He stood quickly. "I'm glad. I thought I had lost it."

He reached for it, but Serassi jerked it away from his hand. "What is this book?"

"Nothing," Rolf said, though he could feel himself start to sweat. "Just where we write down things we remember about child care so we don't forget to tell you later. Right, Nok?"

But Nok's face was even paler. Her fear spread to him like a disease as Serassi started to flip through the pages.

Nok caught his eye. "It's too late," she whispered. "She knows."

But Rolf shook his head. It couldn't be too late. They could always make up more lies. Stay one step ahead of Serassi, just until Cora gave the signal on the typewriter.

Serassi slammed the notebook onto the table, making them both jump. She pointed to a note in the margin. "You. Read this out loud."

"Um." He took a step toward the notebook, even though Nok's eyes were flashing warnings. "Sure." He leaned close, starting to read. "Be sure to remind Rolf that when he lies . . ." His voice faded, at the same time the blood drained out of his own face. Now he understood Nok's fear. She'd written too honestly, never thinking Serassi might find the notebook.

"Continue." Serassi's voice was cold.

". . . when he lies he has a tell." His voice had gone hoarse. "He blinks hard, twice, when he lies about the baby care. S. and researchers might eventually figure it out."

He straightened, and adjusted glasses that were no longer on his face, and cleared his throat. "This is clearly . . . ," he started, "a misunderstanding. . . ."

He looked desperately to Nok, but she didn't even try to lie anymore. She looked like she might burst into tears at any moment, and every muscle in his body just wanted to hold her.

"This is not a misunderstanding," Serassi answered. "You have been lying to us. Making up these false practices in this notebook so we would think you were useful."

Rolf started to protest, but Serassi slammed the book closed.

"This experiment is over."

"No!" Rolf said.

Tears had started to fall from Nok's eyes, as though she had already given up.

"You will come with me," Serassi said to Nok. "We will keep you in a holding cell in the genetics laboratory until we can take the baby."

Nok, crying harder, fiddled with the bow at the back of her apron and tossed Rolf looks for help. He balled his fists. He wanted to punch Serassi so badly. To kick her. To do *something*.

"Leave the apron." Serassi's voice left no room for debate. She took out a set of shackles.

Then a soft sound came from upstairs.

Clink. Clink. Clink.

Serassi didn't seem to notice or care—just another one of the artifacts making noise, like the clock ticking or the microwave that dinged at random times. But Rolf knew that sound. Rolf had been waiting, every moment, just to hear that sound.

The typewriter.

Nok abruptly stopped crying and tossed him a desperate look, her fingers frozen on the bow at the back of her neck. Her mouth opened, but no words came out. This was it. Their escape, and they might not have a second chance! Whatever Cora's message was up there, he had no way of seeing it. *Now,* it might say. Or *The plan is off.* Rolf realized that either way, it didn't matter. Either way, the experiment was over.

They had to run.

"I'm not going to let you take her," Rolf said.

The microwave dinged again, randomly.

Serassi cocked her head. In one step, she crossed the kitchen and grabbed Rolf by the neck, the shackles in her other hand. He sputtered, clawing at her hand, but she was too strong. Nok screamed behind him, clutching one of the plates.

"You do not tell me what to do." Serassi's hand tightened against his windpipe.

His anger pulsed harder. He couldn't breathe. He couldn't see anything but his hatred. What was the use of having honed his body if he was still powerless? No matter how strong he became, or how fast, the Kindred would always be stronger. His muscles tensed and his mind whirled, like the disconnected parts of a car when the gearshift wasn't connected to the central engine. . . .

But wait. That was it.

Connect his mind and his body. It had helped him solve the complicated time equation. Maybe it could help him stop Serassi too. He looked frantically around the room. There was nothing large enough to throw to distract her so they could run. But there was the silver napkin ring from dinner, on the dining room table. And Serassi was standing right in front of the microwave that always malfunctioned. If Rolf could throw the napkin ring at just the right trajectory to hit the microwave button, the door would swing open. . . .

"Nok, duck!"

Before Serassi could turn, Nok ducked, as Rolf snatched up the napkin ring. He only had a second to aim, but this is what he had trained for. His mind quickly worked out the right angle and force to throw it, and his arm obeyed with precision.

It hit the button. The microwave dinged again and the door

popped open, slamming into the back of Serassi's head. Not hard enough to do damage, but enough to surprise her into letting go of Rolf.

Rolf grabbed the shackles and slammed them around Serassi's wrists. They were a material that bound on contact; no keys, no locks. Rolf noticed a small metal tag on a cord around her neck and snatched it, in case it was a key that would unlock the warehouse doors. Serassi's face was still a perfect mask of indifference, but Rolf could practically feel simmering anger coming off her.

"Run, Nok!" He slid the cord over his own head and grabbed Nok's hand. They jumped out through the kitchen's missing fourth wall, landing hard on the warehouse floor.

"We don't know what Cora typed!" Nok said, her legs pumping. "How do we know the plan is still on?"

"We'll find out soon enough."

They reached the drecktube grate that Leon had shown them. Rolf slammed his fists into it, again and again. It wouldn't take Serassi long to get out of her shackles. She would tell the Council. They'd hunt them down, round them up, find out exactly what they were planning. He fumbled with the metal tag on the cord, but it didn't seem to be a key at all, but rather some sort of digital file.

Rolf kept pounding, yelling for Leon to open the door, searching desperately for another way in.

Nok let out a cry. The pink streak in her hair. The yellow ribbons of the apron. Beneath the costumes they were made to wear, he loved her. He couldn't let it end like this.

"Nok. I'm sorry."

She was crying. He felt his heart breaking. He wasn't a hero—he was a weak little *kødd*.

Then, abruptly, the grate swung open. A black-eyed face looked out. Rolf's heart shot to his throat. It was a Kindred, in the tunnels! But—wait. This particular Kindred was familiar.

"Leon?" Rolf said incredulously.

"Don't let the eyes fool you," Leon said. Behind him, Cora's familiar blond head poked out of the tunnel.

Leon snorted. "Bloody hell, Nok, I knew you missed me, but tears?"

Rolf threw his arms around Leon, who mumbled something about getting a room, and hugged him hard.

38

Cora

"WE'VE GOT PROBLEMS," CORA said, as soon as they were in the drecktube tunnels.

"I thought we just escaped our problems," Rolf said, jerking his head back in the direction of Serassi's dollhouse experiment.

"Bigger ones. The Council arrested Cassian. We're on the run now. I can't participate in the Gauntlet. Our only hope is to get off the station."

"What about Lucky and Mali?" Nok asked.

Cora hesitated. Cassian had warned her not to go back for the others. But Cassian hadn't known that Fian would turn on them. Even now, Fian could be leading more guards to the Hunt to arrest them. "I'm going back for them. The rest of you should go with Leon to the Mosca camp. We'll meet there. With luck we can negotiate something with Bonebreak. If he can't take us all the way back to our solar system, at least he could take us somewhere where we aren't being hunted."

Leon's face was unreadable in the dark tunnel. "I'm going with you."

She rested a hand on the rubber shielding over his shoulder. "You can't. They won't make it through the tunnels without you."

She turned before she could change her mind. She crawled on her hands and knees, following Leon's chalk markings of zebra stripes, fighting the claustrophobia creeping into her lungs, until she made it back to the Hunt.

She pressed her ear against the door, listening.

Someone was humming on the other side but paused to giggle.

Pika.

Cora knew that she could trust Jenny and Christopher, and Shoukry and Makayla. But Pika's loyalties were a mystery.

Cora sighed and drew up her knees, leaning against the cold metal tunnel, and waited for the cover of night.

SHE WAS NEARLY FREEZING by the time Pika left, and the sounds of chatter and cell doors closing had died down. She eased the door open and peeked into the darkness.

The coast was clear.

She tiptoed through the quiet rooms and scaled the stairs silently to find Mali's cell. She started to reach for the lightlock, but a hand snaked out and grabbed her.

Mali's face loomed in the glowing light.

Cora pressed a finger to her lips. Mali nodded. Cora closed her eyes and focused on unlocking the door. It swung open, and they both tiptoed back down to the lower level. Mali started for Lucky's door, but Cora held out a hand.

"Wait."

Something didn't feel right. It went back to her argument with Lucky about what would happen after the Gauntlet. He'd said that he wouldn't leave the animals, Gauntlet or not. If she woke him up now, would he still refuse to go?

She chewed on her lip, knowing they were running out of time. She motioned for Mali to follow her into the medical room, where she quietly told Mali everything that had happened. "So now we run," she added, "and hope we can bribe our way off this station, which isn't going to be easy without any money."

Mali's eyes widened for a moment. "Wait here." She scampered off before Cora could stop her, and returned with one of the filthy safari sacks.

"Mali, that reeks."

"Yes." Mali untied the bag as though she was immune to the stench. "Keeps the others away so they do not find this."

Tokens. Hundreds of them.

"They belonged to Dane," Mali explained. "When we swapped Roshian's collection of tails into his cookie tin, we had to empty these out. I told Lucky I would hide them." She closed the bag again. "Will they be enough?"

Cora paused—it was the first time she'd heard Mali state a question like a question. She smiled. "I hope so."

Cora turned around and started rooting through the medical room cabinets. Mali slung the bag over her shoulder and frowned. "What are you looking for?"

"I heard Pika say something once about reverse revival pods. To put agitated animals to sleep. It's for Lucky. There's a chance he'll insist on staying behind. And now isn't the time for him to be noble."

Mali hesitated but then reached into the cabinet and took out a greasy package. "It is this one."

Back in the cell room, they knelt by Lucky's cell. He was asleep with one arm through the bars, the fox curled against his palm. For a second, a part of Cora hated what she was doing. But she pushed past that feeling and set the pod near his face. In a moment the tense set to his expression eased, as he slipped into a deeper sleep.

Cora opened his door, and they dragged him over the dirty floor.

"He will be mad when he wakes," Mali warned.

"Yeah," Cora muttered as she heaved his sleeping form down the tunnel. "But he'll also be alive."

CORA'S ARMS ACHED BY the time they'd crawled halfway through the tunnel, but she didn't dare stop. Lucky's body was too heavy to lift over the cleaner trap triggers, so they'd had to double back and take different tunnels until her vision blurred from the thin air.

She paused to catch her breath. From the nearest grate came the sounds of heavy boots and flat Kindred language.

"Do you understand what they're saying?" Cora asked.

Mali wobbled her head. "A little. They are looking for us."

Cora's heart started thumping harder. She prayed the tokens would be enough to convince Bonebreak to let them on that ship. She dragged Lucky down turn after turn, following

Leon's chalked marks on the walls.

"Move to the side!" Mali yelled. "Now."

Cora tossed a look at a package that was floating behind them. Not fast, but faster than they were crawling with an unconscious body. Mali pressed herself into one of the tunnel alcoves, clutching the sack of tokens tight against her chest. Cora glanced at Lucky, then at the nearest alcove. Not enough room for the both of them. She shoved him as far back into the alcove as she could and, just as the package nipped at her heels, dived into the empty one across from him.

Every moment felt like eternity as Cora waited for the package to float past. There was a crack in the alcove and she pressed her ear against it, listening for the sounds of more Kindred guards hunting for them.

There *were* Kindred voices, but quieter. She almost thought she heard a few words of English, and pressed her eye against the crack.

Beyond was a cell.

Six feet by six feet. It could have been the exact one they'd put her in after her failed escape attempt. The same toilet. The same sink. But there was an examination table in the center. A figure shifted on it, and she gasped.

Cassian.

She pressed a hand against the wall. He was unconscious, strapped to the table. Tubes snaked through his skin and ears and nose, pulsing. On a small screen next to him, a three-dimensional projection showed flashes of images. Fian and Tessela. Serassi and her equipment. Cora. The dice and cards they'd used to train with. The machines were dissecting his thoughts. First was a projection of him playing go fish with Mali on a beach. And then one of him trying to draw a dog in the privacy of his quarters.

And then, the kiss they'd shared just hours before.

Suddenly Cassian hissed, and she realized he wasn't unconscious. They were doing something to him, probing his mind, and it was tearing him apart, just as it was tearing *her* apart to watch.

One of the doctors must have heard her gasp; he looked around. She jerked away from the wall crack, breathing hard.

Across from her, one more package drifted by.

"It is clear," Mali whispered.

Cora's heart was pounding so hard she wasn't sure she could talk. "Go. I'll catch up." Mali gave her an uncertain look, but she shook her head. "I'll be right behind you."

Mali gave her a long, steady look but left. Cora spun and pressed her eye back against the crack. There was equipment on the wall she hadn't noticed before. It was all the length of her arm, and it ended in sharp needles and blades. She didn't have to know what the instruments were for to know that Cassian would likely never walk out of that room unchanged.

When he had confessed to her crimes, he must have known that this would be his fate.

"I'm so sorry," she whispered quietly.

Below, the medical officers inserted another snaking tube into his vein, and he let out a scream.

She choked back a sob and pressed her hands to her face to hold in tears. She couldn't do this—stay here and watch him be tortured. Mali and Lucky and the others were waiting for her. Even now, Kindred guards were scouring the station for them.

And yet she couldn't tear herself away.

She had always accused *them* of being the monsters, but she was the reason he was suffering now. She traced her eyes along his lips, blue now with lack of blood flow. His eyes, mostly cloudy with half-uncloaked thoughts, rolled back and forth. She had thought he was an angel once. There were no such things as angels—she knew that now. But he wasn't a demon either.

"Cora." It was Mali, at the far end of the tunnel. "There are more guards in the hallways. We must go now."

She wiped the tears away and stumbled back from the wall. Her heart pounded even harder, each beat an accusation. "I'm coming."

Tears were coming faster, but Mali didn't ask the reason, just picked up Lucky's legs and dragged him too, until he started to mumble incoherently as he slowly woke.

"Lucky." Cora slapped him lightly on the cheek. "Lucky, can you hear me? Can you walk?"

But he didn't answer.

They reached a higher tunnel where, stooped over, they could move faster. They each wrapped one of Lucky's arms around their shoulders and dragged him, still half asleep, mumbling words that made no sense. Cora tried to put the scene of Cassian's torture out of her head, but it was impossible. At last, they reached a gate that was marked with Leon's signature sign for the Mosca camp: a broken bone.

Cora pounded on the door until it swung open into a dank, chalky room with poor lighting, and she drew in deep lungfuls of air. There was just light enough to make out Leon arguing with a Mosca underling. Against the far wall, Nok was handing a bottle of water to Anya, who took it gratefully, speaking a few words Cora couldn't hear.

"Anya is awake!" Mali slipped out from under Lucky's arm. Without Mali's help supporting him, Cora buckled under Lucky's weight until Leon jumped up to help lay him flat on the ground.

"Great. We just get that crazy girl awake and how *he's* out cold?" Leon asked. "What happened, a guard knock him out?"

"It's a little more complicated than that." She knelt beside him, shaking him gently. "Lucky, can you hear me?"

He mumbled groggily but didn't wake.

"Listen, I'll explain everything," she said, though she wasn't sure if he could even hear her. "Right now we just need to—"

"Well, well."

Cora froze. It was a voice she had never heard before, and yet she instantly knew who it belonged to. Those stunted words. That wheezing, like someone breathing through a mask. She turned to find the most hideous creature she had ever seen.

Bonebreak folded his hands, drumming his fingers together. "More little childrens." He turned to Leon. "I hope your friends are rich, boy. Because there are Kindred guards just outside the door. They know you are here. And protection from them will be very expensive."

She dragged over the sack of tokens. She tore at the knot until it opened, and then upended the bag so they spilled onto the floor. "Is this rich enough for you?"

39

Cora

THE ROOM WENT SILENT.

The only sound was Lucky mumbling in his sleep, Bone-break's delighted cackling as he appraised the mountain of tokens, and the pounding of Kindred guards at the door. Was the Council there too, beyond the gate? She looked around frantically, wondering where Bonebreak's ship was. The echo of Cassian's scream was still in her ears. They had to get off this station *now*.

"You didn't tell me what good friends you have!" Bonebreak said to Leon, and then turned back to Cora. "I will be happy to take your money, girl."

"This isn't just to keep those guards out." Cora knelt next to Lucky, brushing the hair off his forehead. "I want a ride off this station. If you can't take us to Earth, take us as far away from here as possible."

Bonebreak went still.

"Uh, Cora," Leon started, "I wasn't supposed to tell you about that—"

She couldn't see behind Bonebreak's mask, but a growing shrill wheeze came from behind it, until he erupted and spun on Leon.

"I will break your bones!" Bonebreak roared. "I will dance on them until they pop!"

Leon backed toward the door.

"Wait!" Cora threw herself between Leon and Bonebreak. "Listen, let's focus on the money here. That's a lot of tokens. Think of everything you could do with that amount. All the, um, vodka you could buy."

Leon clamped his hands over his head as if he knew how screwed they were. Stacked beside him were odd-shaped boards that, she realized, exactly matched the shapes of the bruises all over his body.

Maybe Cassian had been right all along, when he had said that the Mosca couldn't be trusted.

"A deal?" Bonebreak almost sounded amused. "You are offering me a deal? How cute. However, the Kindred on the other side of that door are offering a deal too. All of you, for a lifetime of trade passes. That sounds like a much better deal to me. Plus they will let me do whatever I want to *that* one."

He jerked his finger toward Leon, who went pale.

Bonebreak raised his arms. "Get them!"

Other Mosca came skittering in from other rooms. They grabbed Nok and Rolf. One stood guard over Lucky, prodding his unconscious body with the point of his toe. Cora recoiled as one that smelled like sulfur grabbed her.

Leon was cursing everyone in sight, but the two Mosca holding him were strong for their size, and he couldn't break free.

Bonebreak started for the door that held back the Kindred guards. It had a blue sensor, like the others, and a manual lock too—Mosca technology—so that the Kindred couldn't unlock it with their minds alone. Bonebreak placed a hand on the lock and chuckled as he started to slide it open.

"Wait!" Cora tore away from the underlings and threw herself against the door. "We can offer you a better deal than they can. I promise."

Bonebreak snorted. Up close, he smelled gassy and rotten. The skin where his mask was sewn to his face was scarred and black around the edges, and it turned her stomach.

"You are human," he said. "They are Kindred. They will always have more to offer than you." He shoved her aside, but she shoved right back.

"That isn't true! They're bound by a moral code that we aren't. We can do all kinds of things for you—lie, steal, kill, cheat. Give us a chance to prove how valuable we can be."

Beyond the door, the Kindred guards had stopped shouting, but there was an ominous thunking sound instead, as though they were using heavy machinery to break inside. Bonebreak's head cocked.

"Hmm . . . ," he mumbled.

Cora's heart beat faster. She curled her fingers around the lock, squeezing it impatiently.

"Nah," Bonebreak said.

He reached for the lock again. Cora's vision started to

fracture. Her fingers, slick with sweat, glided off the lock. On the other side of the door, the Kindred had started talking again, in a way that was slow and confident. Whatever tools they were using to break down the door kept thunking.

"That's it," Leon announced. "Time for negotiations is *over*."

He gave a bellow. It shook the room as he seemed to draw into himself and then thrust out his arms like he was ripping space itself. The two Mosca underlings holding him were thrown backward to the floor. They scrambled, but with their flat back armor and spindly legs, they only skittered around like overturned beetles.

Mali launched herself at the nearest Mosca. She moved so fast Cora couldn't follow the arc of her arms and legs, and in seconds the Mosca's neck was twisted, its masked head flopping unnaturally.

In the space of one breath, it was a battle.

Mali tore Bonebreak away from the door. She was half his size but quick. Anya still looked slightly dazed, though she managed to twist out of the Mosca underling's grasp.

"Cora!" Nok called. "Get the door!"

In a daze, Cora turned her eyes toward the massive lock. It was opening on its own, little by little. Whatever the Kindred guards on the other side were doing was working. She threw herself on the lock, shoving it back into place. It bucked against her hand.

"I can't hold it for long!"

Mali came charging across the warehouse room to help, dodging Leon, who was rolling on the ground with two of the Mosca, but one of the overturned Mosca snaked out a hand and grabbed her ankle. As she slammed to the floor, the Mosca pulled out a knife.

"Mali, watch out!" Cora yelled. She fought the instinct to let go of the lock and dive for the knife. Even now, it took all her strength to hold the door.

Nok and Rolf were trying to drag Lucky to the safety of the hallway, but at Cora's cry, Nok's eyes latched onto the knife in the Mosca's hand, and she hurled herself at it.

"Nok, be careful!" Rolf let go of Lucky, who slumped against the wall, barely conscious. Rolf wrapped his hands around the Mosca's neck, pounding his fist against the creature's head. Nok sank her teeth into the Mosca's wrinkled gray skin. The Mosca let out a scream and dropped the knife, but another one picked it up before she could grab it. Lucky blinked awake just long enough to stretch out a leg, tripping the Mosca before it reached Nok. The Mosca fell on top of Lucky's midsection, hard. There was a crack like a bone breaking, and Cora winced.

"Keep an eye on Lucky!" she yelled, though everyone was occupied except Anya, who stood in the center of the room, watching everything with big eyes. "Anya, help!"

Anya looked at Lucky, who'd fallen unconscious again, but didn't move.

The lock cut into Cora's palm. Her muscles couldn't take much more.

"It's giving!" she yelled. As she pressed against the door, she threw a look over her shoulder to make sure Lucky was okay, but then the lock slipped, and she shoved against it harder. Behind her, Mali had knocked out at least three Mosca and was launching herself at another. Leon's right arm was covered in blood, as he swung his left fist with a roar. Nok and Rolf were trying to hold off the rest with the knife that they'd finally managed to wrench away. And Bonebreak . . .

"Where's Bonebreak?" Cora yelled.

A half second later, a figure barreled out of the shadows. Bonebreak threw himself against her. The lock slid open two inches before Cora could shove it closed.

Bonebreak straightened—as much as he could with his hunchback—and flexed his massive fist. He raised it, and time seemed to slow. Beyond him, the fight was turning in the Mosca's favor; Mali was breathing so hard she looked faint. Leon's pace had slowed. Anya still stood wide-eyed in the center of the room. One of the Mosca got the knife from Nok and pinned her and Rolf to the ground. Leon's bloody arm hung limply by his side.

A terrible certainty gripped Cora.

We're going to lose.

She spun toward the only person left and yelled, "Anya, do something!"

Time sped back to the present, just as Bonebreak swiped up one of the planks and slammed it down. Cora hurled herself toward the floor, throwing herself over Lucky to protect him from the plank.

She braced for impact as memories assaulted her.

The cherry blossoms.

Lucky.

Home.

The impact never came.

After a few surreal seconds, she dared to look up. Bonebreak was standing perfectly still, the plank frozen in midswing; even the expression on his face was as frozen as a wax statue's. One by one, the other Mosca turned to statues as well, as though a witch had cast an enchantment over them. The one hurling a fist toward Leon slowed in time until the fist stopped an inch from his face. Leon scrambled out from under it, shaking himself like a dog. The ones holding Nok and Rolf to the floor looked like immovable bookends. Mali took the opportunity to kick one to the ground, where it clunked heavily.

"What the . . . ?" Cora whispered. She clung to Lucky. He was mumbling aloud, though his breathing had a sort of hitch to it—he'd definitely broken a rib when that Mosca had landed on him. "Hey, stay with me. We're going to patch you up."

The door lock suddenly jerked.

She turned with a gasp. Whatever had frozen the Mosca hadn't worked on the Kindred guards beyond the door. The lock groaned until it was nearly open. Cora lunged for it, but her feet slipped on a slick of blood—was that *Lucky's* blood? Was it worse than just a broken rib?

"No!" She scrambled toward the door on all fours, but it was too late. The door lock groaned one more time, and then—*click.* Horror filled her as it began to open. An inch. Then two. Kindred faces appeared. Black eyes and copper skin. Hands reaching toward her.

She balled up in terror, her hands over her head.

Suddenly Bonebreak dropped the plank. It cluttered to the floor harmlessly. His hand curled into a fist and in two jerky steps he shoved the door closed with explosive power. The Kindred guards pounded on the other side with renewed force, but Bonebreak braced the lock with impossible strength. His jaw still had the wax-sculpture slackness. His movements were strange and twitchy, as though he wasn't in control of his own body.

Cora reached out a shaky hand to grab Lucky's shirt, worried by his halting breath. He winced and pressed a groggy hand to his ribs; she cupped his cheek, trying to see into his eyes.

"Lucky. Stay with me. Say something."

"Ouch," he mumbled.

She let out a cry of relief just to hear him speak. But then, without warning, one of the other frozen Mosca—the one with its fist an inch from Leon's face—lowered its hand and stood at attention like a toy soldier.

"Uh . . ." Leon poked the Mosca, which didn't move. "What the hell is going on?"

"It's Anya," Cora breathed, clutching Lucky tighter. "She's doing this, isn't she? She's taken them over."

Mali gently pressed a hand on Anya's shoulder. Lucky still hadn't opened his eyes, and Cora didn't dare leave his side.

"How's that possible?" Nok asked.

"She's psycho," Leon said.

"I think you mean *psychic*," Rolf said. "And highly telekinetic, apparently. This ability exceeds anything we've seen the Kindred do."

"Call off the Kindred guards," Mali said to Anya. "Use the other Mosca to lead them away."

Anya's head turned robotically. The wax-sculpture Mosca underlings started to move. It was as unnatural as the way Bonebreak had moved. Foot over foot. Bodies swaying. Arms hanging uselessly. Like a puppet master, Anya conducted them over the uneven floor as they moved in jerky steps toward the exit. A sound came from one of their mouths—something like a garbled scream that sounded really, really pissed off.

"That's it!" Nok said, clapping. "She's doing it!"

"Make them scatter throughout the nearby hallways," Mali instructed. "They must distract the Kindred guards away from the door."

Anya's face flickered with strain. Her small fingers shook with a bad tremor, but she managed to move them like she was working controls, as she choreographed the Mosca underlings to sashay toward the exit, where they stumbled through the door with clomping footsteps. The Kindred must have either heard them or sensed them, because the pounding at the door stopped.

Nok pressed her ear against the door. "It worked," she said, and then made a face as she got a whiff of Bonebreak, the only Mosca remaining in the warehouse. "Now we seriously need to get out of here."

Lucky was groaning a little. Waking, which was good. Cora started to reach for his jacket to get a better look at his wound, but footsteps sounded behind her.

Anya was pointing her trembling hands at Bonebreak, making him walk.

"Time to go," she said aloud.

It was the first time Cora had heard her real voice, which matched the whispers in her head. Singsongy, childlike, as though all this was just a big game. Step by step, Bonebreak headed around the corner of the warehouse, to a large flight room that contained a ship. Nok and Rolf parted uneasily to let him pass and then followed behind. Anya steered him to the ship, where his hand mechanically traced a symbol on the hull.

The ship's door hissed open.

Slowly, Bonebreak took jerky steps up the ladder and disappeared into the ship. There were a few seconds of silence, and then a rumble, and then the ship's lights flickered on.

"What now?" Nok asked, looking stunned.

Cora dug her fingers into Lucky's shoulders. She had seen his eyes flicker open for a second, but they were closed again. She gently tucked a stray piece of his dark hair behind his ear.

"Now?" she said. "Now we go home while we have the chance."

40

Lucky

LUCKY WOKE WITH THE worst headache of his life.

It wasn't like a hangover. It felt more like he'd been running a marathon every day and hadn't slept in weeks—so tired even his bones felt exhausted. Waves of pain rippled from his ribs, and he tried to sit up but nearly passed out. This was worse than the time he'd been kicked in the shoulder by a horse. Worse than the time he'd crashed his motorcycle into a ditch and ended up with four broken bones and twenty-seven stitches.

He blinked his eyes open, unsure what he was looking at. A ceiling. White. Smooth. Not like the ceiling of his cell at the Hunt, which had been bars. Not like the Kindred's austere church-like hallways. He tried to blink through his swimming vision and saw Leon nearby, cradling a shoulder that bulged out like it was dislocated, and Nok climbing up through some sort of hatch. There were two chairs in the room, facing a wide screen, almost like in an aircraft. A dripping sound came from places he couldn't see.

He closed his eyes again, trying to remember what had happened. He'd been in his cell. Writing in his journal. And then something about a fight. Cora, brushing his hair off his face. Maybe they were hiding out in this aircraft. He must have been wounded at some point—that pain in his ribs was killer.

Someone—well, some*thing*—was sitting in one of the chairs. It wore a mask and a dirty red jumpsuit, and from the way it was hunched, it didn't look human.

Lucky rested his head back against the floor. A crumpled teddy bear with half the stuffing poking out sat inexplicably next to him. Was he . . . hallucinating? He didn't have the strength to reach out to the bear; just that one small attempt to sit up had nearly made him vomit.

"Get us out of here," someone was saying. He blinked until he could see Mali standing over the alien in the chair. "This ship is Axion technology," she said, drumming on the curved interior walls with her knuckles. "Stolen, I think."

Ship? Why would they hide out in a ship?

"Kid snatchers," Leon grumbled, rubbing his sore shoulder and pointing to some cages that had been soldered to the walls. "Bonebreak must have retrofitted the ship for runs to Earth."

Lucky closed his eyes again. So that creature in the chair was Bonebreak. Waves of blackness shivered over him. He winced through the pain until he saw Cora climb up through the hatch and close it behind her.

Cora.

The others.

They were all safe. All together.

Bonebreak grumbled from behind his mask, and Lucky

opened one heavy eyelid. It sounded something like *dogs* or *logs*, but then a girl he didn't know, tiny, short hair, nine or ten years old, jerked her fingers—she was missing two and her hands were shaking badly—and Bonebreak's voice turned to garbles again. That must be Anya. But when had Cora freed her? How had ... how had he even gotten here?

Anya twitched her small fingers again, and Bonebreak jerkily removed his glove, then traced a few symbols into the control panel; other controls seemed to move on their own—either Bonebreak was moving them with his mind or Lucky was truly hallucinating now.

Leon was pacing unsteadily, cradling his shoulder like it was hurt. "How's she know how to work the controls?" he snapped, jerking his head toward Anya.

"She does not know how," Mali answered. "*Bonebreak* knows how. His mind is still alert. She merely commands him what to do, and he is using his own knowledge to do it."

"Can you get him to make the windshield visible, Anya?" Cora asked.

Anya concentrated on Bonebreak. His fingers stiffly worked a few more controls, and the windshield flickered.

Cora sank into the second pilot's seat, eyes wide. "My god ..."

The others went running to the front to see. Lucky tried to stand, but just the thought of moving was painful.

"Kindred," Leon grunted, looking at the screen. "Those bastards have made it into the flight room. Dozens of them."

"They are well armed," Rolf observed. A second later, as though to prove his point, the ship rocked violently. Nok let out a cry, then smacked Bonebreak in the shoulder.

"Get us out of here already!"

Bonebreak let out another tense grumble of disapproval. It was louder this time, almost a full curse, as though he was regaining control over his body.

"Anya cannot sustain this level of mental control much longer," Mali warned. "Her mind will give out eventually, as well as her hands. The Kindred drugs damaged them."

"She has to keep it up." Cora spun around in the second pilot's chair. "At least until we're out of here."

The ship rocked again, as something hit it from the outside. Their voices began to fade into the background, like that mysterious dripping sound. Lucky's ears had started ringing. He readjusted his hold on his ribs.

Damn, but it stung.

Suddenly the ship rumbled. Nok cried out and tried to grab ahold of something, but the walls were perfectly smooth. She and Rolf stumbled over to where the cages had been retrofitted in and clutched onto the bars.

"That's a good idea," Cora said. "Everyone hold on to the bars."

Lucky reached out to halfheartedly grab at a cage, but his fingers didn't reach. The ship rumbled again. The teddy bear slid slowly toward the left. He felt a sudden wave of dizziness, and his head hit the wall.

"Ow."

"Lucky, you're awake!" Cora sank to his side. Her soft hands touched his forehead. She reached gently toward his bloody jacket, which he refused to let her touch. How did she always manage to smell like flowers? "You have to hold on to something too," Cora whispered. "We don't know how fast this thing goes."

Lucky pressed a hand harder against his ribs. The idea of crawling over to the cages seemed impossible. His legs were still attached—he could see that when he lifted his head, even with his blurry vision—but for some reason he couldn't feel them.

"Where are we going?" he muttered, voice sounding distant.

Cora scooted over to cradle his head in her lap—when had he slumped to the floor?—and had one leg pressed against the captain's chair to brace them steady. Her fingers brushed his hair back tenderly. Should he tell her that this was his dream? Sitting like this under the cherry tree, his head in her lap, back on his granddad's farm?

Ow.

There was pain in his cheek. Someone was slapping him. "Stay with me," Cora was saying.

He coughed violently. If only this damn bullet wasn't in his side. He couldn't even remember which guest had hunted him— was it Roshian? Cassian? No, that wasn't right, Cassian never hunted. Wait, they were still in the Hunt, right?

". . . going home," Cora said.

The words sank into him like a punch, and his heart began to thump with panic. Home. *Home?* He tried to sit up. No, no, there was something wrong about home. Some reason they weren't supposed to go back, but he couldn't quite remember.

"Wait. I think . . ." He fumbled until he found Cora's shoulder, and traced it up to her face. "I think we were . . ."

"Shh." Around them, the world rocked and bucked, but not here beneath the cherry tree. In the distance, Rolf lost his footing and smacked against the wall. His head connected with a crunch, and Nok shrieked.

Anya's face twisted harder in concentration. Bonebreak's hands snapped back into position, moving faster. The world jolted as the ship lifted, and Lucky's fingers fumbled against Cora's face.

"You'll be okay," she was saying. "Bonebreak says . . . emergency medical kit . . . once we're away from the station . . ."

The teddy bear slid back the other way and stopped by his face. He felt a sudden welling of panic. *Wait.* It wasn't a teddy bear. It was that little fox that liked to chew on wooden statues he stole from the lodge, only someone had torn out all its stuffing, and there was so much blood that he felt he couldn't bear such pain.

Then he remembered why they couldn't go home.

"This is wrong. The animals—"

"We're flying!" someone yelled.

Cora twisted around to look, and fear shot through him that she was going to pull away. He dug his fingers into her shoulder and forced words up his throat. "I tried to tell you. We shouldn't leave, don't you see? Earth doesn't need us. They need us here. The animals. The kids. Where's Pika? And Shoukry? We can't just leave—"

Cora was saying something he couldn't make out. Something placating and reassuring about having no choice but to leave, about Cassian being arrested, about the Kindred finding out she had killed Roshian.

She didn't understand!

"No!" he spit out. "No, there's another way." He reached a bloody hand into his pocket for Dane's torn-out journal pages. "We'll regret it if we leave them. You think we'll go home and just forget everyone we left behind?"

She stared at the blood-stained journal with wide eyes.

Other voices crackled nearby.

"... don't see any exit or bay ..."

"How are we ...? Oh ... *shit.*"

The voice morphed into a scream. Lucky's stomach shot to his throat as his head swam. They were falling. Plunging into nothing, rapidly. He'd been on a roller coaster before—the free-falling kind. This was a hundred times worse. The teddy bear tumbled away. So did the journal. Cora was clutching him, or maybe he was clutching her. Falling, falling ...

And then they stopped abruptly.

The screaming stopped, but the ringing in his ears didn't. The ship didn't seem to be falling anymore, though it vibrated in a rumbling sort of way, like a train over tracks.

"Space!" someone yelled. "Look! We're ... stars!"

A *thunk* sounded.

And then—

"Anya!"

Lucky's vision was blackening around the edges, and the angles all seemed wrong and he couldn't tell who was talking. Was Anya walking on the wall? No ... she had collapsed. She was unconscious on the floor.

"Oh god, is she dead?" someone else shrieked.

For a second, a horrifying second, Cora was gone. The cherry tree smell turned to smoke; the petals landing on his ribs singed him with little jolts of pain. He reached out a hand for the fox. Or for Cora. Or for one of the many faces that came to him, the animals and the kids all mixed together.

"Look out for Bonebreak!" someone screamed. "He's getting control again!"

There was a swirl of commotion, but it mostly stuck to the black edges of his vision. He saw a knife in Nok's hand. Rolf and Leon hurling themselves toward Bonebreak, who was out of his chair now and had stopped moving in that robotic way.

Mali leaning over Anya's limp body, shaking her.

Lucky tried to speak. *Let him take us back, they need us there! We can fight!*—but a ricochet of pain silenced him. No one was paying attention to him anyway. Another searing wave of pain hit his ribs. For the first time, Lucky peeled back the jacket and looked at his side. The safari uniform had split down a seam; there was dark, gooey blood. When he moved, more blood came. He picked at one of the shirt's knots until it came loose, and pain shot through him, as something else seemed to tumble out of his side. Was that *bone*?

"I . . . I think I'm dying."

His voice sounded surprised even to his own ears.

Cora twisted to him, her beautiful blond hair whipping around like wheat on his granddad's farm. The color of sunlight. The color of warmth.

She looked down at his jacket and screamed.

Then the black around the edges of his vision poured into the center, and there was only darkness.

41

Cora

"NO!"

Cora collapsed onto the floor next to Lucky. A second ago, Bonebreak's regaining control of his body had been her worst nightmare; but that was nothing compared to the bloody mess spilling out of Lucky's jacket.

She slid her hands around his neck, scared to touch him too hard. "Lucky. Wake up!" His body felt so heavy. "You have to wake up!"

Behind her, Nok gave a surprised cry. Cora glanced around just long enough to see the others trying to wrestle Bonebreak back under control near the front of the ship. Leon was as good as useless with his dislocated shoulder, and Nok and Rolf each weighed about as much as one of Bonebreak's legs. They needed help, but Cora didn't dare tear herself away from Lucky.

"Mali!" Cora yelled. "You need to wake up Anya *now*."

But one look at Anya's splayed body, blood caked in her nose, said she wasn't waking soon. Cora's mind spun. Anya . . . Bone-break . . . Nothing seemed to matter as much as this boy bleeding out on the floor.

"Lucky," she choked. "Please, talk to me."

A few words garbled up his throat. His body spasmed and suddenly he was breathing again, though blood came up with his gasps for air.

"The journal," Lucky said in a weak voice. "I need it. Notes inside . . . could help . . ."

The journal? She looked around blankly. That notebook he'd taken from his pocket . . .

She shoved to her feet, searching for it in the chaos. There—under Bonebreak's foot. Cora darted for it. She had to duck as Bonebreak got a hand free; she slammed her fist into his shin and snatched the journal from under his foot, then scrambled back to Lucky.

"Here. I've got it. You're going to be okay. Just tell me what to do."

The book felt too small in her hands; surely a few scribbled notes couldn't save him. Her eyes widened at the mess of his mid-section. The skin was torn; gone in some places. Half a rib jutted out, the end broken off.

"The torn-out pages . . . ," Lucky muttered. "It's a manual override."

Manual override?

How was an override going to save his life? She flipped anxiously to the last page and skimmed over handwriting that wasn't his. There weren't any descriptions of medical procedures for stopping bleeding, only a diagram of symbols like the ones the

Kindred used to open locked cabinets.

"You have to go back." He coughed. "Dane wrote the notes. The manual override codes open a compartment in the medical room. There are weapons, in case the animals get out of control."

"Weapons?" she whispered.

"I was only going to use them as a last resort. Put the animals out of their misery . . . if . . . things got bad." He strained for breath. "I still had hope for the Gauntlet. But now . . ." He winced and shook his head. "There's kill-dart guns. Powerful enough for an elephant. Powerful enough for a Kindred, I'm sure."

She sank to the floor, stunned.

What did she care about weapons now, while he was dying? She had hoped the scrawled pages contained information to save him. She could barely even think about the station now, or what weapons would have meant.

He coughed louder.

The journal fell out of her slack hand. It slid away as the ship lurched, but she didn't lunge for it.

He was going to die.

She collapsed over on top of him, not worried about being too fragile now. Warm blood soaked into her dress.

"Cora!" Leon bellowed. "We need you!"

The others didn't know about Lucky. From the corner of her eye, she saw Bonebreak by the control panel, twitching as if he still wasn't used to his own body. He squeezed his fingers into a fist, again and again, until his fingers obeyed his head. Dread sweated down Cora's face.

She turned back to Lucky.

His lips moved; blood came up, not words, and she pressed

a finger to his mouth. "Shh. Don't try to talk."

"Go back," he choked. "You can't leave the others behind. Use the weapons."

There was such utter conviction behind his voice. As though he'd crawled back to life—just for this second—because this one thing was so very important.

"Shh . . . ," she started, but unsure this time. "We can't go back, Lucky. A few dart guns aren't going to make a difference. They'll arrest me just like they did Cassian. The Gauntlet and everything else . . . it's over. Cassian was right. Not giving up is noble only as long as it doesn't get us killed. At some point, we have to think logically."

"Logic?" Lucky said. "No. We're not Kindred. We don't give up when it's something that matters. This is our place. This is our cause." His fingers clenched onto her as though someone was trying to rip her away. "Go back, Cora."

She stared in stunned horror. Go *back*? She thought of that glimpse she'd had of Cassian, screaming in pain as they tortured him. Of Fian, who had turned on her. Even if there really were weapons they could use, how could she possibly go back to that chaos?

She let out a sharp exhale. A tear landed on Lucky's cheek.

"I can't," she pleaded, though she didn't know anymore who she was trying to convince. Lucky's eyes were closed. His hand—fingers so weak, like an old man's—slid down to cradle her hand. "We have to give up."

He took in a long breath, then breathed out.

And he didn't inhale again.

"No!" she threw herself back on top of him. "No, you can't leave me! I can't handle this, Lucky. I can't do it . . . I can't go back there." She sobbed into his bloody chest. It wasn't true, the things he was saying. At some point, the battle was too great to be fought. Besides, she *did* have a purpose on Earth. Being with her family was as good a cause as any, wasn't it?

Another sob shook her. She thought of her dad watching the news on the downstairs television; her mother drinking wine on the porch. She could see it so clearly. There would be framed photographs of her on the walls, a shrine of cards and newspaper articles. They had lost their child; wasn't that cause enough to go back to them?

Wasn't it?

His body was still warm. If she closed her eyes, she could pretend he was just asleep, but the taste of blood reached her mouth and she gagged.

A slow sound started to come from Bonebreak's mask. It started as a high-pitched note; then it grew louder and louder: ". . . kill you childrens!"

And then he was lunging for her—a shadow out of nowhere, fractured mask eyes and clawing fingers. She screamed and rolled out of his way. His hands were still sluggish, but he was moving rapidly, fury propelling him forward.

"I will kill you!" he hissed. "All of you childrens! I will break your bones!"

He lunged for her again. The inside of the ship was too tight; there was nowhere to go. Lucky's body. So much blood.

Bonebreak loomed over her. He held up his fist with glee.

Mali lunged forward to help, but the ship pitched sharply with no one at the controls, and she fell back against the wall.

A teddy bear tumbled across Cora's line of vision. *What*

the . . . ? She felt like she was in a dream; no, a nightmare. It was all wrong. Lucky . . . She couldn't even look at him. And his words in her ears: *This is our place. This is our cause.*

The teddy bear tumbled onto something silver. Cora's heart thumped. The gun! Anya must have had it. She scrambled for it. Bonebreak was hissing behind her, tailing her like a shadow. At last, her fingers curled around the familiar shape. It was smaller than the ones she'd fired with her dad at the NRA rally, but it couldn't be that complicated. Aim. Squeeze. Fire.

She spun around, aiming the gun at Bonebreak. He came hissing to a stop, but then cackled. "That is Kindred technology. You cannot operate it."

"Try me," she hissed back, hoping the lie sounded convincing, and jerked her head toward Anya's unconscious body. "She moved you around like a toy, or don't you remember? She isn't the only with those abilities."

Bonebreak's head cocked slightly, as though considering her words. Something warm seeped into her clothes; Lucky's blood. It had rolled all the way to the other side of the ship, and her stomach lurched, but she forced her hand to keep the gun steady.

"Yes. I remember." Bonebreak's voice turned hard. "But none of the rest of you are capable of telekinesis, or else I wouldn't have gotten my mind back." He chuckled to himself, a grating high-pitched wheeze.

The blood thumped in Cora's ears. He'd called her bluff. She tried pulling the trigger, but nothing happened. She prodded the inside of the gun with her mind, wrapping her thoughts around the intricate mechanics. If Anya had figured out how to fire it, then surely she could too. But Anya was a prodigy. A few sessions with

Cassian and a pair of dice hadn't prepared Cora for this.

"Cora," Nok said, low and warning. "Your nose."

Cora tasted the bite of her blood on her lips but ignored it.

"I *can* fire it," she insisted, spitting blood.

Bonebreak snorted. "Then fire."

Her mind prodded and prodded. How did it work? Magnetics? Moving parts? She thought of the training steps: moving the dice, then levitating them. She had barely made it past nudging, let alone . . .

Levitation.

The last time she'd trained with Cassian, she'd levitated a die six inches. A far cry from a five-pound gun, but it was a starting point. Concentrating as hard as she could, she took her index finger off the trigger. Then her middle finger. The gun was heavy, but she gritted her teeth and focused. She removed her ring finger. Then—taking a deep breath—her pinky and her thumb.

The gun hovered in the air.

Cora was so shocked that she nearly forgot to breathe. "You see?" she hissed. "I *do* have abilities! I can fire this gun too; and I will, unless you get us back on course."

Bonebreak let out a surprised grunt, and her fears thundered in her ears. Did he sense the bluff?

The ship was silent, save for the sounds of Nok's labored breathing and a hum of machinery. Cora's blood pulsed harder. It took every ounce of her concentration to keep the hovering gun aimed at Bonebreak. Her attention was slipping. Cassian said she needed to be able to levitate an object for thirty seconds, but only five or ten had passed, and her mind already ached. She couldn't hold on forever. . . .

Bonebreak sat heavily in the captain's chair. He cracked his knuckles, then wiggled his fingers in the air, getting ready to operate the controls. When he spoke, his voice was light and jovial, as though all this had been a prank.

"Earth?" he said. "No problem. I wanted to go to Earth anyway—didn't I mention that?"

Cora reached out for the gun a second before it fell. Her mind let go all at once, and she slumped over, trying hard not to reveal how much it had cost her. She wiped her wrist under her bleeding nose and collapsed in the second pilot's chair next to Bonebreak, trying hard not to think about the boy on the floor.

"Then get us out of here. Now."

42

Cora

THE SHIP GAVE A low rumble as it glided through space. For hours as they flew, the same image showed through the viewing screen: blackness with stars in the distance, the halo of a nearby moon on the right side of the screen.

Bonebreak worked the controls wordlessly, lazily spinning a finger on a trace pad, occasionally flipping levers with his mind. If he was furious, it didn't show. *Everything is a whim for them . . . betraying a promise or keeping it,* Cassian had warned. Cora just hoped Bonebreak's calm lasted until they reached her solar system. In her own heart, calm was the last thing she felt.

Once the others had realized that Lucky had died, they'd all fallen into denial, and then a sort of shock. Nok had helped her clean up the blood and drape a tarp they found in the ship's facilities room over his chest. Now they all huddled near the captain's chair, faces expressionless, no words exchanged. Cora stroked Lucky's dark hair, picking out the dried crusts of blood, trying to ignore how cold his skin had grown.

"How long until we get to our galaxy?" Rolf asked Bonebreak quietly.

Bonebreak flipped another lever. "Settle in. I hope you brought snacks."

Rolf's fingers tapped anxiously against the floor. "This trip is very risky, when we do not even know if our planet is there."

"It's there," Cora said softly.

"How are you certain?" Rolf asked.

"A boy named Chicago overheard the Kindred talking about the algorithm having been changed. Cassian looked into it for me." She pressed her lips together, thinking of that awful scene of him tortured. "He said there's almost a seventy percent chance humans haven't destroyed Earth."

Rolf reflected on this for a moment. "Almost seventy is not one hundred."

Nok placed a hand on his shoulder. "Sometimes it's not about the numbers. It's about faith."

Cora kept stroking Lucky's hair. She still clutched the gun in her other hand—just to remind Bonebreak who was in control. The tear in the back of her head was throbbing, low and dull, but persistent. She glanced over her shoulder. Mali had laid Anya flat and was rubbing the girl's feet with a circular motion that she explained promoted blood flow. Leon had removed his Kindred uniform and managed to reset his shoulder himself, and was now sewing up a wound on his arm with the Mosca's black thread.

Cora kissed Lucky on the forehead and then drew the white tarp over his face. She scooted back against the wall and squeezed his journal tightly.

Mali watched her from across the room.

"Did you know about this?" Cora asked, holding up the journal.

Mali nodded. "I hear him writing sometimes. At night. It was a gift from Dane."

Cora sat in the second pilot's chair, ignoring Bonebreak's smell that kept the others away. Her mind turned to riding in a car, years ago. Her father behind the wheel, her head on the cool glass window, as they drove home from a political fund-raiser. The night he'd had too much to drink. The night that she had lied to protect him, which had kicked off a series of events that had led to this very moment.

Squeezing Lucky's journal, she let her chest rise and fall.

They were going home—but at a heavy cost.

A sob started to crawl up her throat again. She felt herself on the verge of shattering, and knit her hands together to keep them from shaking.

A fantasy played out in her head:

Lucky, alive and well, appears at her side, looking worn out but stable as he drags a weary hand through his hair. "Did we actually . . . did we actually do it?" His eyes sparkle.

"Yeah," she whispers, smiling. "Yeah, we did."

His grin mirrors her own. He lets out a breath, shaking his head like he still can't believe it. "I just . . ." He lets out a laugh. "I can't . . ." He raises his hands in wonder.

Cora grasps his hands, squeezing tight. She meets his eyes. "I know. We're going home."

He pulls her out of the chair, wrapping his hands around her back. She leans into his chest, breathing deep. "How are we going to explain where we've been?"

"We pretend we don't remember." His breath is reassuring as it whispers against her ear. "And we'll have each other. You and me. We'll make sure we remember."

Bonebreak let out a garbled sneeze beside her, and Cora flinched out of her fantasy. Coldness started to creep back in as she glanced at the tarp. Shakily, she opened the notebook. In addition to Dane's instructions about the weapons, Lucky had written his own thoughts in it too, and she imagined those long sleepless nights backstage, all the fears and hopes that must have been running through his head.

Today I brought a gazelle back to life. . . .

Cora trained again today with the Caretaker. She won't talk about it. . . .

I keep thinking tomorrow will be my birthday. No, tomorrow. No, tomorrow . . .

And then:

How can we just leave them all behind?

She slammed the journal closed. Panic was crawling up her throat again, as his words kept ringing into her ears. This is our place. This is our cause.

She picked at her lip, looking out the viewing screen at the stars hanging in the blackness. One of them might be their sun.

One of them might even be Earth. It was out there, waiting. She could feel it. But why was there that little nag in the back of her head?

"How many humans are on the Kindred's stations?" she asked Bonebreak.

He shrugged. "A few thousand."

"And animals?"

He thought for a moment. "Double that."

Cora knit her fingers together harder, thinking. The Kindred's tattoos on her palms flashed. Even now, they had their mark on her.

She wiped at the marks on her fingers, wishing she could rub them away, especially the ornate one on her ring finger. Why had Cassian altered her markings, if not to make some twisted declaration of love with a ring? She kept rubbing. There was more than black on her hands. There was blood there, too.

She remembered Cassian's final words. *This is where you give up, Cora.*

She squeezed her fingers together harder. She had never really noticed before that the way her fingers interlaced formed a sort of natural zigzag. Strangely, the black lines of the markings at the bases of her fingers matched up, too. They met at the same place her fingers met, forming a zigzag exactly opposite the one formed by her fingers.

She drew in a sharp breath.

It made a double helix—the symbol of the Fifth of Five.

And the circular symbols at the base of each finger, which she had dismissed as incomprehensible coding, formed a series of circles in the center of that double helix. And maybe the symbols *were* true coding—after all, all the other humans had something similar—except for the larger circle on her ring finger that no one else had. She'd accused Cassian of designing it like a diamond ring. But now she saw the truth.

The double helix.

Five circles in the middle.

The last one—the one on her ring finger—radiating not like a diamond, but like a star. The *fifth* star. Humanity.

She clenched her hands together to hide the markings and pressed her fists against her mouth. All this time she had thought the markings were some elaborate puzzle, Cassian still manipulating her, and it *was* a puzzle. But it wasn't about twisted ideas of love, like she and Lucky had thought.

It was a message of hope.

A promise.

I believe in you, Cassian had said. *In all humans. Your species has the capacity for such rich emotions; selfishness and greed, yes, but also truth and forgiveness and sacrifice. When you believe in a cause, nothing can stop you. If anyone deserves to be the fifth intelligent species, it is you.*

She pictured that final image of him strapped to the table. A pain started somewhere beneath her ribs, and she shifted in the chair, but it didn't go away. She gripped the edge of the control panel, searching the stars for the pinprick of light that might be Earth.

She had earned home, hadn't she? She needed home, didn't she? *But,* Lucky's voice whispered in her head, *does home need you?*

She let out a shaky breath. Lucky had been delirious. It wasn't fair of him to hold her to impossible standards. Noble missions were for people like him. Like her father.

She looked down at the secret symbol on her hands again.

Cassian, who had risked so much already, had risked this small defiance too.

Over her shoulder, she saw Nok and Rolf holding hands, in silence. Mali was still massaging Anya, who had started to mumble. Lucky's tarp was so terribly, tellingly still.

She clenched his notebook. Did he truly believe that their purpose was back on that station?

Did *she*?

An overwhelming wave of panic gripped her. She ran a hand over her forehead, shaking her head back and forth. This was crazy. The only factors they had working in their favor were a cache of dart guns and a few humans who'd covered for them before. And yet, wasn't that what it meant to be human? To take chances that weren't always logical? To not give up, if there was even the slightest hope?

She spun around in the chair. Leon frowned at the look on her face. Mali stopped rubbing Anya's feet. Nok and Rolf blinked with grief-stricken eyes.

"I've been thinking," Cora blurted out.

Her voice caught up to her all at once. She cleared her throat and looked back at her knit fingers that displayed the Fifth of Five symbol.

"I think we should turn around."

THE SHIP PITCHED SHARPLY to the side without warning. Cora's head connected with the control panel with a starburst of pain. She reached out a hand, feeling for the wall. The others were yelling, but her ears were ringing too loudly to hear them. The ship pitched again and her foot connected with something large as she tumbled to the ground.

The ship abruptly righted again.

"What are you doing?" Nok yelled at Bonebreak.

"Girl says turn us around," he answered. "I turned us around."

"We need to discuss this first!" Rolf said.

Cora blinked through the black dots until her vision began to clear. There was a pale shape in front of her with sweat-soaked hair. Her stomach clenched—she had tripped over Lucky's body.

Nok spun on her. "Are you crazy? Why would we go back?"

Cora pulled herself back into the second pilot's chair and gripped the seat tightly. "Just hear me out." She spoke cautiously, knowing how unpopular the idea would be. "This is bigger than us. This is about proving that we're more than the Kindred think we are."

Bonebreak chuckled.

Cora threw him a sharp look. "Just keep steering."

"Cora is right." It was Anya, her eyes cracked open, though her gaze still looked hazy. "Running away solves nothing."

"Says the girl who's been drugged for years," Leon muttered. "No offense, kid, but you have some catching up to do."

"Just because I was drugged," Anya countered, "doesn't mean I didn't know what was going on. I saw it all. Every corner of the station. Even *yours*."

That shut Leon up.

Cora went over to where Anya sat. "You can really tell what's going on throughout the station, just with your mind?"

"Not all the time," Anya said, rubbing her forehead. "But when I was drugged, I could. The Kindred thought drugging me would dull my mind, but it just showed me how to unlock it in new ways." She looked down at her trembling hands. "Even if it did leave me damaged."

Rolf pushed up from the floor. "You're all forgetting the most important thing: it will be impossible to beat the Gauntlet now. We've missed it. Today is the day it began, and besides, guards will arrest you—*all* of us—if we go back."

Nok tucked a pink strand of her hair behind one ear. "Rolf's right. There's nothing we can do."

Cora tapped a finger on Lucky's notebook, taking a deep breath. "There *is* something we can do. Lucky had codes to access a weapons cache. He was planning on using it after the Gauntlet to rescue the animals from the Hunt. But we can use it too."

"What, to fight?" Nok cried. "Six of us against a Kindred army? That's crazy!"

"There are hundreds of Kindred loyal to Cassian on the station too, already in place to launch a revolution. They're called the Fifth of Five. We just have to get to them."

"So . . . you're suggesting suicide," Leon said. "For us *and* for them."

Cora threw him a look. "I'm suggesting we finish what we started."

"And you think partnering with some rebels means we'll be safe?" Rolf asked. "There's a reason Cassian was doing all this secretly—he knew as well as we do that the Council doesn't want humans on their level."

"Stop. Just stop." Nok sank into the second pilot's chair that Cora had vacated. "I understand that it isn't easy to leave all those people back there, yeah? Maybe we could help them and maybe we couldn't . . . but we *can't* go back." She pressed her hands against her abdomen. "There's no way I'm having my baby there."

"She's right," Rolf said. "It's one thing to ask us to risk our lives and our freedom, but you can't ask us to risk our child's too."

Cora paced, rubbing her aching forehead. She kept throwing glances at Lucky's body, unable to believe he was truly gone. She slumped against the wall.

"Ah, screw it." Leon stood up. "I'm with you."

43

Mali

MALI LOOKED IN SURPRISE at Leon, who was still clutching his banged-up shoulder. "You are?" she asked.

Leon jerked his chin toward Lucky's body. "The Caretaker said we each were the best at something, right? You know, Rolf's smart and Nok's hot and I'm the most perfect physical specimen out of all the people in the world—"

"I'm not sure those were his *exact* words," Rolf muttered.

"But then there was Lucky. He was supposed to be the moral one. And those first few weeks, I never got it. Moral? I don't know what he did back on Earth, but it wasn't bake sales, eh?" He rubbed his shoulder, eyeing the white tarp. "But now I get it. Giving up always sat uneasy with him. He was a fighter. He would have fought for this."

A strange sensation was happening inside Mali's chest. She had never quite experienced it before; it was like her heart was not beating steadily when she looked at Leon. It was both uncomfortable and strangely pleasant at the same time.

Was this how falling in love felt?

Leon waved toward Nok and Rolf. "If you don't want to help, fine. Stay on the ship."

"I don't want to be alone with him!" Nok threw a finger toward Bonebreak.

"She is right," Mali interrupted. "We should not separate. It has taken us a long time to finally be together again. And also I think we are stronger as a group." She paused. "A *hell* of a lot stronger."

She smiled to herself, proud of her first successful use of cursing.

Anya reached out and squeezed her hand. Strength in numbers was an idea Anya had often talked about, back when they'd been trapped by the same private owner. Even at a young age, Anya had cared enough about freeing humanity to fight for it. At the time, Mali hadn't wanted to listen. She had survived for years by being on her own. But now, as she looked around the room, she understood the importance of friends.

"I won't let anything happen to Sparrow," Cora said to Nok. "I promise."

"What about you two?" Leon asked, jerking his chin toward Mali and Anya. "You in?"

When his eyes met Mali's, she recoiled a little bit as that odd heartbeat sensation grew stronger. Suddenly her mouth felt dry. She knew exactly how risky it would be to go back. She knew that if she agreed, she might never have a chance to see the desert where she was born—those hazy memories of camels and bright sun. But she also knew that the human thing to do would be to agree.

"Yes," she said, and Anya nodded as well.

Nok paced uneasily and exchanged a long look with Rolf. She sat nervously in the second pilot's chair. "I still don't like it, but I'll hear you out."

"Yeah, so what's the genius plan?" Leon said.

Cora paced across the floor. "Fian is a traitor, but Tessela isn't. If we can get back to the Hunt, we can get the dart guns, and she can alert the others. The Fifth of Five will join us."

"*That's* the extent of your plan?" Leon laid his head down on the teddy bear. "I'm regretting my decision already."

"The boy is, for once, correct," Bonebreak said. "You are thinking like a human, not a Kindred. Even if there are some loyal to your cause on the station, fighting will do nothing but get yourselves killed. They will always be stronger than you."

"It's the only option we have," Cora said.

"It isn't," Bonebreak said cryptically. "I can offer a better option that will not result in a war."

Mali whipped her head around to him and narrowed her eyes. "Do not trust a thing he says," she started, but Cora held up a hand for her to be quiet.

"Go on." Cora nodded for Bonebreak to continue, and Mali scowled.

Bonebreak drummed his fingers together. "Your skinny friend with the pink hair is right." He pointed a pulpy finger at Nok. "The six of you couldn't make a dent in the Kindred's army, even with weapons, and even with your little mind tricks." His voice grew cold as he glanced at Anya. "Your original plan to run the Gauntlet was wiser."

"Didn't you hear Rolf?" Cora said. "It started today. We

missed it. The module won't return to the station for another twenty years."

Bonebreak drummed his fingers together faster. Mali couldn't see his face behind the mask, but she pictured a grin that matched the creepy delight in his voice. "That is true. The Gauntlet will not return to the Kindred aggregate station number 10-91 for six hundred rotations. But that doesn't mean it doesn't go *elsewhere*. Once it leaves the Kindred's station, it happens to be headed for a Mosca planet named Drogane. I spent some time there in my youth—a lovely place. I could take you. One of you could still run it, free your species, much celebration."

The ship was so quiet that Mali could hear only Bonebreak's raspy breathing behind his mask. She curled her hands into fists. "He already betrayed us once. He will again."

Cora nodded. "Mali makes a good point, Bonebreak."

"It is true that I was going to turn you over to the Kindred, but not on a whim. They were simply offering a better deal. And I am always loyal to those who offer me the best deal. Just ask that one." He jabbed a finger in Leon's direction.

Leon snorted. "Sure, but what if it's a deal we don't want to make?"

"Just listen to my proposal, childrens. I take you to Drogane. My brother lives there; he will shelter us all in his house with his own little childrens. You must have a sponsor—I will fill this role. I will help prepare you for the Gauntlet tests, girl."

"What's in it for you?" Cora asked.

Mali paced, fighting the urge to yell at all of them that it was a very bad idea to even be considering accepting his help.

Bonebreak stood. Hunched over, he was barely taller than

Mali, but his chest was so wide he was nearly twice her size. "Exclusive trade rights. If you beat the Gauntlet, humans will be free to barter and participate in commerce. The Kindred and the Gatherers are too formal for our tastes, when it comes to business transactions. And the Axion—not even *we* like to work with them. They're frighteningly brilliant, always scheming something. You humans don't care as much about the rules—I like that. If you agree that I will be your exclusive trading partner once you gain autonomy, I will help you beat the Gauntlet, and we will all make mountains of money."

Mali kept waiting for Cora to say no. To realize that nothing was worth placing trust in Bonebreak. But Cora kept running her fingers over Lucky's journal, as though she couldn't quite get away from what he had said.

"Okay," Cora said, sounding slightly hesitant.

Shit, Mali thought, and didn't even take the time to congratulate herself on her second successful use of cursing. She spun on Cora. "This is a mistake."

"Ignore the angry one," Bonebreak said, sweeping his hand in Mali's direction. "You are making the right choice. Now, on to Drogane. It takes a half rotation, so we will need to refuel. And purchase a gift for my brother; a Mosca never sees family empty-handed."

"We don't have any more money," Cora said.

Bonebreak glanced around the room, rubbing his chin beneath the mask. "We could always chop up your friend. The dead one, I mean. He doesn't need his body anymore, and I know a black-market dealer not far from here who—"

"No!" Cora looked horrified. "Don't *touch* him."

Bonebreak cocked his head. "Your hair, then. That will pay for fuel and landing fees."

Bonebreak slid a knife out of his pocket.

"Deal." Cora grabbed the knife and strode to the facilities room in the back of the ship, slamming the door behind her, as though she was afraid she would lose her resolve.

The slam reverberated, ending the conversation in the main section of the ship. Nok and Rolf looked at each other uneasily. Leon started picking at the shielding and thread on his shoulder.

Mali paced, fears rumbling in her mind. Part of her agreed with what Lucky had said. Every time she looked at the scars on her hands she was reminded of how much humans deserved better.

But trusting a Mosca wasn't the way. The last time she had trusted a Mosca was back on Earth, when she had been four years old and watching the goats on the dunes near her family's camp. A hunchback man in a strange mask had told her a goat had run away, but he could take her to it. Not long after, she had awoken chained to a stake in a Mosca marketplace.

If you have no owner, the Mosca had said, *then I claim you for my own.*

She paced over to Anya, arms folded tight. "I do not like this," she whispered. "We have no private owner. We have no paperwork. There is nothing to stop Bonebreak from claiming us as his own property the moment we land on his planet."

Anya thought about this for a moment. "Do you remember how we got away from that Mosca scum on station 3-06?"

Mali had been twelve years old. Anya only five, but already

tough. They had been caged together by a private owner who had made them fight with other girls and a chimpanzee.

But then they'd figured a way out.

Mali nodded. "Yes. I must tell Cora. It is our only chance of ensuring that Bonebreak will not cheat us."

44

Cora

THE SHIP'S FACILITIES ROOM had no mirror, but the walls were made of a dull reflective material that projected back a murky image of her face.

She looked awful.

The oversized safari clothes she'd grabbed hung limply on her frame. They looked almost like the plain khaki uniform she had worn in juvenile detention. Her eyes were red with lack of sleep, and her face looked gaunter. Her hair was a nest of long, tangled curls.

She squeezed Bonebreak's knife in one fist and tilted her head to the left, so her hair spilled out to one side. She twisted it into a tight, thick coil that she could cut through with one slice, and set the blade against the outside strands.

It's just hair.

But it didn't feel like nothing. If she did this, it would trigger a new series of events. Bonebreak would take them to his brother's planet. They'd have to figure out how to work with him—and she'd have to continue training, without Cassian now. This was more than one slice of the knife. This was, maybe, cutting off her last chance to go home.

Sadie with her floppy old-dog ears. Charlie's bedroom that always smelled like gym clothes. The view of the woodpecker-holed maple tree outside her window.

The only way to know if home was even still there was to set the knife down and stay on this ship. The thought filled her with a new worry—had she decided to turn back because she couldn't face the reality of what they might find? A nearly 70 percent chance wasn't one hundred, as Rolf had said. Her heart thumped, hard. No. *No.* She could still feel the warmth from that sun. In her heart, she knew that Earth was still there.

She snapped her eyes open. Her reflection looked back at her with cold determination. Lucky, out of all of them, had been the one with a cause. And now it was her cause too.

She set the knife's blade against her rope of hair, just below her left ear, and started to saw.

Someone banged at the door.

Cora cursed, the knife skimming away along with only a few strands of hair. "What? I nearly stabbed myself."

Mali's face looked back. In the shadows, her eyes were hooded, and the lines around her mouth seemed heavier.

"I need to talk to you," Mali said.

Cora glanced out at the ship's cabin, where the others were discussing logistics. She nodded for Mali to come in.

"I have come to talk about Cassian."

And just like that, Cora's tension returned. Only now it was met with the guilt that pounded hard, as she remembered seeing him through the crack in the tunnel. "I saw Cassian," Cora admitted. "When we were fleeing the station in the drecktubes. They were interrogating him with some machine; it looked like torture."

The guilt pounded harder. Cassian was Mali's friend. She might never forgive Cora for just having left him there to suffer.

"I am not going to chastise you for leaving him," Mali said, as though she could read her mind.

Surprise made Cora straighten. "You aren't?"

Mali held up her scarred hands. "This is why I wish to speak to you. These scars are because I trusted a Mosca. It is a mistake to believe Bonebreak will adhere to his deal. If he gets a better offer, he will sell us the moment we set foot on his planet."

"He doesn't own us. We're wards of the Kindred state."

"Not since we left the station. We are unowned by anyone, which means Bonebreak could do whatever he wishes with us. Anya and I were once in a similar situation. We fled from our previous owner and trusted in a Mosca trader to take us to a safe preserve. He didn't. He took possession of us himself and planned on selling us back to the same owner."

The space was so tight that Cora could smell Mali's scent: salt and cotton. "What did you do?"

"We sold ourselves to someone else first. Anya coordinated it with one of the Mosca trader's underlings. He was not very clever. We were able to convince him to betray his commander. We said we'd be worth twice the price our previous owner would have paid. He fell for it, and stole a small vessel that would take us back to the Kindred's station. But the first time we stopped to refuel, Anya and I spread a rumor that there were thousands of tokens on his ship. Dozens of other Mosca swarmed to steal from him, and in the chaos, we were able to escape again." She lowered her hands, flexing the scarred fingers. "My point is, we must sell ourselves to someone else. Someone from an intelligent race who will not let Bonebreak betray us. Someone we trust."

Cora hugged her arms tightly. "Cassian."

Mali nodded. "He is the only one we can rely on." She held up Lucky's notebook, which Cora had left on the control panel. "Perhaps the weapons Lucky describes are not enough against an entire Kindred army, but they might be sufficient to free Cassian."

Cora blinked in surprise at the possibility.

"But we already talked about this," she stammered. "We can't go back there. I'll be arrested."

"*You* cannot," Mali said. "But the Kindred are not looking for me or Leon. We could go back, he and I, and free Cassian with the weapons cache."

"You've discussed this with Leon?"

"No, but he will come. He will do what is right. I know it." She lowered her voice. "Armstrong preserve is on a moon not far from here. We will pass close to it. Have Nok and Rolf insist that they be dropped off there. It will be a convincing argument that they would prefer to have their baby there, among other humans, rather than in the unpredictability of a Mosca planet. While we are there, Leon and I can sneak off. Kindred supply ships make frequent runs. We can find a way to board one back to the station."

"Armstrong?" Cora squeezed the knife harder. "That's the place Dane was talking about. He said it was a paradise, but Cassian warned me about it. Are you sure it's safe for Nok and Rolf?"

"It is the only choice we have."

Mali opened the door behind her and disappeared.

With a shaky hand, Cora set Lucky's notebook on the counter. A part of her wanted to pore over every page right then, soak up every last bit of him, even from beyond the grave. But there would be time for that; time to absorb every word, remember every detail.

She squeezed the knife hard, looked in the mirror, and cut through her hair in one slice.

It came away uneven from her shaking hand. Her reflection showed a messy asymmetrical cut, starting just under her left ear and hanging nearly to her right shoulder. She returned to the main cabin and tossed the rope of hair on the control panel in front of Bonebreak. The others paused in their conversations.

"Here. It's done. But I want to stop at Armstrong first." From the corner of her eye she saw Mali whispering the plan in Rolf's ear. "For Nok and Rolf's sake, and also to bury Lucky's body."

She squeezed the notebook harder. This was one last thing she could do for him, make sure his body rested in peace.

Bonebreak shrugged. "We need supplies anyway. To Armstrong we go, then, childrens."

He shifted the controls and the ship veered sharply upward. Cora braced against the back of his chair as he hummed a strangely melodic little tune to himself in his crackling voice. For a while, the ship rumbled on through space. An hour passed, maybe two, and Cora clutched Lucky's notebook the whole time.

"Hold on tight," Bonebreak said at last. "Entry into Armstrong's atmosphere can be bumpy."

"We should sit in a circle," Rolf said. "If we hold hands, it will provide stability."

Leon snorted. "I'm not doing that 'Kumbaya' shit."

"A circle is the most stable shape," Rolf said, and sat next to him. He held out his hand to Nok, who scooted over between him and Anya and held out her hands. Mali scooted in too, and everyone linked hands. Cora looked over her shoulder at the white tarp, and a sharp pain stabbed through her.

"Come on, Leon." She reached out.

He grumbled again as he scooted over, taking her hand in his right and Rolf's in his left. The ship suddenly pitched to the left, and they all held hands tighter, swaying with the movements.

"So what's this Armstrong place like?" Nok asked cautiously.

"It's where they send humans who turn nineteen and have been obedient," Cora said, trying to sound optimistic in case Bonebreak was listening. "Like a reward. It's a sort of nature preserve where they can govern themselves and live how they want."

Bonebreak glanced over his shoulder; she couldn't read his expression.

"Another fucking zoo," Leon grumbled.

"No," Cora added. "There aren't any bars, and the people there aren't being watched. It's the size of a small moon, and it's habitable."

"But if it's habitable," Nok said, "why don't any Kindred inhabit it? Why leave it for us?"

Cora could feel the uneasiness in Nok's words, and she felt uneasy too. She lowered her voice. "We won't leave you there if it isn't safe, Nok. I promise." And then she raised her voice for Bonebreak to hear. "The Kindred are an astral species, not terrestrial."

But that uneasy feeling reached the tear in the back of Cora's head, throbbing. She hoped she wasn't leading Nok and Rolf—and all of them—into a situation even worse than the one they'd just come from.

The ship dipped sharply. Nok shrieked, and they gripped hands harder. Bonebreak leaned forward, scratching his head, and then shoved a control upward. The ship pitched again. Cora had the feeling of free-falling. That awful rise of her stomach that made her just want to push everything down, to ball up tight, but she didn't let go of either hand. Then the free fall ended abruptly, and there was a rumbling that made her legs and arms jiggle.

"Ever flown before?" Leon barked to Bonebreak.

"I *did* kill the best pilot," Bonebreak muttered at the controls.

The ship keeled sharply to the right. Cora couldn't see the viewing panel from her place on the floor, but the colors had changed. No longer the dim shine of distant stars, but bright flashing colors, as if they were flying straight into a sunrise. Pressure built in her ears. It was the same pressure as when Cassian had materialized her out of the cage, making her body feel like it was breaking up into thousands of tiny particles, until it was all she could do to squeeze her eyes shut.

Then, abruptly, it stopped.

The ship made a winding-down sound, and the temperature cooled back to normal. Bonebreak hit a few more buttons, seeming rather satisfied with himself. "There," he said. "Perfect docking."

The ship lurched to the right, and Nok screamed.

Bonebreak adjusted a lever, and the ship righted.

"*Now.* Perfect docking."

"I think I'm going to be sick," Rolf muttered, looking pale.

Bonebreak hit a few buttons, and the door opened. A curious sound came from the open doorway.

A *sh, sh, sh* that at first Cora thought might be ocean waves. A gust of wind suddenly blew up through the hold, carrying fine, sandy dust and thin, but breathable, air. The sound was the wind—in a space station devoid of anything but artificial breezes, she had missed the wind. She closed her eyes and let it wash over her.

Real dust.

Real air.

For a second, she wondered if Armstrong wouldn't be so bad. Maybe not the paradise Dane had described, but maybe not awful either. She didn't care if it was dusty and hot, as long as it was a safe haven.

The fresh air seemed to have the same effect on all of them, except for Bonebreak. He grabbed a bag from under the control panel and slung it over one shoulder. "I'm going to find something to drink."

"You've been here before?" Cora asked.

"No. But I have never found any inhabited space in the universe, even desert planets run by lesser species, that didn't have a bar." He dropped down the hole.

The others stared after him.

Nok squeezed Cora's hand. "Come on," she said. "Let's see what's out there."

45

Cora

THE DUST NEARLY BLINDED Cora as she jumped down the hatch; Leon caught her, wiping the dust from his own eyes.

"Not looking so much like paradise, sweetheart."

Cora pushed her hair out of her face—its new length meant it kept blowing in her eyes—and squinted into the dust. "Maybe everone here lives indoors, or underground."

"I think this is just what's left of a dust storm that already came through," Nok said. Her 1950s-housewife apron kept billowing in the wind. "One of the models back in London was from Morocco. Used to tell me about the sandstorms there, and how the wind howled." She coughed as the others climbed out of the ship. "Maybe the dust will settle soon."

She was frowning, and Cora didn't blame her. It wasn't a place she'd want to raise a daughter either.

The shadowy silhouette of low mountains hung in the distance—rounded and ancient. And a sun that was bigger than theirs on Earth, which was probably why it was so hot. Bonebreak was walking off toward a collection of dark shapes that might have been buildings. He seemed to move and breathe just fine, and for once she envied him the mask.

"We should catch up with Bonebreak." She took a step, but her legs felt heavy with exhaustion.

"It's the gravity." Rolf came up beside her, stooped over, like it took effort just to stand up straight. "This must be a very dense moon to have gravity this strong. That's why those mountains are so low. And the air—they must have manipulated the atmosphere."

Cora glanced behind her. Anya had stayed on the ship, her head still aching, and Mali stayed as well to take care of her. Mali and Leon exchanged a few words before parting. Mali suddenly stood on tiptoe and kissed his ear.

When he came over, he looked as off-kilter as if she'd slapped him. "Right," he said, a little discombobulated. "She said me and her are doing a rescue mission."

"You okay with that?"

He rubbed at the ear she'd kissed. "Oh, yeah."

Cora rolled her eyes, and they started trudging through the dust after Bonebreak, toward the hazy structures that were getting more visible in the clearing dust.

"What do we say to them?" Nok asked nervously, bobbing along next to Cora as they caught up to Bonebreak. "That Rolf and I are going to be their new neighbors, and by the way, I'm pregnant?"

"I think we start with hello," Cora said. "And then see where that takes us."

The ground was uneven and fissured and marked with

spiny vegetation, and Cora had to be careful not to trip. Her lungs burned; the air didn't quite seem right. She felt light-headed, which didn't match with the heavy gravity. The structures came out of the dust in a wavering sort of way, and for a moment the angles didn't seem right. For a terrifying second she thought she was back in the Kindred's cage, where angles had been distorted illusions, but then she stumbled upon a clapboard hut, and she reached out and touched it.

Solid.

The wooden siding was rough-hewn; it must have been made from trees chopped in a nearby forest. A tin bucket of muddy water sat beneath a cloth tarp.

"Vegetation," Rolf observed. "Water. Breathable air. Your friend didn't lie about there being ample resources."

"I wouldn't call Dane a friend," she muttered. She ran her fingers along the board that formed the corner of the hut, and a splinter came off in the pad of her finger. She broke into a grin. "Look—it's real!"

"Hooray," Nok muttered. "The wonderful world of splinters. It'll probably be too much to hope for a day-care center?"

The dust had nearly settled, and the village was taking shape. The hut was one of about twenty that were constructed with primitive but attentive craftsmanship. A few had flower boxes in the windows holding big-petaled flowers with thick round leaves, though they were all currently coated in dust. There was a covered clay ring that looked like a well, and some beaten-flat areas where maybe the Armstrong residents held dances. Everything was made of wood or clay, with a bit of tin glinting on the roofs. It had a pioneer kind of quality to it, and Cora felt proud, despite her reservations. Even far from home, humans had a knack for surviving.

Rolf's eyes went big. "It looks like how I always imagined America's Wild West."

"A bit, yeah," Nok said, toeing the bucket of muddy water. She rubbed the back of her neck, looking at the village. "Should we just knock?"

Bonebreak shook a finger toward the only building that was more than one story high. "I always say, go with the tallest structure and hope it's where someone important lives."

They followed him across the dusty town, trampling a sort of thick-stemmed succulent grass, to the porch of what they thought must be the town hall. Cora shook the dust from her hair and brushed it off her shoulders, aiming for a halfway presentable appearance, and then knocked.

No answer.

She knocked again. Nothing.

"Where would they be?" Nok asked. For the first time, unease crept into her voice. "You don't think the Kindred knew we were coming and rounded them all up?"

Everyone shot a hard look at Bonebreak, who held up his hands. "If there was a way of communicating with the Kindred or Mosca, little childrens, I would have called for backup when you had a gun pointed at me."

"Then where is everyone?"

"Sleeping," Bonebreak said. "Farming. Picnicking. How should I know what humans choose to do with their time?"

Leon gave a frustrated sigh and pushed forward, throwing the door open. "Hey! Anyone home?"

"We're friends," Cora added. "From Earth, by way of Kindred aggregate station 10-91."

She waited, but there was no response.

"No one home," Rolf observed.

It looked like some sort of makeshift municipal building. There was a big entrance hall with a desk by the front door, and a hallway to the left, probably leading to offices. If it was Armstrong's sheriff's department, there didn't seem to be any jail cells, which was good. She'd be happy to never see another cage in her life. She picked up a book left facedown on the desk and smiled. *Gone with the Wind*. Beneath it was a fat, dusty set of leather-bound pages.

"I guess we wait," she said, flipping open the leather cover and scanning the pages. Nok and Rolf headed off down the hallway to investigate.

"Uh, guys?" Nok's voice came uncertainly from down the hallway.

Cora started to close the folio, but something written across the top of the first page caught her eye.

It was divided into columns. Numbers were listed in the left-hand column like a calendar, but the months only had ten days. In the other columns were series of numbers that didn't immediately mean anything. The first entry read *25/12/12/1*; the next, *30/15/12/3*; and the next, *27/0/2/25*. She flipped the page and froze.

On the next page, someone had written out the column headings:

Total New Slaves / Of Which for Manual Labor / Of Which for Wives / Dead.

She froze. Total New Slaves? Given the dates, that had to be new arrivals on the moon . . . the Kindred's regular delivery of good samaritans to Armstrong.

But slaves? And dead? And *wives*?

Someone had scrawled in the margin:

Ask Kindred next time, need more wives. Keep running away. Say it's for reproduction—they always fall for that.

Cora slammed the notebook closed, her heart pounding. She stumbled through the hallway with legs that felt too heavy until she found the others in a small office. They were gathered around a pile of ancient-looking chains, the kind you'd fasten around someone's ankles if it was 1850. On the other side of the room were bins filled with clothes—baseball uniforms, Middle Eastern robes, frilly dresses—the fake kind of clothing the Kindred gave them to wear.

"What does it mean?" Nok asked in a high-pitched voice.

A tickle started in the back of Cora's throat. No—this couldn't be right. The *Kindred* were the ones who imprisoned humans. Why, when given freedom and ample resources, would humans possibly enslave their own kind?

"Bonebreak," she called, her voice sounding a little desperate. "Bonebreak!"

There was no answer. She ran back into the main room, but he wasn't there. She went to the door, squinting into the bright day. The dust had all but settled; she could see the whole village now, but it was still empty.

"He left us," she said.

"What if he went back to the ship?" Nok asked, anxiously twisting the pink streak in her hair. "He might try to leave without us."

"Anya and Mali are still there," Cora said. "They'll stop him."

Nok paced nervously and then went still, staring at something far off. She had always had the best eyesight out of the group; Cora twisted to follow her line of vision. A single column of dust rose skyward in the distance.

"What is that, another storm?" she asked.

But it was too small, and too concentrated.

"It's a truck," Leon said. "Coming fast."

"What do we do?" Nok asked. "Run?"

But the truck was getting closer. Cora turned around, scanning the horizon. There was nothing but the ship; they'd never make it to those far mountains in time. Hiding in one of the buildings would only trap them.

"No," she said, and pressed a hand against Lucky's notebook in her pocket. "We came here for a reason. We need to find out if this is a safe place." She exchanged a look with the others that she hoped didn't look too worried. "However we have to."

Leon cracked his knuckles.

Rolf pushed at the imaginary glasses on his nose, blinking hard.

Nok's hand fell from her hair.

Cora took a deep breath and watched the cloud of dust approach. Whoever these people were on Armstrong, they were human. They too had been stolen from Earth and caged by the Kindred. They knew what it felt like to be treated like animals.

That had to count for something.

That had to count for everything.

Because if not, she might have just gotten them all into deeper trouble than they'd ever imagined.

ACKNOWLEDGMENTS

I'VE BEEN FORTUNATE TO work with a brilliant team on this book. My editor, Kristin Rens, who has believed in Cora's story from day one, and the entire Balzer + Bray team for supporting us, including Kelsey Murphy, Alessandra Balzer, Donna Bray, and HarperCollins's fantastic team of designers, copyeditors, and marketers. I'm also grateful to my agent, Josh Adams, who inspired Mali's awesome ninja moves, and Megan Miranda, who read countless drafts and helped make each one better.

A special thanks as well to Jesse, for long walks brainstorming about alien planets, giant dollhouses, and twisted safaris.

And, as always, to my readers. Without you, my words would be hollow.